Ninth Daughter

by

Sonja Hutchinson

Five Realms Series

Ninth Daughter

Cover Art by *Teddi Black*

The Wild Rose Press, Inc.
PO Box 708
Adams Basin, NY 14410-0708
Visit us at www.thewildrosepress.com

Publishing History
First Edition, 2024
Trade Paperback ISBN 978-1-5092-5892-5
Digital ISBN 978-1-5092-5893-2

Five Realms Series
Published in the United States of America

Dedication

To David: your encouragement means everything.

Chapter One

Most people celebrated their birthdays, but this year mine meant my funeral.

I wasn't going without a fight, though. I knelt before the bronze statues of the moon goddess—one deity, three identical forms. "Sirini." My fingers trembled, and the marble floor dug into my knees. "Save me. I'll feed the hungry and tend the sick. Or maybe Father can foist me off on some faceless noble. The eligible princes are here for the Courtship Event, and I'll take whomever you choose." I hadn't paid them any attention, since the petty sea god had claimed me at my birth, but marrying beat getting tossed off the Ridge.

I wiped my cheeks. *Maelstrom always collects his sacrifices before their twentieth birthday.* Mine was tomorrow, and I was doomed.

Worshipping the goddess resonated deep within me. I lit a lavender incense stick and placed it across her outstretched hands.

The spicy vapor rose, swirled around my face thrice, and drifted out the window.

She heard me? I touched my forehead, lips, and heart. "So be it."

Papa had summoned me, which meant Maelstrom wanted me today. But Sirini had answered my prayer. Was I saved? My stomach churned. Did I have a future?

The familiar scuff and tap of Grace's limp echoed in

the hallway, and she entered with an armload of clean linens. "Princess Calilee—oh, you're dressed." She tossed the sheets into the wardrobe. "Let me do your hair." She gestured to the padded bench in front of the looking glass.

I sat and clutched my fingers in my lap. "Have you heard of anyone escaping Maelstrom's claim?"

Rose-scented soap wafted from Grace's skin. "No one expects your sacrifice."

"Then I can join the enforcers."

"That's for commoners." She reached for the hairbrush. "Why don't you wear your purple dress, lamb? It complements your complexion."

I stroked the cascade of sapphires around my neck. "Russet is Father's favorite."

She tsked. "His Excellency won't be swayed by a frock." She pulled my boring, brown hair back and pinned the sides. "Though I admit it doesn't hurt. Now, no dawdling. And no maudlin thoughts. You're a princess of the Five Realms. Your father promised to spare you."

How could Papa disobey a god? He'd bring the wrath of the pantheon down upon himself. I swallowed the sour taste in the back of my throat. "Has Maelstrom been sighted in the city? Are the priests gathering?"

She patted my hair. "You must move, Princess. The emperor waits for no one, not even his youngest daughter."

I hid my shaking fingers in the folds of my dress.

"Hurry." She picked up her skirt and waddled toward the door.

I stepped out into the amber glow of the mage-spelled guide stones and joined my sisters. The only difference between us was our birthright tattoos, hidden under our bodices. I hugged Daffi, whose sandy-gold gown complemented my russet one. Rosewater scent wafted around her, the same fragrance I'd dabbed on my own throat. "Trust us to color-coordinate."

She blinked. "Irrelevant. Has that abhorrent god arrived?"

Rosi, dressed in black, wrapped her arms about us. "Cali, why are you so calm? Priests flow through the city." She tightened her grip. "Aren't you scared?"

Like a cornered duck under Cook's knife. "Sirini gave me a sign."

"Truly? Describe it."

"The smoke curled around my face three times." I stepped back. "She's going to save me." *Maybe. Hopefully.*

Daffi's face paled. "I scoured the texts. There is no reprieve. The ninth daughter and youngest identical triplet of every family belongs to Maelstrom. You qualify in both categories."

"We may lose you today." Tears left tracks in Rosi's rouge.

I smoothed them with my thumb. "Trust Sirini. Maybe this summons regards the Courtship Event. Almost everyone has arrived. Or perhaps I'll be joining the enforcers, and you'll be pledged to Sirini's temple. No matter the reason, we will meet our destinies with dignity." If I faced death, I'd never give Maelstrom the gift of my tears, the rotting slug.

Daffi nodded. "I prefer your pragmatism to Rosi's emotional outbursts."

A knot formed in my throat, and my stomach churned butter. This could be my last day with my sisters. Would they find joy in serving Sirini? Would they miss me? Or would they forget me? No, that was too dark.

What about the street children? Rosi would feed them, and Daffi would teach them their letters, but who would protect them? I'd sent notes to Captain Dariel multiple times, but his people were overworked.

I took a deep breath and squared my shoulders. "Papa will send guards for us if we're late." I winked. "And not the handsome ones."

Daffi raised her eyebrows. "Masking your anguish with humor is unbecoming."

Yet it kept me from weeping. "Let's hurry."

We headed to the main staircase, our maids trailing behind us, Rosi first, then Daffi. The oak stair treads were polished for the maximum slippage.

I gripped the wrought iron banister and performed a kick-step that flicked my skirts out of the way. More than one lady had tumbled down this grand ankle-breaker, and it never ended pretty.

"Cali, that is most undignified!" Grace displayed the proper technique of lifting her heavy hem with both hands, took one step, and slipped off the tread. She fell on her plump bottom with a little "oof."

I held out my free hand. "Please mind your aging bones."

She pursed her lips and hauled herself up. "Yes. Well. Perhaps I'll have a word with the maids regarding the polishing."

Wouldn't do any good. Prime Wife wanted everything to gleam, including the floors and stairs. What use were billions of candles and guide stones if the light didn't refract off every surface? Grace and I finished our descent without further embarrassment.

The shouts of an angry mob thundered across the entrance chamber, vibrating in the soles of my slippers. *What is going on?* I opened one of the doors.

Three guards stood with swords raised. "Stay inside," one ordered over his shoulder. "They're savage this morning." A tomato hit him in the arm, and the stench of burning pitch clogged the portico.

Rosi and Daffi joined me. I soaked in the vitriolic shouts.

"Send out the ninth!"

"Everyone must tithe, even the emperor."

"Maelstrom demands his due."

An icy finger crept across my scalp, and an iron band clamped around my chest. Today was the last day Maelstrom could claim me. These were my people whom I served daily, and now they demanded my death? If they defied Maelstrom, he'd ravage our port. Long ago, he'd destroyed a village because the tithes were too lean. What would he do if I didn't leap into the sea today?

A guard swatted aside a burning chunk of wood. "Inside! Now."

Daffi hauled me back and slammed the door. "Pay them no heed. They're bloodthirsty. There hasn't been a tithe ceremony in years, and Maelstrom is apoplectic."

"In other words, angry."

Rosi's cheeks faded to a sickly tint. "Stop it, Cali. You're not funny."

If my dark humor kept the tears away, I'd use it. "They do not hold my fate." *In truth, I need a miracle.*

Rosi led the way. We crossed the green salon, bypassed the breakfast room, hustled down a side hallway, and arrived at a tertiary entrance to the throne room.

My heart pounded.

Two guards stood at attention, their brown surcoats brushed to a suitable sheen. Prime would be pleased.

From the shadows drifted a lanky figure with bulging eyeballs. Maelstrom's priest. He glided across the stone floor as if he had tentacles instead of feet. He nodded at us, the stench of seaweed and rot swirling off his blue-gray robes. "I am Dreaf. It is a pleasant day for a tithing ceremony. Maelstrom has waited twenty years for his servant."

My chin quivered, and I clenched my teeth. It was finally happening. My life was forfeit. I'd miss the Courtship Event. Dancing with handsome princes, flirting, holding hands, maybe even getting a first kiss before I was mercilessly tossed into the sea. I'd miss the marriages of my siblings, the births of nephews and nieces—

"Princess?" Dreaf lifted his bushy eyebrows.

What can I say? That I'd be honored to leap off the Ridge to appease Maelstrom's ego?

Daffi's eyes narrowed. "Depart, fiend! We belong to Sirini."

Three of her priestesses hurried toward us. The one with white streaks in her hair glared at the priest. "The goddess will judge your wicked deeds, demon. Begone and quit frightening her children."

I let out a breath. Sirini loved me. That's all I needed.

The guards opened the door for Dreaf, and he disappeared into the throne room.

The tiny blonde priestess presented a wooden bowl of prayer tokens. "Pay no attention to that brute, sisters.

Draw upon the strength of Sirini."

"Thank you." Rosi plunged her hand into the pool. Her fingers swished until she plucked out a worn coin. Daffi picked one off the top. I dug to the bottom for mine.

Rosi held hers to the light and whimpered. "Mercy."

Daffi opened her fist. "Order."

They looked to me.

"Service." Well, certainly, for the last hours of my life, I'd be pleased to serve the bloodthirsty citizens. *Apologies, Sirini. Please save me. I will serve you.*

The oldest priestess prayed for us, our father, and the ferocious people outside.

"So be it," we whispered.

Rosi, Daffi, and I followed the three women into the throne room. My heart thundered, but I took even breaths. I'd savor every remaining moment with them.

The guard announced us. "Princess Rosilee the Seventh. Princess Daffilee the Eighth. Princess Calilee the Ninth."

I ground my teeth. *Stupid names.* As if our only worth rested in our birth order. They should be Rosilee the Compassionate, Daffilee the Intelligent, and Calilee the…*I don't know.* Ninth Daughter was accurate, in my case. It could have been Calilee the Enforcer, but too late for that.

My father, the Most Excellent Emperor Rhys Acoris of the Five Realms, dominated his throne in sapphire-colored silk that contrasted with his auburn hair and beard, now streaked with white. His First Wife, Empress Bronwyn, aka the Prime, sat stiffly to his right on a smaller chair. Second Wife—Duchess Dorana—and Third Wife—Duchess Eilee, my mother—sagged on a padded bench, leaning against each other.

The goddess had blessed Father with three wives and four sets of triplets. *Today, one of his blessings will die—and I'll never see them again.* My eyes burned, but I banished the tears. *A thousand curses on Maelstrom, may his eyes be nibbled out slowly by barbed fish.*

And that thought was unbecoming of a princess.

The rest of Father's brood wore sapphire blue, the emblem of our realm. Bronwyn's oldest children, Batch One, waited beside her. No. Our brother Rhygan was absent. Bronwyn clenched her jaw, cracking her usual neutral expression. Her distress had nothing to do with me. Where was Rhygan? He should be here.

Batch Three, Bronwyn's second litter, finished the lineup on Prime's side of the dais.

On the other side, standing by the bench, Batch Two sobbed, matching handkerchiefs dabbing at their pale eyes.

Other nobles, arrayed in their realm's finery, stood in rows along both sides of the room. These young people and their parents had gathered for the Courtship Event, the six-week party to find a suitable wife for Rhygan. It was a pity the first day of the festivities began with my death. Since no one knew when Maelstrom would call for me, Bronwyn had scheduled the festivities to coincide with our twentieth birthday tomorrow.

Ambassadors, advisors, guards, and palace staff filled the rest of the space—a massive crowd to witness my glorious sacrifice.

A draft swept through the room, tugging at my hair and skirt. Rosi, Daffi, and I filed through the gauntlet of royals to the dais. We curtsied, arms outstretched like chickens taking flight. The scents of crushed cedar boughs, peppermint tea, and rank body odor wafted across my face with each gust. My thighs burned. *How long will Father keep us like this?* No matter, we'd hold.

"Rise, daughters."

We complied. Rosi took the lead. "Greetings, Father. We await your good pleasure."

I nodded at the wives. Dorana offered a smile, more a show of perfect teeth than a greeting. I raised my eyebrows at my oldest sister, Rindi. She shook her head, and her eyes cut to the left where Rhygan should be standing.

Why wasn't he here? Something was wrong.

Father stood. The hall fell still. Even the silence held its breath. He glanced at one of the guards, and every door to the throne room slammed. Heavy steel bars thunked into place.

Several nobles winced.

"I have multiple announcements today. While we are gathered here, soldiers will search the palace."

Gasps and whispers flitted through the room.

I glanced at Rindi again. Were they looking for Rhygan?

Father continued. "They will be thorough. Messes are inevitable."

"What are they searching for?" A young, dark man dressed in yellow stepped forward and offered a deep bow to the emperor. "If I may be so bold to ask, Your Imperial Majesty."

Father pursed his lips. "Introduce yourself."

The man, scarcely older than I, swallowed. "Prince Xavier of Tulya, at your service."

Father's eyes narrowed. "Rumors circulate of civil unrest in your lands. Is there truth behind them?"

The knot on Xavier's throat bobbed.

Poor guy. He should have kept his mouth shut. But it prolonged my life for a few more minutes, and I welcomed the news from the north.

He cleared his throat. "I have heard them, Most Excellent—"

"Skip the formalities. Odds are you'll be family before summer." Father glanced at his bevy of daughters who wouldn't be tossed off any cliffs today and thus would need husbands.

I squeaked. Rosi shot me a look—*no noises!* Right. Set aside my fear and watch this prince get squashed beneath Father's protocol.

Xavier straightened. "I remain your faithful and loyal servant, and I promise my father is rooting out any pockets of…unease." He glanced in the direction of an older man on the far side of the room. They shared the same coloring. And noses. Probably the King of Tulya.

Father grinned. "Your diplomacy skills are coming along, Prince. But you shouldn't promise that which you cannot deliver."

Wisely, Xavier nodded and stepped back. His sister, also in yellow, scolded him with a glare.

She thought like me. We could have become great friends if I wasn't being tossed off a ridge today.

Father addressed the assembly. "Crown Prince Rhygan has disappeared."

Chapter Two

Tru shielded his eyes against the sun rising behind the Evening Inn. Shadows hid the cobblestone courtyard. At the west end of the yard, the kid goat bounced and chased dust devils. Chickens clucked in the coop, pecking the dirt. Rabbits poked their noses out of their hutch, ready for greens. The early spring breeze carried the scents of fresh-tilled loam, wildflowers, and apple blossoms.

Goddess be praised, what a blessed life. Another two years, and he'd have enough saved up to buy his own stable, maybe in Rigolan where wild horses still roamed. *Won't that be something to see.* He hooked a hay bale and headed for the pens.

The new hand, Yarrow, and useless Oakley leaned against the paddock rail, doing nothing. "Hey, Hawk," Oak yelled, his arms crossed over his rounded belly. "A couple priests rode through town yesterday, hollering about a tithe ceremony in the capital today. They're tossing someone off the Ridge."

Hawk emerged from the stable, a pitchfork in hand. "Nobles don't get sacrificed. Some servant will go to Maelstrom, and the intended victim will hide out until ever'body forgets they're supposed to be dead."

What a waste of a life. If Tru had power, he'd end the sacrifices.

"If we left now on Lightning, we'd be in time for the

show." Oakley grinned at his uncle. "How about it?"

"How about ya get to yer chores?" Hawk handed the pitchfork to Oak. "If ya want a show, visit the tavern tonight." He glanced at Tru. "You got this covered?"

Tru nodded. "Yes, sir."

Hawk strode through the back door of the inn and slammed the door.

Oak dumped the tool in the weeds and smirked at Tru. "Bootlickers aren't invited."

What a layabout. As if Tru wanted to see some girl die. He crossed to the pen and whistled. Three goats, the kid, and four sheep ran up, bleating and straining against the posts. He scratched heads before dumping their hay into the trough. "How are you girls this morning?"

"Quit talking to 'em like they can understand ya." Oakley spit in the dirt.

"Quit standing around when there's work to be done." Tru pointed to the coop. "Collect the eggs."

Oakley glared but grabbed the basket.

Yarrow kicked the pitchfork into the air and caught it. "Oak, did ya see that?"

He was too busy scowling.

Tru picked up two empty buckets and waited until the lazy scab entered the chicken pen. Too bad Hawk'd never fire the git.

Tru scattered feed, filled water troughs, hauled hay, and kept half an eye on Oakley and Yarrow mucking out horse stalls slower than molasses in winter. A breeze dried the moisture at the hollow of Tru's back. The other two men hadn't even broken a sweat. The horses stomped and snorted, tails twitching.

Thirty minutes later, Eve hollered for them.

Tru pointed at the filthy stalls. "Finish this after the

meal."

Oakley glowered, dropped his tool, and headed for the kitchen. *Hopeless loiter-sackin' fopdoodle…what a waste of air.* Yarrow propped his shovel against the wall before scurrying out. Tru picked up the pitchfork and stowed it where it belonged. No one would trip over a tool in any stable he ran.

He entered the warm kitchen filled with yeasty bread fumes. "Morning, Evening." That joke hadn't grown stale, even after eleven years.

She scowled. "Just Eve." She ladled boiling-hot grains into dishes and placed them on the table. The scent of onion and sage set Tru's mouth to watering. Oakley, Yarrow, and Eve's husband, Hawk, dug in, elbows bobbing and mouths slurping. *Disgusting.* Tru's guardian would have boxed his ears if he'd eaten like that. He picked up his bowl and leaned against the outer wall. Eve had added sausage, onions, and beans to the porridge for a hearty meal. "Smells amazing."

She nodded, her version of "thank you," and laced her fingers over her round belly.

He winked.

The corners of her mouth twitched. Even if it took another eleven years, he'd coax a smile out of her.

Hawk belched. "Did you lads finish the morning chores?"

"Yeah, I fed the animals and cleaned the cages." Oakley scraped the last remnants of his breakfast and licked his spoon.

The stench of dandelion greens and curdled milk rose from Oak, and Tru swallowed a lump of sausage whole. *Gods, liars are the worst.* Couldn't trust their words or their character. Had Sirini gifted him with his ability to detect lies? Possibly. He'd been doing it all his life, and his nose sniffed them out better than a hog hunting truffles. "*I* fed the animals and scoured the cages. You collected eggs and picked your arse."

Yarrow laughed.

Oakley scowled. "Whatever." He shoved his bowl across the table. "More."

Eve gave him another ladleful of mash. "That's it. I gotta have enough for guests. If you're still hungry after that, I'll make ya eggs."

Oakley grimaced. "I hate 'em."

"Not my problem." Eve filled a serving tray with bowls of porridge and mugs of beer. "The patrons in rooms two and three are departing this morning. Make sure their horses are ready." She hefted the load and balanced it.

Tru shoved off the wall. "Want help with that?"

"No, I got it." She used her ample rear to open the swinging door separating the kitchen from the inn's dining hall and disappeared.

Oakley and Yarrow wandered out the back door, leaving their dirty dishware on the table.

Hawk snagged a fresh honey wheat roll off the pile. "Barn about clean?"

"Almost." Tru scrubbed his dishes in the soapy water. "I'll have Oak and Yarrow exercise the horses next."

Hawk nodded. "Good. I gotta fix a busted shutter. Can ya ready the guests' mounts?"

"Will do. The black and the dappled?"

"That's them."

Tru headed outside. He found Oakley and Yarrow leaning against the tack wall, laughing. "Did you finish mucking the stalls?"

"Not yet." Oakley cleared his throat and spat on the floor. "Getting to it."

"Now. Then exercise the bay dun and the sorrel." He waited until they moved, then crossed to the main entrance of the barn. He collected the black horse and gagged. Manure coated its hooves and pasterns. "Oakley!" *Inept. Absolutely useless.* He should be out in the fields where he couldn't injure a man or beast. "Oak!" Tru turned to find both stable hands had fled, tools abandoned on the floor. They hadn't taken an animal with them, either.

He didn't have time to track down the loafers. It'd serve them if Hawk came to check and found them idle. Tru led the black to the pump and washed off the crap. "That feels good, doesn't it?" A curl of hair flopped into his eye, and he blew it aside. A half hour later, he had both horses groomed, saddled, and waiting at the door of the inn for their owners.

The first man out wore fine clothing. Maybe a minor noble or a merchant. He tipped Tru a copper and rode off on his gleaming black. He hooked a left at the main highway, heading toward the capital—and the sacrifice.

A few minutes later, the dappled's owner appeared. He smiled, offered his mount a head scratch, and heaved his rounded body into the saddle. "She looks beautiful. Thanks for the care." He tossed Tru two coins, nodded, and took off.

Three coppers. *Not bad for the morning.*

Better than that poor tithe, for sure. Losing her life before it even got started. If bedamned priests tried to throw him off a cliff, he'd end his life when they came to collect him—spend eternity with the true goddess, not that bloodthirsty sea bastard.

"Sirini, please stop the sacrifice and Maelstrom's cruelty." That was all he could do for today's victim. He had horses and Oakley to supervise—if the slug hadn't taken Hawk's fastest horse and set off for the capital.

****

Shouts and cries echoed around the room, and I blinked. Rhygan wouldn't have left the palace without guards or telling anyone. This was the reason for the summons—unless Papa was also announcing our fates.

Emperor Rhys's voice filled the crowded room. "Crown Prince Rhygan has not been seen since last night. If you have information, speak."

Multiple voices cried out questions or invoked the goddess, but no one came forward. The noble daughters of Rigolan, dressed in their kingdom's traditional silver and onyx, fixed their gazes on my father. In citrine, the Tulya twins huddled around their sister. The dark-haired woman from Kurik with ice-blue eyes and a malachite gown stared at me.

My eyes burned. Those ladies should have discussed perfumes before gathering. Rose and honeysuckle worked together, but who wore lemon?

Father held up his hand. The crowd quieted. "Do not panic. He will be found. Until then, our guests will be made comfortable."

Translation—*None of you are leaving until Rhygan is located.*

Prince Xavier's eyeballs bulged. Most unattractive.

Father continued. "The event begins this evening, and I trust everyone is prepared."

If something goes wrong, you'll all pay. And Rhygan had better be there. Me, too, for that matter. That was so unfair, to be sacrificed before I got my first kiss.

"We are expecting the delegation from Olerio this afternoon. Please greet them warmly."

We need these allies; treat them like family.

Father glanced at Batch Two. "The triplets will be attending. Make them feel welcome."

Ladies, flirt like mad because those men are your best shot at finding spouses without being split apart.

Olerio hadn't sacrificed their youngest triplet because Maelstrom had no power in that kingdom. That's why Momma gave birth to us there. *Oh!* Maybe that would save me.

Father continued. "Our first event will be a dinner, followed by cards in the parlor."

With all the eligible in attendance, let the scheming begin.

I'd been looking forward to the dancing, bantering over meals, and long walks in the gardens. I wouldn't have found a husband, being ninth and therefore unimportant. But it would have been fun. A weight like a wet wool blanket settled on my shoulders. *I don't want to die!*

Dreaf glided up and bowed. "Majesty, the people await your decision."

Father scowled. "They will be disappointed. I only have three daughters by my third wife, so the tithe does not apply."

"The law clearly states the ninth daughter of every *man* belongs to Maelstrom, so he has claimed her." He inclined his head to me. "And she meets the identical triplet criteria."

"She was born in Olerio, not Acoris."

"Yet she lives here." Dreaf's gaze narrowed. "She

benefits from my lord's blessings."

All the air whooshed from my lungs. Sirini hadn't saved me, and Father couldn't. I was doomed.

Father's fists clenched. "It is a barbaric practice! I cannot abide by it."

The priest's eyeballs bulged. "If you do not offer the sacrifice, your people will revolt." He waved his arm behind him. "The streets will run with the blood of innocent townspeople. Your soldiers. Your family. Do you wish to lose more than one child?"

Father's jaws bunched. "Did you take my son to guarantee the tithe was delivered today? I demand you return him!"

Dreaf smirked. "And Maelstrom demands his due. What will it be, Emperor? Your daughter or civil unrest and the loss of your heir?"

I drew a shallow breath. Father had no choice. He had to deliver the sacrifice, and all the power of the Five Realms could not spare me. I would not be serving as an enforcer, righting wrongs in the city, flirting with foreign princes, or enjoying the births of nieces and nephews. Instead, my death would quell riots and bloodshed and save the next emperor.

Papa straightened and turned his glossy gaze to me. A muscle in his cheek twitched. "Pri—" His voice wavered. He cleared his throat. "Princesses Rosilee and Daffilee will pledge to the Temple of Sirini at a time of their choosing. Princess Calilee…will serve Maelstrom."

The weight of a thousand moons settled on my chest. Tears welled. My nose dripped. I pulled a handkerchief from my sleeve and blotted. I'd die today to save my family and my city.

Rosi sank to her knees and wailed. Daffi clung to

her.

Momma launched herself at the priest, but two palace guards raced to intercept.

Father descended to wrap Rosi and Daffi in his powerful arms.

But not me. Not solid, unwavering, independent Cali. She didn't need a hug. An icy draft whipped about my ears, drowning out the uproar. Father couldn't rescue me. The goddess ignored me. The citizens demanded my blood. The entire city was in chaos. I couldn't even help the enforcers track down Rhygan's kidnappers.

My token was service. How could I serve Sirini by dying? That didn't make sense. Although a willing sacrifice counted as a double favor. Maybe that was it. To save Rhygan and Acoris, I had to claim that blessing. Otherwise, I was as worthless as a single stocking. I lifted my chin. "I will comply."

The crowd murmured. My sisters wailed. The guards pulled Momma away from the priest. He straightened his torn robes and glided farther away on his hidden tentacles. Father cradled Rosi and Daffi in his arms.

Didn't they hear me? I raised my voice. "I volunteer to serve Maelstrom!"

Everyone froze and stared. Momma let out an ear-piercing screech like a hunting hawk swooping in on prey. Prime collapsed back in her throne. Father caught my gaze and mouthed, "Thank you."

I blinked and squared my shoulders. I would *not* cry. I was a princess of Acoris, born to duty. I would minister to my family and my people willingly and with honor.

Dreaf smiled. "A willing tithe. Excellent." He reached for my hand. "Let us appease the god and the worshipers."

"No!" My mother wrenched one hand free of the guards and swiped at him. "You can't!"

"It has been witnessed." The priest licked his lips. "It will be done."

A flash of light shot through the throne room, reflecting off Prime's ultra-polished walls and windows. A blast of wind whipped my skirts.

I whirled.

The three moon priestesses stood behind me, arrayed in ivory and gray robes. The blasting air lifted them to hover above us. Their eyes blazed with an eerie silver glow, and their hair floated like ribbons in a breeze.

I dropped to one knee. Moments later, so did every other mortal. Except the idiot Dreaf.

The priestesses spoke in voices that echoed as a multitude. "I abhor this vile sacrifice. Maelstrom has no claim on my children. Begone, foul beast."

I chanced a peek.

Dreaf smirked. "Speak your will to the people, Goddess, but they will not relent."

"Superstitious rabble." Sirini hissed through three pairs of lips. "I will destroy your repulsive cult and this travesty." The priestesses turned in unison to survey the crowded throne room before settling on me. Their eyes blazed, and heat flared in my sapphire necklace as if struck by lightning. "I will not be mocked. The sacrifices will end."

Dreaf laughed. "Princess Calilee will serve Maelstrom. Return to your moons for another long slumber, crone, and leave the Five Realms to its true ruler."

Three sets of eyes narrowed. "You will die for that insult, worm." The light flashed again, and the goddess vanished—yet the foolish priest still gloated. She hadn't touched him.

The priestesses settled to the flagstones, their eyes normal. The tiny blonde moaned and dropped the bowl of prayer tokens. The coins crashed to the floor.

Three of them rolled on their edges to my feet and spun on their axes.

Whispers and wails filled the hall.

Holy moonbeams, what was all that? Sirini hadn't spoken through her servants in over one hundred years. Why had she chosen now to condemn the tithe?

Father raised his voice above the clamor. "The goddess has spoken. Remember this day and repeat her words. It is a sign of blessing that she would speak in such a…dramatic fashion."

The tokens continued spinning beside my toes. Too creepy. I scooped them up.

The crowd hushed. Everyone stared at me, faces pale, eyes wide. A few of the noble ladies had already performed the obligatory swoon and were attended to by servants.

Father cleared his throat. "Read your coins, Daughter."

I opened my palm, and my stomach clenched. All three tokens lay face down. I flipped the first one, a piece of wood. "Retribution." I turned the bone tile. "Retribution." Last one, the metal coin. A chill skittered down my spine. "Retribution."

Was that good for me or disastrous for the realm?

Chapter Three

Tru dunked his head under the flow from the pump, washing off sweat and grime.

Hawk strode out of the main barn. "Did you scrub the stalls with vinegar? Smells clean."

"Had to." Tru smoothed his hair back with his hands. "Manure was packed in every crevice. Took me three hours to set it right." Oak had been mucking down the center of each stall but neglected the edges and corners. *Inept slug*.

"Muckin' is Oak's job." Hawk squinted. "Where is he?"

"No idea." Tru rubbed a sore spot on his lower back and angled his body to catch the breeze. It dried the sweat and water trickling down his neck. "Haven't seen him or Yarrow since breakfast."

"I'm going to fire that boy." Hawk whirled toward the barn. "Is Lightning here?"

"Yes. I brushed him down after I scoured his stall."

"What's left of the morning chores?" Hawk asked.

"I haven't even set foot in the secondary barn yet, other than to feed Lady and Noble. I still gotta muck their stalls and exercise all the horses. I'll be at it the rest of the day." His shoulders tensed. Another day of interrupted chores. But flexibility was part of his job as lead stable hand. Cleaning the tack could wait until tomorrow.

Hawk squinted at the sun. "Take a break and enjoy a meal in the hall. On me. I'll track down those two snails and make them polish the second barn to my standards." He smirked. "Then maybe I'll have them shovel the privy and churn the compost heaps. Teach them to think twice before taking off without permission."

Tru wiped his palms on his leather trousers. Perfect punishment. "Thanks. A break does sound good. I won't be long."

"Take what time you need. You earned it today." Hawk stomped off toward the paddock, cupped his hands to his mouth, and hollered, "Oakley! Yarrow!"

Tru stepped into Eve's kitchen and the scents of fresh baked bread and grilled onions. The worktable was filled with baskets of winter produce, mounds of rolls, a wheel of cheese, and two haunches. Looked like goat stew for dinner tonight.

Eve looked at him. "What do you want?"

"Hawk said he'd cover my midday meal."

She nodded to the hall. "Eat in there. Got no room for ya in here."

"I can lean against the wall."

"You're afraid of Charity?" Her mouth twitched. "For Sirini's sake, tell the girl you're not interested. You've never had trouble speakin' your mind afore."

He rubbed his nape. "I don't want to hurt her feelings."

Her eyebrows climbed. "You don't think keeping her waiting for ya isn't hurtin' her feelings?" She gestured at the door. "You're eating in there. Ignore her, for all I care, but I don't want ya underfoot in here."

Great. He'd eat fast. He pushed through the swinging door and stepped into the dining hall. Twelve tables lined the room in three rows. A guest—the man who'd brought in the gray mare last night—claimed the spot closest to the front door with loggerheads Oakley and Yarrow. They were whispering, heads close. The patron had his cloak on and the hood up like he'd be inconspicuous.

Of course they were lazing. "Hey! Hawk's looking for you two."

Oakley glared, but his fat arse remained in the chair.

Charity flew at Tru like a chickadee to seed and wrapped her arms around him, pressing her breasts against his bicep. "So nice to see you again! Are you here to dine?" She batted her lashes, her brown eyes bright.

"I need to eat quickly. Got work to do." He cleared his throat. "Just gonna sit by the window." He withdrew his arm from her and headed for the farthest table. A breeze fluttered the white curtains and chased out stale air. Tru dropped into a chair, his back to the room.

Charity bounced to his side, her assets threating to pop out. She leaned toward him, offering a view most men would pay for. "The house special?"

"Sure. And ale, thank you." He studied the dirt lane outside. If guests entered, she'd have to serve them and leave him alone.

She went to fetch his food. Her hips swayed, and her brown hair danced in loose curls across her back. Eve was right. He was a first-class heel for not telling Charity how he felt. If he did, maybe she'd turn her attentions elsewhere. Or knowing his luck, she'd double her efforts to win him over.

She was lovely, but his heart didn't skip a beat for her. He couldn't imagine spending quiet evenings in their home. They'd have nothing to say. She enjoyed fashion, dancing, and royals gossiping. He liked working with horses, fixing things, and stargazing.

Chairs screeched across the plank floor behind him. He glanced over his shoulder. Oakley, Yarrow, and the cloaked man headed for the door.

Gods, it'd be sweet if Hawk was waiting in the lane now.

He wasn't. The guest turned north, toward town. The two knuckleheads came back inside. Charity emerged with Tru's food.

Oak grinned. "You're looking tasty, Char. Sit on my lap and let me sample your lips."

"Nice try, slug." She set a platter of grilled meat and vegetables before Tru with a mug of ale, a board with bread and soft cheese, and utensils. The scent of garlic and peppercorn filled the hall. She sat in the chair across from him and smiled. "I don't have other customers, so we can chat."

Tru's shoulders dropped. What could he say that wouldn't make her cry? Nothing. He'd ignore her, and eventually she'd get the hint. He picked up his knife and fork. Savory spices on the thin slices of meat mingled with the juices and butter from the greens, and his stomach growled. "Thank you." He loaded a forkful and shoved it in. The salty, spicy, meaty goodness melted on his tongue. It was so tender it fell apart without any chewing.

Oak plonked into the chair beside Charity and stared at her cleavage. "Bring us some of that, love." The overpowering stench of stale sweat rolled off him.

Yarrow took the seat next to Tru. "You gonna eat that bread?"

"Yes." He stabbed at Yarrow's reaching fingers.

"Hands off."

Charity leaned away from Oakley and hiked her blouse up. "You got any silver?"

"No."

"Then no food."

Good for her. At least she didn't struggle to voice her emotions.

Eve shot through the swinging door and advanced on Oakley and Yarrow. "Which of you turds broke the gate latch on the chicken coop?"

Yarrow's eyes bugged, but he said nothing. Oak gazed at Charity.

Tru grinned and took another bite. This show was worth the wait.

"Had to be one of you. If Tru or Hawk had busted it, they'd have fixed it immediately."

Oak tore his gaze away from Charity's chest and addressed Eve. "I didn't do it."

The scent of bitter dandelion and curdled milk wafted across the table. Tru chased away the odor with a swig of ale. "Liar."

Eve crossed her arms and stared at Oak. "Fess up, or no more free meals."

Oak's jaw clenched, his eyes narrowed, and he glanced at Yarrow.

"Don't blame him," Eve said. "I want the truth."

Oak shoved back in his chair and stalked out. He chose to pay for all future meals rather than speak up. That spoke volumes about his character.

Tru tore his bread in half and slathered it with cheese. "I'll fix the latch after I eat."

Eve settled her hand on his shoulder and squeezed. "Thank you. You're a blessing to us, Tru. I appreciate ya greatly."

He choked and stared after her walking back to her domain. Had he imagined that? She'd never thanked anyone aloud in the eleven years he'd been working here. He met Charity's gaze. "Did you hear that?"

She grinned. "You're the favorite. And who can blame her? You're a wonderful person."

He stared at his plate. "Thanks. I gotta hurry and get back to work."

Charity sighed. "You're always working. That's a fine trait, but it leaves no time for me."

What could he say? Nothing. He shoveled his food down, wiping up the juices with the last of his bread, and downed the ale. "Delicious, as always. See you later."

He reached for his dishes, but she was quicker. "This is my job. You go make sure the world is right and everything functions properly."

If only he could. He'd start by turning her heart somewhere else.

****

All three coins read "Retribution." Had anyone ever drawn the same three tokens before? The odds were…impossible. And "retribution" wasn't a blessing or a prayer. Why did the priestess's small bowl contain multiples of them?

Whispers echoed through the throne room, and two women swooned. Again.

Retribution. I held them on my palm, the cold tiles biting. Searing. If I flicked them off, would circles of scorched flesh mar my skin?

"This isn't fair!" Rosi slapped my hand, and the coins flew into the pile on the floor. "Somebody do something!"

Daffi helped the priestesses collect the coins into the vessel.

Father glared at the priest. "You heard the goddess. She wants the tithes to end. Now."

Dreaf shrugged. "That old crone took no action. Maelstrom demands his due, the citizens clamor for it, and if you cancel now, you'll face riots and bloodshed. It is your choice."

Sirini made her demand to us, but she hadn't spoken to the populace. They still required a tithe. Father could deny the priest all day, but it wouldn't calm the city. I had to do something. "Father, I volunteered. It will keep the peace." And hopefully return Rhygan.

His jaw clenched, and he lifted me off the floor in a monstrous embrace. "My sweet Cali Cub," he whispered. "Always thinking of others first. If I could take your place, I would."

"I understand." I clung to his neck, my feet dangling, and cemented this memory in my mind. The scruff of his beard against my cheek. The scent of applewood and sword oil. His massive size and the unspoken promise of safety in his arms.

A knock sounded at the main door. Father set me down.

Two soldiers unlocked the bolt and ushered in the captain of the guard. He knelt before Father. "We were unsuccessful."

Father raised his voice. "Until Crown Prince Rhygan is located, no one leaves this palace without an armed escort. All incoming and outgoing messages will be read." He scanned the visiting nobles and mounted the dais. "Guards, send the word to every town and village in the Five Realms—information about the prince's whereabouts will be rewarded."

Bronwyn rose to join him, porcelain face neutral. "Anyone guilty of harming my son will be executed."

Xavier cleared his throat. "May we aid in a search of the city?"

"No." Father signaled for soldiers. "My security will handle it. I appreciate the offer, but you are honored guests. You will be treated accordingly."

Translation—*You're valuable prisoners; enjoy your stay*.

I should be out there searching for him with the enforcers. He had to be found.

"It is time." Dreaf held out his hand to me.

"I cannot serve Maelstrom in this gown. I'll change into suitable attire and bid my family farewell."

"You have one hour. Meet me on the portico." He slithered away, probably to announce the great news to the ravenous crowd.

Rosi, Daffi, and Momma wrapped me in their arms and wailed.

The other siblings hung back, staring, fidgeting. Jerys, the closest sister to our age, joined in the embrace. Prime and Dorana slipped out a back door, followed by Batch Two. The Batch One sisters crowded around Father, blurting out whispered questions and demands.

This couldn't be happening. How could my life be over already? I hadn't done anything worthwhile. Tears welled, but I blinked them back. My life was in service to Sirini. Either she'd save me or she'd use my death for her glory, but I wouldn't meet Maelstrom with reddened eyes and salt on my cheeks. That would please him. I took a deep breath. "I don't have much time. Come help me prepare."

We hurried up the polished staircase, sniffling Grace leading the way.

We entered my bedchamber, and my stomach rolled. "If I'm to serve, I'll look the part. Grace, I need a maid's outfit. Daffi, unbutton my dress. Rosi, help me with my boots." I sank onto a padded footstool and hiked my skirts. The boots were my favorites, and submersion in saltwater would ruin them.

And that was the most ridiculous thought I'd had all year.

Momma perched on the edge of my bed. We had her dark-brown hair, tan skin, green eyes, and slight stature. "Cali, this is madness. You can't go."

"I have to." I pulled my right boot off and tossed it at the shoe shelf. "If I don't, the people will riot. Innocent people might perish. And what if they break into the palace and grab Daffi? Or Jerys?" Rosi sat unmoving, so I tackled my left shoe. "What if they took Rhygan to guarantee my cooperation? It's the right thing to do."

"No, it isn't." Rosi grabbed my hands. "Maybe you won't die. Maybe Maelstrom will give you the ability to breathe beneath the waves and you'll live in his underwater temple."

"There's no such thing." Daffi finished the last button and peeled the frock off my shoulders. "Who could visit? Fish?"

"Maybe he wants a wife," Rosi said.

I would *not* marry that beast. I stood and dumped the gown onto the floor in a swoosh. "That's a vicious thought." No, this was my destiny. I'd known it all my life. Though I really thought Papa would find a way to save me.

"Marriage is better than death." Daffi hung up my

dress.

"I disagree." I waved at the wardrobe. "Split my clothing between you. For the Courtship Event, you'll never appear in the same outfit twice for the entire six weeks."

Rosi blinked. "I'm not going to attend. I'll be closeted in mourning."

"As will I." Daffi settled beside Momma.

Grace and my sisters' maids returned with the simpler garments.

I smiled at the younger girls. "Valora, Dia, thank you for helping me."

They bobbed quick curtsies and retreated to Grace's adjoining room.

I held up the long-sleeved shirt. It had a slit at the neckline, but did it tie in front or back?

"Back." Grace helped. The blouse rode high enough to cover my birth tattoo and sapphire necklace. "You forgot to remove this." She fumbled for the clasp.

I clutched the gems. "I'm keeping them."

Mother's eyebrows rose. "Whatever for?"

For courage. A sense of belonging. A piece of home. "I love them." And it'd infuriate Maelstrom, who despised items from the dry. His counterpart, the goddess of the land, frequently teased him by tossing things from her domain into his waters. I might as well join the fun.

Momma teared up again.

"No, don't cry. I won't get through this if you do." I pulled the sleeveless blue dress over my head. It hung from my shoulders like a billowing curtain, the excess puddling on the floor. I kicked it. "Who wore this last? A giantess?"

No one spoke.

"Grace, fetch your cutters. I can't have this tangling my feet in the ocean."

They all sobbed.

I'd said the wrong thing. Again. I picked up the monstrous apron. The white cotton edges met in the back instead of on my hipbones. The last owner must have been twice my girth. I tied it and turned to the looking glass.

Absolutely ridiculous. Like a little girl playing dress-up.

I braided my hair, knotted it at my nape, and secured it with two slim wooden pins imbued with magic to stay until I drew them out. More dry land products to taunt Maelstrom.

Grace rushed in with her sewing kit, followed by Daffi's maid. "We'll have to work fast."

I climbed onto the padded stool. "No hem. Just cut it above the ankles, please."

"But it'll fray."

"I can live with that."

Daffi welled up again.

Bad choice of wording. "Stop crying! I won't get through this if you don't."

Daffi nodded and rubbed her eyes, smearing colored powder across her temple.

Grace attacked the bottom of the dress.

The cold metal cutters brushed my bare foot. "Don't make it straight and neat. I want to look the part of a despairing victim."

She hesitated for a moment, winced, and shifted her wrist for the next slice.

"Momma, did you witness the last tithe ceremony?"

She shook her head. "I could never bear the

mother's agony of losing her child. Why?"

"I don't know what to expect. Will the priest throw me off? Am I expected to jump?"

And again. Momma, Rosi, and Daffi collapsed into each other. My throat closed, and my eyes burned. I should think before I speak.

"I witnessed it." Grace crawled to the far side of the stool to finish the cut.

"Tell me what happened."

"Maelstrom demanded an infant, not even six moons old."

I hopped down. "The priest threw the baby into the sea?"

Grace stowed her cutters in the sewing kit. "And the people cheered, pleased as gluttons on feast day."

"That depressing story doesn't help." I sat and donned a pair of lightweight tan suede slippers with blue ribbons. *Oh lovely, color coordinated for my adoring fans.*

Grace helped me tie the laces. "I heard a tale, from long ago, of a nineteen-year-old girl. She fought the priest at the lip of the Ridge. He pushed her, she caught the edge of his robe, and they both plunged to the sharp rocks below. Their bodies lay there for hours until the tide took them."

Momma wailed.

I swallowed. Lesson learned—jump out to clear the rocks. "Thank you, Grace. What a gruesome story."

She hugged her kit to her chest. "Do you need anything else?"

Poor love. Maintaining a proper distance between servant and master even through her misery. I embrace her. "Thank you for caring for me all these years."

She dropped the sewing bag and wrapped her arms around me. "You do your parents proud. I'll miss you."

"And I you."

She ran to her room, wiping her face with her sleeve.

I turned to my family. "I'm out of time. Will you attend with me?"

They splashed cool water onto their faces, reducing some of the puffiness and clearing the smeared powders. It didn't help much.

I led the way down the hall and froze. Father, Bronwyn, and Dorana stood at the landing. People lined both sides of the staircase, leaving a narrow path down the center. Half-siblings. Father's advisors. Royal visitors. Ambassadors. Guards. Palace staff.

All here to witness my final humiliation and say goodbye. How was I supposed to walk this gauntlet without bawling?

Chapter Four

Momma pushed by me and clung to Father.

"Be strong, Eilee." Dorana patted Mother's shoulder.

I blinked. Get creative. Pretend I was attending a costume ball. Or rush, as if late for breakfast—which I'd missed. I'd perish with an empty stomach.

Dorana embraced me. "The goddess be with you."

"Thank you."

"Your kingdom loves you," Bronwyn said without the usual condescension in her tone.

Father kissed me. "Hold your head high, Cali Cub. Show them how royalty meets duty."

I nodded and stepped by him to the head of the stairs.

Rindi and Rhyada hugged my neck. "We love you."

I clenched my teeth. Rhygan should be here to say farewell. I took the next step.

Batch Two—Palama, Pensie, and Prescia—crowded the tread. "We'll miss you."

Sure. Who would they torment after their favorite target died? I moved on.

Justyn and Jayson held out hands to help me. Justyn kissed my fingers and pressed them to his heart. "You're braver than I am."

A fat tear rolled down my cheek. *Stupid brothers.*

"Make him suffer before he takes you. Remember what we taught you?" Jayson asked.

I nodded. "Go for the soft spots. Eyes, cheeks, throat."

"Groin." Justyn grinned. "Fight like a beast, Cali." He tapped a pin securing my braid. "You've got weapons. Use them."

"I will." I continued.

Jerys threw her arms around me, sobs shaking her tiny form. "Don't go."

I buried my face in her gorgeous auburn hair. "I have to." I pulled away and took another step, wiping my face with my hands. I'd made it through the family and hurried down the rest of the stairs. Royals from other kingdoms murmured to me.

"Fear not, my lady."

"The goddess will guide you."

"Make those fools regret their demands."

On and on they went. Advice, well-wishes, sorrow. Tears from palace staff. The corridor of people ushered me to the entrance doors, ten feet of burnished mahogany, inlaid with alabaster and carved with an oceanic theme of seaweed, sea stars, seahorses, and fish. I'd spent hours as a child running my fingers over the designs, wishing I was a mermaid. *Guess I'll be there soon.*

Two guards opened the doors.

I stepped out onto the portico to a crowd.

They cheered. Whistled. Tossed flower petals. Shouted my name.

Inhuman leeches.

Rosi and Daffi grasped my hands and stood with me shoulder to shoulder, them in silk and lace, me in servant's cotton.

The smirking priest slithered forward. "I'm

surprised I don't have to search for you."

As if I'd flee and plunge my realm into civil war or threaten Rhygan's safety. Not that Dreaf would be able to find me if I'd hidden in the secret passageways. "I'm ready."

Dreaf presented me with a long string of black pearls, each separated by a tiny, silver bead. "A gift from your new master."

What a treat. He'd get them all back when he killed me. I draped them over my head. They hung to my belly, so I knotted them at my breastbone. The fortune looked ridiculous against the simple dress.

The slimy priest glided toward the crowd. They parted for him, still cheering and shouting my name.

I followed, my sisters at my sides, chin high. The sun blinded me, the heat baked my shoulders through the thin cotton dress, and my slippers scraped along the cobblestones counterpoint to Rosi and Daffi's bootheel clicks. The scents of clematis, tulips, brine, and unwashed bodies coiled around us.

Beyond the palace courtyard walls, guards with vehicles waited to ferry us out to the Ridge. I climbed into an open wagon with Rosi, Daffi, Momma, and Papa. I tapped the driver. He flicked the reins. The two horses hauled us through the crowded city streets, the cart swaying and dipping.

Some of the townspeople wept and reached out to touch us. Others smiled and shouted thanks. Hundreds of priestesses, in groups of three, followed us, admonishing the crowds and calling out curses on them.

We passed the flower market where we bought fresh blossoms for our rooms. The millinery Daffi loved. The fountain in the square featuring bronze statues of Sirini, their faces tranquil with lips slightly upturned. We rode by vendors selling cakes glistening with sugar crystals and golden meat pies. Taverns. Inns. Jewelry and dress shops. All places where I'd been welcomed—until they all turned on me.

The city ended at the ruins of an ancient temple on the pointy southern tip of the Ridge.

It'd taken us forty-five minutes to arrive. My fingers ached—Rosi and Daffi held on too hard. My vision blurred. These were the last moments of my life, and I wanted to soak it all in and treasure every moment.

We hopped from the wagon. Mother and the girls huddled in Papa's strong arms. The rest of my family gathered around them.

I followed Dreaf.

He slinked up the crumbling steps to the lone jagged pillar and raised his arms. Other blue-gray robed priests joined him, hands buried in their sleeves, hoods concealing their faces.

It was creepier than a cluster of newly hatched spiders on my pillow.

The crowd shushed.

He raised his voice. "Citizens, we gather for another glorious tithing ceremony!"

The throng cheered. Some booed. A ragged shoe smacked him in the chest.

I smirked. Not everyone welcomed the barbaric tithe.

Momma mounted the stairs and turned to the crowd. "Which of you would willingly give your lives to Maelstrom?" Her red-rimmed eyes sparked with fury. "My precious daughter *volunteered* so the god would bless you, as if he needed a blood payment to do good."

She pointed her finger at them. "Yet you all stand there and cheer for her death? Are you monsters?"

"Our nets come up empty," someone shouted.

"The trade ships sink before they reach the harbor," another called.

"We need the tithe!"

A green tomato landed at Dreaf's feet. "Maelstrom's a slug!"

Papa wrapped his arm around Momma and hustled her down the stairs.

Dreaf continued with his speech.

While he droned on about honoring the fiddling god of the sea, I studied the place. The temple had been built over a thousand years ago on the promontory overlooking the bay. Originally, it was a perfect open-air cube with grand pillars and a roof. But time, saltwater, and wind had eroded the cliffside foundation until one corner hung suspended in midair above the surf. A massive chunk had sheared off and plunged into the ocean. The roof had collapsed, leaving behind a small, jagged triangle of marble floor. The priests assumed Maelstrom wanted it thus and didn't repair it.

Soon I would jump into the crashing waves to become Maelstrom's newest servant. I swallowed. *Death, here I—* Although, if I ran, how far would I make it?

No. I had to do this for Rhygan.

Beyond the Ridge, in the hazy distance, the Pearl Islands gleamed like green jewels on the turquoise water. My mother's birthplace. Maybe my uncle, the governor, would take me in. Could I swim that far?

Definitely not. I shuddered.

The priest finished his speech. The people cheered.

Rosi and Daffi wailed.

I mounted the steps to join the priests. Two of them reached for my arms, but I jerked back. "Don't touch me!"

They parted, creating a blue-gray passageway funneling me to the edge.

I tucked the pearls inside my dress, took a deep breath, and squared my shoulders. I could do this. It was my duty as a royal daughter. Forget the people. This was for Rhygan. Face tilted toward the sky, I shouted, "Sirini, give me the strength to accept my fate!"

A gull cried. The surf crashed into rocks. A breeze tugged at my skirt.

Sirini didn't answer.

Fine. I'd worship her in death as I had in life, with all my might. I sprinted for the edge, slippers rasping against the floor, and dove off the broken slab of white marble.

I hung suspended above the frothy surface far below, my arms steepled, my back straight. Wind tore at my hair, clothing, and skin. My heart pounded in my ears. I sucked in briny spring air—and speared into the chilly water.

****

Tru headed for the chicken coop with his toolkit. How much more crap could Oakley dish out and not have it splash back on him? Bad enough he wouldn't work, but now he was breaking things?

The chickens gathered, a vortex of loose feathers, dust, and sharp claws. "Afternoon, girls. No feed this time. Just here to fix your house."

The gate hung canted, leaving a gap at the bottom for the smallest birds to sneak through. He nudged a brown hen back in. "Nice try." The latch wasn't busted, though. The top leather hinge had been stretched. Oak must have heaved on it.

"Easy repair, ladies. I'll be done in a minute." Tru pulled the nails and repositioned the leather until the gate was plumb.

Something slammed into his temple with a burst of pain, and he sprawled to the ground.

"Whoreson freak!" Oakley kicked Tru in the thigh. "You got me in trouble!"

Tru rolled to his feet, brought up his knee, and blocked the next kick with his boot. "You got yourself in trouble." He backed toward the paddock. "I had nothing to do with it."

Oak threw his right fist.

Tru danced out of reach, then darted forward and punched Oak. A sharp crack split the air. Coppery blood spewed out, coating his tunic and the ground.

Oak cursed and cupped his broken nose, his eyes watering. "I'll kill you."

"That's it!" Hawk stomped toward them and slapped the back of Oak's head. "Bad enough you're my worst employee, now you attack my best? I'll drive that arrogance and laziness from ya even if I have to beat it out." He grabbed Oak's ear and twisted.

He cried out and fell to his knees.

Hawk looked at Tru. "Are you injured?"

Tru rubbed his aching knuckles. "I'm fine."

"Run cold water on 'em. Nice punch." He dragged Oak toward the barn. "You're gonna learn some respect, by the gods, or I'll turn ya out, nephew or not."

Tru's head thudded. Maybe finding another place to sleep for a time would be wise. If Oak came creeping around for revenge, the loft was too exposed. Tru picked up his hammer, adjusted the leather hinge, and drove in the nails. "Good as new." The chickens scraped at the hard-packed dirt. He caged the two escaped hens and returned to the barn.

One of the horse stall gates stood open, blocking the main path down the center. Tru sighed. How many times had he told them not to do that? *Utterly worthless*. He'd have less to do if he worked alone. The gray mare was gone. The guest must have left. Tru closed the gate.

The clop of multiple hooves and snorts echoed through the open barn doors. More clients? Tru headed out.

Four magnificent black stallions trotted down the lane. Their riders wore sapphire blue, but the lead man showcased an embroidered scale on the gambeson.

Gods above—the emperor's enforcers. Tru stepped back. No one messed with them.

They dismounted. The leader's bald, sunburned head gleamed. His gaze swept the main building, the stable, and the strip of shops on the other side of the street. Analyzing. Cataloguing. Judging. His eyes narrowed, and he stomped toward Tru. "Do you work here?"

He nodded. "Yes, sir. May I be of service?"

"We're seeking a man who rode through here yesterday on a gray horse. He wore a green cloak with an onyx pin. Did you see him?"

"He arrived late last night and departed around noon. I tended his mare."

The enforcer squinted. "Is someone inside who might have spoken to him?"

"Earlier he was speaking with Oakley and Yarrow,

our stable hands. And Charity, the barmaid, probably served him."

The enforcer stomped inside. The other three stood in the street, scanning.

Tru was burly enough to take on brawlers, but no way would he tangle with enforcers. What had the man with the gray mare done? Had he broken a law? Was he a thief? A murderer? Tru would keep watch and protect his people.

Chapter Five

Entering the water was like getting punched in the throat.

At least I'd cleared the rocks. The riptide pulled me into a somersault, and my knee slammed my cheekbone with an explosion of pain. Saltwater seeped through my lips. The current tossed me sideways, then down. I spit out a mouthful of brine.

A bonfire flared in my chest. Black dots danced in my eyes. I needed air, but where was it? Everything blurred. My heart thudded in my ears. I pumped my arms, kicked my feet, and aimed for the bright pinpoint of sunlight in the distance. The undertow slurped me down. I thrashed but was flung about like a dry leaf in a tornado. I inhaled water, coughed, and repeated.

My strength evaporated. My lungs burned. This was it. My short, pathetic life was over before I'd even done anything worthwhile. I'd failed.

The sea spat me out.

I landed belly down on a rock shelf, gasping like a beached fish. Gray walls engulfed me. A cave? I hacked up more saltwater. *Thank you, Sirini, for saving my life!*

A black maw opened in the side wall. Was that a staircase? A way out? I'd investigate as soon as I had my breath.

I shut my eyes. So tired. So much pain. *Just need to rest…*

A wave crashed over me and yanked me back toward the cave mouth. I yelped and scrambled for a handhold, but the rock was slicker than polished glass.

A hand grasped my ankle and jerked me into the water.

I rolled in the swirling currents. Another hand grabbed my hip, then I faced the green-skinned god of the sea. I gasped, sucking in saltwater, and spewed it in his face.

"Yu wll be ine." His lips moved, showcasing pointy teeth. His eyes blazed like fire opals. Gill slits at his neck undulated in the current.

This is for you, Jayson. I shoved my thumbs in Maelstrom's eyeballs.

He cried out and shot away, a thin stream of blood trailing him.

I stroked my arms and kicked my feet, now tangled in the stupid blue dress, and popped to the surface, sucking air.

Maelstrom seized me and pulled me under. His lips moved, but I couldn't make out his words over the pounding surf. One webbed hand encircled my neck and squeezed.

My sapphire necklace heated like a fiery coal, and lightning shot into Maelstrom's chest, blasting him backward.

His mouth gaped like a bug-eyed flatfish, then he shook his head and came for me again.

I whirled and kicked away.

Something tugged at my waist. He'd grabbed my apron. He wrenched me toward him through the churning water.

Why won't he let me go? I used the momentum and

slammed my fist into his throat.

His bleeding eyeballs bulged.

I pulled one of my magic wooden hairpins and stabbed him in the shoulder.

He wrapped his webbed fingers around it and yanked, but it didn't budge. Blood trickled from the wound.

What does it take to get rid of him? I jammed my knee into his tenders.

His skin pinkened, and he drifted away, one hand clutching his neck, the other cradling his gonads.

I kicked my feet and shot out of the ocean, gasping for air. A stiff breeze battered my face, and dark clouds blotted out the sun.

Gale, the god of storms, blasted down from the roiling black masses, looking like someone's angry, muscular grandfather. The winds whipped his white hair and fluffy beard around his face.

Maelstrom rose up beside me and shook his fist at Gale. "She's mine!"

Gale pointed, and lightning bolted from his fingertip into Maelstrom's face.

He screamed and exploded from the water, hurtling at Gale like a harpoon. They grappled in midair, tumbling on the winds now stirring the sea into frothy waves.

Thank you, Gale! I swam away, my arm muscles burning. An incoming wave snatched me and hauled me under. I thrashed, kicked my feet, and broke the surface again. I sucked in air and spit out brine. Slowly, I made my way toward shore, though the currents had pulled me far from the Ridge.

The storm clouds raced south. I scanned the skies,

but they were clear of Maelstrom and Gale. *Fine by me*. Finally, the sun emerged, though much higher in the sky than it should have been. I'd been in the drink for over an hour? Not possible. I cracked my shin against a submerged rock, and my leg went numb. Kicking with my good leg and pumping with both arms, I swam for the rocky coast.

I thrashed my way out of the current and floated face up on gentler waves, my body bobbing and throbbing. My limbs slackened. The Ridge loomed far to the west, empty. I must have fallen asleep in the cave. Or passed out. No way had I fought Maelstrom for hours.

There was no sign of him now. Had Gale won the battle?

I grinned. *What a lousy sacrifice. Oh, damn!* I was supposed to die to save my brother and our city. Would Maelstrom take out his wrath on them now? *Useless!* I couldn't even perish properly.

Or maybe he didn't want me since he didn't return for me. Surely, he'd been victorious. He was stronger than Gale.

My elbow scraped a rock, and I rolled to my hands and knees. I'd been carried beyond the river mouth to the sandy beaches of Kurik, the neighboring realm. Crawling out took more physical and mental stamina than running off the Ridge, but I hauled myself up into the sea grasses, collapsed, and fell asleep.

I awoke at midday, the sun directly overhead.

Alive. That was a colossal failure. I'd botched my own sacrifice. *Absolutely inept*. Now what? I couldn't go back to High Point. The people all believed me dead and the tithe satisfied. If I showed up, they'd assume Maelstrom wasn't pleased with his offering and demand

Rosi or Daffi. Or kill Rhygan if they had him.

No, my old life was gone. I'd have to find a new one. By myself.

My chest tightened, and tears welled. I'd never been alone before. I'd always been surrounded by siblings, servants, guards, friends, even strangers who looked out for my well-being. Well, aside from screaming for my death.

Could I do this? I had no choice. Unless I returned to Maelstrom. Although Sirini wasn't speaking idly when she condemned him. That lightning from my necklace had to be her. I'd never shot anyone else with it.

But if she wanted him dead, why hadn't the strike killed him? I'd have to hide from him for the rest of my life or risk his wrath.

This lopsy-daisy attitude was unbecoming of a princess. I was an Acoris! I couldn't let a little thing like losing my family, friends, and home stop me from doing what was right. I'd find a new place to serve Sirini. I could still help innocents seek justice, though not as an enforcer, but there had to be something I could do. First step, walk to the nearest village.

My tongue had swelled and stuck to the roof of my mouth. My lips were dry and cracked. Dampness clung to my hair and clothes. Sand and salt encrusted everything, leaving my skin tight. I needed fresh water. The river was a short trek to the west, so I set out.

I found a shallow area and stretched out full-length in the chilly flow. Blessed be! I washed and drank deeply, rehydrating my abused body. *I'd be sore later, for sure.*

But I couldn't sleep here. The day was warm, but at

night, it'd be too cold. I hauled myself out of the water and stood, dripping, on the sandy bank. Squinting northward yielded no results. The town of Borderline lay up there somewhere, straddling the Emperor's Highway and the bridge that connected Kurik to Acoris. As a major trade hub between the two realms, Borderline was larger than most villages. I should be able to find work if I could make it by nightfall—providing no one recognized me. Dressed as a servant and lacking guards and matching sisters, I'd blend in. Probably.

I took a deep breath and set out. The groundcover transitioned from sharp, spiky grasses to short, fat-bladed wild varieties and half-buried rocks. Tangles of purple and white wildflowers dotted the prairie. The three slivered moons hung low on the horizon.

The goddess hadn't restored me, Maelstrom hadn't taken me, and the sea had spit me out like a rotten oyster. I was so useless.

That thought was dangerous. I needed to press forward and not give in to despair.

The sun blazed, baking the damp from my clothes and heating my skin. I tied the apron over my head, shielding my scalp and face.

What were Rosi and Daffi doing now? Were they weeping? Sorting my things and clcancd out my room? Being entertained by Batch One and Jerys? Mending? Preparing for the event? Napping?

Lazy birdies. While my feet ached and my breath rattled in my chest, they were probably cuddled in a downy bed, sleeping off the crying jags of this morning. What I wouldn't give for a pillow and a soft place to lie. Or a drink of water. My tongue was a roll of cotton batting in my mouth.

I mopped sweat off my face with the apron and veered toward the river for another sip.

I stopped short. The land had been gently climbing from sea level. The river hadn't. A huge drop from the bank to the river taunted me—no handholds, no roots or grasses, just a nasty fall into a raging current. I'd be swept back to the sea.

To the north, the land continued to rise. Behind me, I'd have to hike back an hour to reach a safe place to drink.

I was less than two hours from the village. I could make it.

A half hour later, I staggered into the farmlands south of town. They were newly plowed and planted. No little leafy heads popped up to announce their identity. I grinned. Good for them, or I'd be tempted to eat their little heads. My stomach growled. Far to the east, partially obscured by heat haze, a house squatted beneath the only two trees on the plain. But the distance between the house and the village looked about equal, so I continued north.

My slippers scuffed at the dirt, and I stubbed my toe on half-buried rocks. My arches burned. My thighs quivered. My belly cramped. My breath rasped. My tongue… If I didn't find water soon, I'd drop and never rise again. I trudged on.

Something moved ahead, and I squinted. A figure stood beside a fenced paddock.

I stumbled toward him, wheezing. He flickered, disappeared, then reappeared. I blinked. *That's foolishness. People don't flicker.* I caught my toe on a clod and dropped to one knee. *Ow.* I giggled. That wasn't a proper curtsy at all. Rather clumsy. I braced my hands and pushed. My butt rose into the air, and my forehead hit the ground.

Really, this was undignified before an audience. Grace would admonish me and demand I rise. *Right away, Grace*. I straightened and brushed grime off my palms, hair, and…the dress was caked with mud.

My tongue snaked out and scraped against cracked lips. I staggered forward several more steps, veered into a row of newly planted peas or beans or…I didn't know what they were. Poor little things. Best stay on the path. My leg buckled, and I slammed to my hands and knees.

"Miss?"

He was way out there.

"Miss?"

Closer now.

I fell to my side, ear pressed to the dirt. Thudding footfalls echoed through the ground, running toward me. My heart pounded harder, which was stupid. He would help me, or he would hurt me. Nothing I could do about it.

A shadow draped over my face, then he squatted beside me. "Are you all right?"

"Wrrr." My shaky voice mangled the word.

"I've got you. No worries." Faster than a puppy gobbling a table scrap, he whisked me into his arms and set off for the village.

Praise the goddess. I was safe.

He broke into a jog.

I shut my eyes.

Water gushed somewhere close. The man was priming a pump with me balanced on one knee. Clear liquid flowed from the spigot. I buried my face in the stream and gulped.

"Easy." He held my waist so I wouldn't topple into the grate over the cistern.

Sated, I leaned back into him. "Thank you." I ripped my apron off my head and wiped my face and hands. The white fabric came away streaked with grime. "Amazing what difference a drink of water can make." I smiled. "I look quite frightful, don't I, but I am grateful for your assistance." I tied the apron around my waist.

He grinned, flashing dimples on his weathered cheeks. "You're a might pretty, if I may be so bold, despite the dirt." A sandy-blond curl flopped into his green eye, and he shook his head, dislodging it.

He was much younger than I'd thought. Maybe midtwenties?

"My name's Truthful, but everybody calls me Tru."

"What a wonderful name. Mine is—" I couldn't blurt out my real one. I was supposed to be dead. "Calla."

"Like the lily?"

"Yes."

He hoisted me to my feet. "Praise the goddess I saw you weaving through the bean field, Calla. Your clothing tells a desperate story. Were you shipwrecked?"

Close enough. "The waves tossed me onto the beach. Borderline was the nearest village."

He whistled. "That's a long way to walk. What happened to the others on your ship?"

I had to stick truth-adjacent, or I'd have to keep track of a bunch of lies. "I'm the only one who came out of the water."

His eyebrows scrunched. "I'm sorry for your loss. Where are you from?"

My mother's home. "Pearl Islands."

"You don't have any way to pay for passage back,

do you?"

I shook my head. "I'm not interested in returning. Are there any shops in town that need a worker?"

"What can you do?"

Princesses didn't learn marketable skills. If someone needed a dance partner, I could tread the hardwoods all evening. But I didn't know anything exceptionally useful. Oh, except one. "I sew. Mending, embroidery, things like that."

Tru pursed his lips, and his olive-green eyes flecked with gold drifted across the dirt yard. "I don't think so. Can you scrub? My employer lost her kitchen help two days ago and hasn't filled the position."

"I can do that!" But I had one other need to attend to before applying. "Is there a privy nearby?"

His eyes widened, and his tanned cheeks colored. "Oh. I'm so sorry. Yes, this way."

I followed him to a coffin-sized box standing upright near a barn. I'd never been in one of these, but the royal stables had a few. I'd learned to hold my breath if passing anywhere near them. This one was no different. I hurried and finished.

Tru waited several steps away, his back turned.

"Thank you." I smoothed my skirt and patted my hair. "I should not beg for a job in this grubby state."

His gaze ran down my body, and heat flooded my face.

"I'm not gonna lie. You're a fair bit dirty. There's a bathhouse across the way if you've got a copper."

"No coins."

"Don't worry about it. Most of the folk around here arrive at a similar state by the end of the day." He studied my face and shrugged. "I'm at a loss to boost your spirits."

I laughed. Even stray mutts received mercy sometimes. Maybe Tru's employer would take pity on such a sorry sight. "Guess I'm ready, then."

He offered his arm, and I took it. And paid better attention to my surroundings. The path led between the stable and the paddock to the cobbled courtyard with the water pump. A massive three-story building squatted to the east, perpendicular to the barn, with a wing jutting out in the north to enclose the patio. To the left were noisy animal pens, a garden, an orchard, and the bank of the river. A dirt lane separated the property from other buildings. The Emperor's Highway and the bridge lay beyond them. "What is this place?"

"The Evening Inn. There are rooms for rent and a dining hall. Locals come in for food and ale." Tru headed for the largest building on the right. "Hawk and Evening run it. If you get the job, you'll be working for her. She goes by Eve." He waved me in through the open doorway.

I stepped into a stifling kitchen and the enticing aromas of meat, onions, and bread. My stomach moaned loud enough to attract the attention of the plump woman stirring the stewpot.

She sneered. "I don't give handouts. Get out."

Chapter Six

Handouts? As if I'd accept charity. I'd work for my bread.

"This is Calla," Tru said. "She was shipwrecked and walked into town. You need help; she needs work and a place to sleep."

Eve's gaze ran down my body. "She's too skinny to work."

"I'm stronger than I look." Puppy-dog eyes wouldn't move the battle-axe's heart. I squared my shoulders. Then my stomach rumbled loud enough for the guests on the third floor to catch, and my face heated. I clasped my hands over my belly.

"You're half-starved." Tru guided me to a bench at the long worktable. "Two bowls of stew, Eve. I'm buying." He tossed a silver coin onto the grimy table surface. "We can talk about employment after we eat."

Tears puddled in my eyes. "You're being so kind to me, Tru. I can't repay you."

He patted my hand. "Don't bother. You're in sore need of assistance, and I'm pleased to help. I know what it's like to be in a strange place with no money."

Eve glared at me but dished out goat stew, followed by a couple of honey wheat rolls, a cup of soft yellow cheese, and two mugs of ale. Simple food, but glorious.

I bowed my head, closed my eyes, and offered a quick prayer of thanks. Nothing had gone as expected today, but Tru was surely a gift from the goddess. I opened my eyes.

He was staring at me.

"What?"

"Who did you pray to?"

"Sirini."

He nodded and dug into his meal. "Nice."

"Why?"

He blew on a spoonful of stew. "If you'd said Maelstrom, my opinion of you would have plummeted. We don't venerate him here."

I shuddered. "I wouldn't worship Maelstrom if my life depended on it." *No irony there*. I matched Tru's pace in downing the best meal I'd ever eaten.

Eve pointed at a basin in the corner. "Clean up."

He rose, but I stopped him. "I'll do it."

Eve watched me with narrowed eyes.

I scrubbed the dishes, dried them, and stacked them on the table.

"Hmmm." She crossed her arms over her chest. "You're a mite slow but thorough. Now scour the worktable."

Tru grinned. "Does she have the job?"

"For now. For five hours of labor, I'll give you a place to sleep tonight and a silver."

He stepped forward. "That's a bit cheap, even for you."

I grabbed the rag from the washbasin. "I accept. Thank you, Mistress."

She glared. "Eve will do."

Tru smiled at me. "You'll be fine. I'll come fetch you when your shift is over."

Warmth spread through my chest. "Thank you. I

don't know what I'd have done without you."

"I'm glad you survived. See you later." He walked out the back door.

The lie prickled, but the truth was too dangerous. I rinsed the rag, found a scrubbing brush, and tackled the filthy work surface. I swept the bluestone floor after that, then the dining room began filling with patrons.

A lovely young woman hustled through the swinging door and shrugged off her cloak. "Sorry I'm late." She hung the garment on a wall peg and turned to me. "I'm Charity. Who are you?"

I had to think for a second. "Calla."

"You're the new helper?"

I nodded. "For tonight."

Her smile widened. "Fantastic! I hate scrubbing floors after serving meals all night." She tied an apron around her waist, tugged the bodice of her tunic down, and fluffed her curly dark-brown hair so it brushed the tops of her pale breasts. She winked. "Better tips when there's a display worth viewing."

"Are you going to work or just primp?" Eve pulled fresh rolls from the oven.

Charity gathered cups and filled them with soft cheese from the vat. "You're new in town?"

"Chat later." Eve ladled out brimming bowls of stew.

"The floors are finished." I bobbed a curtsy. "Now what should I do?"

"Assist her."

I prepped trays. Charity would carry them out to waiting diners, return with dirty dishes, take out mugs of ale or wine, and come for more bread, stew, or cheese.

Two hours into my shift, pain speared through my

heels and up my calves, and my thighs trembled. But I was earning my way, surviving on my own, and making friends.

****

Dirt or no dirt, Calla was the prettiest woman Tru had ever seen. And strong! She'd survived a harrowing experience, walked for hours, then impressed Eve enough to get the job. Being alone and afraid in a new place could buckle anyone, but Calla stood. Amazing.

He began his evening chores.

Her shipwreck tale was horse crap. Her words were tinged with a faint dandelion. She'd been in the sea. The Pearl Islands was a half-truth. Her name was also a fib, but he wasn't one to judge. He had no clue what his birth name was, either. But she'd left out certain specifics. Anyone else would have been suckered by her story.

Why had she been in the water? Had she jumped off a ship to escape a harsh taskmaster? Was she a slave? That vile practice was illegal in the Five Realms but not in other lands. And why did she feel the need to lie? Lying was the worst form of treachery.

He snorted. Why should she trust him? He was a stranger, an unknown. She was probably wary. He'd have to prove himself worthy. And he would.

He climbed into the loft for his toolkit. After Oak's punishment, would he come looking for revenge? Tru'd haul the ladder up into the loft. Easy enough. Then he could sleep with both eyes closed. A weapon might be welcome, too. He grabbed his hammer and a pair of cutters and hid them in his blankets.

The sun sank, and shadows grew. The tack still needed scrubbing, but it could wait. An ale for his parched throat would top off this crap-filled day. If any guests showed up after dark, Hawk would fetch Tru.

He crossed the barn and stepped into the empty street. The secondary barn glowed with lantern light. Surely, Oak and Yarrow were finished. There were only four animals, including Tru's mare. A chill skittered down his arms. Had Oak taken his vengeance out on Lady?

Tru dashed across the lane and entered. Lady nickered, and he sighed. "Hey, girl. Did those brutes treat you right?" He rubbed her nose and released the latch. "Come on out so I can see you." She snorted and surged forward, her ears loose and relaxed, her tail raised. "Aw, I'm happy to see you, too." Her coat and eyes gleamed. Her legs were clean. Tru checked her stall. It was scrubbed, with fresh hay laid down. "Amazing. Hawk whipped them into shape, didn't he?"

Lady brushed her lips over Tru's hair.

He chuckled. "I know. I need a haircut. Into your place, and I'll give you a treat. Tomorrow we'll go for a run. How does that sound?" If he missed another day of exercising her, she'd grump for a week.

Lady backed into her stall and nipped his tunic.

"I'll fetch you an apple." The basket of last fall's harvest hung on the wall. He grabbed a withered specimen and took it to her. She didn't care if it was bruised.

At the scent of fresh-cut fruit, a cacophony of nickers filled the space, and four beautiful horses poked out of nearby stalls.

The enforcers' mounts. They were staying the night.

A few minutes later, Tru entered the dining hall and found a seat. The soldiers weren't in attendance, but locals packed the place. Charity brought him an ale, and he smiled. "Thanks."

She winked and waded into the fray, swinging her hips and bending over to chat with customers. She'd earn good tips tonight.

"Tru! Axle left; now we need a fourth." Indy paused his card shuffling to point at the empty chair by him. "Come join us. No coppers."

"Sure." He took the seat. "What's wild?"

The front door opened, and a blast of cool air swept through the room.

"Shut the door, ya git!" Indy hollered.

Oak stood in the doorway, nose swollen, eyes blackened, and filthier than the underside of a privy seat. He scowled and pointed at Tru. "Watch yer back. I'm coming for ya."

Tru snickered. "Crawl away and lick your wounds, cur."

Oak slammed the door behind him.

"You shined his eyes?" Indy asked.

Tru nodded. "He blindsided me, but I gave it back."

"Good on ya," someone else said. "That shite deserved a good beatin'."

Charity brought a pitcher and refilled the mugs. She leaned down to whisper in his ear. "I know you can handle him, but please be careful. I've never seen him that angry."

"I'll be fine."

****

At the end of my shift, I clung to the table's edge, my legs trembling and throbbing.

Charity sat beside me and rested her chin in her hand, eyes closed. "I'm half dead."

Eve appraised me with narrowed eyes. "I'm

impressed. Didn't think you'd make it." She flipped a silver coin at me.

I caught it. "Thank you. Shall I return tomorrow?"

"Yes!" Charity opened her eyes. "Please, Eve. We need her."

Eve nodded. "We'll see how you do. Come at noon prepared to work a full eight hours."

My thighs quivered. "Thank you. I'll be here."

Charity groaned. "I'll wipe down the tables, then I'm going home. My feet are killing me."

Eve grunted. "You should be accustomed to the labor by now. You're too soft."

"I'll toughen up."

Tru entered the back door. "Evening, ladies."

Charity smiled. "Greetings, handsome. Are you free to walk me home?"

"Come to collect Calla." He looked to Eve. "How'd she do? Are you hiring her?"

"For tomorrow. Show her to the loft. She can sleep there tonight."

Charity's smile slid off. "What? She's with you?"

"Just met her today. Come on, Calla, I'll help you settle."

Charity's eyebrows furrowed. "But—"

A cleaning rag smacked her in the chest. Eve pointed to the dining room. "Work first, then jealous squabble. Out."

Charity glared at me and slipped through the swinging door.

Lovely. Now she thought I'd poached her man. I'd clear that up tomorrow—before she thought up ways to get me fired.

Tru took my arm. "I imagine your feet are aching."

I leaned on him. Pain shot from my heels to my hips, and I winced. "I'm forever saying thank you, but I mean it."

He led me out the back door. I shivered and huddled closer to soak in his heat, taking ginger steps across the courtyard illuminated by hanging lanterns. Tru opened a side door in the barn, and we entered. Comforting warmth and the scents of hay, horses, and manure swirled around me.

"You get used to the smell." He grabbed a lit lantern off a hook and crossed to a ladder. "You first."

I climbed, stretching my aching arches on each rung, and made it to the loft without falling off or tangling my ankles in my dress. Up here, the sweet hay odor overpowered the unpleasant manure.

Tru ascended one-handed and hung the lantern. "It doesn't look like much, but this is a great place to sleep."

Faint light spilled onto a makeshift sleeping area. Three walls of stacked bales surrounded a narrow alcove. A wool blanket served as a bed, and hooks held articles of clothing. A pair of fine-though-scuffed boots rested at the pallet near my feet.

This space wasn't for me. "Who sleeps here?"

"I do."

Oh no. Not happening. I stepped back, close to the edge of the loft, heart pounding. He blocked the exit by the ladder, but I'd jump before being used in that manner.

Tru gestured to a lone bale inside the makeshift room. "Have a seat. Enforcers arrived today, and I need to check their horses. Then I'll make a place for you on the far side. Be right back." He scurried down the ladder.

Father's enforcers were here? I was supposed to be one of them.

I slumped against the hay wall. They all knew me. If even one of them spotted me, I'd be hauled back to High Point, and Maelstrom would get me. Or one of my sisters.

Chapter Seven

I couldn't go back home, and Tru seemed like an honorable man. I'd simply tell him that I wasn't the type of girl to share his blanket.

Tru returned. "Sorry about that. I was thinking how inappropriate this looks, with me sleeping up here, too." He ran his hands through his hair. "I assumed Eve would give you a room in the inn. If I'd known she was bunking you here, I'd have been prepared." He let out a deep breath and grabbed a hay hook. "I can't offer you a door or a lock, but you'll be safe here tonight. Honest."

What a relief. He wasn't demanding…good. I stared at him, his features hidden in shadow. He'd been kind. I'd have to trust him now or brave the streets to find another place to sleep. For a silver. I nodded. "Thank you."

He began shifting bales in the dim light. Horses in the bays below made snuffling noises.

My feet cramped into tight knots, and I held my breath. No crying now.

Tru approached. "Come tell me if this is acceptable." He offered his hand, pulled me upright, and handed me the lantern.

I crept down the hay-strewn planks to the far end of the loft.

He lit a second lamp and hung it from a ceiling beam. "In there." He pointed at an opening in the wall.

I stepped through the gap.

He'd hollowed out a narrow, private space. One bale rested beside the doorway for a seat. I collapsed onto it, feet throbbing. Two hay hooks protruded for clothing. As I owned only the garments I wore and wouldn't dream of removing them with a strange man sleeping nearby, the hooks were thoughtful but useless. "This is lovely. Thank you."

He smiled and took the lantern from me. "Open flames close to hay is courting disaster." He hung it beside the other. "Be right back." He flew down the ladder, banged around below, then reappeared with two blankets slung over his shoulder. He tossed one down in the center of my alcove and smoothed it out.

I pulled off my shoes and rubbed my aching feet.

"They smell like horse, but they're soft and warm." He flicked the second blanket to cover the first and stepped back. "If you need something, holler."

"I couldn't possibly ask for more." Like a washing cloth and fresh water, a comb, a sleeping gown, a pillow… "Again, thank you." This was beyond weird. My first night away from home, my sisters, and my usual routine. Tears welled, but I blinked them back. How was I supposed to relax when everything was new, unusual, and uncomfortable?

Tru ran his hand through his curls. "Then I'll let you sleep."

"Wait."

He paused. "Do you need anything else?"

"Would you—could you stay and talk for a few minutes?"

He sat, resting his back against the wall of hay. "Your first night in a strange place, away from friends and family, unsure about your future. I understand. If you were home, what would you be doing now?"

I grinned. "Chatting with my sisters while we brushed our hair."

"I've got a comb. Want me to get it for you?"

"No, I'll be fine until I can purchase my own." My feet throbbed, my thighs spasmed, and my lower back ached like someone had pummeled me. If I awoke tomorrow morning able to walk, it'd be a miracle. "Take my mind off my suffering. Talk to me."

"About what?"

"Why do you live up here? How old are you? Do you have family?"

He snickered. "Sleeping in the loft is a perk of my employment. I'm twenty-five years old, or close to it, and have no family."

"You're not sure how old you are?"

"Not really. I was abandoned in a forest as a babe. A hunter found me, took pity, and raised me."

I'd heard of people abandoning infants in the wilderness, but never thought I'd meet someone who'd survived. "Where is the hunter now?"

Tru shrugged. "He disappeared eleven years ago."

"I'm sorry."

"Thanks. He did well by me. Taught me to read and write, how to care for myself, even got me this job. He slept up here with me. We worked all day and drank ale all night."

"When you were a child?"

"Why not?"

Not a standard upbringing. "What happened to him?" *Brilliant, Cali. Way to ask inappropriate questions.* "Never mind. You don't have to answer."

Tru shredded a sliver of hay between his fingers. "I don't mind sharing. One night he and I were playing cards in the dining hall when two strangers came in looking for rooms. Gray—my guardian—took one look at them and ducked like he'd dropped something. When he rose, he whispered we were leaving through the kitchen and to wait for his word. Soon as the men were seated, Gray and I snuck out. He packed his bags and said he'd be back for me when it was safe. I never saw him again."

"That's awful. Have you ever tried looking for him? Did he have a home somewhere?"

"Not that I know of. As long as I can remember, we wandered the Five Realms, camping at night, taking odd jobs, never staying in one place longer than a few days. He bought me a mare when I was old enough, and we didn't need anything else. When we lingered here for two weeks and took employment as stable hands, I thought he'd decided to make this our home."

"After he left, Eve let you stay?"

"She's had a touch of softness for me since the first day."

I laughed. "I've met Eve. She doesn't have any softness about her."

"It's hidden, but she's a sweetheart." He winked. "Give her time. You'll see."

I stretched, flexed my feet, and yawned. "Thank you for sharing."

"Now you."

My shoulders sank. I should have expected that. *What can I say?* Princess Calilee the Ninth was dead. I cleared my throat. "What do you want to know?"

"You mentioned sisters. How many?"

"A hundred or so."

He laughed. "I imagine large families can make a house feel cramped. Must have been nice, to have that many people love you."

"Yes. I miss them terribly."

"And you were a seamstress? Were you an apprentice?"

"No, I made things for my siblings and the household. I enjoyed it whereas my sisters showed more interest in"—history, fashion, royal bloodlines, charity work—"other subjects." My heart compacted to the size of a pebble.

"Maybe I could hire you to fix a rent in my other shirt?"

"No need to pay. I'll do it willingly." I yawned.

"That's my signal to leave." He rose and smiled. "Good night." He turned down one lantern outside my alcove and took the other with him. Wood scraped against wood. Had he pulled the ladder into the loft? The light dimmed.

I pitched forward onto the blankets and stretched out. Everything ached and spasmed. My remaining hair pin was jabbing my skull. I yanked it out and set it aside, along with the pearls and my sapphires.

If I were home, I'd be lying on a soft mattress with linens and warmed quilts in a comfortable sleeping gown, my hair re-braided, my face scrubbed. My sisters—

Tears welled. *No! No crying.* I couldn't return, so dwelling on them would make me more miserable. This was my life now.

Tomorrow, I'd work my shift for Eve and prove I was a worthy employee—if I wasn't too sore to move.

I'd find a new purpose. I was no longer a useless ninth princess. I had a friend, Tru. Maybe Charity, too, if I could clear up the misunderstanding.

Tru's soft snores carried across the loft. I closed my eyes and drifted off.

I awoke to the snuffling sounds of the horses and someone banging around. I bolted upright, heart pounding. Who was it? I crawled to the edge.

Tru stood below, talking to a horse.

I sighed. Not a stranger.

He looked up and smiled. "You're awake. How do you feel?"

"Great." Which was odd. I'd been so sore last night I could hardly move. But nothing ached, throbbed, or complained, thank the goddess. "How are you?"

He laughed. "Fine as corn silk. I laid out a few things. Come down when you're ready."

I turned and spotted a basin of fresh water, a washing rag, a clean pair of stockings, and a comb. *Bless you, Tru!* I carried the treasures into my room. My face and hands scrubbed up well, but the dress was ruined. Eve would never send me into the dining room in it—which was great if the enforcers were still here.

Today was my twentieth birthday. Jerys and Rhyada probably woke Rosi and Daffi early as a prank   No. No more thinking about them. I'm Calla now, a kitchen helper, a shipwrecked girl from the Pearl Islands.

After combing hay from my hair, I braided it in two tails, wrapped them against my head, and secured them with the wooden pin. I hung the sapphires and pearls around my neck and tucked them into my shirt. I folded the blankets, piled Tru's things on the bale, and emerged.

Tru met me at the base of the ladder. "Let's eat—

breakfast is always free for the hired help—then you can plan your day. Do your feet hurt?"

"No, they feel great. A good night's sleep put me to rights."

He opened the side door to a splash of bright sunlight. "Beautiful day, if you want to explore town before your shift begins."

"I need to purchase a few things." No telling what a silver would buy. Did they sell used clothing here? They'd have fabric to make my own, which would be cheaper than buying pre-made. I'd require shoes, too. The heel on the right one had worn so thin it'd split soon. I walked beside Tru toward the kitchen, squinting.

Searing pain blazed across my forearms. I stopped and brushed my hand over the red spots. Had I been stung by an insect? The redness spread—on both arms— radiating outward to my wrists and elbows. The scent of cooking meat rose from my skin. What was happening? My face heated, started itching, then burned like a firebrand pressed against my cheeks. "Tru?" I touched my chin.

Tru turned, his eyes widened, and he ran to the pump. "Wet down." He primed it and worked the lever. Cold liquid spouted from the faucet.

I thrust my searing arms under the spray and whimpered. The chilled liquid soothed my blistering skin.

The water changed direction and splattered my face.

I sputtered and blocked the flow with my hands. What was going on? How was that possible? Water shouldn't stream sideways.

Chapter Eight

I ducked and turned away, but the water followed me.

"How did—" Tru stopped pumping. "Whoa!"

Water spewed sideways from the spigot, drenching my hot face, then changing direction to drill me in the chest. The force shoved me back, and I landed on my bottom. "Shut it off!" I coughed, twisting my face away from the spray.

"I did!"

It knocked me over and drove me across the paving stones. They scraped my burned flesh, and my dress tore up to my knee. I screamed.

Tru picked me up and raced for the kitchen.

The water stopped.

He shouldered through the door, kicked it closed, and set me on the bench. "Your face is blistering. How are your arms?"

Eve scowled, her fists deep in raw bread dough. "What's going on?"

"She's burning." He gently took my hands and examined my skin. White blisters covered them.

I blinked back tears. "How? I've never been sunburned before." I inherited Momma's tan island skin. My fair-skinned, red-haired siblings had to be careful, but not me.

Tru reared back and stared.

The blisters faded, and my skin transitioned back to light brown. Within seconds, my arms were normal again. I rested my fingertips against the spot. The heat was dissipating. "How's my face?"

He pursed his lips. "Almost healed."

"What happened?" Eve grabbed my chin with her flour-dusted hand and turned my face toward the candles suspended from the ceiling. "She looks fine to me."

"I swear to you, she was burning." He ran his hand through his hair. "And the water from the pump attacked her!"

She rolled her eyes. "It's too early for hysterics. Do you want breakfast or not?"

He stared at me.

I dripped on the flagstones. "Yes, please."

"Did you anger Beck somehow?" He sat on the other bench.

I shook my head. I'd never worshipped the god of fresh water, much less prayed to him. I'd certainly never made him angry, so why had he attacked me? "Is there a Beck temple here?"

"No." Eve set bowls of porridge in front of Tru and me. "Nearest one's in Heartside."

Probably some tiny village up in the lake region. I should have paid better attention in geography class, but Palama said education was wasted on someone promised to the sea, and I'd believed her for several years until Daffi convinced me otherwise.

But my missed lessons wouldn't bother Beck. I'd need to fix it before he sent something more dangerous after me.

My mouth watered at the savory scent drifting up from my bowl, and I dug in. It was mostly cooked grains with chunks of egg, ham, and onion. I'd finished half my portion before Tru stopped staring and tucked in to his.

Eve continued kneading bread at the other end of the table, shaping rolls and loading them onto a wooden peel.

"You've offended Beck and Zelos." A curl hung in Tru's eye, and he shook his head, dislodging it. "What did you do?"

"Nothing."

"You didn't curse their names or mock them?"

"No. I wouldn't do such a thing." Though I'd attacked Maelstrom. A chill skittered across my arms. Had Gale been aiming at me with that bolt? No, he wouldn't miss his target. He'd hit Maelstrom. Maybe he'd complained to the pantheon when I escaped? What if he'd turned all the other gods against me? How could I survive that?

"You worship Sirini?" Tru asked.

I nodded.

"You should go to her temple and ask a priestess for advice." He scraped his bowl and crossed to the washbasin.

My meal sat heavy in my stomach, but I finished what I'd been given. Wasting food would insult Eve, and I couldn't afford that. And Tru was correct. I should ask Sirini's blessing on my new life and offer a sacrifice.

"I'll be right back." He darted out the door and slammed it behind him.

"Mind the hinges!" Eve shouted.

He wouldn't want to be anywhere near me after that, and I didn't blame him. I'd lost my only friend. My eyes burned, but I blinked. No feeling sorry for myself. I washed my dishes.

Eve hefted the full peel to the oven, slammed the door, and tossed the empty paddle onto the table. "If you're going to live here, visit the temples of Sprout and Xyla, also. This town don't prosper without them."

"Thank you. I'll do that." I'd never worshipped the god of plants and farming or the goddess of the hunt, but my new life could use the deities' blessings. Especially if Zelos and Beck were furious with me.

Tru burst back into the kitchen with a dark-blue cloth and handed it to me. "Here."

I blinked. He'd come back? He wasn't angry? I shook out the hooded cloak. "What for?"

"To protect you from Zelos."

My face heated. *Of course*. I couldn't walk to the temple without stepping outside. I flung the garment over my shoulders and settled the hood. "Am I covered?"

"If you keep your head down. Let's go."

"You're going with me?"

He grinned. "Do you know how to get there yourself?"

"No."

"Then let's go."

I tucked my chin and followed him outside. Breath held, I waited. Nothing happened. I sighed. "Seems to work."

"To the temple." He headed north, hugging the shadow of the building. "No problems with the sun?"

"No." This might be a good opportunity to handle my other business, as well. "Do you have a jeweler in town who will buy…things?"

"What things?"

I had to trust him. Working would take too long to save up for the items I needed. I glanced over my shoulder. *Good, we are alone*. I pulled out the pearls. "I want to sell a few."

Tru's eyes widened, and he cradled the necklace on his fingertips. "This is worth a fortune! Where did you get it?"

"It was given to me before I jumped into the water." Technically true.

"Your mistress gave you this?" He nodded. "Trying to save her jewels, not caring if you perished weighed down with unnecessary items. Did she give you anything else?"

I cringed at his misunderstanding, but my sisters' lives and mine depended on me being dead. "This is all I have." He didn't need to know about the sapphires. I'd never sell them, and they were all I had left of my family.

Plus, they might zap someone like they did Maelstrom.

"There is someone in town who'll probably buy a couple of these, but I doubt he could afford them all. You'd have to go to the capital for that."

"A few should do, but I don't want to show him the entire strand. Do you have cutters?"

"No."

"Take me to a sewing store first, please. I'll buy a small kit, then we can visit the temple, the jewelers, and shops for clothing, shoes, and a grooming set."

"We'll be hard-pressed to handle all this before your shift begins."

"Can you spare a few hours? I don't want to get you into trouble."

He shrugged. "I have two assistants. They can do the morning chores, and I'll work late tonight. No worries."

We crossed the stone patio—stopping briefly at the

goat pen for Tru to scratch the kid that bounced toward him—and stepped into the dirt alley. My suede slippers weren't meant for outdoor use, and every pebble in the path poked my soles. I peeked around my hood at the village, but the backs of buildings gave no clue to the contents.

My toes slipped into a divot, and I pitched forward.

Tru caught my elbow. "Watch your step."

"I didn't see it."

Dirt swirled around my slippers, and the hole widened.

I stepped back. What was happening?

The depression widened. A whirlwind of dust rose to my waist, and the pit grew deeper and wider, stretching to swallow my feet.

I scrambled back and coughed.

Tru grasped my hand and pulled me to the side.

The entire path disintegrated, leaving behind a deep, gaping chasm.

I screamed. Was the earth trying to consume me?

****

Tru cursed. The gods were furious. "Run!" He raced east, hauling Calla behind him, then darted into a passageway between two buildings. Several strides in, he glanced back.

The chasm followed them between the shops, picking up speed and spitting dust.

Sirini, save her! If Calla fell into that abyss, she'd never crawl out again.

The dirt beneath her heels collapsed, and she stumbled backward with a cry.

Tru yanked her forward, hauling her behind him. What had she done to deserve this?

A wooden boardwalk lined both sides of the Emperor's Highway. Maybe she'd be safe once off the ground. They hopped onto it and turned right, running alongside the heavy traffic, their feet pounding against the slats.

She looked back and gasped. "It stopped."

He pivoted and returned to the alley.

Hard-packed dirt, pebbles, a few weeds—it was all normal. No chasm leading to the depths, no swirling dust, not even a scar where it'd been opened moments before.

"Did we hallucinate it?"

He stared at her. "You did something bad. Now Zephyra and Tera are after you, too?"

"I swear, I don't know why sun, water, breeze, and land are angry!"

Chapter Nine

"The gods are after you." Tru crossed his arms. "Did you let your mistress drown in the accident? Curse the gods as the ship sank? Dishonor them? Tell me what you did."

A woman passed them, a grass basket in one hand. Men on horseback and several donkey-drawn carts creaked down the highway in both directions. A foreigner hurried by, his fluffy red tail held high out of the dust. No one paid heed to them.

Calla clenched her trembling fingers.

Tru nodded. "I can see it on your face. You know what you did. Tell me. Otherwise, I can't help you fix it."

She snorted. "How can I make this right? I doubt offering sacrifices at all the temples would undo—"

"Undo what?"

Tears welled, and her face scrunched. "I battled Maelstrom."

Normal spring scents perfumed the air, not curdled milk or dandelion. It was the truth. "Like an argument? You shouted at him?"

"No. I gouged his eyeballs. Punched him in the throat. Stabbed him in the shoulder with a hair pin. And kneed him in…a more sensitive area."

He smiled. "Seriously? He tried to take you under, and you fought him?"

She nodded. Tears tracked down her face, and she wiped them away. That moment in the sunshine left her hand reddened. "He grabbed my ankle, and I didn't want to die. My brothers taught me self-defense, and I reacted automatically. I didn't mean to offend the pantheon."

She hadn't been on a sinking boat. She'd been sacrificed to Maelstrom in the place of her mistress. And survived. No wonder she'd lied about her identity—she didn't want to be tossed back in to finish the tithe.

She'd struck the god! Tru laughed. "You're amazing. Sorry, that's not helpful. I'm picturing you in the water, punching that sot in the windpipe. But striking him wouldn't have offended Tera, yet she's the one who attacked you in the road back there, so there's something else going on. We need to visit Sirini's temple."

"Cutters, first. I want to offer her a few of these silver beads."

Tru pointed east. "This way, along the boardwalk."

They passed the apothecary on the corner and stopped at the earthen cross street for a man on a ram to ride by. Would Tera open the dirt and attempt to swallow them again? She hated Maelstrom, so Calla's battle with him would probably make her joyous, if she'd heard about it. And how did any of the gods know about that fight? Did Maelstrom whine to them? They'd be more likely to mock him than feel pity.

"Are you afraid to try it?" Tru asked.

She nodded. "We should run."

"You first."

She took off, and he followed. The ground beneath her feet shifted, but she made it across the lane and leapt onto the boardwalk. The building on the corner contained two shops, a used clothing dealer and a seamstress.

Calla hurried inside and gaped. "Oh, how lovely. I could stay here for hours."

"We shouldn't, though."

"Of course." She found a simple sewing kit with two sets of cutters. All the tools fit nicely in a leather case with straps. She chose four spools of thread and handed over her only coin, the silver. With no pockets, she knotted her apron into a bag.

He slipped his hand into his pocket and fingered the bone button he'd spotted near the water pump earlier. It'd popped off Calla's dress when Beck attacked her. Tru'd give it back. Eventually. "The temple is two streets north." He led her back to the highway. Carts and horses traveled in both directions. They'd have to wait for a break to cross. She'd never make it. The distance was too great, and if the land goddess opened a rift, a lot of people would be hurt. Or killed.

The way cleared, and Tru whisked Calla into his arms. *Tiny thing weighs almost nothing.* She clung to his neck, and he crossed at a run.

"Sorry." He set her on her feet. "I didn't think we should chance an accident."

She nodded. "Good thing there are wooden boardwalks."

The corner they stood on featured a farmer's market that wouldn't open until next week. An ancient elm tree spread new leaves over the southwest edge of the block, offering shade for them and camouflage to the pixie nest in the canopy. The bazaar sprawled across the block, filled with rows of shuttered stalls and empty tents. Permanent buildings lined the far edges. The boardwalk ran all the way around the district, but dirt, grass, and a few paving stones littered the shopping area. If she ever wanted to visit, she'd need to be carried. He hid a grin. He'd volunteer for that duty.

She squatted in the safety of the elm, her back to the street, and slid the necklace into her lap. Tru'd never seen a tithing ceremony, but he'd heard the victim always wore a gift from Maelstrom. What a blessing Calla had not only survived but saved the pearls. That damned god could support her financially.

Each pearl and bead were separated by tiny knots, so clipping the string wouldn't send expensive baubles rolling in every direction. With a few strategic cuts, she freed three silver beads and three black pearls from the strand. She put everything back in her apron purse and tied it around her waist. "I'm ready."

He led her north, his hand on the small of her back. She had to be frightened. Could he fight a god? No telling, but he'd protect Calla with his life if need be. *Deities, bring it on.*

****

Tru was warm and strong and far more helpful than I deserved. If something happened to him while he protected me, I'd never forgive myself. Saving my useless life wasn't worth his.

A hearty gust of wind slammed into me. I let out an embarrassing squeak and stumbled into the street—and the path of a rondecka beast. The startled rider yanked back on the reins. Sharp cloven hooves loomed above me. The road dirt swamped my feet as if I'd stepped into quicksand. I screamed, and dust filled my mouth.

Tru hauled me out.

I clung to him on the boardwalk.

He held me tight. "Were you injured?"

"No." My heart pounded in my chest, and my eyes burned, but I fought off tears. Who knew the goddess of breezes could blast hard enough to toss me into the street? That was more like— I looked up.

Dark-gray clouds closed in from the south, rolling and spitting lightning. Gale raced toward me. The gusts of wind buffeting Tru and me were the prelude to the real battle.

"Run!" He grabbed my hand and tugged me down the boardwalk, past the open-air market and the furrier at the far end. He didn't check for traffic but darted across the next lane and entered the temple grounds.

Our footfalls pounded against the granite walkway, the only path through the wide, concentric rings that surrounded the building—an outer border of gray stones the size of my fist, a middle of white gravel, and an innermost ring of fine silver sand. In the center lay the massive, round building with a domed roof.

For half a moment, I stared at the marvel, the grandeur, the sheer breathtaking beauty. Granite steps led visitors to a portico with three painted statues of the goddess, each standing twice my height. Above them, alternating bands of moonstone and white marble marched like exotic jewelry up to the polished silver roof, which was topped with a moonstone carved into a crescent shape.

No doors barred entry to the temple. An arched opening beckoned us inside.

None of the other gods would dare enter this sanctuary, not even to pursue me. As proof, Gale's storm whipped through the city streets, but the winds didn't penetrate Sirini's grounds.

I touched my fingertips to my forehead, lips, and

heart and raced up the steps to the portico.

"Look."

I turned. The clouds were shredding and dissipating like tufts of wool pulled through a comb. Gale had canceled his attack on me, as had Zephyra, the breeze goddess. Good. "Let's go in."

The clunk of Tru's heavy work boots and the rasp of my slippers against the granite floor echoed in the foyer. Creamy pillars funneled us into the immense central worship chamber.

Diffused sunlight from opaque windows in the ceiling—four stories up—bathed the hall with light. Three life-size marble statues of the goddess stood at the far end of the circular room, shoulder to shoulder, hands outstretched for offerings. Round stools filled the space for worshipers. A massive cauldron of prayer tokens sat in the center, below the moonstone crescent on the roof. Priestesses in white, gray, or silver robes hovered nearby.

An ancient woman with long hair parted from the group and approached. "Greetings, daughter. I am Prudence, the high priestess of this temple. I see a heavy burden lies upon you."

That obvious? "Greetings, Prudence. I have somehow angered the gods and wish to appeal to Sirini for…" For what? Guidance? Protection? A weapon?

Prudence grinned. "I know what you seek. It was foretold in the Writings. Come. We will read them together, and you will find answers."

Just what I needed. I glanced at Tru, his eyes the size of stew bowls. "May my friend come?"

Prudence nodded and walked toward the three statues. She stopped before the figures and touched her fingers to her forehead, lips, and heart, then crossed behind them.

Back home, I'd never ventured beyond the stools. I'd draw my prayer token from the central cauldron, pray with a priestess, and give my offering. But approach the goddess? I'd never dared. Tru and I followed Prudence, but my steps slowed. My heart pounded to be near the marble statues.

Tru's hand on my lower back pushed me beyond them to a narrow corridor. Prudence waited for us beside a tall podium. The Holy Writ of Sirini, a book thicker than my thigh and bound between two carved wooden plates, covered the entirety of the stand's surface. While I clenched my trembling fingers, Prudence opened the tome. Dust and the scent of old paper rose in a delicate cloud.

Tru nudged me closer.

Beautiful script, artwork, and vibrant colors filled the pages. I crept forward, drinking it in: illustrations of people, large blocks of text, and decorative borders. What tidbits of wisdom did it contain? What marvels would I discover if allowed to browse the words handed down from the goddess? To touch one of the sheets or linger over an image for more than a few moments?

Prudence stopped at a page near the back, her index finger trailing down the text. "Here it is. Give me a moment." She skimmed, then smiled. "This is my first encounter with your kind."

My jaw dropped.

Tru to the rescue. "Her kind?"

Prudence clasped her hands. "Today is your twentieth birthday?"

I nodded.

"What?" He gave my ear the traditional tug. "You didn't tell me. I would have bought the sweet bread."

Precisely why I didn't tell him. Without Rosi and Daffi, the customary celebration would break my heart.

Prudence ignored his interruption. "And you are the youngest of identical triplets?"

I nodded.

Tru stepped back. "You were the sacrifice, not a servant sent in her place."

My eyes burned, but I blinked. "I fought him and escaped."

Prudence smiled. "Well done, child. That eel deserves a pounding."

Tru clenched his teeth, his gaze locked on my face. "You lied."

My chest tightened. Had I lost my only friend? "I misled you."

"Still lies."

Prudence snapped her fingers. "You should discuss this later. For now, you must know your life is in danger. Sirini has gifted you with a spark of divinity. Maelstrom claimed you for his own, so the other deities couldn't interfere before your activation. But he lost you, and now the other gods want it. Any god who successfully takes it will grow stronger."

Tru stuck out his hand. "Wait. How do they take it from her?"

"Her death will release it."

I laughed and gasped at the same time, and it came out as a snort. "Sirini gave me *what*?"

"A spark," Prudence said. "You have the potential to become a goddess. You have twenty-eight days to find your counterpart and complete the process. Until you locate him, the other gods will try to steal it. Except Sirini, of course. None of the others may harm you if you are in one of her temples or under her moonlight."

A goddess? That's ridiculous. Me? Calilee the Ninth, a single stocking, worthy only of sacrifice—and I'd botched that. And who was the other person? Prudence had said "him." Was it Tru? No, he wasn't a triplet. Or maybe he was, and he didn't know it. Could it be him?

His brows were still furrowed, and his lips pursed. He hadn't forgiven me yet.

"What happens if I don't find my counterpart within a month?"

Prudence cocked her head, and her eyes softened. "You will perish, and the spark dissipates."

I leaned against the wall and slid down.

Chapter Ten

I had one lousy month to locate a strange man. Was his life in my hands, too? If I failed, we'd both die?

"Where will she find her counterpart?" Tru asked.

"One of Sirini's temples." Prudence scanned the book. "He will feel drawn to them, as you were, to seek answers."

"And he'll also be attacked by the gods?"

"Yes."

"And he was born on the same day as Calla, the youngest of identical triplets?"

She nodded.

Tru couldn't be my counterpart. He was five years my senior.

The whole thing sounded like a fairy tale or something maids told their charges to incite creativity or relieve boredom. Sirini orchestrated simultaneous births of three boys and girls? Why not spark the oldest? Or the middle? Why not all of them? "This is madness."

Prudence patted my head. "It's been a thousand years since a spark reached maturity. Galc and Zephyra found each other within days, though Tera almost succeeded in stealing one."

I swallowed. "How many people with sparks have died during those years?"

"I don't know. Maybe the answers lie in other temple books."

"They aren't all exact copies?" Tru asked.

"Oh no. Sirini speaks when she wishes, to different priestesses. When we hear her words, we write them down. She rarely repeats the same information twice." Prudence flipped to the back of the book and showed Tru the blank pages. She returned to the last entry. "I wrote this twenty years ago. I haven't heard from Sirini since."

"She appear—" No. I couldn't tell them about the throne room display without giving away my identity. I cleared my throat. "Tales say she appeared in person over one hundred years ago."

"Some say it's been longer." Prudence shrugged. "I hope to see her someday, but if it's not meant to be, I am content."

My heart fluttered like a colony of bats taking flight. I didn't want the spark. Who'd want to worship me? I'd make an awful goddess. Besides, the pantheon was full. All the elements had been mastered. Was I supposed to take someone's place? I couldn't kill a goddess if my life depended—no, not going there.

"What's she the goddess of?" Tru asked.

Uselessness. Single stockings. Bungled sacrifices.

"Let's find out." Prudence shooed us with her fingers out of the alcove.

He hoisted me to my feet, and we followed Prudence to the massive cauldron of prayer tokens in the center of the sanctuary.

She gestured at the pot. "This is the easy part. Choose three."

The sea of tokens beckoned. If I leaned over the rim, I couldn't reach the other side. Should I stand in one place and select all of them, or move around the vessel? Or climb in? I snickered. Those coins were filthy. Then again, so was I.

"They will call to you." Prudence's skin glowed slightly. Not lantern bright, but luminous like a moonstone.

I shivered. Was Sirini here now, witnessing my actions? Reading my heart and mind? Or directing my hands to the correct blessings? I plunged into the cauldron, elbow deep, swishing through the discs. The collection was an odd mix of mediums: wood, bone, metal, and stone. Most of them were cold, but I encountered a bit of warmth. I shifted to the right, bumping Tru with my hip, and sought that heat again. There. One white-hot ember called to me. I snatched it.

My blood pounded in my ears, and I stared at my hand, closed around the now cold prayer token. Did I dare look? I dropped it onto Tru's palm, then dipped back into the cauldron. I moved around the pot, reaching toward the center, stretching. I stood on my toes and immersed my arm, chasing the coin. It was too deep. I dove in and found it.

I surfaced and caught Tru laughing, his hand clamped over his mouth.

"Enjoying the view?" I shifted, hips buried. My graceful movements had probably flashed my bare leg beneath my ripped skirt. I held out my hand to Prudence, who took the second coin.

The moment it left my hand, the last token blazed to life near my elbow. I snagged it and began the journey of climbing out.

Tru extended his hand and hauled me out with one tug. "That was entertaining."

"Read the coins." Prudence opened her hand and studied the bone disc. "Justice."

Tru pinched his metal token between two fingers. "Justice."

I stared at mine, wooden and dark with age. "Justice."

I'd wanted to be an enforcer, to bring equity to my city and the downtrodden who'd been ignored for far too long. Now I'd become the goddess of justice for the entire Five Realms—if I managed to survive and find my counterpart. My knees buckled, and I collapsed.

****

She sprawled on the floor, face pale, staring into nothing.

"Calla?" Tru knelt.

Her glazed green eyes looked right through him.

"What's wrong with her?"

"Shock, I imagine." Prudence collected the three coins and tossed them into the cauldron. "Pick her up and follow me." The old priestess left the sanctuary and headed down the hallway of pillars.

He picked up Calla and hurried after Prudence. She swept into a long, curved hallway full of doors and entered the second one. Tru followed into a cramped, dim room. Three candles on the wall gave enough light to reveal a narrow bed, a desk, a chair, and a shelf. The comforting scent of beeswax and lavender filled the tiny space.

"Lay her here." Prudence stepped aside.

Tru squeezed by and laid Calla down. If the priestess demanded one more person to enter the room, they'd be hard-pressed to obey.

"I'll send someone to tend to her care. You may wait here or in the foyer."

"I'll stay." He pulled the chair close.

She walked away, leaving the door open.

Tru brushed stray hairs from Calla's face. She had a pretty mixture of dark-bay and chestnut tresses with strands of buckskin, lightened by the sun, and soft as corn silk. Her chest rose and fell, the barest whisper of movement. Occasionally, she blinked. But she didn't see him, didn't respond to his fingertips stroking her cheek.

Was this shock dangerous? Would it take her life? Or was it more like sleeping with her eyes open?

Maybe she was absorbing the information. She'd be a goddess. A being with the power to enrich the lives of people or to bring devastation if they deserved it. And justice! That was sorely needed throughout the Five Realms. The emperor's enforcers kept watch in the larger towns, but they were too large to guard properly. Villages fended for themselves.

Plus, he'd heard rumors of troops amassing near the northern borders. Tulya and Rigolan threatened revolution. A goddess of justice could end the war before it began.

What powers would Calla have? Would she fly on glowing white wings, dispensing justice with a fiery blade? Or would she sit on a lofty throne and demand people come to her? Maybe she'd create a special band of enforcers, roving the countryside, stamping out inequity, corruption, and cruelty in her name. Would her appearance change, as Maelstrom's had? Would she become invisible, to watch over the realm impartially? Or transform into a giantess? The possibilities were endless.

Any of those would be spectacular. He'd worship her all the days of his life. She was breathtaking, with a sweet character, an impeccable work ethic, and a delicious sense of wry humor. And an odd penchant for lying, but surely, she had good reasons for them. Watching her climb into that cauldron headfirst, feet kicking, hips wiggling, he'd bitten his lip to keep from laughing. She didn't care that people were looking. Maybe she hadn't noticed when several worshipers gathered. Either way, she'd sought out her destiny with zeal—literally dove into it—not whining or complaining or crying like a pampered child. She didn't argue or deny her fate or beg for a change. She accepted the truth.

Unless this shock was a delayed rejection. He couldn't blame her. If he'd learned he was to become a god, he'd have braced his feet and said, "Sard, no!" He wouldn't welcome the danger, the responsibility, or the attention. Being a god meant worshipers.

Calla wouldn't struggle to find those. They'd be drawn to her like bees to pollen, like flies to horses. Like he was to her. He caressed the bone button in his pocket.

To survive, she'd have to leave Borderline and tour the Five Realms until she found her counterpart. He didn't want her to go, but he also didn't want her to die. She didn't have any other option. Could he watch her walk away? Or ride away, as a horse would be better, considering she couldn't place her foot on soil anymore. And she'd probably have to travel at night. Zelos couldn't burn her then, and Sirini's moonlight would protect her from storms, high winds, wild animals, fire, ice, water, rocks, and maybe aggressive plants. Gods above, a lot of dangers awaited a young woman with a divinity spark.

A priestess with long black hair and ice-blue eyes swept into the room, carrying a laden tray. She was built like a mountain. Tall, muscular, and probably capable of taking him down in a fistfight. She set the tray on the desk. "How is she?"

"No change." At some point, he'd taken Calla's hand, so soft and tiny.

"I'm Jasmine." She opened a palm-sized tin and passed it to Tru. "Wave that under her nose."

He sniffed it and turned away, his eyes watering. "That's awful." Like a mixture of garlic, skunk, and goat piss.

"It may wake her. It's worth a try." She took a step closer to him. "I'll do it if you can't abide the smell."

"I've got it." He waved the foul pot before Calla's face.

She blinked, her face scrunched, and she jerked away from the nauseating odor, her hands clutching her nose. "Faugh! What is that horrific stench?"

Tru gave it back to Jasmine and hauled Calla into his lap. "You're awake, thank the goddess."

She froze. "Tru? Where are we?"

"The Temple of Sirini." He stroked her arm. "You...went away for a while."

Calla fisted his tunic and pulled her knees to her chest. "Did I dream it?"

"No. I'm sorry."

She jolted. Was she holding back sobs? Then she stilled. She took a deep breath, let it out, and relaxed into him. "All right. I'm calm. Now what do I do?"

"I brought food and drink." Jasmine poured water into a mug and handed it to Calla. "Regain your strength before you plan your next steps."

"Thank you." She sipped it, cradling the cup.

So like a child, adorable and trusting. Warm. Curvy. Sitting in his arms in her filthy blue dress, she was definitely a woman. And she'd notice his response if she remained in his lap. He shifted her to the bed and leaned her against the wall.

Jasmine set the tray of food on the mattress within Calla's reach. "I brought flat bread, stewed pears, a wedge of cheese, and leftover roast from last night's meal. I can vouch for the quality of the cooking at the temple."

Calla stared at the meal. "I don't wish to be rude, but I can't eat now."

Jasmine sat on the end of the bed and patted Calla's dusty suede slipper. "Very well. The High Priestess told me of your fantastic news. You must feel overwhelmed. I'm here to help."

Calla sighed. "There's the problem. I don't know what I need."

Poor Calla. With the temple's backing, what could he possibly hope to do for her other than wish her well and wave goodbye as she rode out of town? His chest tightened. She'd leave him, like everyone always did, and he'd be alone. Again.

Chapter Eleven

I huddled in the corner. No more working for Eve, not as a target with a tasty prize for the deity who killed me first. No wonder Maelstrom drove the citizens to demand me. He'd been devouring sparks for centuries, growing stronger with each one while the other gods missed out. Maybe that's why Gale attacked Maelstrom. And his greatest enemy, Tera, had to be salivating at her chance to obtain mine.

She couldn't have it. I'd escaped Maelstrom. I would escape all the others, find my counterpart, and take my place in the pantheon.

I fisted the blanket beneath me. As the goddess of justice, I could finally help Flick. He'd waited fourteen years already.

Flick ducked and raised his arm, shielding his head. I screamed, but the merchant ignored me. His cane smashed into Flick's hand with the loud crack of breaking bones. He wailed and curled around his mangled fingers, his other arm still caught in the vendor's grip.

"He didn't do it!" I lifted my skirts and kicked his shin. "That was unfair."

As justice, I could stop other incidents like that. And really, what choice did I have? I could perish, but what use would that be?

I didn't want to leave Tru. He'd been so kind, and I

had no one else. But I couldn't ask him to go with me, yet I couldn't remain here. I'd endanger anyone near me.

But I was wasting time. I had twenty-eight days to find a stranger, or I'd never see my sisters again. I handed my mug to the priestess. "I need to go."

Her eyes widened, but she took the water. "Where?"

"To purchase supplies. Tru, do you have time to guide me around the town?"

He brushed a clump of hair from his eyes. "Sure. Anything you want."

"Or I could take you." The priestess gathered the uneaten food and stacked it on her tray. "If you'll give me two minutes to put these things away, I'd be happy to assist."

Did she realize the potential cost of her offer? "That's kind, but I don't want to take you from your duties here."

"What duties? We have too many priestesses and not enough work. Please let me go! I'm dying of boredom."

Tru grinned at me. "We might need help keeping you safe from the elements."

Endanger this sweet young woman for my benefit? Never. "It's too dangerous."

Her eyes glinted. "I am a temple guard, and I've been trained in self-defense. Not all our visitors come to peacefully worship, and I've fended off angry or drunk men who intended havoc and chaos. Trust me. I can be most useful."

I could use all the help I could get. "I accept. Thank you. I appreciate your willingness to brave the gods on my behalf."

"They won't mess with me. I carry Sirini in my

heart."

That sounds promising. "If I become a priestess of Sirini, would I also receive her protection?"

"You can't do that now."

"Of course not. Why would anything be easy?" I sighed. "Let's move."

Tru held out his hand.

I took it, and he hauled me off the bed like I weighed nothing, comforted me with tenderness, and at some point, he must have forgiven me for the lies I told—or rather, the omissions. He was an absolute blessing from the goddess, and I wouldn't have survived without him. I must thank Sirini for him. "I need to visit the sanctuary first."

The priestess led the way. "I'm Jasmine, by the way."

Pretty. Most commoners took names from nature. It was a sweet tradition. Why didn't the nobles do that? Calilee was made-up, a mashing of calla lily and the last half of my mother's, unique to me, and sure to be recognized if I ever said it aloud. "I'm Calla."

"Pleased to meet you." Jasmine gestured with her chin down the columned hallway. "The sanctuary is that way. I'm going to put this food up, then I'll join you on the portico." She disappeared down the arching corridor.

Tru still clasped my hand, and heat flooded my face. My cheeks were probably red. Was he afraid I'd collapse again? Or was he as drawn to me as I was to him?

"What did you need in there?" he asked.

"To give an offering." I pulled free of him and opened my apron purse.

He stood behind me, solid and protective.

I approached the marble statues of Sirini. Gray veins

and silver flecks wove through the white stone, dancing across folds in her dresses and the bare skin of her arms. Her eyes were carved moonstones, ice-blue and luminescent, with glinting black mica for pupils. She gazed down at me with affection and a sly grin, amazingly life-like. I half expected those glorious faces to shift and speak to me, then I'd respond appropriately by dying of fright.

Thankfully, she didn't move.

Each statue stood with hands outstretched and cupped to receive her offerings. I placed a tiny silver bead into each pair. "Thank you for Tru and Jasmine. Please keep us safe and guide me to my counterpart quickly. Sustain my courage and grant me strength." I backed away, head bowed.

Jasmine waited for us on the portico, wearing a light-gray cloak that matched her priestess robes beneath. "Where to first?"

"Jewelers."

Her black eyebrows lifted, and she pointed west. "This way."

I followed her down the granite path to the end, Tru at my side. He hoisted me into his arms to cross the street. The scents of leather and horse clung to him like a heady perfume, and I soaked it in. He was so handsome. Lovely cheekbones, strong jaw, an adorable cleft in his chin, and I could get lost in his olive-green eyes.

He plunked me down on the wooden walkway. "Only half a block to your destination, my lady."

"Thank you."

Jasmine fell in beside me. "Why do you need the jewelers, if I may be nosey?"

"I'm going to sell a few pieces of my necklace." I fished around in the apron purse for the three loose black pearls. They were huge, about the size of my thumb pad, and flawless.

Jasmine's eyes widened. "Those are gorgeous! Where did you get them?"

"They were a gift."

She stopped and scanned the street, then leaned close. "If I may, I suggest you allow me to handle the sale. The temple frequently receives offerings as grand as this, so the proprietor of the shop will not ask where I obtained them. Whereas you, dressed as a servant, might draw his curiosity."

She was right, yet I hesitated. Why was she being so helpful? I trusted her—she was a priestess of Sirini, so how could she not be trustworthy? But my skepticism rode high after I battled Maelstrom and suffered attacks by the pantheon.

Her pale-blue eyes flared with silver light momentarily, then faded.

A chill skittered down my back. Was that the sun glinting off her face? Or had Sirini given me a sign to trust her servant? I handed the pearls to Jasmine. "Thank you for your gracious offer."

Tru squeezed my shoulder. "It's a great idea."

I glanced up at him. Had he seen it, too?

Jasmine took off at a brisk pace. We followed.

The jeweler's shop sat at the back end of the builders' area, surrounded by the mason, carpenter, blacksmith, and armorer's shops. The boardwalk led us directly to the front door. I didn't have to brave Tera's wrath of dust devils and sudden pits. An armed guard greeted Jasmine with a nod. He ignored Tru and me.

We exited with far more gold than I thought I'd receive and a promise to sell more pearls, should any others be offered at the temple. I had enough to finance my journey.

A heavy weight settled on my shoulders, and I leaned against the building. I had to leave. Plan the trip, purchase supplies and clothing, and say goodbye to Tru. My eyes burned, and I blinked. *Stupid tears.*

"What's wrong?" He hovered, his gaze darting over the streets at passersby.

"I'm scared. I don't want to go. Or be alone."

He took my hand, his brows furrowed. He had no encouraging words.

"I'll go with you," Jasmine said.

I snorted. *Oh, real ladylike.* Grace would scold me. "Why?"

"I've always wanted to visit the other temples and see new places." She grinned like she had a pocketful of gold—which she did. "I've lived here my entire life and have never left, unless you count the day I crossed the bridge to stand in Acoris on a dare from friends. *Please* allow me to go with you. I'll be helpful. Highwaymen won't accost us when they see my robes. Priestesses are hallowed."

"We just met. You want to spend a month with a stranger?"

"You won't be a stranger after we chat, and I can tell you're a lovely person. Sirini wouldn't have given you that gift if you weren't worthy."

"She gave Maelstrom a spark."

Her eyes bugged. "I didn't think of that."

Truthfully, I wouldn't survive a single night if I didn't have a companion. A man on a horse rode by. I didn't own one or know how to ride, but walking to the next town was sheer folly. "The gods are trying to kill me. I can't step foot on dirt or pump water without being attacked. I don't know how to cook a meal or start a fire—which would be foolish to try, as Sear would burn me. Are you certain you want to be near me?" She wasn't a servant to wait on me or a palace guard to protect me. The journey she'd volunteered for would be perilous.

She shrugged. "Life is always dangerous. It's a risk I'm willing to take."

"Will Prudence allow you to leave?"

"We're not chained to the altar. Priestesses come and go, transferring to other temples or living out in the world to offer aid to the poor and sick. Technically, I don't even need to ask for permission to go, although I'd never be so rude to her."

My shoulders dropped. I'd have someone to talk to and ease the burden of traveling alone. "Thank you. I accept."

She bounced on her toes. "I can't wait. When do we leave? Are we walking or riding? Where are we going first?"

"Do you know how to care for a horse?" Tru asked.

"No. Why?" Jasmine looked to me. "Is it difficult?"

"I was going to suggest you take a cart, but if you can't tend the animal, then it'll be more trouble than it's worth."

"I can't walk, not with Tera threatening to swallow me whole." Plus, my feet would ache. Which reminded me I needed new shoes. And clothing. And a million other things.

"Can I pull the cart?" Jasmine asked.

I laughed. "I'm not sitting while you play beast of

burden."

"I can teach you to care for a horse," Tru said, "if you can put off leaving for an hour."

What would I do without him? He'd been a friend and constant support since the moment I arrived. Saying farewell would break my heart. I ground my teeth and blinked. Gods, I'd never get through the next hour, much less the next month. "Can I afford those things?"

"Easily. You have a year's wages. And you won't need to buy a horse. I'll lend you mine."

"I can't take yours. She's all you have left of your life with Gray."

Tru shrugged. "You only need her for twenty-eight days. After that, you'll be a goddess, and you can return Lady to me." He dropped his gaze to the boardwalk. "It guarantees I'll see you again someday."

Jasmine grinned. "Excellent! We purchase a cart and supplies now, learn how to care for the horse, then leave by noon. Are we going northeast or west?"

"Northeast." If I stepped foot in Acoris, I'd be recognized.

"Then let's go." She handed me the gold she'd collected from the jeweler.

I stuffed it in my apron purse. One of my first purchases would be a cloak with pockets. "Where's the cart shop?"

"We'll make better time if we split up," Jasmine suggested. "If I may, Tru, you buy the wagon while we get the food and cooking items."

"And clothes," I added.

Her face lit up. "We're buying clothes, too? I love shopping!"

"I'm not sure splitting up is wise." Tru scanned the

busy streets. "How will you cross the highway without me to carry you?"

"I forgot about that." Jasmine pursed her lips. "If I may, you help her get to the clothing district first. We'll have boardwalks most of the way back to the inn from there."

A dust devil whipped down the street, a whirling vortex of dirt and bits of grass. It swelled, then a head formed near the top. Shoulders. A torso and arms. Legs and feet. Tera, the goddess of dry land, ran toward us, elbows pumping, brown hair flying back from her face, her dark eyes pinned on me.

Can I outrun her?

Jasmine braced.

Tru stepped in front of me. "Bring it on, dust face."

Go for the soft spots. My brothers had drilled it into my head a thousand times. It'd worked on Maelstrom. I clenched my trembling fingers into fists.

Tera screamed, leapt onto the boardwalk, and barreled right at me.

Jasmine stuck out her arm and caught Tera below the chin, shifting sideways to absorb the impact.

Tera's feet flew out from under her. She landed with a breathy "oof."

Jasmine stomped on Tera's chest. "Back off! Calla is protected by Sirini now."

Tera curled in on herself, eyes bulging, mouth gasping.

"Run!" Jasmine took off.

I froze.

The goddess writhed on the wooden planks. Dust and dirt sloughed off to blow away in the breeze.

Tears welled. She'd come to kill me, but I stood by

while Jasmine took care of the threat. *Useless!* No, worse than that. Worthless. I couldn't even defend myself.

Tera collapsed into a pile of silt and filtered through the boards.

My stomach roiled, full of swarming bees. This was my life for the next month? Physically battling the entire pantheon?

Jasmine had seriously hurt Tera. Served her right. She shouldn't be attacking people; she should be serving us with her gifts. How dare she try to murder one of the people under her care? She should be punished—but could I do it, even after I ascended?

Tru grabbed my hand and pulled. We crossed the narrow street and raced toward the boardwalk lining the empty open-air market.

"Look." He pointed at the road.

I slowed, then stopped. My filthy suede slippers rested on hard-packed dirt. No dust devils nipped at my ankles. No divots tried to swallow my feet. "She gave up?"

"For now." Jasmine stood on her toes to see beyond Tru. If she had another two fingers of height, she'd look him right in the eye.

I had the adorable view of his collarbone, currently peeking between the laces of his shirt.

"How'd you learn to fight like that?" He kept my hand and pulled me onto the boardwalk. "And does your arm hurt?"

Jasmine rotated her shoulder. "It aches, but that'll fade. And I told you. I'm a temple guard. Hand to hand, sword, quarterstaff, you name a weapon, I've probably trained with it."

"Would you teach me?" I'd had some training from

my brothers, mostly to fend off or disable handsy suitors and unwanted advances. But no bladework.

"I'd be happy to. But let's finish our shopping first."

We headed toward the highway. Thank the goddess Jasmine took over the planning for now. My brain couldn't focus on much beyond the looming farewell to Tru. He wouldn't volunteer to go with me. He had a life here. But my heart would rejoice if he did. No, I was being selfish. He had a job he loved, people he cared for. He wouldn't give it up for me. We just met yesterday. It's not like we'd fallen in love and pledged ourselves to each other. Though I'd do that, if he asked.

Goddess, where had that thought come from?

"We're heading there." Jasmine gestured at a series of small shops on the far side of the street. "Give Tru some coins, and we'll part ways."

I fished two gold pieces from my apron. "Will this be enough?"

He whistled. "Plenty. You'll get a deluxe model and some extra perks."

"Can you buy us some barrels for water, too?"

"Sure." He pointed to the far end of the block. "Past the seamstress, baths, and leather shop is the overflow stable for the inn. I'll meet you there."

Jasmine grinned and wrapped her arm through mine. "Let's spend money!"

Traffic cleared, and we walked across the highway on solid ground. With luck, Tera needed a long time to heal. But what about the others? Would Beck follow me into a clothing store? I'd soon find out.

Chapter Twelve

Calla walked away with someone else, and Tru's chest tightened. For the briefest time, she'd needed him. Some protector he was. A temple priestess took down Tera with two moves, leaving Tru standing around like an extra post. Jasmine could protect Calla against the gods, and with a cart to travel in, she didn't need to be carried over dirt areas.

She hadn't even asked if he wanted to go.

Gods, yes. If she even hinted that she'd welcome his company, he'd quit his job and follow her anywhere. But he couldn't intrude.

Jasmine literally begged to go on the journey, and Calla agreed. If Tru asked… But if she said no, his world would crumble. Better not take the chance. Better to offer his horse, knowing he'd see Calla again when she returned the mare.

All he could do now was help her get underway. He rubbed his aching chest and set off.

The carpenter/wheelwright's yard had no customers. The shop mostly repaired broken vehicles, but they had a few new models artfully parked at an angle near the highway so passersby could view their dream buggies. The wagon on the end looked promising. It was large enough for the two women to sleep in if they couldn't find an inn, had an oiled canvas bonnet— currently folded neatly on a bench—and best of all, it had those innovative coiled springs recently invented in the capital. Those would make for a smooth, comfortable ride.

After a bit of haggling, Tru dragged the cart onto the highway.

A rider on a stallion laughed. "Lost yer horse?"

Tru waved and headed west, dodging road stinks, potholes, and wheel ruts. At the Ale Huntress tavern, he hung a right, pulled it past the brothel—ignoring the ladies hooting at him from the upper windows—and parked by the cooper's shop. He had plenty of coins for supplies.

He should ask. The way she'd looked at him in the temple, and the way she clung to his hand, she'd welcome his company. Wouldn't she? But if she wanted him along, she would have asked. The best way to make a fool of himself was to jump in where he didn't belong.

He made two more stops, dragged the loaded wagon to the secondary stable, and parked in back.

Jasmine and Calla rounded the corner, bags hanging off their shoulders.

Calla gasped. "It's beautiful!" She stacked her packages into the cart, then circled it. "I can't believe how big it is. You bought this with two gold pieces?"

She loved it. That's all that mattered. "I brought back a few coins, too." He fished them from his belt pouch and placed them in her palm. His fingertips brushed her soft, warm skin, lingering for a moment.

She turned bright-green eyes up to his face. "Thank you."

"You stuffed hay bales under the benches. Is that for the horse?" Jasmine climbed in. "It's got a bonnet. We can ride in any weather." She fingered the curved ribs arching over her head. "This is the prettiest wagon I've ever seen. Oh, look! A trap door." She lifted the ring, revealing a small cubby under the bed. "Is this for hiding valuables?"

"Or holding tools and spare parts for the wheels and axle assembly."

Calla cried out. The ground beneath her feet shifted, and her arms flapped for balance.

Tru picked her up and set her in the driver's box. The dirt settled back into place.

"I guess Tera's recovered." Calla rubbed her fingers, her brows furrowed.

He climbed up and slung his arm around her shoulders. *Ask her now. Yeah, like a heel when she's vulnerable and endangered.* "We'll keep you safe. Did you find everything you need?"

She nodded. "I'm sure I've forgotten something, but I can't think what it might be."

Jasmine jumped off the back and peered down the street. "There's something happening."

Tru hopped down, swung Calla into his arms, and crossed to the front of the barn. He set her on the boardwalk.

"You!" The enforcer and his men stomped across the dirt lane. Two of them grabbed Tru. "You are under arrest."

"For what?"

"Perjury and treason."

A tremor raced through him. The penalty for perjury was a few hours in the stocks, which he could handle. But treason carried a death sentence. They had the wrong man. "There must be some mistake. I'm loyal to the emperor."

108

The lead enforcer looked down his nose at Tru. "I have three witnesses who state you not only interacted with the spy, but you exchanged money and helped him escape."

"The man in the green cloak? Who said I spoke to him?"

"Your co-workers, Oakley, Yarrow, and Charity."

This was Oak's revenge. Should have seen it coming. But Charity? Why had she turned on him? "They lied. They're the ones who aided him. I cared for his horse, nothing more."

"That's for the emperor to decide. You're going with us."

Tru's heart rate kicked up. How could he escape?

Calla stepped between them. "Dariel, may I say goodbye before you take him away?"

He glared. "Do I know you?"

"No, but everyone knows your name and your reputation for equity. Please. Allow me to say farewell."

His eyes narrowed. "Fine." He glanced at his men. "Don't let him loose. I'm not going to chase him all over this gods-forsaken backwater."

She walked to Tru and lifted her arms for an embrace.

He held his breath. What was this? Did she expect a hug or a chaste peck on the cheek? Did he dare to kiss her? And what was that mischievous spark in her eyes? He settled his hands on her narrow hips, and she grinned. He leaned down, inhaling her sweet scent one last time, and touched his nose to hers.

Her cheek slid across his, her breath tickled his ear, and she whispered, "I'm going to create a diversion. Meet us at Jasmine's."

Heat flooded his face. If he'd kissed her— Wait. Was that an invitation? He buried his lips in her glorious hair. "I'm coming with you?"

"I can't leave you here, can I?"

He tightened his hold, as much as he could with two enforcers holding his upper arms. "Gather my things? My money pouch is hidden in the hay."

"I will."

The burly enforcer on the right yanked on her arm. "That's enough."

She planted a warm kiss on Tru's cheek and stepped back—into the roadway beside Burly. Dust swirled, dirt fled, and the lane dimpled beneath her feet.

Was she brave or merely foolish? The entire street could cave in, taking all of them into the depths. As far as diversions went, though, it was glorious—provided she survived it.

She held Tru's gaze. The divot widened. Deepened. Her shoes slipped down the incline. "Help!" She clutched Burly's arm. He released Tru and caught Calla.

Jasmine crept up behind the dark guard with the goatee.

Tru stepped into the roadway and reached for Calla, as if to assist her in escaping the growing orifice. Goatee, still holding Tru's arm, joined him.

Jasmine slid between the two men and cried out, her toes on the edge of the gaping pit. "Help!" She pitched forward into the maw of the expanding crater.

Goatee let go of Tru to save her.

Tru whirled and dashed into the barn.

****

My diversion worked!

"Stop him!" Dariel drew his sword.

Now I had to delay the enforcers and survive Tera's attack.

A tornado of dust, hay, and twigs formed behind me. I had to point my toes to keep a connection with the ground, but I wouldn't need the shifting dirt once Tera materialized.

Dariel stopped, eyes wide and lips parted, watching the creepy transformation of the whirlwind into a woman.

Tera took shape, and the other enforcers froze. She glared and stomped toward me, her brown hair streaming after her like tree fronds in a storm.

"Help!" I tugged on the soldier's sleeve. "She's going to kill me!"

He drew his sword. His partner did the same.

I took several steps back, skirting the edge of the now stable pit, and reached for Dariel. "Save me!"

Jasmine bit her lip and threw herself at the fourth man. "Don't let her hurt us!"

Without breaking stride, Tera swatted dirt into the faces of the two closest soldiers. The hole in the road filled moments before she stepped in it, her gaze cemented on me, and she closed the distance.

The fourth, a smaller man with bulging arms, went down on one knee and bowed. "My goddess."

Great. A true believer. He wouldn't be much use. I fisted my hands in Dariel's tunic. "Do something!"

He scowled and shoved me behind him. "Stay back."

Tera raised her palms, burying the kneeling man up to his hips in soil, then splayed her fingers at Dariel.

His left arm blocked the bulk of the sediment coming at his face. He stepped toward her, and his sword lashed out. The point raked across her throat.

She stopped, eyes wide, and clamped her hand over the fine sand gushing out of the wound. It flowed over her fingers and puddled at her feet. With one last look of hatred thrown at me, she dissolved into a puff of dust and scattered on the breeze.

That worked! Tru got away, and Dariel eliminated Tera from my life for another hour—or more.

A horse screamed, and two black beasts exploded out the barn doors. They turned south, racing for the farmlands and ocean. Another two followed, only they went north.

Dariel cursed. "After them!"

Two soldiers went south, blinking dirt from their eyes. Dariel and the worshipping soldier took the other way.

I glanced at Jasmine. "That was exciting."

"Let's go before they blame us."

"I need to grab Tru's things. Come with me." I led her to the hay loft in the larger barn.

"Hurry."

Tru had few personal items. Jasmine piled them in the center of the blankets. I hunted for his valuables. My fingers brushed a loose bit of straw in the seam between two bales, revealing a well-hidden cavity. I pulled out a heavy money pouch, a book, and a box secured with string, and handed them to her. "Add these."

She tied the ends of the blankets together and hefted the bundle to her shoulder.

I knelt to grab Tru's spare boots and toolkit. What was in it, fist-sized ingots of iron? I grunted and hauled it to my chest. "How am I going to get this down the ladder?"

"Over here." She crossed to the hook-and-pulley system and lowered everything to the barn floor below. "Go down. I'll be right behind you." She secured the rope to the cleat, jumped, and swung down like an acrobat.

I gaped. "Where did you learn to do that?"

She picked up the toolkit like it weighed nothing and waved. "Get down here!"

I scurried down the ladder. "I need to speak to Eve. I'll meet you at the cart."

She flipped the blanket bundle to her shoulder and left the boots for me. "Got it." She peered out the door, checked both directions, then darted across the street.

I grabbed the boots and ran to the kitchen.

Eve stood in her usual spot before the fire.

The scent of fresh baked bread, warm applesauce, and roasted carrots wafted at me. "Tru's been falsely accused of a crime by Oakley and Charity, so now he's on the run. I'm going with him. We won't be back. Thanks for everything." I closed the door behind me.

"Oakley!" Eve hollered loudly enough to rattle the windows on the second floor.

I grinned. She might be able to get Tru out of trouble. I rounded the corner of the inn and headed for the lane. It was empty. The gaping crater meant to swallow me was filled in like it'd never existed.

What were the odds another of the gods would attack me before I made it out of town? Best not to think on it. I darted across the street, tossed Tru's boots in the back of the wagon, climbed into the driver's seat beside Jasmine, and stared at the wooden arms jutting off the front. We looked at each other and laughed.

No horse.

Jasmine jumped down. "Come on. We'll haul it ourselves." She grabbed one of the supports. I took the other. The cart needed three heaves, but we got it moving.

Now to move it to the temple, collect Tru, and begin our journey.

Should be easy.

Chapter Thirteen

We rolled the cart between the leather shop and the Evening Inn and approached the highway at a good clip. Draft beasts and carts passed up ahead in both directions, not watching for runaways from the side. And we were moving fast.

This could get tricky. "Can we stop in time?"

"Hope so," Jasmine said.

We braced our feet. Small rocks dug at my soles through the thin suede slippers. Jasmine's shoes slid across the hard-packed dirt, and she laughed.

Was this funny? My hands slipped. I whirled, planted them on the driver's seat, and braced my heels.

"Do you ladies need help?" a male voice called from the boardwalk.

Jasmine laughed again. "Yes!"

Three young men hurried over and stopped the cart.

A farmer in a hay-stacked wagon passed us with less than a handspan of space between his rig and ours, his eyes wide.

"Where are you headed?" The biggest man in our pack of saviors watched the oncoming traffic for a break.

"The temple." Jasmine pressed her fingers to her forehead, lips, and chest. "Bless you all for diverting a colossal accident."

"We'll get you home." The men hoisted us onto the driver's bench, picked up the wagon handles, and dashed across the highway. We passed the Ale Huntress tavern at a nice jog.

The gentle breeze tugging at my hair grew more snapping. Biting.

Great. Zephyra blew in our faces, and the men fought to keep our forward momentum.

Jasmine leaned toward me, eyes squinted and shielded with her palm. "You'd better run. I'll be right behind you."

The moonstone crescent peeked over the shorter buildings of the market, less than a block away. If I could make it to the grounds, Zephyra couldn't hinder me. Plus, running would take her attention off Jasmine.

I leapt off the slow-moving cart and dashed away.

Zephyra blasted me from behind.

I staggered forward and fell to my knees. *Come on, Cali. Pretend it's a footrace against Jayson.* I braced my back foot and took off. Bits of dirt and hay swirled around my eyes. I blocked it with my arm, hoisted my skirt with the other hand, and sprinted. I passed the furrier, feet pounding on the boardwalk, and rounded the corner. The temple cast an immense shadow across the narrow lane. Almost there.

Hands settled on my shoulders, fingers fisted my dress, and I was hauled into the air.

I shrieked and looked up.

Zephyra, goddess of the winds, stared down at me with a gleam of triumph in her pale-gray eyes. "You're mine."

I screamed, kicked my feet, and clawed at her.

She veered from the temple grounds and flew higher, following the street.

Don't look down…and go for the soft spots. Justyn

and Jayson had drilled it into me how many times? I couldn't reach her eyes or throat from this position. But I found other targets. I punched up, two quick jabs to her belly.

She gasped and cradled her stomach, leaving me dangling from her left hand. She also lost a bit of altitude.

I hauled out my sapphire necklace and mashed it into her skin.

A jag of white lightning blasted her wrist.

She shrieked and released me.

I fell, screaming my throat out.

****

Tru pumped his legs, running down the roadway, his gaze tracking Calla. *Sirini, no!* The goddess wouldn't be this cruel. If Calla hit the ground from that height, he'd lose her. Not happening. He sprinted, arms outstretched. He would not let her die.

Her scream echoed around him.

Almost there. He had her. He'd catch her. He lurched forward, reaching.

She smacked him rump-first in the chest. *Yes! I saved—* Tru's lungs emptied, his feet tangled, and her weight dragged them down. He somersaulted over her and landed sprawled on his back.

That sarding hurt! His biceps burned like he'd tried to lift Lady, and he'd pulled a muscle in his thigh. But thank the goddess, no broken bones. He sucked in a deep breath, rolled to his side, and hauled himself up. "Calla?"

She lay in the dirt on her back, arms flung wide, staring at the sky.

He knelt beside her. "Calla? Are you all right?" Why wasn't she moving? Had she hit her head on the cobbles? "Where do you hurt?" He ran his fingers along the back

117

of her head. No blood. Her exposed face started to pinken, then burn. Her borrowed cloak's hood was bunched up at her nape. He tugged it back up into place and leaned over, casting her face in shadow. Her skin faded to her healthy tan.

She blinked.

Jasmine dropped to her knees beside Calla. "How is she?"

Indy, Axle, and Wander rushed up. "Good catch."

"Thanks." Tru brushed hair from Calla's smooth cheek. Gods, he'd come so close to losing her! He couldn't imagine never seeing those beautiful green eyes again or her ready smile. His heart thumped, and his arms trembled. She was alive, and that's what mattered. "I don't see blood. Check her legs."

Jasmine felt Calla's hips and thighs. She didn't flinch or scream, so that was good. No bones poked out anywhere. "She's breathing." Jasmine probed Calla's ribs. "Nothing broken."

Calla sucked in a deep breath and reached for him.

He took her hand and helped her sit up. "Are you hurt?"

She grabbed him in a fierce hug. "You saved my life. Thank you."

"You're welcome." Heat poured off her body like a blast furnace. "Where did you get these?" He ran his finger over the sapphires.

"They were a gift." She tucked them back into her bodice.

Maelstrom didn't give land-based baubles. But she hadn't lied. They must have come from someone else. Sirini, maybe? "How do you feel?"

She pulled away. "Like the luckiest woman in the

world! How did you come to be right where I needed you?"

"I was standing on the temple grounds when Zephyra grabbed you. I chased her down the road." He swallowed. "When I saw you fall—"

"You could have been crushed." She swatted him, then groaned and rubbed her shoulder. "That hurt."

"Need help getting her inside?" Indy asked.

"No, we can handle it." Jasmine rose and turned to them. "Thank you for your assistance. The goddess will bless you for your good hearts."

In unison, they pressed their fingers to their foreheads, lips, and hearts.

"Happy to." Indy slapped Tru's back. "See you around?"

"No. And you didn't see me here. Right?"

Indy's eyebrows rose. "Sure. Take care." They walked away.

"Help me up." Calla held out her hands.

Tru threaded his arm around her waist, careful to not bump her injured shoulder, and lifted her to her feet. His arms ached, but he could take it, for her sake. "Can you walk?"

She nodded.

A gust of wind struck them from the east, and Tru whirled. *Not again.* "Get her to the temple! I'll handle this."

Zephyra rode the breeze, her gray dress flapping wildly behind her, arms outstretched. Her right hand was red and swollen. She swooped to a lower altitude but still out of Tru's grasp.

He bent his knees and braced. That bitch wasn't getting a second chance.

The goddess flew over his head, gaze cemented on Calla's fleeing form.

Tru ran beneath Zephyra, jumped, and hooked his hands around her hips. *Yes!* His arms burned and trembled, but he fisted his fingers in her dress. His body weight pulled her down, and his boots hit the roadway.

She shrieked and clawed at his skin, hovering above him.

He yanked. She landed belly-down on the street with a muffled *whumpf*. He planted his knee in her back and scanned the area. Was Calla safe?

Jasmine loomed, a fierce gleam in her eyes, and kicked Zephyra in the temple. "Calla's under Sirini's protection now."

Zephyra twitched, went limp, then dissipated on the breeze.

Tru searched the skies for her.

"She won't be back soon." Jasmine held out a hand to help him up. "She'll need to heal."

He grabbed her hand, gained his feet, and brushed dirt from his palms. "Calla made it?"

"Yeah. That was a bit of excitement to spice up a fine morning."

He headed for the temple, his injured leg throbbing. "I don't suppose that's the last of it?"

"Not until Calla finds her counterpart." She fell into step beside him. "We won't have to face Zelos or Blanche, as they're both too lazy to leave their homes, but I'm certain we'll see the rest of the pantheon before the month is out."

Tru glanced at the sky. Zelos might not show up in person, but the sun would burn her. And Gale could spit nasty storms. Who knew what the other gods would throw at them? "We'll deal with each attack as they come. Or maybe a few of them are chasing the counterpart." He stuck his hand in his pocket and sighed. He hadn't lost the button.

The men had parked the cart in front of the temple. Lady was tethered to the porch of the priestess's living quarters in back. Tru grabbed one of the traces, Jasmine grasped the other, and they hauled it around the block.

"Hey, girl." He scratched Lady's nose. She seemed content to graze on the grass. He picked up the saddle and blanket where he'd dumped them earlier and tossed them in the wagon.

Jasmine slapped his shoulder. "We should leave soon."

He nodded. "Sure."

"And get out of sight. No sense letting anyone else see you here."

It hit him like a punch to the throat. He was on the run from the law. Uprooted. Homeless again. His job, friends, even the hope of Gray—

"I'll be back for you, boy." Gray flicked his hood up, concealing his face. "Obey Hawk and Eve. They'll care for you until I return."

Tru's guts soured, and he swallowed. If Gray came back, would he give up or keep searching? He wouldn't know where to begin.

Blast it, Oakley! The slug had ruined Tru's life for good this time, and it wasn't even for something he'd done. It was pure spite—betrayal—that left him in this…this…*sard*. He clenched his fists, but there was nothing to punch.

He had to find a way to prove his innocence. But not until after Calla found her counterpart. *Oh*. His shoulders dropped. She'd clear his name. He let out a deep breath and stretched his fingers. He'd help her now, and she'd return the favor later.

Jasmine grabbed several bags from the back of the wagon. "Calla needs time to recover and clean up, and I must pack. Twenty minutes?"

Tru nodded.

"Come with me." She gestured with her chin at the long, low building where the priestesses lived.

"Am I allowed in there?"

Jasmine rolled her eyes. "You need to get off the street. Grab your stuff."

Tru gathered his gear and followed her up the steps to a covered porch lined with wooden chairs. Nice place to sit at the end of the day and enjoy the sunset and a breeze off the river. Though breezes didn't hold the same appeal now.

Jasmine stepped inside to a wide foyer with blue padded benches and four grinning priestesses.

A short girl, maybe twelve, bounced on her toes. "May I feed your horse? Please? I won't spook her." She held up a red apple.

Tru grinned. "Sure. Her name is Lady. She likes ear scratches."

The girl ran out.

The other priestesses, closer to Calla's age, converged on Jasmine. "We're ready to help. What do you need?"

"Come with us." Jasmine ducked through a door to the right and entered a dark stairwell.

Tru and the others followed down the stairs to a guide-stone-lit tunnel. Tru had to duck and tuck his elbows, but before he cracked, it spit them out into a massive room.

Padded couches, chairs, candelabras, and small tables lined the curved walls. Wooden stairs hugged the farthest edge and climbed up to the main level of the temple. Calla stood with Prudence at the bottom.

Tru dropped his bundle and rushed toward her.

"What happened?" She met him halfway, hands outstretched.

He took them. *So soft!* "I held her down, Jasmine kicked her, and Zephyra disintegrated." He inhaled Calla's scent, a hint of lavender mixed with sweet hay and dirt. "How do you feel?"

"I'll be fine."

"I've got your new clothes." Jasmine bumped elbows with Calla. "Follow me for a bath."

Calla's eyes lit up. "That sounds divine!" She squeezed Tru's fingers. "Be back soon."

"I need my cloak."

She drew it off her shoulders and handed it to him, then followed Jasmine.

Her sweet floral scent clung to it.

The next twenty minutes were a flurry of activity. Someone offered Tru a rucksack to repack his clothing and personal items. Three priestesses ran to collect supplies for their journey. Another volunteered to help Tru strap Lady into the struts and put up the bonnet. He wore his hood, but thankfully the enforcers didn't ride by.

Tru tossed his gear into the cart. The priestesses returned with three wooden crates of food and a canvas sack of assorted equipment. He stowed them. Hopefully, they had everything they needed.

"Tea? Or almond cookies?" The blonde priestess

had a wine-colored birthmark on her cheek. "Fresh baked."

"Sounds great." His thigh throbbed on the walk back through the tunnel to the basement, and he took a seat by a table. Riding on a cart while Lady did the work sounded perfect. He kneaded his sore leg and stretched it out.

The blonde brought a plate of cookies and two mugs of peppermint tea.

"Thank you."

She joined him, cradling her mug. "Do you know where you're heading?"

"No idea." He sipped the hot beverage and relaxed.

Calla entered the room.

Tru's breath hitched, and his gaze skimmed the length of her body. Black boots climbed her slim calves to her knees. Leather leggings encased her shapely thighs. Leggings! A milky white shirt contrasted with her tanned skin, and the soft brown suede tunic was laced tight to lift her— His cheeks heated. He raised his eyes to her face, and she grinned. Gods above, had he ever seen anyone more gorgeous?

"What's left to do before we leave?" She started braiding her thick, wet curls.

"Your chariot awaits."

Jasmine entered, multiple satchels, rucksacks, a longbow, and a quiver hanging off her shoulders. "I'm ready— Are those cookies?" She dumped the gear and crossed the room. "Aster, you're the best! Can we take these with us?"

The blonde snatched one more from the plate. "Sure."

Jasmine stuffed cookies in her pockets and gathered

her equipment. "Let's go."

Tru rose from the chair, gritting his teeth against the leg pain, and held out his hand. "Let me take those for you."

"I've got them." She headed for the tunnel entrance. "Calla, don't forget your cloak."

Calla tied her braid with a strip of leather and grabbed her new garment off a chairback.

Tru helped her don the blue-green tent. It was threadbare in places, had several holes, and the bottom edge was torn. "They didn't have anything closer to your size? Or in better repair?"

"This one's perfect. I'm going to alter it, so I need all this extra fabric." She raised the hood to cover her wet hair. "Is there any tea left?"

"I've only taken one sip of mine." Tru grabbed the mug and offered it to her.

"Take it with you." Aster put her hand on Calla's shoulder and herded her toward the door. "Hurry."

Tru followed Calla and Aster into the bright noon sunshine, squinting at the drastic change. To the north, blue sky beckoned. To the west, dark clouds blotted out the far horizon. A storm was raging in Acoris. Was that merely a spring squall, or was it Gale trying to cut off Calla? *Hah*. They were headed the other way.

Jasmine stowed their gear and perched on the driver's seat with the reins. "Come on! The day's moving."

Tru helped Calla with her mug of tea into the back, then climbed up beside Jasmine and released the hand brake. "Have you ever driven one of these?"

"No, but how hard can it be?" She flicked the reins, and Lady took off.

Aster and several others waved from the front porch.

Tru peeked around the edge of his cloak. The lane was empty. As they rolled by a side street, he glimpsed a black horse with a single rider, and his heart pounded. He pulled his hood down farther and slumped on the bench.

He'd get back at Oakley someday.

Chapter Fourteen

"Where are we going?" Jasmine asked.

"No idea." Tru turned. Calla knelt behind him, the hot tea cradled to her chest. "What's our destination?"

She shrugged. "Is there a temple in Shadow Wood?"

"A small one," Jasmine answered. "That'll be a lovely two-day trip along the Crystal River."

Tru taught Jasmine the basics of driving. She had the hang of it within minutes and directed Lady down a quieter street parallel to the highway. At the edge of town, they merged into the heavier traffic on the main thoroughfare. She fell in behind a carriage with two giggling children and set an easy pace.

"I've got this." Jasmine waved at a young man on horseback riding toward them. "Hi, Moss!" She elbowed Tru in the side. "You should stay out of sight until we're far away from anyone who'll recognize you."

"Holler if you need help." He ducked through the opening of the bonnet, squeezing by Calla, and sat on a bench.

She leaned against the other one covered in crates.

With all their equipment, there wasn't much room for people. "Are you comfortable?"

"Sure. And I have work to do." She pulled out her sewing kit and unfastened her cloak. "I'm altering this."

"Do you have everything you need?"

"Plenty. I found a full rag bin, and the lady was

selling them twenty for a copper. I bought the entire drum." She toed a bulging bag leaning against Tru's bench. "Dig through there and find me the suede leggings, please."

Sunlight streamed through the front and back hatches of the bonnet, but the white canvas also allowed in indirect light. Tru opened the sack and found a brown item at the top. "This?"

"Yes."

The garment had been leggings for a large man, but it was too holey to be a rag. At least it smelled like soap. "What are you doing with this?"

"Making patches." She stuck her finger through a hole in the cloak and wiggled it.

She was amazing. And clever. They faced a long, uncomfortable journey, and she'd found a project. "Can I help?"

"I need two circles of good suede." She handed him a pair of cutters.

The wagon springs eliminated most of the jolting, leaving them with a swaying ride that was relaxing and nap-inducing.

She jabbed her needle into the fabric, and the steel flashed in the stray sunbeam streaking through the bonnet opening.

"Have you thought about how you're going to find your counterpart?"

She winced, examined her stabbed finger, and sucked on it. "He just celebrated his twentieth birthday, and he's the youngest of triplets. We can stop at temples and ask the priestesses if they know anyone of that description. And if they have information about sparks. We continue from town to town until we succeed."

"Talk louder so I can hear you!" Jasmine hollered over her shoulder.

Tru grinned and handed Calla the patches. "Now what?"

"Cut rags into strips the width of your thumb. Don't use threadbare or ripped parts. Only good fabric."

"How long?" He grabbed something off the top. "And do you mind stains?" The garment looked like a sleeping gown for a child with a frayed hem and a brown spot across the chest.

"They're fine. The length doesn't matter; just make them the same width." She rummaged through her satchel and pulled out an empty cotton bag with a drawstring top. "Put the strips in here. The scraps of unusable fabric will become stuffing in a pillow."

He looked at the gown in his hand. She trusted him? "Are you sure you want me doing this? I don't want to ruin your project."

"You can't. We can chat." She smiled. "The hours will fly by."

He'd gladly spend all day gazing at her glorious face. Pale-green eyes, framed by hair in a hundred shades of brown, pink lips, now parted and slightly moist, and the tiniest dent in her delicate chin. How he'd earned the blessing of being in her presence was a mystery.

She nudged him with her booted toe. "You're staring at me. Do I have cookie crumbs on my face?"

"No. Enjoying the view."

Pink flared in her cheeks, and she ducked her chin. "Sweet talker." Her head whipped around, and she crawled to the gap in the fabric at the rear of the wagon. "Someone's coming."

He slid down the bench and squinted. "Two riders

129

on black horses."

She gripped his hand. "Enforcers."

****

No time to panic. I shut the curtain and turned, slamming my ribcage into his knees. "Hide!"

"Where? Move the hay bales and crawl beneath the bench?"

"Too obvious." The space was too cramped to stash him anywhere. Maybe I could disguise him. "Up front." I crawled forward and grabbed the bag of rags. "Curl up."

He wedged himself into the corner and lay on his side, huddled under his cloak.

I dumped the bag over him and spread the garments, scattering them around the wagon, even tossing a few onto the benches and crates. I leaned back against the mound. Tru's elbow dug into my ribs.

I wiggled to dislodge him. "Be still."

The galloping hooves slowed behind us. "Pull over!"

I pulled my cloak into my lap, spreading part of it over the pile.

Jasmine brought the cart to a stop. "Enforcer, may I help you?"

"We're searching for the stable hand you were with earlier this morning."

I recognized the voice. My father's Commander of the Enforcers, Dariel.

"I haven't seen him since then," Jasmine said.

"Do you know where he went?"

"I just met him today, sir. I have no idea where he is."

The lies slid so easily off her tongue. I swallowed.

If they questioned me, could I do it?

"Who's in the wagon with you?" Dariel asked.

"My friend."

Horse hooves clattered over the hard-packed dirt. The curtain whipped open, and Dariel stuck his head in. I flinched. His gaze tracked over the mess: barrels, hay bales, wooden crates, rucksacks, a saddle, satchels, scattered garments, and me with my massive stash of fabrics at the front end.

"What are you doing?" Dariel asked.

My heart thundered. "Mending. I'm a rag-picker."

The toe of Tru's boot peeked out of the pile.

I picked up a chunk of gray fabric and held it out for Dariel. "I make them into new items, like quilts, rugs, or pillows." I casually dropped the tunic atop Tru's boot.

Dariel's eyes narrowed. "You look familiar. Do I know you?"

He'd been serving at the palace my entire life. Of course, he recognized me. I shook my head. "We just met this morning, sir."

"What's your name?"

"Calla."

"Where are you from?"

"The Pearl Islands."

He stared at me.

I plunged my needle into the fabric. "What can I do for you, sir?"

"Have you seen the stable hand?" Dariel shifted a bale, peered under the bench, then shoved the hay back into place.

"No, sir." Sweat beaded in my palms, and I clenched my cloak. "I heard him mention High Point, though."

Dariel checked beneath the other bench, scowled,

and nodded. "Sorry to disturb you." He hauled on the reins, turned his stallion west, and took off with his partner beside him—back toward Borderline.

I sighed. "Jasmine, let's go."

She flicked the reins, the wheels creaked, and we were underway.

Tru sat up, dislodging rags. "You're amazing."

"I was terrified."

"Thank you. Your ease of lying just saved me."

I bit my lip. He still hadn't forgiven me. "Should I have handed you to them?"

He snorted. "No. I approved of that one. It just surprises me how good you are."

That stung. But I deserved it. "Some are for the greater good. I have my reasons."

He laid his hand over mine. "I can see that, and I appreciate that you protected me. But I hope someday you'll trust me enough to tell me the truth."

The more people who knew, the higher my sisters' risk. I couldn't chance it. "Someday."

Jasmine stuck her face through the gap. "Tru, the danger's over. If I may, you could join me up here. Calla, I could use a bite to eat."

I'd never prepared a meal in my life. This should be interesting. "I'll see what we have."

Tru helped me stuff the rags back into the rucksack, then climbed over the divider.

I crawled to the food crates. What goodies had the priestesses bought for us? We had bags of flour, sugar, and cornmeal. Were we going to bake bread over a campfire? Obviously, they'd never planned meals for a road trip. A thick slab of smoked bacon. I pulled out more items. A crock of butter. *Seriously?* It'd go rancid.

I selected a few things and repacked the rest. Now for the biggest question—did we have a sharp knife and plates?

Ten minutes later, I served slices of cold ham and cheese wedged inside split buttered rolls on rag napkins.

Tru laughed. "I'd have never put these together, but it's easy to eat. Thank you." He squished it flatter and took a bite.

Jasmine handed him the reins, and he took them in his free hand.

I leaned back and enjoyed mine. A little too much bread, but otherwise tasty.

A man on a horse galloped toward us from the south, closing in fast. He passed us with a wave and a cloud of dust. A light rain would be nice to matt down the dirt, but then we'd be facing mud.

I tapped Tru's shoulder. "Can we stop soon?"

"For what?"

I choked on my bread and swallowed. "A privy?"

Jasmine laughed. "None of those out here."

Pink spread across Tru's cheek. "I'll find a place."

"If I may, how are you going to set foot on the ground for this outing?" Jasmine asked.

I hadn't thought of that. "Maybe Tera's still healing and doesn't have time to bother me?"

Jasmine chuckled. "This'll be interesting."

More like embarrassing. Bad enough I had to point out the delicate need to Tru, but now we were all discussing the mechanics of me keeping my feet off the ground while I… *Lovely.*

The prairies of southern Kurik stretched around us. No trees or low hills to hide behind, just grasslands. Tru was a gentleman—he wouldn't peek—but I'd be flashing skin to anyone riding by.

Tru pulled over at the edge of the highway, jumped out, and hurried to scratch Lady's ears.

Jasmine circled to the back. "I'll be ready, just in case." She yanked two latches, and the rear panel of the wagon swung down.

I put on my cloak, scooted to the end, and hopped out.

The dirt stayed beneath my feet. "One less thing to worry about." *Oh, the aches!* I stretched and yawned.

Tall grasses and wildflowers spread out in all directions, but twenty paces to the west, a low-lying clump of lavender created a semi-private place. I rushed toward it and fumbled with the ties at my waist. I'd never worn anything other than skirts. The leggings were comfortable and offered amazing freedom of movement, but this should be easy enough.

Jasmine blocked Tru's view should he turn away from his horse. "Hurry up; I need to go, too."

I pulled down my garments, squatted—and a field mouse scampered into my clothes. I screamed and fell back into the lavender, feet in the air.

"What's wrong?" Jasmine held her hand out to me.

I pointed. "Mouse! Get it off me!"

Jasmine rolled her eyes and waved back Tru, who'd headed for us. "You're afraid of a little thing like that?"

My bare skin started to pinken. I had to get out of the sun.

Another rodent ran up my leg and bit my thigh.

I screamed again and loosed in the lavender.

"Hey! Watch the boots." Jasmine skipped back, then chased the first beast through the fabric bunched around my ankles.

Three more mice swarmed.

Jasmine swatted them off. "You're burning."

"I know!"

A pile of loose dirt formed beside my hip, and a shrew popped out. His little claws raked my skin, leaving four pink marks.

That hurt! I pounded him. "Xyla is attacking. I must get out of here."

Jasmine found the mouse in my clothing and tossed him aside, then hauled me to my feet. "Better run." She stomped on a vole mound that appeared by her foot.

I bent to pull up my leggings, giving Tru a sight he'd never forget. Hopefully, he was facing the other direction. A fluffy brown rabbit hopped toward me, and I toed it away, tying my drawstrings. The grasses around us swayed. "Incoming." I bolted for the cart.

"I'll be there in a sec," Jasmine called out.

Tru stood on the far side of the wagon, his view of the prairie blocked by the bonnet. "What's going on?"

"Goddess attack."

A hawk screech split the air.

A chill skittered down my spine. *Do I dare look up?*

"Look out!" Tru yelled.

Chapter Fifteen

I somersaulted.

The hawk swooped, talons spread, and missed. Barely.

Tru plucked me off the ground and ran for the wagon. "Are you hurt?"

"Not much." I clung to his neck. *Don't cry.* Not for a stupid mouse bite, a couple of scratches, and some blisters. It could have been worse. It could have been spiders. Or wolves.

The hawk circled.

Tru dumped me in the back of the cart. "Hand me the bow."

The bird screeched. *Will it return?*

I passed him Jasmine's longbow, but where was the quiver? I shifted a bag and found the arrows. "Here."

He popped the lip, grabbed a bolt, and scanned the skies.

I crawled to the edge. *Can he hit it?*

Jasmine ran up, her robe flapping behind her. I stifled a laugh. She wore leather leggings and a tunic beneath. "Want me to do it?"

"I've got it." He tracked the bird and released.

The hawk shrieked and dropped like a stone.

Jasmine snatched her bow. "Fantastic! Now fetch my arrow." She climbed in, and I moved back. "How are your legs?"

"They don't hurt." I rubbed my hand down my thighs and winced. "Except here. Mice have sharp teeth."

Tru jogged up and handed her the arrow.

"Can you drive? Calla needs medical attention, then I'll come forward."

Tru's gaze cut to me, his brows furrowed. "You're injured?"

"Animal bite." I pointed to my leg. "Nothing major."

He nodded, locked the back panel in place, and got us moving again.

Jasmine drew the curtains at both ends. "Let me see."

Ten minutes later, I had salve and a bandage over the tiny puncture wounds, and Jasmine climbed into the driver's seat. "We won't make it to Shadow Wood until tomorrow evening. I suggest we stop at the way station by the river bend for the night."

I gathered my cloak and sewing kit and leaned against the front wall behind Tru. Weren't way stations dangerous? Travelers were often robbed. "Is it worth the risk?"

Jasmine frowned. "What risk?"

"Brigands?"

"I'm a temple guard. Between Tru's brawn and my sword, no one will mess with us."

"You have a sword?"

Her eyebrows rose. "Of course. I've also got knives." She patted her thigh. "And I throw a mean punch."

She was certainly built for fighting. I'd never seen a more muscled woman. I bet she could beat half the palace guards in a training battle. "Let me know when we're getting close, please."

Another hour of stitching left my hands cramping, and I stowed my sewing kit. Our wagon was a mess. I wasn't utterly useless. I could tidy this, arrange it better, and make our lives easier. Multiple pegs stuck out from the wooden ribs of the canopy, perfect for hanging things. Two hooks up high near the back were probably designed for lanterns. *Do we have one?* I got to work.

A short time later, I dusted off my hands. Everything had a place, and we'd save time hunting for needed items. I smiled and leaned out the back, allowing the breeze to cool my face. I'd contributed—

A horse nickered behind us, and I squinted. A brown animal galloped toward us, kicking up plumes of dust. Not an enforcer, thank the goddess. The rider was slight and wore a bright-red cloak. Most likely a woman. I ducked and watched.

She drew closer, passed, and blocked the roadway.

I crawled to the front and crouched. My belt knife might be small, but one good slash would slow her down.

A chill skittered across my arms. Could I harm another person, even in self-defense? That was allowed under the law, but was it true justice?

Gods, what if I was as useless at defense as I was at everything else?

****

Tru hauled on the reins, and Lady snorted. What was Charity doing here? She'd betrayed him and ruined his life. What more could she want? Had she led the enforcers to him? The road was empty. He swung his gaze back to her and narrowed his eyes. "I know what you did."

She directed her mare to Tru's side of the wagon. "I

can't believe I caught up to you. I've been riding for hours."

"What do you want?"

"To apologize." Her horse pranced beside Lady.

"Not interested." He flicked the reins, and Lady hauled them forward.

"Wait!" Charity matched the wagon's pace. "I need to explain."

"No." He clenched his jaw. "You betrayed me, falsely accused me of a crime, ruined my reputation, cost me my job, and left me homeless *and* hunted by enforcers."

She leaned from her saddle and laid her hand against his wrist. "I didn't know the charges were so serious."

He jerked away from her. "Even if it was a 'pissing in public' charge, you *lied* about me. You know I hate lies."

The wheels hit a patch of grass and lurched. Tru and Jasmine pitched forward. She grabbed the reins and directed Lady back into the roadway. "I'll drive. You yell at the barmaid."

Charity sighed. "Stop and talk to me. Please."

Jasmine pulled to the side of the road. "Go. We'll stretch our legs."

Tru jumped from the wagon and stalked into the grass. No way could she justify what she'd done. What a waste of time. They had to reach the way station before dusk. This stunt could mean traveling in the dark—too dangerous. He turned and slammed into Charity.

She stumbled back.

He grabbed her arms. "Make this quick. We can't linger."

Her chin trembled. "First, I'm sorry. When Oakley

asked me to say what I did, he swore it was a joke, but it wouldn't work if I didn't play along. And I was mad at you, so I agreed." A tear trailed down her cheek. "I didn't know the charge was treason! I thought it was something stupid that'd get you an hour in the stocks. And then I could comfort you and keep you company—"

"And you thought that would be funny. Seeing me in the pillory."

"Well, no, but…looking back, it was foolish and mean. Which is why I'm apologizing."

He threw his hands in the air. "Do you realize what you did to me? I'm on the run now!" He turned away, jaws clenched, and took a deep breath. *Calm down. Keep control.* She was trying to make things right, not stir him up more. "What you did wasn't a harmless prank. You left me a wanted man. I lost my job. My home. You *know* what that place meant to me, and you ripped it away in your jealous rage."

She winced. "I tried to fix it. I told the enforcers I'd lied, that it was the other two. Oak and Yarrow were arrested, and I had to stand in the stocks for lying—and it was so awful. I'll never wish that punishment on anyone, even if they deserve it. The enforcers told me they'd track you down for further questioning, so I don't think they believed me."

"And now you want forgiveness because you feel guilty?"

"Yes." She brushed away more tears. "No. I don't deserve it. But I regret my actions, and I'll do anything to regain your favor."

"The damage is done. I believe you when you say you're sorry because you're not a mean person. But you went too far. And I'm the one paying the price. Right now, I have no forgiveness to offer you."

She grabbed his hands. "Please. I love you! I can't bear the thought of you leaving angry and never seeing you again. I want you to love me in return, marry me, and grow old with me."

This part lay squarely at his feet. He'd been a coward, but now was the time. He stepped back. "I should have said this sooner, so I apologize. I'm happy to be your friend, Charity. You're a lovely lady. But I'm not the right man for you. You deserve someone who will worship you like a goddess, who'll look forward to time with you every day, who'll want to spend every waking moment by your side. Give up on me and find another man."

She crumpled to the ground, sobbing.

Jasmine approached. "I'll help her now. Go back to the wagon." She knelt and pulled Charity into an embrace. "I know it hurts. Let it out."

Tru walked away. He'd spoken the truth, but his guts knotted. He'd caused her pain. If only she'd taken all the subtle hints he'd thrown her way over the years. Why did she have to be so stubborn? Why didn't she turn her attentions to Indy? He'd been in love with her since they were all children.

Tru hopped into the driver's seat and picked up the reins.

Calla popped her head out. "What's going on?"

"An issue with Charity. She'll be leaving in a few minutes."

"Why's she lying in Jasmine's lap?"

"I said some things she didn't want to hear." He pivoted and found himself nose to nose with Calla. "It's my fault. I should have told her the truth." He winced.

Omitting the truth was just as bad as false words.

"Did she tell you why she betrayed you?"

"Oakley told her it was for a joke."

"And she believed him?"

"She was angry at me."

Calla laid her hand on his arm. "Why?"

Her touch sent a shiver to his core. "Because sometimes I'm a fool."

"Did you work it out with her?"

"She apologized, and I broke her heart. Now I feel like a heel."

Calla looked over his shoulder. "They're heading this way."

Tru turned. Charity's eyes and face were red, but she'd stopped crying. And she refused to meet his gaze.

Jasmine took the reins of Charity's mare. "It's too late for her to head back to Borderline, so she's coming with us. I'll tie Bonny to the back and get Charity settled, then we can be off."

He closed his eyes. Great. Now they'd have to walk on eggshells, probably with awkward silences and tension. But she couldn't travel alone at night. He'd be polite.

Jasmine climbed into the seat next to him. "I'll drive." She clucked, and Lady hauled them onto the road.

He peeked into the back. "How is she?" Charity sat beside Calla, cutting fabric strips.

"Fine." Jasmine elbowed him. "You did the right thing."

"Sure. I feel fabulous."

She grinned. "If any other women chase you down, we'll need a bigger wagon."

"Shut up."

"I estimate two hours before we reach the way station."

He glanced at the sky. Three hours until sunset. Then the eggshell walking would begin.

Chapter Sixteen

Jasmine hooked a left off the highway and headed for the way station set back from the road.

Tru shielded his eyes against the setting sun. Despite Jasmine's statement that these places were safe, Tru wasn't taking chances. He'd sleep in the wagon and guard their gear.

This shelter provided a covered area for the animals, though only three walls. The front lay open to the elements. A dun gelding was tied to the hitching rail. The women would have to share the space with a stranger. "Jasmine, take only what you need."

She nodded. "There won't be trouble." She set the hand brake and jumped out. "Grab your gear, ladies."

Tru released the rear gate.

Charity hopped down, a small bag hanging off her shoulder. "Two hours seated in this is brutal!" She stretched her arms over her head, then bent to touch her toes.

Tru held his hand out for Calla. "Are you doing all right?"

"Fine, thanks."

He swung her to the ground. The dirt started to filter away beneath her feet, and he hoisted her into his arms. "I guess Tera hasn't given up yet."

She smiled at him, and warmth spread through his chest.

"Why can't she walk?" Charity asked.

"I'll explain later." Tru stepped inside the shelter and set Calla on her feet.

The room was wide with a fireplace set in the middle of the back wall. Two rough men in well-worn clothing were spreading blankets in the left corner, close to the blaze they'd started. A table and four chairs hugged the opposite wall.

Tru addressed them. "Greetings. You'll share the space tonight?"

They stared at Calla. The one with long, oily hair nodded. "Of course."

The second man had a beer gut that strained the seams on his tunic.

Damnation. Could Tru leave her alone in this room with them?

Charity pushed past him and scanned the room. "We have to sleep on the floor?"

"You'll be fine." He hurried out to Jasmine. "Two men. I'm not sure about this. Maybe we should camp closer to the river?"

"No." She hoisted her bag to her shoulder and snagged a crate. "Did you see the work Calla did in here? Everything's organized."

"I'll take care of the horses and join you as soon as I can."

"We'll prepare dinner. No worries, Tru. The goddess watches over us."

It wasn't the goddess he was anxious about.

He unclipped Lady and led her to the hitching rail at the back of the lean-to. Behind it, a pump over a trough provided a major convenience for travelers. Nice. They wouldn't have to break into their water barrels tonight.

Tru filled the wooden vessel, and Lady plunged her nose in. The gelding strained toward it but couldn't reach. He was tied too tightly. What kind of idiots stabled this poor beast? Tru circled Lady, but the gelding skittered away.

"It's all right. I'm a friend." Tru held his hand out for a sniff. Once the gelding quieted, Tru scratched his neck and loosened the ties. "Your owners didn't treat you well tonight, did they?" They hadn't bothered to remove the saddle. The horse rubbed against the side wall, then dove into the water.

This was taking too long. He led Charity's horse to the rail and secured her, then turned for feed. The shared wall with the shelter was packed with baled hay. He hauled one down and spread it beneath the rail, offering plenty to the gelding.

He was rubbing against the wall again.

"What's the matter?" Tru released the straps and took off the saddle. *Sarding fools shouldn't have a mount if they can't care for it.* He pulled on the blanket padding.

It stuck. *Disgusting.* The matted fabric adhered to the horse's body. "Filthy buggers!" He picked at the edge and peeled it back. The gelding let out a squeal and shifted its weight from hoof to hoof. "Calm down, I'm here to help." He stroked the animal's neck until he quieted, then tried the blanket again. Four quick tugs, and it came free.

The poor beast had sores over its ribs.

Tru'd give those two loiter-sacks a proper scolding later. He hauled the wagon into the stable, barely squeezing it between the hay bales and Bonny, and arranged his blankets on the floor of the cart. He went inside the shelter.

The women had positioned the table in the center. Calla and Charity were seated, pulling food from the crate. Jasmine handed him their cooking pot. "Could you fetch us water, please?"

Tru glared at the men, propped against the side wall atop their blankets, and hurried to the pump. If they so much as looked at Calla, he'd pound them. He returned, set the pot near the fire, and turned to them. "I fed and watered your horse since you couldn't be bothered."

Beer Gut grunted. "Didn't ask ya to."

"You're welcome." Tru turned and checked the blaze. *Amazing*. They'd built it properly to burn all night. Satisfied, he sat at the table with the women, positioned so he could keep an eye on the two slugs.

Calla leaned toward him and whispered, "Were you rude on purpose?"

"They've abused that poor animal. I restrained myself."

Charity's gaze darted between Tru and Calla.

Jasmine joined them. "Let's thank the goddess for our meal."

The women bowed their heads. No way would Tru close his eyes.

Jasmine finished. "Let's eat. I'm starving." She'd carved the pre-roasted chicken and paired it with bread rolls and slabs of cheese.

Jasmine chatted as they ate. Charity refused to look at him. Calla's eyelids drooped, and she chewed slowly. Poor lady was bone weary. Tru watched the travelers. The one with oily hair stared at the chicken, licking his lips and scratching his beard. Probably had fleas. Beer Gut leered at Calla. Tru ate. If that asswipe didn't tear his gaze off her soon, Tru would do it with his fists.

Her warm hand settled on his forearm, and she whispered, "He's not hurting me."

"I don't trust them." He didn't bother lowering his voice.

"You glaring won't help. Please." She squeezed his arm.

He turned his palm up, and she slid her hand into his. Warmth flared in his chest. Did her pulse race when he was near? Did her heart flutter like his did? They'd only known each other two days. Was that long enough to mean anything?

He glanced at Charity.

She shifted her gaze to her food.

He pulled his hand away.

Jasmine leaned back in her chair. "That was fabulous. I'm stuffed."

"Priestess, by chance do you have any scraps?" Beer Gut asked.

She gathered an uneaten chicken leg, the carcass with some meat on it, and two chunks of cheese. "Here. May the goddess bless you."

They descended on it like they hadn't eaten in days.

Disgusting. Tru crossed his arms. No way could he rest, knowing the women were sleeping in the same room. He caught Jasmine's gaze. "I'll stay in here."

She grinned. "Admirable, but unnecessary. We'll be fine."

"Are you sure?"

Beer Gut gobbled the chicken leg and glared at Tru.

"Where are you headed?" Jasmine asked the two meatheads.

"The border of Rigolan." Beer Gut gnawed a bone. "Some noble is hiring men for a militia. We figured to apply."

Jasmine's eyes narrowed. "I thought news of a civil war was gossip. You'd fight against your own countrymen for a traitorous cause?"

He shrugged. "Need a job."

Jasmine stood and stretched. "I'm ready for sleep. The Traveler's Truce of way stations makes this place safe. Sacrosanct. No violence may be offered within these walls." She glanced at the men. "You know the rules."

Beer Gut rubbed his forearm over his greasy lips. "Breaking the truce brings blood debt, Sister. We ain't dumb."

Jasmine nodded and smiled at Tru. "See?" She patted the knife strapped to her thigh and winked. "Go."

He stood. "Do you need the lantern, or may I take it?"

"What lantern?"

"We didn't bring one?"

She shrugged. "I didn't find one."

Charity's eyes widened. "What kind of fool doesn't pack one for a long journey?"

He snorted. "Did you bring one?"

She flushed.

"It's one of the many things we forgot," Jasmine said. "We'll pick one up tomorrow in Shadow Wood."

Easy for her to say. They had a fire to illuminate the room. Tru had a sliver of moon to find his way. "I'll see you all in the morning." He stalked out the door.

If anyone screamed in the middle of the night...well, they'd better not. He climbed into the wagon. If there was trouble, he was only six steps away.

****

I shifted, sleep addled. The wooden planks dug into my hip bone. *Come back, Dream Tru.* His warm fingers gently closing around mine as we walked through a sunlit meadow, occasionally sniffing wildflowers. If the floor was a bit softer—

A calloused hand clamped over my mouth.

My eyes flew open to a dim room.

"Don't scream." The fat man stood over me, a knife at my ribs. "Come with me."

My heart pounded, and my limbs froze. Go with him to be ravaged? I'd rather be stabbed. But Jayson had taught me well. I tossed back my blanket as if complying and jerked my knee up into Fat Man's bollocks.

He screamed and doubled over. Then his head jerked back, and his body followed.

I rolled to my feet.

The world slowed to a crawl.

Jasmine hauled him away, her left hand buried in his hair. Her eyes glittered in the dim firelight, icy blue and luminous.

Greasy crept forward, knife at his side. He slashed at her.

She pivoted, dragging Fat Man into the path of the weapon. It scored across his throat. Blood gushed, dousing Greasy.

He gaped, eyes wide, jaw dropped.

Jasmine punched him with her knife-filled right hand, three quick jabs, in the belly.

He clutched his wounds, fell to knees, and keeled over.

In less than five seconds, it was over.

I covered my mouth. "You killed them."

She released Fat Man and cleaned her weapon on his

150

leggings. "They broke the truce and paid the blood debt." She tossed their knives on the table. "You want their clothing for your rag collection? They're blood-soaked."

"No, thank you."

Charity sat up. "What's going on?"

"Housekeeping."

The door flew open, and Tru rushed in. "What's going on? I heard a scream."

Jasmine checked the bodies. "They attacked Calla. Nothing worth saving. Their boots are trash." She grabbed their tunics and dragged them toward the door. "Step aside, please."

Tru hurried to me and wrapped me in his arms. "Are you all right?"

I breathed deep his leather, horses, and hay scents. "I'm fine. I got in one solid kick before Savage Jasmine finished them."

She returned, holding her robes out from her body. "I got blood on my clothes. I need cold water."

"I'll get it." Tru headed outside with the pot.

Jasmine gingerly shrugged out of her robe.

"What did you do with the bodies?"

"Dumped them behind the privy." She stoked the fire and stared at the floor. "We should probably clean this up while it's wet, too."

Charity whimpered. "Don't look at me. I didn't make that mess."

"Maybe there's something salvageable in their gear." Jasmine set their rucksacks on the table. "Oh, how convenient. They have a lantern. No glass or oil, but usable. Calla, do you know where our cooking oil is?"

"I hung it on a peg."

"Think you can find it?"

Sure. After that harrowing ordeal, the dark wasn't so frightening. And with the moon out, no deities would mess with me.

Jasmine had killed two men! For me. Sure, they deserved it, but it was so…permanent. And gross. I almost threw up. All the blood. Now we had to clean it up. I shuddered. It was justice, something I'd be dishing out in twenty-eight days. Could I do it?

Tru emerged from the stable with a pot of water. "Where are you going?"

"To get oil. Jasmine found a lamp."

"I'll go with you." He helped me into the wagon.

I found the oil and my sack of rags. And I needed the privy, despite the bodies behind it.

Tru lit the lantern. In less than a half hour, the floor was scrubbed, Jasmine's robe was blood-free, and my rag collection was short three pieces. I didn't want them back. Jasmine rinsed them and laid them out to dry beside the fire, then we all crawled back into our blankets for a few more hours of sleep. Tru took the lantern with him.

It was only my second night away from home, yet palace life was a lifetime ago.

Several hours later, morning sunlight streamed through the eastern window and baked my face. Literally. My skin itched and started burning. I hauled the blanket up over my head.

Day two. Would I survive twenty-seven more days of living like this? Hopefully, I'd find my counterpart soon. Was he risking sunburn now, too? Or avoiding water pumps? I grinned. Did he have a priestess to carry him to the privy during daylight hours?

"Rise up, you lazybones," Jasmine called. "The day

has begun."

I sat up and hurried into my cloak.

Charity stared at me. "You are so odd. Why do you hide from the sun and avoid stepping on dirt? Are you royalty or something?"

I snorted. Was that irony or just a lucky guess? "The pantheon is trying to kill me. Zelos burns my skin. Tera tries to swallow me. Zephyra once carried me into the sky. Xyla's wild animals bite me. Beck and Maelstrom both tried to drown me, and Gale spits lightning at me."

Charity scooted away, eyes wide. "What did you do to warrant their hatred?"

"I'm becoming one of them."

Her jaw dropped, then she laughed. "You had me believing. Very funny."

"It's the truth." Jasmine set the empty pot on the table. "If I may, Charity, would you fill this and wake Tru? Calla, I could use your help getting a meal ready."

"Coming." I rolled my blankets and secured them to my pack.

Charity's eyebrows scrunched. "So we're all in danger traveling with you?"

"Yes. Tru and Jasmine came along to defend me."

"May I travel with you to Eldritch?"

"Do you want to take that risk?" I rummaged through the food crates and pulled out bacon and eggs. "Jaz, do we have a frying pan?"

"No." She poked at the fire. "Add it to the shopping list."

Cold ham, cheese, dried fruits, and bread for breakfast, then. I added bowls, plates, and eating utensils to the list.

Charity grabbed the pot and headed outside.

Must be nice to walk in the sun. But I was above petty jealousy. "How far is it to Shadow Wood?"

"We'll be there before sundown." Jasmine piled our gear beside the door. "They don't have an inn, and the temple is too small to accommodate us, but we can camp behind it."

Charity returned with the water, followed by Tru.

"The horses are fed and watered." He chose the chair that faced the door.

Always on guard for danger. I smiled. "Good morning."

Charity yawned and stared at the food. "I'd rather sleep for another twenty minutes."

"Suit yourself." Jasmine sliced a thick slab off the ham and handed it to me. "You can grab a snack later." She served herself and Tru. "Let's thank Sirini."

I bowed my head but peeked at Tru. His gaze was locked on that door, as if strangers could burst in at any moment. So admirable. Did he have soldier's training like Jasmine? Or had he simply learned to fight because life had been difficult?

"I might as well eat." Charity sifted through the dried fruits for a strawberry. "Calla, where are you from?"

"Pearl Islands."

Tru choked on his water and pounded his chest.

"Need help, big guy?" Jasmine asked.

"No, I'm fine." He grabbed his ham. "I'll hitch Lady to the wagon and saddle Bonny. Be ready in ten minutes." He left.

Charity ran after him. "Tru! Don't." She closed the door behind her.

Jasmine sighed. "This may be a long day."

Tru hated my lies. But I couldn't share the truth. Could I? He'd already endangered himself to protect me. He wouldn't betray me.

I should tell him. Soon.

Chapter Seventeen

Tru entered the stable. The stench of Calla's answer had left his eyes watering and ruined his appetite. She had to keep some things from strangers, especially Charity. He didn't want to cause Calla any more pain by reacting to her fibs, but gods, he hated them! If he knew the truth, he'd know how to better protect her. Why couldn't she see that?

"Tru?" Charity stood behind the horses, wringing her hands, staring at the ground.

"What?"

"Did you hear me?"

"I answered, didn't I?"

She winced. "Someone woke up in a foul mood. I asked you not to saddle Bonny."

"Why not?"

"Because I'm not returning to Borderline. I'm going with you."

Tru hauled the wagon from the lean-to. "Shouldn't you go home?"

"There's nothing for me there. I'll find work in Eldritch."

He untied Lady and led her to the cart. "Does your mother know you're not returning?"

"No."

Her ma must be sick with worry. Why didn't that bother Charity? Was she not thinking this through?

"Where did you get Bonny? She's not yours." He hitched Lady to the traces and snugged the ties.

"I borrowed her from my kinsman."

"And he doesn't want her back?" Tru untied the gelding. Might as well take him with them. Maybe they could sell him in Eldritch.

Charity blocked his path, still staring at the dirt. "Please."

"It's your decision, Charity. I'm not trying to dissuade you. I'm just worried about your family."

"Thank you. I could send Ma a note."

He patted the horse's neck. "Do Jasmine and Calla need your help inside?"

"I guess so." She left.

Tru tied the gelding's saddle to the side of the wagon. The blanket was useless, so he kicked it to the corner of the lean-to. He led Bonny out. With four people and all their gear, it'd be too heavy for Lady to pull on her own. Could he attach Bonny and the gelding to the traces? He grinned. Work in Eldritch. As a barmaid. No support network, no family to call on if she needed help. Did she not realize how hard it would be? She'd be headed back to Borderline within a week.

He cinched straps on Bonny and attached her to the left trace. It wasn't ideal. She'd pull to the right if they weren't careful. The gelding balked. Tru dug through his bag for salve, added a clean blanket to his back, and tightened the straps. Without harnesses, this would have to do. Though it looked ridiculous.

Jasmine stepped out and tossed bags into the wagon. "We about ready?"

"Just need to load up."

Charity held out a food crate. "Can you stow this for

157

me, please?"

"Happy to." He lowered the rear gate, shoved Jasmine's bags to the front, and stacked the crate on the bench next to the other two. Charity and Jasmine brought out the rest of the gear. Tru jammed it all into place and hopped out.

Calla stood in the doorway, fingers laced, eyebrows scrunched like she'd lost her puppy.

She'd said some lies were for the greater good. Hopefully, she'd realize she could trust him and share it. Until then, he'd be supportive. "Do you need a lift?"

She nodded.

He picked her up, set her inside the cart, and crossed to the driver's seat.

It was occupied. "Sit in back with Calla," Jasmine said. "I need a chat with Charity. We can swap out later."

"Yes, ma'am." He climbed into the back.

Jasmine flicked the reins, and they were off.

Calla started rearranging the gear, hanging things on pegs, and clearing space. "Are you angry at me?" She took off her cloak, sat on the floor against the front wall, and grabbed her sewing kit.

He stretched out his legs, resting his feet on the bale beneath the other bench. "You're not from the Pearl Islands."

Calla glanced up front. They were talking. She lowered her voice. "How do you know?"

"Sirini gave me a gift. I can smell lies."

Her eyes widened. "I've never heard of such a thing. What do they smell like?"

"Dandelion greens and curdled milk." He leaned toward her. "When someone lies, that stench coats the back of my throat."

She poked her needle into the fabric and pulled it out. "I have my reasons."

"And I'm sure they make perfect sense to you. But I wish you trusted me. I would never hurt you, Calla."

"I know."

"Can you at least tell me your real name?"

She sighed and met his gaze. "I want to confide in you. I trust you. But other lives are at stake, and I can't risk it. If anyone else finds out, my family would suffer further."

"You're that well known?"

"I've been the tithe for twenty years! Everyone knows my name. They were chanting it as I rode to my death three mornings ago. They aren't likely to have forgotten me so quickly."

"Why would your family die if people found out you survived?"

"Because the citizens would assume Maelstrom wasn't happy with his tithe and demand another daughter." Her voice cracked on the last word, and she blinked several times. "I can't take the chance they'll sacrifice one of my sisters."

"I understand."

"Thank you."

She was a minor noble from High Point, not Pearl Islands. He tossed Jasmine's bag out of the way and sat beside Calla. "I'm sorry. I wish I could do something to make your life easier."

"You're doing plenty."

"I would never betray you."

She leaned into his shoulder. "My life has been in your hands from the moment I met you. If you meant me harm, I'd be dead already."

She was being hunted by the pantheon and facing death if she didn't find her counterpart in time, yet here he sat, worrying over a few lies. *What a sarding heel.* She needed sympathy and friendship, not pressure. "You were close to your family."

"Very." She picked up her cloak and continued with her stitches.

"What's your favorite memory of them?"

She grinned. "Footraces through the gardens. Meals around the table. Stitching in the salon. Playing pranks on each other. Just spending time together."

"Sounds nice." She grew up with parents and siblings. He'd never even *seen* a salon. They were from two different worlds. One of the many reasons he shouldn't hope for a future with her. She'd be a goddess. What would he be to her? If he was lucky, maybe a priest. Or just another worshiper in the horde. She'd never truly need him, not with so many others around.

"Do you have a favorite memory from your childhood?" she asked.

"The day I got Lady." *What a great day.* "I was eight and too big to ride with Gray on his horse. We stopped in Eldritch for a week and worked in the malachite mines. Made enough money to buy Lady from a rancher, who had six horses for sale. Lady walked up to me and nuzzled my hair, and I knew she was mine."

"That's sweet. Wait. You were employed in the mines?"

"Nasty place. Only did it that one time."

She clamped the needle between her lips and rolled to her knees to dig through her pack.

Her leather leggings hugged her form gloriously. What would it be like to run his hand down the swell of her hip— No. Too dangerous. She was minor nobility or maybe a merchant's daughter, and soon to be a goddess. He was a commoner. Not that it should matter, but it did.

He shifted his gaze out the back. Prairie stretched to the horizon, bright spring green with dots of white and purple flowers. The scent of lavender rode on the breeze. Same as it had eleven years ago when he and Gray traveled this route to reach Borderline. They'd camped next to the river. Gray didn't trust way stations, which didn't make sense, because they're safe. Well, aside from last night's problem. Camping was more fun, anyway. Gathering wood, building a raging fire, cooking a fresh-caught trout, or roasting apple slices. It was an adventure. Never in one place for too long.

Gray was obviously running. Hiding from someone, always moving, isolated, never making friends or settling down. Always distrustful of people getting too close to them. Until he recognized those men in Eve's dining hall, and he'd fled, leaving Tru behind.

Ironically, unless he cleared his name, he'd also be on the run, fated to live out the same existence as Gray. Where was he now? Still fleeing? Or had he been caught? What had he done? And why hadn't he returned for Tru?

Calla settled beside him, her apron/purse in hand.

"What are you working on?"

"Pockets," she said around the needle, then held up her cloak. She'd sewn multiple small compartments to the interior along the seams of the front openings. "To hold these." She plunked a black pearl into one and poked it down with her finger. "To protect against thieves. They'll have to take my entire garment to get my wealth." She flipped up the bottom edge to showcase more of her work. The hem, which had been ragged and threadbare, was now reinforced with the same brown suede she'd used as elbow patches. The new seam held slots running along the length of it. "See?" She pushed a coin into one of the sockets. "I'll store my gold coins here, the pearls in the upper pockets, and my smaller denominations in my belt pouch. Thieves might steal the easier coins, but my hoard will be safe."

He laughed. "You're so clever! But I hate to be the bearer of bad news—thieves won't get anywhere near you while Jasmine and I are around."

"Just in case." She carefully cut the pearls from the knots and stored them in her cloak. She put the silver beads into a small drawstring bag and tied it to a loop she'd added inside the garment.

Tru sorted the gold from the other coins and tucked them into the hem.

"Now for the test." She rose and donned it.

Amazing and breathtaking. She'd started with a ragged tent/cloak and transformed it into a work of beauty—a coat with sleeves that covered to her fingertips and wooden buttons down the front. The bottom edge hit her mid-calf, and the weight of the coins aided the drape of the fabric over her luscious figure. The blue-green tint matched her eyes.

"You're beautiful."

Her cheeks colored, and she grinned. "Thank you."

"Where did you find the buttons?"

"One of the shirts in my rag bag." She took off the coat and hung it on an empty peg. "Now that it's finished, I can work on my next project."

"Which is?"

"A surprise." She sat beside him and bumped his

shoulder with hers. "For you."

Charity stuck her head through the gap in the bonnet. "We're stopping up ahead for a rest, in case you want to get out."

Calla shivered. "The last time I got out for a break, I was attacked by rodents."

Charity shrugged. "Then stay here."

Poor Calla. Even the simplest of tasks was complicated. "I'll carry you."

"No, thanks. Way too embarrassing." She tucked her chin to her chest.

The wagon lurched, and she crashed into him.

He threw his arms around her. "What's going on?"

"Sorry," Jasmine called out. "I pulled off the road. Didn't realize there was a ditch."

Wind smacked them, bowing the cover. A second blast shoved the bonnet back along the ribs, exposing Calla to sunshine.

She sprang up and donned her coat.

What was going on? Tru grabbed the edge of the canvas and tugged it—

Zephyra flew through the back opening. She knocked him aside and tackled Calla.

She screamed. They hit the wagon's front wall, slammed into Jasmine, and tumbled into the driver's seat.

Zephyra clenched her fist and raised it.

"No!" Tru grasped her wrist.

"Get her out of the sun!" Jasmine handed the reins to Charity and put Zephyra in a headlock. "I've got her."

Tru drew Calla into the bed and tossed a blanket over her. "Are you all right?"

The wagon lurched again. Charity cried out and

163

brought the wagon to a stop.

The blisters on Calla's face began to fade. "I'm fine."

Tru poked his head out the bonnet. "Need help?"

"No." Jasmine's biceps bulged as her forearm dug into Zephyra's throat. "Sirini says you elementals aren't immortal. What's it take to kill one of you?"

Zephyra's eyes widened. "Don't. Please."

Another gust rocked the wagon, and Tru shielded Calla cowering in the corner beneath the blanket.

A tornado of dirt and grass flew up the roadway, heading toward them. "Incoming! Another goddess," Jasmine said. She had Zephyra under control.

Tru would handle Tera. He strung Jasmine's bow and nocked an arrow. If he fired now, would the bolt pass harmlessly through the swirl? He aimed and released. The arrow was sucked into the twister with the grass and dirt.

"Crap." He grabbed Jasmine's sword. "Calla, stay down." He wedged her farther into the corner, blocking her with his legs.

Jasmine shouted, "Xyla is closing in on us, too."

How were they supposed to fight three goddesses?

"Hand me my bow and quiver," Jasmine demanded.

Tera was gaining on them. Tru tossed the equipment up front and braced to take her on.

Her body took form in the swirling dust. Instead of vaulting the rear gate, though, she circled to the right. What was she doing?

Tru turned and almost skewered Zephyra still grappling with Jasmine in the driver's seat. "Tera's coming up behind you!"

Jasmine's eyes blazed silver. She pivoted and

shoved Zephyra off the driver's bench. She crashed into Tera, and they tumbled across the grass.

"She's mine!" Tera tossed dirt in Zephyra's face and punched her in the stomach.

Zephyra gasped. "I saw her first." She grabbed two fistfuls of Tera's hair and took flight.

Tera growled and scratched at Zephyra's hands and arms. They continued rising. "You can't have her. It's my turn!"

A woman with long brown hair ran toward them from a grove of scrub oak in the north. The goddess of the hunt, in form-fitting leather leggings and a tan tunic, nocked an arrow.

Jasmine shot first.

Xyla dodged the bolt and unfurled massive white-and-gray wings. She took three running steps, launched into the air, and aimed at Jasmine.

She drew a knife from her thigh sheath and threw it.

Xyla banked, but the blade scored her leg. She screeched like a hawk and fell. Her body hit the ground with a muffled whump and a plume of dirt.

"Is she dead?" Tru mounted the exposed side of the wagon where the bonnet had pulled free. Xyla lay on the ground, her bent wings twitching. She would need time to heal from that. But what about the others? Tru scanned the sky.

Zephyra spiraled over the treetops of the grove, Tera dangling by her hair.

Jasmine nocked an arrow, tracked the moving forms, and shot Zephyra in the chest. She plummeted like a stone. Tera shrieked and turned to dirt, scattering on the breeze. Zephyra crashed into the canopy of trees.

She hadn't taken her wind form. Was she dead now?

Or merely wounded? And where was Tera? Tru scanned the horizon. She wouldn't give up that easily.

Calla stood, the blanket held over her head. "Is it over?"

"Not yet. Get down."

A large rock smacked Calla in the temple.

She collapsed.

Chapter Eighteen

Blood trickled from Calla's wound, and an egg-sized welt sprouted on her temple.

Tru knelt beside her. "Calla, can you hear me?" Her chest rose and fell.

"How is she?" Jasmine leaned over the front wall.

"Not dead." He patted her hand. "Calla, wake up."

"She's back!" Charity screamed.

Tera stalked toward them with a sly grin, another stone in hand.

"You bitch!" Tru grabbed the sword, jumped onto the sideboard, and launched himself. Her rock hit his chest. He plummeted and took her to the ground, dirt swirling in his face.

She jabbed her fingers in his eyes. "She's mine!"

"You can't have her!" One swift thrust drove the blade into her side below the ribs.

Her eyes widened. Her mouth gaped. Her hands fell limp. She exhaled.

And didn't inhale again.

Tru scrambled back. She didn't filter into dust and blow away. She didn't leak sand. She just lay there, staring sightlessly into the sky.

He'd killed the goddess of dry land?

A hand came down on his shoulder, and he sprang away, reaching for his belt knife.

"Easy, wolverine." Jasmine grinned. "It's me." She

pulled her sword from the body and examined it. "Odd. No blood." She wiped the blade in the grass.

A chill raced across his skin. "I killed a goddess. Oh crap. What have I done?"

Jasmine cocked her head. "I'd say she deserved it."

"Will Sirini punish me? Is the balance of power skewed toward Maelstrom now?" He ran his hand through his hair. "I wasn't thinking. I was so angry that she hurt Calla, and—" Would Sirini discipline Calla for his foolish action? He sprinted for the wagon, clambered over a wheel, and hopped in.

Calla lay between the two benches, eyes closed, head wound clotting. Still breathing.

He sighed.

Jasmine climbed in. "We should put a compress on her head." She dug through Calla's rag bag and pulled out a chunk of cotton. "Can you get some cool water?"

"Sure." He crossed to the barrels at the back, opened the side spigot, and filled their cooking pot halfway. "It's not very cold."

"It'll work. Thanks." Jasmine dipped the rag, squeezed it out, and laid it across Calla's temple.

"I didn't realize it'd be so easy to kill a goddess. I thought she was immortal." Tru stared at Calla's slack face. Her skin around the wound was turning purple. Maybe it was a blessing she was asleep. He rubbed the spot on his chest where the rock had impacted. He had a bruise, too.

"They're not gods, you know." Jasmine wadded up Calla's coat and gently placed it under her head. "Fix the bonnet so she doesn't burn again."

Tru yanked the edge of the canvas back over the ribbing. The cotton straps that tied the cloth to the wagon had ripped. That's how the fabric had peeled back from only a small gust of wind. "Charity, can you sew?"

"Yes." She huddled in the driver's seat, holding the reins to her chest.

"Could you reattach these ties?"

Charity set the brake. "Hand me the sewing kit."

Tru handed it to her and sat beside Jasmine and Calla. "What do you mean, they're not gods? They have powers. They're worshipped."

"And they're mortal." Jasmine waved toward the body in the grass. "Sirini is the only true deity. She made sparks and set them in humans, changing them into beings different than us but not all-powerful. They can't be in all places at once. They aren't all-knowing. They're created, same as you and me. They heal faster, they are stronger, they all have unique gifts, and they could live forever if they weren't stabbed through the heart. But they aren't infallible."

"What happens when one of them dies?"

Jasmine shrugged. "Not sure. I assume that Maelstrom, as Tera's counterpart, might weaken due to her death. Or maybe her spark passed to him, and now he's stronger. I'll have to ask around at the other temples."

He'd been lied to his entire life about the pantheon. *Figures*. Every day was a series of lies and half-truths piled together. "Why are they worshipped if they aren't deities?"

"Because they impact the citizens' lives. Maelstrom demands reverence and sacrifices. In exchange, he uses his powers to ensure safe passage for ships, rescue drowning sailors, drive fish into their nets, things like that. If the people stop worshipping him, he withdraws his protection." She rewet Calla's compress. "Same with Sprout in Olerio. The people worship him, and he ensures that their crops are the richest in the Five Realms. They grow wealthy and credit him. But enough of this. We need to move. Eventually, Zephyra and Xyla will heal, then they'll be back." She hopped out. "I've got to piss. Would you water the horses?"

A few minutes later, they were underway. Tru rode in the bed, cradling Calla's head in his lap. He dampened the rag often, and the swelling on the side of her head diminished. Did she already have some of the healing properties of the other…what were they? Not gods. Demigods? Super-beings? Didn't matter. He prayed that Calla would awaken soon and be fine.

He ran his fingers down her cheek. So silky and soft. She'd never worked full days in the fields. Surely, her tan skin was her normal tone, which made her tale of the Pearl Islands home plausible. Maybe her parents were originally from there.

"What are you doing?" a voice said over his shoulder.

He turned to find himself nose to nose with Charity. She'd climbed in behind him. "Hoping to wake her up."

"By petting her face?"

"Do you need something?"

"Food. Mind if I take something up front for Jaz and me?"

He waved at the crates. "Help yourself." No way was he eating another slab of cheese until next week. But they were welcome to it.

At midday, Calla's eyelids fluttered, and she opened her eyes.

He smiled. "Good afternoon, beautiful. How do you

feel?"

She brought her hand up to her temple. "My head hurts. What happened?"

He helped her sit up and told her of the rock, the fight, and Tera's death.

Calla paled. "You did that for me? What if the other gods seek vengeance?"

"It was worth it." He took her hand. "Anything to keep you safe."

She blinked. "I'm not worth all this trouble. You could have been hurt. Or killed!"

"I will stay with you, no matter how many deities attack." Her beauty enticed him like a lavender blossom gathered bees. Her laugh never failed to coax a smile out of him, and her sense of humor would probably leave him with permanent smile creases on his face. But what drew him above all else was her courage. She faced every challenge bravely, more so than anyone he'd ever met, and without complaint. She was no weak damsel who needed rescuing. And her desire to do good in the world, to give more than to take, gave him faith in the human race again. Made him want to be better and to do better.

"You're staring at me again."

****

"I can't help myself."

I rolled my eyes, and the flutters in my stomach grew wilder. "You're slathering it on thick." Were my cheeks coloring?

"Just the way you like it." He waggled his eyebrows.

I laughed. What had I done to deserve his attention? I'd gaze into his olive-green eyes all day and not grow weary. Run my fingers down the planes of his stubbled cheeks to the adorable chin dimple. Trace the lines around his tempting lips.

But he was so much more than a handsome face. His gentle, tender soul manifested in his care of the people around him and the horses in his charge. He always wanted to help. I'd been a delirious, filthy servant girl sprawled in the bean field, but he didn't hesitate to lift me into his arms and see me to safety. He was both a savior and a sweet friend. He risked his life taking on the pantheon for me.

He'd killed a goddess for me. How could I even begin to repay him?

I didn't deserve his attention, yet he freely offered, and I'd cherish it as a gift. We'd have twenty-six more days together before I ascended. Or died.

He held my hand, rubbing his calloused thumb across my skin. Unless I was the world's worst at interpreting body language, he wanted me. But he was a gentleman, waiting, offering subtle hints and not-so-subtle smoldering glances. His gaze danced over my face like a hungry man at a banquet.

I was starving.

Should I kiss him? We had less than one month, but it could be glorious. Even with two chaperones. And it could last beyond that. Couldn't we stay in touch after my ascension? Surely, some of the other gods had a human they favored.

It was risky. What if he didn't welcome a kiss? What if he backed away?

No, I wasn't reading him wrong. His lips were moist. Tempting. He was staring at my mouth. Heat speared to my core, and my heart pounded.

I leaned toward him. His gaze caught mine, and he

froze, eyes wide. I shifted closer, our noses almost touching. His hot breath caressed my skin. I was trapped in the sweet agony of the moment, needing to taste, to feel, to experience, even if just this once.

I brushed my lips across his. Sampling. Inviting.

He pulled me into his lap and deepened the kiss, one calloused hand caressing the skin on my arm, the other anchored around my waist. His touch, his warmth, the sculpted plane of his broad chest—he was intoxicating. I wrapped my arms around his neck, cupped the back of his head, and ran my fingers through his unruly silken curls.

His tongue parted my lips, and fire blossomed in my nether regions. *Great goddess, I'll combust in his powerful arms!*

Charity gasped behind us.

I shot out of Tru's lap.

She bounced a chunk of bread off his forehead. "I guess she's fine." She turned to Jasmine. "Can you pull over please? I need to get out."

"Make it quick." Jasmine guided the horses off the road.

Charity hopped out before the wagon came to a stop.

Jasmine looked at us. "What's going on?"

Tru ran his hands through his hair. "She caught us kissing."

Jasmine rolled her eyes. "I've got this." She followed Charity.

Tru thunked his head back against the ribbing. "I'm a heel."

"We both are." I took his hand. "I regret that it hurt her feelings, but not the kiss."

"Nor do I. Will there be a repeat?"

I leaned toward him. "Innumerable repeats." Our lips met, sweet and slow, utterly divine. I pulled away before we got caught again.

His finger stroked my wrist. "Calla—"

"It's Cali. But please don't call me that in front of others."

His gaze softened, and he drew me to his side, his arm slung around my shoulders. "That's a beautiful name. Thank you for trusting me with it."

"You don't recognize it? You don't know who I am?"

"I don't even know the names of all the Kurik nobility, and I've lived here half my life. Why should I recognize an Acoris noble?"

I smiled. "It doesn't matter. I'm Calla now."

Jasmine climbed into the driver's seat. "We're ready. I've got to pick up the pace if we're to make it before sundown, so brace yourselves and hang on." She shut the curtain. "Come on, Charity. Let's move."

She mounted the step, shifting the wagon slightly, then we were underway again.

Tru turned to me. "It's not much privacy, but enough for me."

I grabbed his face and leaned into him.

Jasmine made excellent time, and we arrived in Shadow Wood a couple of hours before dusk. She set the brake. "Everybody out."

I donned my coat and crawled to the rear of the wagon, muscles protesting. Sitting for so long, no matter how enjoyable with Tru, left me stiff and achy. At least I wouldn't have to worry about the dirt. Tera was dead, and the ground was safe again. I hopped out and stretched.

We were parked on the north side of a building under a lean-to. I walked around front and studied the village. Although that word might be an overstatement.

Shadow Wood was a collection of seven buildings erected along the Emperor's Highway. The edge of Woodland Forest, Xyla's hunting grounds, loomed over the four businesses on the far side of the road: blacksmith, carpenter, tavern, and general market. Three squat structures hugged the waterfront: a miller, a tailor, and the temple where we parked. Dwellings spread out along the banks of the Crystal River.

Sirini's temple wasn't anything like the grand ones in High Point and Borderline. Built of gray wood, it looked like all the others. Nondescript. Ancient. Was it leaning slightly? The crescent moonstone above the lintel was the only clue to its identity.

"Let's go. Daylight's waning." Jasmine led the way. We followed her inside.

Sunlight filtered through high windows, illuminating a gray sanctuary. A tapestry of the goddess hung above an offering table. Hand-hewn benches, highly polished, created a half-circle seating area. In the center stood a tall stool with a bowl of tokens.

A white-haired priestess in a matching robe greeted us. "Blessings in Sirini's name. I am Amity. Welcome." She touched her fingers to her forehead, lips, and heart.

Jasmine repeated the gesture. "Greetings, Sister. We've come seeking knowledge and a place to spend the evening."

Amity smiled. "I'm pleased to provide both. There is a covered area out back with a firepit. You'll be safe. May I suggest you set up your camp while the sun lingers in the sky, then return here to ask your questions."

"Thank you. Are you alone here?" Jasmine glanced around the small room.

"Sister Tulip is preparing our evening meal. Would you care to join us?"

"Your offer is kind, but we brought our own provisions." Jasmine bowed. "We'll be back in an hour."

"Perhaps you would tell me the subject matter now so I may prepare?"

Jasmine grinned. "Sparklers."

Amity's eyes widened. "Intriguing!" Her gaze shot past Charity and Tru to me.

Jasmine herded us outside. "Let's move."

I gave Charity a gold piece to purchase the things we needed. She wouldn't look at me, but she stared at the coin before hurrying across the highway. Tru took care of the horses. Jasmine and I hauled our supplies to the backyard.

Amity's pit could roast half an ox if we had one. Which we didn't. But if Charity found a frying pan, we could dine on bacon and fried eggs tonight.

Jasmine built a fire, drawing freely from the wood stacked against the temple. I visited the privy on the other end of the property. Thank the goddess I didn't have to be carried. I returned to help Jasmine.

A canvas awning stretched between four posts. That hadn't been there when I left for the privy. Had Jasmine pulled it taut? It shaded a patch of new spring grass, thick and soft, a better sleeping surface than a wooden floor. I spread out our bedrolls. Should I place Tru's next to mine? I was no longer Princess Calilee, so her reputation didn't matter. And since I'd slept in a loft with him two nights ago, servant Calla's reputation was already ruined. Besides, who would care? With two others nearby, we weren't in danger of succumbing to our desires.

Charity returned with a proper lantern, a flask of oil, and a frying pan. A boy on the cusp of chin whiskers followed her, carrying the rest of her purchases in a cheap wooden crate. He set them beside the firepit. She smiled and offered him a copper. "Thanks for the help."

He bowed. "Anytime, lady." He ran off.

She gave me the change, still refusing to look at me. "I don't think I forgot anything."

"Thank you." Talk about uncomfortable.

Jasmine lit the new lantern and the rusty one we'd obtained last night and hung them from the roof. "Do we eat first, or do we go inside and find out what Amity knows?"

My stomach rolled. Food would never sit easy until I learned more about my spark. "Questions first, please."

Jasmine turned to Charity. "You stay here and watch our things."

Her eyes widened. "Alone?"

"You're under Sirini's protection. No one will harm you."

"Then our supplies are safe. I want to go with you."

I didn't want to hurt her feelings, but no. She'd betrayed Tru out of spite, and she hadn't looked at either of us since the kiss. "I don't trust you with my secrets."

"Calla's life is in danger," Jasmine explained. "The priestess may have helpful information, we're on a time limit, and you're acting like a child. Guard our gear or visit the town; I don't care which. You're not coming with us." She pointed at Charity. "And if you go to the tavern, don't speak to anyone about us. Not our names, where we're going, where we came from, or what we're doing. Understand?"

Charity's chin quivered. "Yes."

Thank the goddess Jasmine had said it. I'd have caved. I couldn't stand upsetting someone, even if they deserved it. *Some justice goddess I'll make*.

Chapter Nineteen

Amity led us to a tight kitchen area with an ancient oak table, and we sat.

My heart fluttered. What information had she found?

She folded her hands and smiled at me. "I researched. Allow me to share what I learned."

I sighed. A little information was better than none.

"Sirini existed before time itself. She created the world with her spoken word. One of her people, Zelos, worshipped her devoutly, and she rewarded him with a spark of divinity. It gave him new abilities. He could control the sun. He healed quicker than normal men. Most importantly, he could live forever and offer Sirini his undying devotion." Amity tilted her head at me. "You can guess how that ended. He turned from her and demanded worship from mortals. If they would not give it, he burned their skin and crops."

Jasmine muttered, "Asshole."

Amity grinned. "Sirini grew to loathe Zelos and sent him away. Periodically, they try to unite, to mend their differences—the days when her three moons ride the skies with the sun—but they have never reconciled.

"In time, she placed a spark in two new people, this time newborn babes. They didn't change immediately. They needed to find each other to activate the sparks. Sirini hoped that the act of seeking each other out would create a greater bond between them, and together they would balance Zelos. Maelstrom and Tera found one other in their twentieth year but loathed each other. And they were jealous of Zelos. The three fought constantly. Sirini separated them like petty children. Zelos was exiled to the Pearl Islands. Tera was sent to northern Olerio, and Maelstrom made his home off the coast of Acoris."

I raised my hand. "Are they allowed to leave their areas? Because Tera followed me to Kurik."

Amity nodded. "They periodically roam, but the farther they are from their temples, the weaker they grow."

That explained why Tera had been so easy for Tru to kill. Zephyra was only a few days away from her temple, so maybe she'd survived the fall.

A chill shot down my arms. Xyla's home was only two hours from here. She'd be at full strength if she attacked me tomorrow.

Amity watched me; her brown eyes glimmered in the candlelight. "Shall I continue?"

I nodded.

"Sirini regretted giving the sparks and waited several hundred years before trying again. Sprout and Xyla got along and proved helpful to the citizens. They didn't demand worship. They thanked Sirini and worshiped her. Pleased with the success, Sirini changed Beck and Mica."

Amity frowned. "This is where the details grow sparse, but I've heard tales from other priestesses. Maelstrom began requiring sacrifices. He'd discovered the pattern in Sirini's gifts. Sparks are only given to the youngest of identical triplets, a rarity back then.

Maelstrom found a young girl with a spark and killed her. It fled her body, and he grabbed it somehow. It gave him greater strength to venture farther from his temple."

I swallowed. "He's been demanding sacrifices for two thousand years. How many has he stolen?"

Amity shrugged. "No one knows but Sirini. And she changed the requirements again. The counterparts now have a time limit. If they fail to connect, they die, and their spark returns to Sirini." Her chin trembled. "Can you imagine being a parent, not knowing these things, and watching your child perish mysteriously? No sickness, no accident, just here one moment and gone the next." Her eyes watered, and she blinked. "Losing a child is the worst pain anyone can know."

My chest tightened. *Poor Amity.*

And why had Sirini devised such an unjust way of dealing with the sparks? Why not just let the spark dissipate and let them live their lives as normal mortals? Maybe I'd have the power to change that once I ascended.

Jasmine clenched her fists. "Maelstrom has been sowing suffering and fear without repercussions."

Tru asked, "Who was next? After Beck and Mica?"

"That's where my records end. You'll have to search other temples for the rest."

Jasmine rolled her eyes. "It'd be easier on us if Sirini put all this information in one place." She looked up. "No offense, Goddess! You know best."

My stomach had soured. "I have twenty-six days to find my counterpart."

Tru grabbed my hand.

"I'm afraid that's true, child." Amity paused for a moment. "The only multiple births in Kurik are the king's eldest children, but they are a female and two males. You should travel to Eldritch and ask the priestesses if they know of any commoner triplets."

Jasmine nodded. "It's our plan. May we draw blessings before we leave?"

"Certainly." Amity leaned on the table and stood. "Allow me." She led us into the sanctuary. "Help yourselves."

Jasmine plunged her hand into the bowl, swirled, and pulled out a wooden chip. "Protect." She rolled her eyes. "What have I been doing these past few days?" She laughed. "But I'll continue. Thank you, Sirini."

Tru plucked a metal disc off the top and frowned. "Duty. What's that mean?"

"If I may, it is a moral or legal obligation, a responsibility, a requirement."

He glared at Jasmine. "I know what it means. I don't know what I'm supposed to do with it. Do I have a duty I'm unaware of?"

"Toss it back in. Ponder later." Jasmine grabbed my arm and hauled me to the bowl.

I swished my fingers through the tokens, but they were all cool to the touch. No heat to guide me to a specific blessing or message. I chose one. "Home." My eyes burned, my throat closed, and I ducked my head.

Tru wrapped his arms around me. "Once you ascend, you can return to see your family."

"Unless I fail."

"Don't talk like that." He kissed my forehead. "Let's go eat, then I've got a few errands."

We found Charity at the campfire kneeling before a frying pan over the fire. The fried bacon-and-potato scent made my mouth water. A flat griddle with a cover rested over a section of hot coals beside a lidded pot.

I glared at the fire. Would Sear try for me? Or was it safe next to the open flames? Time to find out. I pulled our new plates and utensils from the crate and sat beside her. The fire stayed in the pit like it should. *Good. One less thing to worry about.* Maybe he was off harassing my counterpart. "Charity, that smells—"

Tears streaked her face, and a dirty handprint marred her shirt near a ragged tear.

"What happened?"

She blinked and brushed tears from her cheek. "I'm fine."

Jasmine knelt beside Charity. "Tell us."

She sniffed and poked at the potatoes. "I was a fool. I'm sorry for the way acted." She shot a glance at me. "Especially you. You didn't do anything wrong. I was being jealous."

"I forgive you. But what happened to your shirt?"

Her gaze dropped to her lap. "I didn't want to stay here. I was angry at Jasmine for giving me orders, and I was furious with you for…you know. So I went to the tavern."

"By yourself?" Tru squatted beside me.

Charity nodded. "There were two men." Her voice cracked on the last word. She took a deep breath. "They offered to buy me a drink, and I agreed."

"Oh, sweeting." Jasmine hugged Charity. "Did they hurt you?"

"No. But the ugly one tried to kiss me. Said it was payment for the ale." She wrung her fingers. "When I refused and got up to leave, he grabbed my arm. I jerked away, and my sleeve tore. Back home, I always had Hawk and other friends to ensure patrons left me alone.

I didn't realize how vulnerable I was. Thankfully, the owner saved me. I returned here to stew in my stupidity." Fresh tears fell. "I've been awful. I'm so sorry."

Jasmine patted Charity's shoulder. "I'm glad you weren't injured, as I'd hate to bloody my knife again, but if you want me to head over there and teach them some manners, I will."

Charity snorted. "No. That's not necessary." She wiped her face again and straightened. "I've learned my lesson."

Tru grinned. "Between Jasmine battling way-station wastrels, Calla diving into her own sacrifice, and Charity taking on tavern bums, I'm surrounded by brave and dangerous women." He winked at me. "Lucky me."

Charity's face whipped toward me, her eyes wide. "You were Maelstrom's tithe?"

I nodded.

"You're Pr—"

I covered her mouth. "Please don't say it out loud."

She pulled my hand away. "I've been with you for two days and didn't know!"

"Would it have made a difference?"

She sighed. "Probably. Because I'm too petty for my own good. I promise, from now on, I'll be better." She stirred the potatoes again. "I've been a burden, and I realized I could best contribute tonight by cooking our meal."

"You're not a burden," Jasmine said.

"It smells delicious." Tru lifted the cover off the griddle and whistled. "Homemade biscuits? You made these?"

"You're surprised?" Charity cracked eggs into the potato-and-bacon pan and dusted them with salt. "I'm an excellent cook. Two minutes until it's ready."

"What's in this pot?" Tru reached for the lid.

Charity swatted his hand with the spatula. "That's our morning meal. Beans, onions, and fried bacon."

"Sounds amazing!" Tru looked around at the cooking gear she'd scattered over the grass. "Do you need any help?"

"Hand me the plates."

It was the best meal I'd eaten in two days, and I stuffed myself. While Jasmine and Tru cleaned the dishes, I took Charity aside. "I'd be happy to mend your shirt."

She glanced at Tru, then leaned toward me. "Can you do it without me taking it off? I don't have another one to wear."

"You only brought one?"

"It's all I own."

"Then I'll share." I dug through my pack for the sewing kit and a proper garment for her. "This pink will look much nicer with your complexion than mine. You should keep it."

"Are you sure?"

"Absolutely. Tomorrow morning, we can go shopping. The building next door is a tailor, and I bet he's got new pieces to sell."

Charity ducked her chin. "I don't have any coins."

"I have plenty. If we're going to travel together, we should be comfortable. Wearing the same shirt every day will grow uncomfortable."

"And stinky." She giggled. "Thank you. I'm sorry I've been a pain."

"I'm sorry you were hurt. I can't imagine that kind of heartbreak."

She leaned closer and lowered her voice. "Are you really Princess Calilee?"

"Not anymore. Please don't call me that."

"I have so many questions! Life at the palace, the nobility, who's marrying who."

"Maybe later, but not now."

She nodded and handed me her blanket. "Shield me while I change."

Twenty minutes later, the dishes were clean, I'd mended Charity's shirt, and Tru was ready to head out for his errands.

"Want me to go with you?" Jasmine asked.

"No, I've got this." He turned to me. "May I have a few coins? I'm hoping to find the carpenter. If he can make us new traces, I'll need to pay for it. And maybe a beer."

I dug a gold piece from the hem of my coat. "Is this enough?"

"Two silvers would be plenty."

I handed him my pouch. "Take it. You might think of something else you need."

"I promise I won't spend it all." Tru left, whistling a peppy tune, his hands in his pockets.

Jasmine inspected my coat. "You're brilliant. How did you come up with this?"

We spent a few pleasant hours around the campfire, chatting as if we'd known each other our entire lives. Tru returned with news—the carpenter would be by at dawn to modify our wagon for three horses.

Jasmine finally ordered us all to sleep and dimmed the lanterns. Charity hurried to the privy. Tru banked the fire.

I crawled into my bedroll.

Jasmine grinned. "Don't stay up all night whispering. We leave after dawn." She lay down and pulled her blanket up to her chin.

Charity hurried back. "It's cold away from the flames!" She settled in her blankets.

I rolled to face Tru. The deep red coals in the firepit reflected in his eyes and cast a pink glow on his skin. I ran my finger across his cheek and lips. "Sleep well."

He kissed me and tugged me close. "Not a chance, with you lying next to me."

I snuggled into his arms and closed my eyes. Tomorrow, we'd be heading into Xyla's territory. She had a forest full of creatures to slow us, but she needed to get her hands on me to steal my spark. She controlled wild animals, but what about tame ones? Could she influence our horses? How strong would she be so close to her home? Would we be able to stand against her?

Tru whispered in my ear. "Be calm, my love. I bought a sword and extra arrows at the blacksmith's shop tonight. We're prepared for tomorrow."

How did he know what I was thinking?

"Your heart is thumping. I can feel it." He rubbed my back. "Sleep now."

What had I done to deserve his attention?

Chapter Twenty

Tru woke with the sun, day three of Cali's adventure. She slept with her cheek mashed against his shoulder. Stray hairs curled around her face. So lovely. What would it be like to awaken by her side every morning? If life ever returned to normal, if she wanted his company after her ascension, would he have more of these glorious mornings?

He carefully freed his arm, draped his blanket over her, and began his chores.

The horses had nibbled the grass down to the ground and drained the water trough. He refilled it and checked the gelding's sores. They'd scabbed. Too bad he didn't have his grooming tools, or he'd brush them down. Maybe he'd find one at the market. If not, they'd be in Riverton by the end of the day, and it was a much larger town.

Provided, of course, Xyla left them alone. The odds hovered around zero. They'd have to be vigilant. New traces would help. The makeshift contraption he'd devised yesterday would fall apart under high speeds.

Jasmine rose and stretched her arms above her head. "Good morning." She toed Charity. "Wake up. I call the privy first."

An hour later, they'd eaten, cleaned up the mess, groomed, and repacked the wagon. The women headed for the clothing shop.

The carpenter arrived a few minutes later. The old man had also brought along proper collars for the horses and extra straps. Tru paid more than he thought they were worth but considered the overage a tip for the on-site call.

Finally, they were off. Amity and Tulip waved goodbye, and Jasmine headed north. Tru sat in back with Cali. She'd cut her rags into strips and now stitched them together, end to end, to make one long band.

"What are you doing with those?" He handed her another piece from the rag bag.

"You'll see." Within seconds, she'd sewn that strip on and held her hand out for another. "Have you traveled through this part of the country?"

"Gray and I came through on our way to Borderline."

"Did you enjoy it?"

"Sure." *Aside from waking up alone and frantically screaming Gray's name at the wilderness, wondering if he'd left me or been eaten by wolves or—*

The horses squealed, and the wagon lurched.

Jasmine yelled, "Bow and quiver! Now!"

Tru strung the longbow.

Cali handed the wooden tube through the bonnet opening. "What's going on?"

"Wolves!" Charity hauled on the reins.

Jasmine stood, nocked an arrow, and fired. "Arm yourselves. Xyla brought friends." She fired again. A wolf yelped.

Cali's eyes widened, but she drew her belt knife and crept to the back.

The horses surged, and she stumbled into the stack of water barrels.

"Careful!" Tru grabbed her arm and helped her stand.

A snarling wolf leapt at her. She screamed and jumped back. It fell and smacked its jaw on the rear gate.

Weren't wolves nocturnal?

Tru strung his smaller bow and handed the quiver to Cali. "Hand me new ones. And stay away from the edge."

Charity cried out, and the wagon jolted hard to the right.

Tru loosed another bolt at a wolf, hitting it in the ribs. It fled. Another three trailed them. How many were up front terrorizing the horses? And where was Xyla? He shot another in the neck, killing it. Cali passed him another bolt.

A piercing shriek sliced the air. Xyla swooped down, wings unfurled, and hovered behind them. "You'll die for that!" She fisted her hands in his tunic and yanked him toward her.

He dropped the bow and jabbed the arrow into her shoulder.

She screamed, pivoted, and pulled him from the wagon, dumping him in the roadway.

No! He had to protect Cali.

Two wolves converged on him, lips peeled back, tails erect. He brought up his arm, blocking his throat, and drew his belt knife. He stabbed the smaller black one in the neck, shoved his forearm into the teeth of the larger gray, and rolled to his knees. Pain blasted down his arm. The gray had a tight grip, and its teeth were buried deep. Tru skewered its shoulder, and it fell away. Both retreated to the forest, bleeding.

Tru sprinted after the zigzagging cart.

Xyla clung to the back, reaching for Cali. Four wolves still hampered the horses.

Jasmine shot at one of them, and another jumped at her. Its weight carried her off the other side, and they somersaulted into the grass. The other three pursued Jasmine. She gained her feet and slashed with her knives.

She'd have to hold her own. Cali needed Tru. He put on a burst of speed and launched himself at Xyla, catching her around the knees.

She stroked her wings powerfully, gaining altitude—with her hands fisted in Cali's tunic. She screamed, batting at Xyla, and they rose into the air.

Tru's bulk hampered the goddess, his boots hovering a handspan over the ground. She hung suspended above the roadway, unable to rise farther. He stabbed her thigh. "Let go!" He pierced her leg again, then slashed at her wing. The blood-slicked handle slipped from his grip and hit the dirt. He yanked out a handful of feathers.

Xyla tilted, flapping her wings wildly, and wrapped one hand around Cali's neck.

She gasped and clawed at the goddess's wrist.

"Soft spots!" Tru jabbed his thumb in one of the leg wounds.

Cali punched Xyla in the throat.

She dropped Cali, clutched her neck, and veered sharply to the right.

Tru released and landed on his feet. "Cali!" He knelt beside her. She was sprawled in the street on her back, her face bright red with white blisters. "Are you hurt?"

"I'm fine. Help Jasmine." She rolled to her knees.

He unbuckled his belt, stripped off his tunic, and draped it over her face.

"Thanks."

He helped her up, scooped up his knife and belt, and scanned the meadow.

Xyla was a tiny dot on the horizon, flying erratically.

Four wolf carcasses lay in the grass.

Jasmine limped toward them. Blood streamed from multiple bite wounds, and her left arm hung useless at her side. She staggered, then slumped to the ground, unmoving.

****

I ran toward Jasmine. This was my fault. She was injured because of me. And the wagon with our medical supplies was nowhere in sight. I knelt beside her. "Is she alive?"

Tru rolled her to her back.

She winced. "Don't do that again, or I'll stab you."

I sighed. "Let's bind her wounds. And yours."

"I'm fine." He clamped his hand over the teeth marks on his arm. "She's not."

Jasmine sat up and rotated her neck. It cracked several times. "I'm good. We've got a long walk to catch up to Charity. Provided she managed to stop the horses." She fell back into the grass. "Just let me rest a moment."

Tru shoved her sleeve up. "Your forearm is shredded. Is the bone broken?"

"No. My shoulder's out, though."

He probed it. "You're right. Dislocated."

She sighed. "This is going to hurt. I need something to bite on."

Tru offered his belt.

Jasmine chuckled. "Guess it'll work." She wedged it between her teeth.

Tru set her shoulder in less than a blink.

Jasmine grunted and spit out the leather. "I hate that."

I tore off the bottom edge of her robe with shaky fingers and began binding wounds. She had bite marks on her arms and legs. Two of them needed stitches, but without my sewing kit, I couldn't do anything but stop the bleeding. And the way I was shaking, I couldn't hold a needle, anyway. At least I had the sun to my back, so my shadow shielded my bare hands. My face still stung like a swarm of bees had attacked me.

"Let's get moving." Jasmine pushed herself upright and blinked several times.

"Rest a few more minutes." Tru squinted into the distance. "No telling how far we have to walk or if Xyla will return soon."

I laced my fingers. "We didn't hurt her that badly, did we? I punched her in the throat."

"I stabbed her and yanked out a bunch of feathers. Maybe she bled to death." He scanned the skies again.

They were empty.

He put on his belt, cleaned his knife, and sheathed it. "How's your face, Cali?"

I didn't bother to correct him on the name, but I lifted the edge of his tunic so he could see my skin. "Starting to heal." It didn't itch anymore.

Jasmine rolled to her knees and rose. "I'm surprised Xyla didn't take control of the horses. We need to get out of her territory." Jasmine limped toward the highway.

Tru draped her right arm over his shoulder.

I followed, Tru's tunic hanging off my head. My eyes burned, and I blinked back tears. Why was I crying? It was over. We all survived.

But they'd gotten hurt because of me. Totally unfair.

Jasmine should be in her temple, safe and whole, worshipping the goddess, not covered in bite wounds. Tru should be in his stables with his beloved horses, not holding his left arm awkwardly around Jasmine's waist. If I hadn't botched my own sacrifice, none of this would have happened.

Tears tracked down my face. I couldn't even brush them away for fear my hands would burn in the sun. I had twenty-five more days to find my counterpart. Hopefully, he'd be in Riverton.

Our walking pace was slower than a one-wheeled cart dragged by slugs, but it was forward progress. Twenty minutes later, the snorts of horses carried on the breeze.

If Zephyra attacked us now, I'd kill her with my bare hands. *Bring it on! I'll show you what a princess of the Five Realms can do.*

Thankfully, it was Charity in our wagon. I waved.

She veered off the road, looped around us, and brought it to a stop beside Tru. "Sorry that took me so long. This thing is hard to steer, but I figured it out." Her eyes widened at Jasmine's wounds. "Oh! You poor dear." Charity set the brake and jumped down. "Let's get you inside."

Tru checked the horses. "You two take care of Jasmine. I'll drive." Lady nuzzled his hair. "Hey, girl. Do you need a drink of water?"

Jasmine rolled her eyes. "Let's do this quickly." She hobbled to the back and climbed in.

Tru watered the horses. Charity and I re-treated all of Jasmine's wounds, applying salve before binding them with strips from her robe. It was ruined, anyway. She refused stitches. Good. I wasn't sure I could do it.

We set out again. Charity kept watch at the back, and Tru drove.

I sat with Jasmine, propped against the front wall, our legs stretched out in the aisle between the benches. I'd met her only two days ago, but we'd been through so much together. Battling gods, wolves, and rapists. Shopping. Meals. Endless hours on the road. We shared our thoughts and emotions like sisters. And yet I knew so little about her. "Where did you grow up?"

"Borderline. Born and raised." She grinned. "I've known Charity since we were both babes. We attended classes together, fought over boys, and drove our parents crazy."

"What did you do?"

"Sneaking beer from the tavern, asking indelicate questions at the brothel, the usual things young people dabbled in."

I'd never done any of those things. Leaving the palace required an armed guard and a chaperone. "How did you become a priestess?"

"I was promised to the temple the day I was born, so I grew up knowing my future. And I found freedom in having that path laid out. Charity tried several occupations before finding one she enjoyed, though she'd have preferred to marry and tend house rather than wait tables."

Charity stuck her tongue out. "At least I don't have to remain a virgin all my life."

Jasmine shrugged. "I'm fine with that. Men aren't attracted to women my size, anyway, nor do they appreciate a wife who can beat them at arm wrestling, swordsmanship, or marksmanship with a bow." She shifted and winced, moving her left arm carefully. "I'm quite content serving Sirini as a temple guard."

"I've never even lifted a sword, other than to hand one to you." My brothers had taught me self-defense, but they all refused to teach me blades.

"The first lesson is to never wield a weapon unless you're prepared to use it. If you want to learn dagger play, I'll instruct you. Leave the swords to Tru and me."

I nodded. Truthfully, I'd drawn my knife to take on the wolves, but I'd dropped it when Xyla appeared at the back. I wouldn't have been able to stab her, anyway. "Please teach me how to fight. I must defend myself."

Jasmine lowered her voice. "You don't have palace guards close by now. It's wise to take your protection personally."

A chill shot across my skin. "You know who I am?"

"Of course. Knew you the moment I set eyes on you. Charity isn't the only royal watcher in Borderline."

Great. Tru was the only one who didn't know. I should remedy that soon. "Do you want to go home? This trip has become too dangerous."

Jasmine met my gaze. "I'll stay." For a split second, her pale-blue eyes flashed silver.

I gasped. Was that a trick of sunlight reflecting off her eyes, or was Sirini checking on us? She'd given me a spark, but did she care if I succeeded? In the throne room, she'd been more interested in stopping Maelstrom's tithe than my welfare. But maybe she'd sent Jasmine to help.

Or maybe it was just a reflection of the lantern swinging from the ribs, and we were on our own.

Chapter Twenty-One

We made fabulous time—Xyla didn't return—and pulled into Riverton hours before sundown. Homes, farmland, and animal pens with adorable newborn lambs and goats gave way to the first business, a tavern called the Wild Piglet. We passed more houses, a money lender, and a row of clothing shops.

A grass-covered open-air market made up the town square that featured a three-tiered fountain in the center. I'd keep clear of that during daylight hours in case Beck tried for me again. The bubbling water changed from blue to purple to green, so the town held a resident magician.

Sirini's temple took up the riverbank side of the square. A paved path led from the highway, around the water feature, and up to the temple's entrance.

Tru pulled up in front of an inn. "We'll stay the night here."

"I'm looking forward to a real bed." Charity stood and stretched.

"I'm happy to get out of this wagon." I donned my coat and hopped out. Every muscle in my body ached. Between the long ride and fighting Xyla, I needed a soak in hot water. This inn included a bathhouse, and I'd be in it before nightfall.

A gust of wind slapped me in the face, knocking me back. I groaned. *Not again.*

Jasmine wrapped her arm around me and hustled me through the front door of the inn. "Why don't you get us a room? We'll bring the gear."

An hour later, our horses were stabled, our wagon was parked behind the barn, our things were stacked in a room with four beds, and us ladies were headed to the baths. Tru opted to use the room basin. I patted my pockets. My sapphire necklace, pearls, and coins were all stowed.

We had the bathhouse to ourselves, but Jasmine set up one of the privacy screens. I stripped, sank into the vat of magically heated water, laid my head back, and sighed. "Perfect."

"No dawdling." Jasmine tossed in a brick of soap.

"Can I see your house mark?" Charity entered the tub beside me.

I sat up, revealing the tattoo at the top of my cleavage.

She studied it. "Was it really inked with magic?"

"Supposedly. It didn't stretch or fade as I grew."

"That's awesome. I've never seen one before in real life. Thanks."

"No problem." I dunked my head.

Afterward, we headed back to the inn. "Shall we eat in the dining room tonight?" *How utterly divine, to sit at a table and enjoy a meal that I didn't have to help cook or clean up after.* "I'll pay."

Charity giggled. "You pay for everything. And I'm in favor."

We climbed the stairs to our room, and I knocked. "It's us. May we enter?"

Tru opened the door. "Granted."

Charity dumped her gear on her bed. "We're

heading for a meal. Care to join us?"

I kissed him and put away my things. "Please say yes."

"How could I refuse you?" He offered his arm.

Jasmine rolled her eyes. "Don't make me vomit. Save that stuff for private."

As if he and I ever had alone time.

The dining hall had eight small tables and a large one by the window. Tantalizing smells of roasted meat, stewed vegetables, and seasonings emanated from the kitchen.

Five of the smaller tables were occupied. By their worn, humble clothing, they were locals. Tru led us to a corner spot and pulled out a chair for me. So sweet! He sat with his back to the wall, and Jasmine took the seat beside him.

The barmaid hastened over. "Welcome to the Riverside Inn. Tonight, we're serving lamb stew with root vegetables or roasted rabbit with greens in butter sauce."

We ordered, and she hurried away to fetch the food.

My stomach growled. "I hope the portions here are generous."

A round man with white hair at the next table nodded. "Pardon me for overhearing, but aye, they'll fill ya up."

I smiled. "Thank you. Do you live here?"

"Name's Oli. I run the bakery on the north side of town. You all passin' through?"

What an odd name. "Pleased to meet you. We're heading to Eldritch."

Jasmine toed me under the table. "What time will you open in the morning? We'll stop for provisions."

The barmaid returned with a bread roll and a pot of butter for Oli. "This'll start ya off, Grandpa. I'll have your stew in a few."

"Thank you, dear." He grinned at Jasmine. "I'm open by sunup. Now I'll leave ya to your evening. Didn't mean ta interrupt."

Jasmine leaned toward me and lowered her voice. "It's not wise to tell strangers our plans."

I doubted a local could be dangerous, but I nodded. "Sorry. Won't happen again."

Tru stretched his arm across the table and took my hand. "We'll go to the temple after we've eaten?"

"We could split up and cover more ground," Jasmine suggested. "Calla and I will talk to the head priestess while you and Charity ask around town about our mystery triplets."

Charity frowned. "What are you talking about?"

We'd left her out of the conversation last night because I didn't trust her, so how could she know?

Jasmine raised her eyebrows at me. "Do we tell her now?"

Charity's attitude had improved, she'd been friendly and helpful, and she'd come back for us after Xyla's attack. I turned to her. "I'm searching for a young man. He's the youngest of identical triplets and celebrated his twentieth birthday three days ago. I'd like you and Tru to ask the locals if there's anyone here who meets that description."

Charity grinned. "Born a half-moon after the spring equinox?"

"Yes."

She grabbed my hand. "I know who he is! You should have asked me days ago, and I could have saved us all this hardship."

I stared at her. She knew? And my distrust of her caused—

"Who is he?" Jasmine demanded.

"A minor noble of House Rigolan. He's the first cousin to the princesses. Let me think." Charity looked up at the ceiling, though she was probably scouring her memories, not counting beams. "King Fenton of Rigolan abdicated the throne twenty-five, no, twenty-six years ago to marry a commoner. He was the oldest of triplets. The second brother, Franklin, became king. His wife birthed triplets, a boy and two girls, but the boy died in infancy. It was so sad. Now the oldest girl, Finna, is the heir."

The barmaid set a board of bread rolls and a crock of butter with a spreader knife on the table. "Sorry that took so long. Your meal will be served soon."

"Thank you." I grabbed a roll and took a bite. "Continue."

Charity buttered hers. "Fenton's youngest brother, Fenri, and his wife had identical triplets who were boys, and they were born a half-moon after the spring equinox exactly twenty years ago. I remember because I was four years old, and my mother carried on about how blessed the Rigolan family was to have two sets of triplets. That began my love of royal watching."

Two sets were a blessing? I wondered what she thought of my father. Tru and Jasmine helped themselves to butter, leaving me a tiny bit in the bottom.

Charity grinned. "Don't tell anyone, but secretly, I hoped one of those triplets would ride through Borderline, fall in love with me, and take me away." She shot Tru an odd glance. "No offense, that was before I met you."

"None taken." He winked at me.

"What are their names?" Jasmine asked.

Charity bit her lower lip. "You're taxing my memory here. Let me think. They're really strange, even for royalty. Sh…Shay…Shanen. That's it. Shanen, Shalet, and Shaded."

Jasmine rolled her eyes. "We're looking for a man named Shaded?"

"Yes. And he's incredibly handsome. Blond hair, blue eyes, broad chest—"

"You've seen him?" Tru asked.

"No, but stories circulate." She finished her bread and licked her fingers.

The barmaid served our meals with two mugs of ale and two cups of wine.

"Thank you." I sipped mine and grimaced. Not the best vintage. The lamb stew came in a huge bowl with a biscuit on top, thick savory gravy, carrots, tomatoes, onions, beet greens, and a hearty portion of meat. "Now that we know his name and what he looks like, he should be easier to locate. I hope we don't have to travel all the way to Oakencrest to find him, though. That'd take, what, another nine days?"

"Or ten." Jasmine picked up her roasted rabbit haunch with both hands and took a bite. "Or more, if we have difficulty in The Wastes."

"Pardon me." Oli swiveled in his chair. "I know it's exceedingly rude of me ta eavesdrop, and I truly didn't do it on purpose, but I can assist you."

Jasmine scowled at the man. "That's bold of you."

She had some venom in her tone. I smiled at him. "Please tell us."

"You're looking for those triplets from Rigolan? I seen 'em."

****

Tru tensed. The man was old, overweight, and posed no threat, but he'd overheard their conversation. No telling who he'd pass that information on to.

"When did you see them?" Charity asked.

"Six days ago, they passed through here on their way to High Point. They bought sweet buns in my bakery in the afternoon, and later they ate supper over there." He pointed to a long table. "I sat here and watched them carrying on with the two princesses. My granddaughter had to take them three different meals before they were satisfied."

Six days ago. Heading to the capital. My shoulders dropped. After coming all this way, now we had to turn around? And we'd have to pass through Borderline to reach Acoris, which meant hiding from enforcers.

"Thank you, Oli," Cali said.

He nodded and turned back to his meal. "I won't interrupt ya again. Promise."

Jasmine glowered at him.

Charity beamed. "We're going to High Point? Where all the eligible nobles are making matches for their kingdoms? I heard that Princess Finna is going to marry your—um, I mean, she's supposed to wed Prince Rhygan to keep Rigolan from seceding. There's unrest brewing up north, and a marriage might stave off civil war."

"Yet another reason I must ascend," Cali muttered. She gulped her wine and caught Tru's gaze over the rim of her cup.

What was that look for? "Let me guess. Rhygan

doesn't want Finna."

"Goodness, no," Charity said. "He's been courting Sorka, the Kurik princess. She's so gorgeous. Black hair, ice-blue eyes, tall… I wish I had her coloring. Anyway, Rhygan will wed Finna because it's his royal duty."

"Sounds to me like those poor people are treated as pawns in a political game." Tru drank his ale. "If I was in Rhygan's shoes, I'd be angry if I had to wed a woman I didn't love."

"You don't understand." Charity wiped her fingers. "It'll keep the peace. Rigolan and Tulya both talk of seceding from the Five Realms. Marriages to the emperor's heirs will save countless lives. All the royals accept their duties and submit. And no father wants to see his children miserable, not even nobles, so love matches are sometimes allowed."

Tru finished his stew. "We'll speak to the temple priestess tonight, and tomorrow we'll head to High Point?"

"Yes." Jasmine gulped her ale. "That was fabulous." She signaled for the barmaid. "Do you have sweets?"

The girl collected Jasmine's dirty plate. "We have almond cakes with honey glaze or strawberry tarts."

"I'd like a tart, please."

"Me, too," Charity added.

Tru handed over his dirty dishes and winked. "I'll take one of each."

Jasmine chuckled. "Yes! I want both."

Cali nodded. "I'd like the cake, please."

"Three tarts, three cakes. Be right back." The young woman gathered the rest of the dishes and hurried off.

"Feels great to not be the one washing up tonight." Charity leaned back in her chair and elbowed Cali. "So.

Are you going to tell me why you need to find Prince Shaded?"

Oli propped his chin in his hand, bringing his ear closer to our table.

"Maybe before bed."

A half hour later, Cali paid the bill, left a generous tip, and they filed out of the dining hall.

Brilliant stars twinkled in a dark sky. Sirini's three half-moons gleamed, lighting the walkway with a silvery glow. Tru laced his fingers through Cali's, and they followed Jasmine across the street.

"Is there something you'd like to tell me?"

She sighed. "Yes. You deserve to know. My name is Calilee Elanor Acoris, ninth daughter of Emperor Rhys and Duchess Eilee of the Pearl Islands."

Fire flared in Tru's chest. He stopped short and jerked his hand from hers. *Petite, two-faced deceiver, her father is the sarding emperor!*

She reached back for him.

Bugger that. He retreated a step and linked his hands behind his back. The gurgle and splash of the artesian fountain masked the pounding of his heart.

"Tru?"

"You're not a minor noble."

"No."

Jasmine grabbed Charity's arm and continued toward the temple.

Tru stared at Cali. "You're royalty. So far above my station I shouldn't even look at you, much less touch—" He clenched his jaw. "If your father found out I've kissed you, my head would decorate the palace gates for twelve moons."

Tears welled in her eyes. "Not if I asked for your

pardon."

"You risked my life. If you'd told me at the beginning, I would have helped you, but I'd have kept a respectful distance."

"You're saying if I was a servant girl, my reputation didn't matter?"

"No! I'm saying commoners get *killed* for looking at royals the wrong way. This isn't a difficult concept, Princess. You endangered my life."

"Not on purpose."

He ran his hands through his hair and groaned. "You're not understanding. You've always had privilege and rank to protect you. I have nothing. No family, no status, and absolutely no worth to your father. Just standing out here without a chaperone could earn me a flogging or a prison sentence."

Her brow furrowed. "That's not fair. Station means nothing."

"It means everything when one of us is common. And it doesn't change the fact that I shouldn't be in love with you!"

She gasped. "You love me? You've only known me four days."

"I only needed one!" He turned away and punched the air. "Damnation, Cali. Have I not proven it with my actions, words, and—" He took a deep breath and let it out. "If only you'd told me who you were."

"How was I to know you were trustworthy when we first met? My sister's lives depend on me being dead. And by the way, the princess *is* dead. Now if I'm Calla a servant girl or Cali the goddess of justice, who's going to stop us from loving each other?" She stepped toward him.

He stepped back.

She threw her arms around his waist and snuggled into his chest. "I love you, too. When I'm a goddess, no one will dare keep you from me."

He stiffened. She'd risked his life with her lies, and now his heart was splintered. *She doesn't need me. Sard, she doesn't need anyone*. He pushed her away. "Princess or goddess, I will still be unworthy."

Chapter Twenty-Two

Tru took two steps back. "Head in. Give me a minute."

Tears glittered on her cheeks, but she nodded and walked away.

A few moments later, he followed. Gods he'd been a fool! From the first half-truths, he should have run. But no, the pretty damsel in need wrapped him around her finger like a cotton thread and pulled him taut, weaving him into the weft of her lies so tightly he couldn't escape. At some point, she'd realize she didn't need him, and she'd abandon him. It'd be wisest to leave now. Saddle Lady and ride into the foothills.

But he couldn't, not while she was vulnerable. If she were injured or killed…no. He'd stay until she found her counterpart—the handsome noble who was worthy of her attention—then he'd rebuild a life somewhere else.

His chest tightened. He'd done it before, and he'd survived worse.

The temple loomed above him, a replica of the Borderline tower. The paving stones led to the open doorway beneath a covered portico.

Cali glanced over her shoulder at him and entered.

He stalked up the stairs and into the candlelit hallway. Beeswax and vanilla scents perfumed the air. Cali, Jasmine, and Charity greeted a young priestess in a white robe with the build of a ten-year-old. Maybe Sirini had made a child the head priestess here.

She nodded to him. "Welcome. I am Willow. Please follow me." She turned and led them to the sanctuary with its statues of the goddess and cauldron of tokens.

Jasmine and Cali did the blessing thing before the statues, touching foreheads, lips, and hearts. Cali slipped something into the goddess's hands.

Probably silver beads. She carried a small fortune and never thought twice about spending coins on whatever she wanted. New clothing, cooking gear, hot baths…must be nice to never worry about where the next coin came from, or if she could afford a meal in a tavern, or a night at an inn, or a damn hairbrush.

That was unfair. She'd grown up in luxury and faced the shock of losing her family and her home. The goddess had blessed Cali with the means to at least maintain some of her previous lifestyle. Who was he to complain? Especially since Cali shared her abundance with him.

Willow and Jasmine were chatting, but he'd missed the bulk of their conversation. He took a seat on a bench beside Charity.

Willow opened her book and read from it, repeated most of what they'd heard from Priestess Amity. Then came the new. "Two hundred years passed, and Sirini created fire and ice. After their third attempt to kill one other, Sirini banished them—Sear to the western tip of Tulya, and Blanche to the snow-covered peak of the Three Sisters Range. Sirini withheld sparks from triplets for three hundred years before allowing another."

Charity leaned forward, soaking it all in with widened eyes.

Willow continued. "Maelstrom killed the next two

sparks Sirini created, growing stronger with each one. Sear figured it out and stole the next one. Another pair, Gale and Zephyra, survived long enough to find each other and ascend, but Sirini separated them immediately. Gale was banished to northern Tulya and Zephyra to central Acoris.

"After that, the gods and goddesses raced to locate new sparks, sometimes attacking one other. Sirini demanded they stop, but they didn't obey. Maelstrom demanded the citizens offer their sparks in a tithe ceremony. To disobey would bring his wrath upon their fleets. Sear required a similar sacrifice in his home kingdom, but his subjects would not comply. So Maelstrom grew strong, and the others did not."

Charity interrupted. "What do you mean by 'grew strong'?"

"He gained the ability to travel farther from his temple without his powers diminishing. I've heard rumors that he's been spotted as far north as the Jewel Islands in Olerio and as far east as the tip of the Kurik peninsula."

"We need to stop him." Jasmine clenched her fists. "By the way, Tera is dead. Do you know if that impacts Maelstrom's power?"

Willow frowned. "No. Her spark returned to Sirini."

"What do I do when I find my counterpart?" Cali asked. "Does our physical proximity complete the ascension? What's the process?"

"I do not know." Willow flipped through her book. "It is not recorded within these pages. Perhaps you should enquire in Eldritch? They have four Holy Tomes."

"We're heading for High Point." Jasmine stood and

bowed. "We'll seek answers there."

Willow inclined her head. "If you ever pass this way again, I would love to hear how this tale ends." She gestured to the cauldron. "Please. Draw blessings before you leave."

Jasmine, Charity, and Cali approached the pot. Tru waited near the door, arms crossed.

Charity plucked one and grinned. "Help. Does that mean I should assist someone else, or that I should accept help from others?"

"Both." Jasmine plunged her hand into the vessel and withdrew a bone chip. "Boldness." She laughed. "I've never had a problem with that, but I will strive for more."

Cali swished her fingers through the tokens and smiled at Tru. "I'll draw one for you."

"No, thanks. I don't need one."

"I'll do it, anyway." She pulled a metal coin out and read it. "Home."

He grunted. "That's yours. You drew it in the last temple, too."

She tossed it back in, selected a wooden token for herself, and blanched. "It says Home."

Willow performed the sign of blessing. "You should both turn your thoughts to the merits of family. Belonging. Love."

Easy enough, as he had no family, no place to belong, and no one suitable to love. He met Charity's gaze but turned away. He'd never make her happy. They were too different. They'd end up hating each other.

Besides, his idiot heart resided in an unsuitable place. He stalked out of the temple.

Jasmine caught up to him and matched his gait. "We

should sleep now and leave tomorrow morning."

"Agreed. Do we need any supplies? The bakery will be open at dawn, but the other markets won't until later."

"I think we have enough food to see us through to Borderline."

"We can't stop there. Or at least I can't." He glanced behind them. Cali and Charity chatted, walking arm in arm. Seems they'd become friends since yesterday. "I guess I could hide in the wagon while you buy food." They crossed the highway and entered the inn.

"Too bad we can't drive straight through, day and night, switching drivers, but I know the horses can't take that strain."

"Three days is the quickest we could make that journey, and that's if the gods leave us alone." Gale and Beck had only attacked Cali once. Had they moved to High Point for the counterpart? Mica, Sear, Sprout, and Blanche hadn't shown up at all. Maybe they finally heeded Sirini's commands. Or maybe the counterpart had his hands full with attacking deities.

Jasmine unlocked their door. Four single beds, separated by small tables, lined the wall. She'd claimed the cot closest to the door and put Tru near the window. Not that they assumed anyone would break in during the night. Merely precautions.

But Cali had taken the bed next to his. He couldn't face her yet. "Jasmine, give me the key. I'm heading over to the tavern. I'll be back in an hour or so."

She stared at him for several moments before tossing it to him. "Stay vigilant."

"Always." He checked his coin pouch to make sure he had enough and ducked out without meeting Cali's gaze.

Three days, then he could leave. Maybe he'd find a job in Olerio. Or head to Rigolan. The bristled man out by the marshes had a lucrative business breaking wild horses. The herds had swelled in recent years, so maybe he could use a hand.

Tru headed to the tavern and found a seat in the back. The barmaid fluffed her hair and adjusted her blouse before walking toward him, a swing in her hips. He sighed. Why couldn't these women leave him alone?

"Ale, please." An hour later, after rebuffing multiple advances from the barmaid, he'd learned nothing of value. Tru returned to the room. The women were asleep.

He awoke with the roosters on day four of Cali's twenty-eight and slipped from the room. A stop in the kitchens secured them a meal, extra food for the road, and a flask of oil. At the bakery, he bought bread, rolls, and sweets and headed for the stables. He flipped a copper to the stable boy and asked for their cart and horses to be readied and their new supplies loaded.

He met the women coming down the stairs, their bags flung over their shoulders. Jasmine carried his. He took it from her. "Our meal is ready."

"Morning, Tru." Cali smiled.

He nodded and crossed to the dining hall, selecting the table they'd occupied last night.

"Someone woke up cranky," Charity said.

"Leave him be." Jasmine sat beside him and greeted the server. They ate oatmeal with bacon, onion, and apple and drank hot tea with honey.

"How was the tavern?" Cali asked.

He stared at his meal. "Fine."

"Did you go shopping?"

"Yes."

Jasmine snorted.

Cali reached for her coin pouch. "Do you need me to reimburse you?"

"No." He scraped his bowl, leaned back, and gazed out the window.

A half hour later, they were on the road heading south. Charity sat up front with Tru driving. Jasmine rode in back, watching for attacks.

Charity shielded her eyes with her hand. "Cali told me about your argument."

Did every woman in existence blab about personal issues? "I'm glad you've become friends, but that was a private conversation."

"I know, but she was devastated. Can't you give her a chance to redeem herself?"

"You're feeling compassion for her but none for me? I'm the one whose life is over if her father finds out I kissed her." He flicked the reins and picked up speed.

Charity grabbed the seatback. "She wasn't thinking about that. She assumed her old life was gone, and she had to build a new one."

He glared at her. "You know who she is?"

"Yes."

He grunted. "And Jasmine does, too?"

"Yes."

Of course. "Cali felt safe enough telling you two but not me."

"She didn't tell me. I figured it out on my own. And Sirini told Jasmine."

"And no one thought I should know." His grip tightened, and the horses sped up.

Charity laid her hand over his. "Let me drive. You're going to steer us off the roadway." She slowed them to a safer pace. "And yes, I thought you should know, but it wasn't my secret. Cali asked me not to tell."

"Yet when you saw us kissing, it didn't occur to you to say, 'Cali, I hate to be the bearer of bad news, but he could be hanged for doing that. Maybe you'd better let him decide if it's worth the risk.' "

Charity's lips pursed.

No, that idea never occurred to her because it wasn't her neck in danger. *Damnation!* All three of them allowed him to play the fool without any warnings.

Charity hauled on the reins. "Xyla!"

Chapter Twenty-Three

An arrow thunked into the side of the driver's seat beside Charity. She dropped the reins.

Tru cursed. "We're under attack." He picked up the straps and hauled on them, then shoved them in Charity's hands. "Bring us to a stop."

Xyla sprinted toward them, the rising sun behind her blinding him. He squinted. She nocked another arrow without losing her stride and fired again.

Tru forced Charity down. The bolt skimmed the side of the wagon and deflected, striking into his left shoulder. He hissed. Gods, that hurt! The stone head barely penetrated his skin. He plucked it out, drew his belt knife, and climbed over Charity. "Stay down."

Xyla dropped her bow and ran for the back of the wagon.

He leapt off the side and tackled her. Flames radiated through his shoulder and deadened his arm.

"She's mine!" Xyla pulled a knife.

Tru rolled away and crouched, useless left arm tucked to his chest. "No, she's not."

Xyla slashed at him.

He blocked her wrist with his forearm, numbing his fingers, and sliced her hand on a back swing.

She raked his throat with her nails, leaving four searing trails.

"Back off!" Tru jabbed at her stomach.

She sucked in her gut and thrust out her butt, barely avoiding the weapon, and punched at his ribs.

He twisted his hips and skipped back on his toes, but the knife penetrated his belly like a white-hot firebrand. Grimacing, he lifted his left forearm to deflect the next hit, and fiery waves of pain shot through his shoulder. His wrist collided with hers in another explosion of agony. He cried out and slashed his blade across her throat.

She dropped her weapon, hands flying to the wound. Blood spurted between her fingers and dripped into the grass.

He pivoted his wrist, thrust upward, and severed her brachial artery.

She collapsed and stared at him, blood spurting.

"Leave us alone." He backed away, sucking air.

The greenery writhed, and the scent of fresh dirt billowed. He retreated farther. Rodents gathered around the goddess and swarmed her broken body. A brown rabbit draped itself over her neck wound and melted into her, sealing the gash.

Oh crap.

A mouse disappeared under her arm. A vole sank into her chest, followed by a shrew. A robin landed on her belly and was absorbed.

Zephyra swooped down, blasted by Tru, and spiraled above Xyla.

She sat up. "It's not over yet."

Jasmine stomped through the field, swung her sword, and decapitated the goddess of the hunt. "Yes, it is." She kicked the head, sending it rolling across the grass. "Heal from that, bitch." She raised her weapon to Zephyra. "You want this?"

Zephyra reared back and flew away.

Tru's stomach rolled, and he lost his oatmeal. Beheadings were brutal. And disgusting. Hot bile burned his throat and nose, and his gut clenched again. His side screeched, his shoulder throbbed, and every inhalation sent waves of fire ants through his chest. He sank to his knees, cradling his left arm.

"You're injured." Jasmine crouched and draped his arm across her shoulder. "Let me help you to the wagon." Her hand pressed against the puncture in his side, and he winced. "Sorry." She shifted her hand lower and hoisted him to his feet.

His knife fell from his fingers. She stooped and grabbed it with her sword-filled hand. Blood had seeped through the bandages on her arms, yet she moved as if she had no injuries.

Charity had pulled their rig over.

Cali rushed forward, tears rolling down her cheeks. "I'm so sorry. I never wanted you to get hurt. I hate this. I can't do this anymore."

Blood coated his clothing at his shoulder and his ribs, soaking his leather belt and dripping onto his leggings. "It's not that bad, Cali. I'll live. Don't cry."

She cradled his face in her hands. "You aren't allowed to die. Understood?"

He rested his forehead against her. She was so sweet. He didn't deserve this devotion. "I'm not going to die."

"Your injuries could be dangerous unless treated properly."

"I've been hurt worse by a horse."

Her chin quivered. "You're impossible. Get into the back, and I'll patch you up." She climbed inside and spread a rug over the floor.

That was new. She'd made it with the strips she'd been sewing for the past few days? And now she'd let him bleed all over it? "Cali, pull that back. I'll lie on the floorboards."

"No. Get in." She retrieved her medical kit and her remaining rags.

Jasmine helped him. "I'll clean the weapons. Charity, keep watch!"

"On it," she yelled.

Tru crept forward and collapsed to his back. His side burned like he'd been jabbed with a branding iron. The shoulder throbbed in time to his heartbeat. His left arm hung useless.

Cali crawled by him, packed a handful of rags to his injury, and applied pressure.

He hissed.

She didn't let up. "First we stop the bleeding, then I'll decide if it needs stitches."

"Just bind it and let me rest." He fingered the small hole in his tunic where the arrow had struck. The wound to his flesh was barely a pinprick. Had his collarbone chipped? Or was it just bruised? Either way, time would heal it.

She guided his hand to the packing beneath his ribs. "Hold this." She worked the buckle on his belt, yanked it out, and dumped it to the side. She pulled his shirttails out of his waistband.

At any other time, watching her undress him would be incredibly enticing.

Cali loosened the ties on his tunic, peeled it back, and froze. Her eyes widened. She gasped and sprang away, her hands over her mouth.

"What?" She'd bared his chest, but not the injury.

Tears filled her eyes, and she collapsed near his feet. Her shoulders heaved with her sobs.

What the sard? "Cali, what's wrong?"

Charity climbed in from the front. "What did you say to her?"

"Nothing. She was inspecting my wound and just started crying." He gripped the laces and tugged.

Charity inhaled sharply and spread his shirt collar, baring more of his skin.

He looked down. "What? Do I have another injury?"

"No, you ass. You have a house mark!" She crawled to Cali and held her. "Poor lamb. Let it out."

Tru hoisted himself up onto one elbow, keeping his left hand clamped to the rag at his side despite the fire raging in his shoulder. "Please tell me what's going on."

Jasmine dumped the weapons beside Cali and stared at Tru's bared torso. "You're full of surprises, aren't you, stable boy?"

"Would someone explain what I've done?"

Charity glared at him. "When noble children are born, they're tattooed with a magical process that identifies them."

Never heard of it before, but it sounded like something the idiot nobles would do. "So?"

"So you have one!" She pointed at the blotch on his chest.

He fingered it. "That's a birthmark."

Jasmine rolled her eyes. "It's a house mark. It declares to all the world that you belong to a royal family."

That couldn't be right. "You've made a mistake."

"No." Cali sniffed and wiped at her eyes. "I

recognize it." She pulled at her collar and exposed her own. "Blue for Acoris. The triangle is Rhys's house. Three vertical lines indicate the third wife. Three dots mean the third child. I am the third child of the third wife of Rhys's house in Acoris. There is no one else with this tattoo. It is unique to me." Her tears began flowing again. "As is yours."

"And why does it make you cry now?"

"Because her heart is broken, you dolt." Charity ran her hand down Cali's hair and patted her shoulder. "Because now you're completely gone to her."

He clenched his jaw. "And why is that? Who am I?"

Cali spoke through her sobs. "The olive green indicates Rigolan. One dot. You're the first born. One vertical line. The first wife is your mother. Two concentric circles. Your father is King Franklin." Her shoulders twitched. "You're the crown prince of Rigolan, and because of the civil war threat, to ensure peace, you'll be forced to marry one of my sisters." Her voice cracked on the last word. "And produce heirs." She slumped into Charity's lap, weeping.

Likely story. He wasn't any more royal than Jasmine was. "I'm not marrying one of your sisters, Cali. And I'm not a prince."

"You're the baby everyone believes is dead." Charity stroked Cali's shoulders. "You can deny it all you want, but the proof is on your body."

It wasn't possible. Was it? He rubbed his mark. His guardian, Gray, had told him it was an odd birthmark and to keep it hidden because superstitious people would believe it was evil. Tru had never questioned the explanation, although the sour milk and dandelion scent proved it was a lie. He'd never worked up the courage to demand the truth. Sard, Tru had been fourteen years old when abandoned! Large for his age, but not brave enough to question his guardian.

And how had Gray gotten his hands on a crown prince? Why hadn't he been returned to the palace? Gray had to know what the mark meant. Had he kidnapped Tru and kept him from his birthright for some dishonorable purpose? No, because it was all poppycock.

A chill shot down his spine. Except there was no dandelion lie smell coming from any of the women. They were telling the truth, or at least they believed it—he was the crown prince of Rigolan.

Not that it mattered. "I'm not going to reveal my identity, I'm not moving to Rigolan, and I'm certainly not marrying a stranger." He eased back to a prone position, hissing when the pain clobbered him again.

"You have to." Jasmine climbed into the wagon, duckwalked to his side, and squatted. "It's your royal duty. Your kingdom needs you. Franklin only has daughters, which means the throne might shift to another house if the other nobles object to a female ruler. To ensure stability, you must take your rightful place."

"It's not my kingdom. Has the bleeding stopped?" He peeled back the rag.

"No." She clamped his hand back down over the packing. "Think of all the good you could do. You know how commoners struggle. You could pass new laws to make life easier on them. Be a conduit for change and eliminate corruption."

"No thanks."

Her eyes narrowed. "Think on this. Your mother has believed for twenty-five years that her son is dead. Can you allow her to continue grieving?" The wagon jolted, and Jasmine dove through the front opening. She returned a moment later. "The horses moved to find more grass. They're fine." She dug through Cali's medical kit to make a poultice.

"I don't know the woman, and I'm sure she's not mourning after all this time."

"You're heartless." Jasmine flicked his hand away from the injury, pulled his tunic back, and lifted the bottom edge of his shirt. "This isn't very deep. I doubt any organs were punctured. It could use stitches, though." She glanced at Cali, still crying. "But a poultice and binding will suffice." She packed an herb-stuffed bundle over the wound, added a clean cotton pad over the top, and tied it with strips of gray cloth. She bound his shoulder and put his arm in a sling. "Try not to move."

The sling was part of her destroyed robe. He held out his hand. "Help me sit up."

She settled him against the front wall of the wagon. "Need a drink?"

The taste of vomit soured his mouth. "That'd be great."

She poured him a mug of water, dumped his belt beside him, and hopped out. "We should get moving." She closed the rear gate and flipped the latches. Cali had quieted in Charity's lap and stared vacantly at a hay bale.

"You must have been kidnapped." Charity shot him a sympathetic look. "Since you were never returned, they assumed you were dead."

Dead sounded great right now. It'd be better than watching the haunted expression on Cali's face. He'd lost her forever, but supposedly he'd gained a birthright. Sure. He'd been wanting a family and a place to belong for years. Now it dropped in his lap like a golden apple in one mistimed flash of skin? Unbelievable. Did they think he was so simple to buy their ridiculous story?

Cali believed it. Jasmine had, too. She spotted the mark and accepted it instantly.

He shivered. What if it was true? What if the tattoo allowed him to claim an inheritance and heritage beyond comprehension? Provided him with an instant family? A home? A people to call his own? Father, mother. Siblings. "I have two sisters?"

"Finna and Farras. I've never seen them, but rumors say they're gorgeous. Blond hair, olive-green eyes, dimpled chins…" Charity sighed. "Like you."

He swallowed. If he was a prince, then he had duties, too. A life that wasn't his to direct anymore. People who would depend on him. He wouldn't be allowed to run his own stable someday. He'd be expected to marry and have heirs. His stomach soured. His life wouldn't be his. "Do you remember my birth name?"

She grinned. "Now you're pushing the limits of my memory. Let me think. Started with F, I'm sure. Far…Fen…Fred—"

"Prince Freidrick." Cali sat up and wiped her face with her hands.

Great. Saddled with a pretentious, ancient moniker.

Cali poured herself a mug of water and gulped it down. "You need to present yourself to my father when we reach the palace. It is your duty."

Then kiss all his goals and hopes goodbye. They'd force him into a role he couldn't possibly play. "I don't think so. I'm not a prince."

"You were born one. You've been masquerading as a commoner, and you were raised by someone who obviously had royal blood because he taught you proper manners. You're so different from every other man I've met—the differences are astounding. I should have guessed you had noble blood simply by your dining habits and speech patterns."

Tru grunted. "That makes no sense. Commoners can have good manners."

"No, they don't." Charity shrugged. "I've never met anyone like you, Tru. You're different, and nothing you can say will change my mind. Your guardian tried to raise you as a commoner, but you learned his habits, his bearings."

Right.

"You could stop the civil war before it even began," Cali said.

His chest tightened. He'd have that much power? He turned away and grabbed his belt. "Pour me some water, please. I need to clean the blood off this leather."

Pure foolishness. He would not present himself to the emperor or King Franklin or anyone else at the palace. And he'd never again bare his skin in front of others. He was Tru, a stable hand, and that was good enough.

Chapter Twenty-Four

Between the rocking of the wagon and the numbness in my chest, I fell asleep on Charity's leg. I woke up several hours later. The hollowness had spread. My throat was tight, and my belly felt like I'd swallowed a huge stone.

I'd lost Tru forever. As a ninth, my status wasn't high enough to be his bride. And if I found my counterpart... Goddesses didn't marry princes.

King Franklin and my father would parade Rindi and Rhyada before Tru. Or maybe Palama, though she was a third.

My eyes burned, and tears welled. *No!* Not again. No more feeling sorry for myself. My fate was to die. Surviving beyond my twentieth birthday was a blessing from Sirini. I should be thankful, not mourning.

And if she'd spared me from death, then she had a greater purpose for me. I'd be a goddess. I could help my people—be useful, not a single stocking, but an instrument of justice, aiding my father with disputes. Use my power to better the lives of the citizens, both nobles and commoners. Hadn't Tru said something about the smaller villages having no access to enforcers? Maybe I could travel, assisting those who needed me.

Tru would marry one of my sisters, produce heirs, grow old, and die. I, as an immortal, would eventually forget about him. Perhaps my heart would mend, or maybe I'd be known as the mourning goddess, suffering from eternal sadness.

Oh, good grief! This wallowing was unbecoming. I should turn my mind to something else. I sat up.

Charity groaned and stretched her legs. "My feet fell asleep, but I didn't want to disturb you. How do you feel?"

"Hollow." I poured a mug of water and gulped it down. I glanced at Tru sharpening a knife. "Tru, would you like some?"

He didn't look at me. "No."

Great. Our relationship was ruined. He couldn't even muster politeness for me. Maybe that was for the best. If he was rude or mean, my heart could harden and begin to mend.

I put the mug away. "Where are we?"

"Coming up on Shadow Wood in a few hours." Charity rotated her ankles and bent her knees. "You slept a long time."

My stomach growled. "Did you stop for a meal?"

"No, just nibbled out of the crates." She hauled a bag off the bench and handed me a roll. "This has bits of apple and nuts. It's delicious."

"Thanks." I tore a piece off and ate it. "Did Tru eat?"

Charity rolled her eyes. "He said he wasn't hungry."

He didn't look up from his knife.

"You're going to grind that down to nothing," Charity teased.

He ignored her.

"I need to get out." I hollered for Jasmine to pull over.

Our pace slowed, and the wagon jolted before lurching to a stop.

"Real smooth!" Charity hopped out the back. "It feels good to stretch."

A breeze spat dirt into her face. She raised her hand as a shield. "Cali, get back!"

Zephyra swooped down behind Charity, pushed her to the ground, and hovered outside the bonnet. "Now you're mine." She grabbed my tunic.

Who did she think she was, treating Charity like that? I grabbed Zephyra's dress and hauled her toward me.

Her eyes widened, and she tugged back.

I pivoted, dragging her into the wagon, and slammed her down on the rag rug at Tru's feet.

He jerked back.

Straddling her, I planted my forearm across her neck.

"I need your spark! You don't understand." She swung a fist.

I blocked it with my shoulder. "It's mine."

A gust of wind whipped through the space, but all it did was ruffle my collar and force me to squint.

"But if I get one more, Tera will stop trying to kill me. I'll be as strong—"

I pulled my belt knife and pressed it to her chest. "Listen up, fungus. Sirini only gave you one spark, so live with it. My friends have killed Tera and Xyla. You can be next, or you can leave me alone."

"Tera's dead?" Zephyra blinked. "I'll go. Please don't kill me."

I sheathed my weapon. "You deserve it, after what you've done. You're supposed to help others, not try to kill them." I backed off her. "I don't want to see you again. Ever."

She nodded, clambered out the back, and flew away.

Charity laughed. "Who knew you could be so fierce? That was amazing."

I donned my coat, pulled the hood over my hair, and climbed out. "She made me angry, shoving you like that. Are you injured?"

Charity's smile faded. "I'm fine. You did that for me?"

Jasmine rounded the end of the wagon and hugged me. "Nice work, Calla. I didn't even realize we were under attack until it was over."

"She wasn't armed. If she'd had a blade, I wouldn't have lived through the encounter." I swayed on my feet, my bladder near bursting. "Pardon me." I ran for the copse of alder trees by the water.

When I returned, Jasmine and Charity were watering the horses. Tru had hauled himself to the driver's seat. His face was pale and sweaty.

Poor dear. "Are you in pain?"

He clenched his jaw. "I'm fine."

My eyes burned, and I turned away. *No more crying!* He was injured because of me. I climbed in and settled.

"No need to be rude to her." Jasmine mounted the driver's box, causing the wagon to shift slightly.

"I wasn't. Let's go."

Tru's dried blood stained the rag rug on the floor. I flipped it over and lay down, my head pillowed on my pack.

Charity sat beside me. "Ready," she yelled and wrapped her arm around me. "Another crying jag would do you good."

I let it out, then fell asleep.

The jolt of the wagon leaving the roadway woke me.

"We're in Shadow Wood." Charity crawled to the rear gate, released it, and jumped out. "Hand me the bags, please."

I shifted our gear. Charity and Jasmine grabbed loads and hauled them to our camping spot behind the temple.

Tru hobbled to unhitch the horses and park the cart. One-handed.

I approached. "Do you need help? You're still in pain."

He didn't look at me. "I've got it."

I snagged a couple of food crates and followed Charity and Jasmine. "I slept all day. Let me do the work now."

"It'll go quicker with all hands." Jasmine dumped our bags beneath the pergola. She glanced up. "Not supposed to rain. I think we'll forgo the canvas roof." She headed for the woodpile. "I'll get the fire started. Will you lay out our bedrolls?"

I probably wouldn't sleep at all tonight but spread them out. Then I rearranged them so I wouldn't be next to Tru. New tears welled up, but I blinked. Time to toughen up.

Charity prepared a soup and hung it over the blaze, then began mixing biscuit dough.

I'd never made them before. Technically, I'd never cooked *any* food, pampered as I was. It'd be a good skill to learn.

She stirred the ingredients with a big spoon until it came together in an ugly lump, then flicked wads of it onto the warm griddle resting over coals and covered them. "They aren't as pretty this way, but I don't have a board to roll them out." She leaned back, propped on her elbows. "Now we wait. That soup needs to simmer."

I looked around. "Where's Tru? Is he still caring for the horses?"

Jasmine sat beside me. "He headed to the tavern."

"Is he going to eat with us?" Charity asked.

"I doubt it."

My chest tightened. Our relationship would never be the same.

Charity, Jasmine, and I chatted, ate, cleaned up, repacked the crates, and settled. I tracked the three half-moons chasing the archer constellation through the sky. Charity snored. My eyes burned, and my throat constricted. Maybe when I became a goddess, I wouldn't care anymore.

Tru returned hours later and crept to his bedroll.

Finally, I slept and dreamed of Rindi giving birth to Tru's beautiful triplet daughters with her red hair and his olive-green eyes.

We rose with the sun on day five of my quest for the elusive counterpart. We ate and loaded our gear. Tru still couldn't move his arm, so Jasmine hitched the horses. He refused to ride in back.

Charity climbed in and offered me a sympathetic smile. "Give him time."

I'd survived the attacks so far. How was my counterfeit doing? If Beck stole Shaded's spark, would I die immediately? Or would I live out my full twenty-eight days? I shuddered. Morbid. I curled up on the rag rug and closed my eyes. Sleep would circumvent the pain.

Charity shook my shoulder. "No sleeping now. You'll be unable to sleep at night."

I sat up. "Then what am I supposed to do all day?"

"Let's talk. I've got a billion questions about the royals, and you probably have all the answers. We can pass the time gossiping."

I sighed. "I guess. What do you want to know?"

The hours flew by. I told her about all my siblings, our relatives, and life at the palace. About the Olerios, my father's closest ally, and the triplet sons who'd most likely match up with Batch Two. Charity giggled at my nickname for Palama, Pensie, and Prescia. I talked about the Tulya twins in the far northwest. The oldest daughter would be expected to marry Rhygan if he refused the Rigolan princess, and he would, as they couldn't stand each other. The Tulya prince, Xavier, had had the nerve to address my father in the throne room six days ago. Was it only six? It felt like months.

Jasmine stopped at midday for a break, then resumed our trek. Zephyra left us alone, not even offering a cool breeze to battle the scorching heat. If not for my reaction to sunlight, Charity and I would have peeled back the bonnet. Instead, we took turns fanning each other and continued with our gossip.

Without goddess attacks to hinder our progress, we arrived at the way station near the river bend well before sundown. Thankfully, we had it to ourselves. Once we were settled inside, Tru helped Charity prepare the meal.

I drew Jasmine aside. "Teach me to use a sword."

She crossed her arms. "No."

"Why not?"

"Because it takes too long to learn. How about a knife? You don't have to kill an enemy with it, just do enough damage that he's unable to continue."

"Agreed. Show me." I pulled my weapon and crouched.

She grinned. "Hold on, ruthless. We wrap the blades in leather first."

A few minutes later, we were ready.

Jasmine faced me. "Knife fighting is fast and deadly. If you draw, be prepared to use it."

I swallowed. "Even for defense?"

"Definitely. If an opponent comes at you, he's trying to take you down."

Could I kill someone? When I'd had Zephyra beneath my blade, it was pure bluff. I wouldn't have stabbed her. But if someone came at me, I'd be properly motivated. "Got it."

"The strategy is simple. Stab anywhere you can reach, and don't let go of your weapon." She leapt toward me and rammed hers at my stomach. I tried to block, and her leather-bound blade slid across the back of my hand. "Now you're disabled and probably dead. The hardest part is avoiding your opponent's knife. If your foe has a sword or a quarterstaff, run away. You can't win against weapons with longer reach."

"How do I defend against that move you used on me?"

"You want to duck, dodge, or deflect. Stay out of range if you can. Your enemy is most vulnerable when early in the swing"—she demonstrated by drawing her arm back for a thrust—"or late, when fully extended." She jabbed her blade at me. "Early, you can jump forward and offer your own blow, then skip back. Or use your free hand for blocking, deflecting, and controlling." She showed me several moves.

"Hold on, you're going too fast." I tried to defend against her move and would have lost all four fingers to a naked blade.

"Don't block with your hand. Use your forearm, like this, at my hand or wrist. Avoid my knife edge! Now try again." She slowed her movements so I could follow, then came at me again. "The quickest way to end this fight is to damage my hand so I can't hold my weapon. Once I drop it, you've won. Then you can flee, disable, or kill."

We practiced two defensive moves until I mastered them.

Charity clapped her hands. "The meal is ready." She served soup with toasted bread.

Jasmine set her leather-wrapped knife beside her bowl. "This smells divine! Thank you."

I tossed my blade on my pack and sat opposite Tru. He picked up his spoon and concentrated on his food, still refusing to look at me.

A horse whinnied outside, and Tru whipped around. "That wasn't one of ours."

"How can you tell?" Charity stood.

Tru caught her wrist. "Stay here." He headed for the door.

Jasmine rose. "I'll look. You've only got one arm." She rushed to her gear and pulled out her sword.

My heart pounded. The newcomer better not be a brigand. Or worse, a larger party of rough men. Way stations were supposed to be places of safety.

The door creaked open.

Jasmine leapt forward and blocked the entry of the two men.

Enforcer Dariel scowled at her, his bald head gleaming in the lantern light. "You'd break the Traveler's Truce before we've even entered?"

Goddess, no! They'd arrest Tru.

Chapter Twenty-Five

Tru turned and poked the fire. Could his sarding life possibly get worse? Of course, it could. The moment the enforcer recognized Tru, he was bound for prison.

Jasmine lowered her sword. "My apologies. We were accosted in this station four days ago, so I'm a mite proactive."

The two men stepped inside and closed the door.

Tru couldn't stir the firewood forever. Chin to his chest, he crept back to his chair and hunched over his soup bowl.

Dariel's gaze swept the room and landed on Tru. "You."

That didn't take long. Tru set his spoon aside and nodded. "Evening."

Dariel scowled at the women. "You've harbored a wanted man. You're all under arrest."

Jasmine raised her sword again. "Four against two. Give it a try."

"That's enough!" Cali pushed her chair back, marched up to Dariel, and planted her fists on her hips. "Tru is innocent of any crime, and if you dare try to imprison me, my father will demote you to the cesspits."

Tru shot to his feet. Was she going to reveal her secret to save them? "Please don't."

Dariel looked down his nose. "And who's your father, little maid, that he could do such a thing to me?"

She straightened her shoulders. "Emperor Rhys. And if you don't recognize me now, Commander Dariel, you don't deserve your position."

Dariel's eyes widened, his face paled, and he dipped into a deep bow. "My apologies, Your Highness. I didn't expect to encounter you so far from the palace. Forgive my error."

She glowered at the other man, a tall, lanky bruiser scarcely older than Tru.

Lanky dropped to one knee and bowed his head. "Princess."

Damn, she'd mastered the whole *imperial authority* attitude. Should Tru bow, too?

"Granted. You may rise, Dariel and Newt," she commanded.

She knew both their names, too. Tru grinned. She'd never cease to amaze him.

The enforcers straightened. Dariel's gaze flicked to Tru, then back to Cali. "Princess, why are you here with these people? Where is your guard?" He scanned her attire. "And your wardrobe? Also, pardon my ignorance, but are you Princess Rosilee or Daffilee?"

"Calilee."

He frowned. "You can't be. I watched her dive off the Ridge six days ago."

"I fought off Maelstrom and survived."

His eyes widened. "Praise the goddess. You remembered your combat lessons." Dariel swatted Newt's arm. "Remember Justyn teaching her how to flip someone over her shoulder?"

Newt nodded. "Among other things. How did you escape Maelstrom?"

"I gouged his eyes, punched him in the throat, and

shoved my knee into his groin. Oh." She pulled out the sapphire necklace from her neckline. "And zapped him with this. Sirini weaponized it for me. Then Gale showed up, throwing lightning bolts, and that distracted Maelstrom."

Tru swallowed. The bastard deserved it, and more.

Her eyes narrowed. "But Princess Calilee is dead, for the safety of her sisters, so I'm entrusting you with that secret. Your vow to my father was to protect *all* his daughters, not just me. So now I'm Calla, a simple commoner."

Dariel glanced at the others. "And these people are…"

"Friends. Priestess Jasmine, Charity, and Tru."

Dariel stared at Tru. "I'm still required to take him in for questioning. I can't rely on your word alone, Princess. I need corroboration. Proof."

Charity cleared her throat. "I testified to his innocence. Isn't that enough?"

"Not after your original claims of his guilt."

She rolled her eyes. "I explained that to you. Oakley swore it was a practical joke, to get Tru in trouble. I didn't realize the charges were serious. If anyone is guilty, it's Oak."

Cali returned to her seat. "Dariel, you may trust my assessment. Tru is innocent of anything illegal or treasonous. There isn't a dishonest thought in his head, and that's settled. Would you care to join us for a meal? There's plenty of soup." She took a bite. "Mine's grown cold."

Was it truly over? Just like that? She dipped her spoon, skimming from the center to the far side of the bowl, exactly how Gray had taught Tru as a child. Royal etiquette. Graceful.

She glanced up, caught him staring, and smiled.

"Thank you for the generous offer. We accept." Dariel dumped his pack and dug out a bowl. Newt was quicker. Within minutes, they both sat on the floor, backs against a wall, noisily eating soup and toasted bread.

They'd either not been taught how to eat properly in the presence of nobility, or they didn't care.

Cali's brow furrowed. "Has Rhygan been found?"

"Not that I know of." Dariel lowered his bowl to his lap. "But I've been away for days."

"Maybe he's home already."

"I would hope so."

"How's Merit?"

"Growing like a cornstalk," he said around a mouthful of toast. "He's taller than his mother and gaining on me."

"As we all expected." She looked to Newt. "And Zinnia?"

Newt swallowed. "She's walking now. Wears her mother out by day's end."

Cali tsked. "Yet you're here, gallivanting around the countryside instead of at home assisting your exhausted wife."

Newt winced. "Doing my job, Highness."

Warmth spread through Tru's chest, easing the tightness that bound his heart. He'd never heard of nobles who learned their servants' names, much less their children's. Was Cali's depth of kindness and compassion endless?

Dariel rose to refill his bowl. "Highness, where are you heading, if I may ask?"

"Back to High Point to locate a Rigolan noble."

"Please accept our services in escorting you home." He settled against the wall.

"Traveling with two enforcers, I might be recognized. I can't take that chance." She picked up her dishes and squatted beside the washpot in the coals.

Charity jumped up. "I'll do that for you."

Cali plunged her bowl into the hot water and swished it with the rag. "Why? Am I incapable?"

Charity's eyebrows scrunched, and she glanced at the enforcers. "No. I thought—"

"It's fine. I'm not above menial tasks. You can't treat me like royalty and expect anyone to believe I'm a commoner."

Tru leaned back. Poor Cali, caught between roles. Talk about uncomfortable.

She snatched his bowl and spoon from the table. "I'll wash these for you. How does your shoulder feel?"

He grabbed for the dish, but she danced away. "It aches. And I'm capable of doing my own washing, too."

"Not tonight, you aren't."

The hairs on the back of his neck stood up. No doubt, Dariel and Newt were watching Tru like a roach crawling toward their pantry. He had to act as her servant, nothing more. No displays of emotion. No smiling or flirting. No joking. No speaking unless spoken to.

Definitely no handholding, kissing, or sleeping anywhere near her. He rose and snagged his pack off the floor. "I'll sleep in the wagon and keep an eye on the horses."

"Is that necessary?" Cali asked.

He darted out the door. Between Jasmine and two trained soldiers, Cali had no need for him. Maybe he should saddle Lady and ride out now. Save them both some embarrassment.

****

For a moment, I'd forgotten. No more affection. He was gone forever. Tomorrow we'd arrive in High Point, and Tru would present himself to my father. I'd find Prince Shaded and ascend to godhood.

Could the pain grow worse? I blinked back tears. I'd survived so many hardships in the past quarter-moon. I could survive this.

Jasmine pushed away from the table. "Be right back."

"We'll continue our lesson?" I collected my wrapped blade.

"Sure." Jasmine shut the door behind her.

"She's teaching you knife fighting?" Dariel crossed the room.

"Among other things. We've done hand to hand, as well."

Dariel fingered the hilt at his belt. "May I ask why you need this knowledge?"

"I've been attacked multiple times. Jasmine and Tru protected me, but he is injured, she's still healing, and I should be able to defend myself." I crouched, weapon ready, and feigned a stab to his upper thigh. I scored a kill shot to the major vein.

He stepped back, eyes wide. "Highness, this is…unsettling. How have a priestess and a stable hand kept you safe?"

I jabbed again, striking only air. "Jasmine is a temple guard, and if you two battled, I'd bet on her. She killed two brigands in less than three heartbeats! And Tru had training. Between the two of them, I haven't been injured even once. Unless you count a bite from a field mouse."

"And the rock," Charity added.

"That only hurt for a few minutes." I rubbed my skull where Tera had beaned me.

Dariel's eyebrows scrunched. "A mouse bit you?"

I shrugged. "Don't ask. It's embarrassing."

"Who's attacked you? I'll arrest them."

"Good luck. The two brigands are rotting behind the privy." I pointed toward the back of the building. "And two of the goddesses are dead."

He blinked. "I'm sorry, did you say goddesses?"

"Jasmine decapitated Xyla after Tru dealt her a mortal blow—it was absolutely disgusting." I circled the soldier, knife ready. "And Tru killed Tera." I darted forward and poked at Dariel's belly.

He was prepared and blocked with his forearm. "Why are goddesses attacking you?"

"Long story." I stabbed at his chest.

Dariel knocked my hand away, grabbed my throat, and hauled me toward him. He pivoted and plastered my back to his front, his arm around my neck in a choke hold.

I bent at the waist and shifted my weight. He was supposed to fly over me.

Instead, he pushed me down and planted his knee in my lower back. "Highness, that was sloppy. You're on your belly in an indefensible position. Now what will you do?"

I stabbed blindly behind me.

He yanked the weapon from my hand and tossed it away. "And now?"

I threw my elbow back, into his groin, though I

softened the blow.

He rolled away and laughed. "Excellent move!"

I gained my feet. "This is when I run. I can't take you down."

"Well done, Highness." He rushed me and wrapped his hands around my neck. "How do you break out of this?"

Jasmine walked in and crossed her arms.

I clawed at his skin, but my fingernails did zero damage to his large, calloused mitts. I looked at Jasmine. "What do I do?"

She demonstrated.

Oh, that was brilliant. I shoved my head down, as if bashing my forehead against my knees, and his grip broke. I skipped back.

He darted toward me.

I ran around the table and hid behind Jasmine. "Help."

Dariel followed me and sidestepped by her.

She grabbed his thumb and twisted.

Dariel landed on the floor, his hand buried between his shoulder blades.

"Did you see how I did that?" Jasmine asked me.

Dariel tried to break the hold.

Jasmine planted her hand on the back of his neck. "That's a great way to snap your arm, soldier. Good thing this is a mock battle." She released him and stood up. "Let me show you that move, Cali."

They worked with me for an hour. Charity and Newt watched from the table, cheering my victories and laughing at my failures. About the third time I had my face mashed into the filthy floor, I called for mercy. While I had no desire to put my new knowledge to the test with an attacker, I wouldn't have to. Not with Jasmine and Tru at my back. I should accept Dariel's offer, as well. No one would recognize me if I stayed out of sight, so why turn down extra guards?

Dariel and Newt rolled out their blankets on the far side of the room.

I took off my boots and belt and lay down between Jasmine and Charity. "Jasmine, I take it you couldn't convince Tru to sleep in here?"

She turned to face me. "No, but I convinced him to stay. He was going to leave."

My throat tightened. "What am I going to do without him?"

"Trust Sirini. She is in control."

All of Maelstrom's previous victims might have issue with that statement, yet I had no choice but to cling to it.

At dawn on day six of my quest for godhood, we ate the oatmeal Charity had simmered all night, thick with dried fruit and chunks of ham. Tru hadn't once looked at me and didn't speak. With his arm in a sling, he couldn't help with the cleanup. Instead, he stood by the door, scowling.

"Let me check your shoulder." I moved toward him.

He walked outside, shutting the door in my face.

It'd hurt less if he'd run me through with his sword.

A light fog hugged the landscape, but the rising sun would soon bake it away. I set my hood and darted to the wagon. Charity climbed in behind me, and within minutes, we were off. Newt rode ahead; Dariel took the rear. Both had been warned to watch for incoming attacks from Sear, Gale, Beck, Mica, or Sprout.

We reached Borderline at noon and returned

Charity's borrowed horse. I gave her a gold coin to sooth her cousin's anger, which ended his shouting diatribe immediately. Instead of going home, though, Charity wanted to stay with me. What a blessed friend.

Tru hadn't said anything, but this had been his only home. "Tru, do you want to see Eve and Hawk?"

"No."

Stupid tears. I blinked. Maybe he'd return to this life after he saw me safely to the palace.

We approached the bridge spanning the Crystal River, and Jasmine stopped. "We're vulnerable here. Beck could sweep us off with one wave."

We'd have to split up. "Send Charity and Tru ahead with the wagon. Once they're safe, the rest of us will dash across."

Tru fingered his sword hilt. "Charity goes alone. You need my help if you're attacked."

"You only have one arm."

"I only need one."

"Let's move!" Jaz pulled her bow and quiver from her gear and strapped on her sword.

Dariel and Newt secured their horses to the back of the cart.

I hopped out, hood up, and chewed my bottom lip. Would Beck attack the wagon? Charity could be killed.

She waved and set off across the bridge. She shared it with two other riders, one from each direction.

I held my breath.

She reached the far side, pulled off into the grass, and set the brake.

I exhaled. Though my heart still pounded.

Dariel directed. "Newt first. Tru and Jasmine with Cali. I'll take the rear."

I pulled my belt knife. "Should we run?"

"Fast walk." Newt drew his sword and marched out.

I followed, Tru on my left, Jasmine on my right.

The rails at waist height were thin slats marking the boundary, not sturdy guards against falling in. The swollen river far below frothed and gurgled.

Halfway across, the water began churning. *No, no, no*. Two figures rose, supported by a column of liquid that lifted them to the bridge deck.

Tru shoved me behind him and braced his feet. Jasmine nocked an arrow.

I trembled. For all my brave thoughts of trying out my new moves, I didn't want to fight again or risk my friends' lives.

Chapter Twenty-Six

I swallowed. *Don't panic.*

Beck's skin was eerily transparent. He had short-cropped pale hair, blue eyes, and a handsome face with a powerful build, tall and muscular. His leather leggings and tunic, sans undershirt, were dry despite the droplets clinging to his skin. He scowled at me, though his sword remained sheathed. He gave off a "don't mess with me" attitude that I intended to heed.

The woman beside him—holding his hand, their fingers intertwined—had alabaster skin with gray veining, gorgeous bauxite-red curly hair that hung to her hips, and kind, onyx eyes. Her black, ankle-length dress was dry. She was short and solid, like a marble statue. She was also unarmed. It wouldn't take the goddess of rocks much effort to rain tons of stone down upon me.

Jasmine aimed her arrow at Beck. "State your intentions."

A burbling growl emanated from his throat.

Mica nudged him with her elbow. "Stop that." She locked her gaze on me. "We wish to speak and avoid a battle that will cost you dearly."

I squared my shoulders. "Ask Xyla and Tera about the cost of fighting my friends."

Mica's face paled further. "So Zephyra spoke the truth."

"Heed her warning." I could use Mica's fear. I

sheathed my knife and stepped forward.

Tru caught my arm.

I turned to him. "I can't hear her well, and I don't want to shout. Come stand beside me."

Jasmine flicked her fingers. "I've got you covered."

Swords drawn, Dariel and Newt walked to the edge of the bridge. Tru put me behind them, peeking through the space between their shoulders.

The fountain of water eased Beck and Mica toward us until they stood face-to-face with me, the flimsy guard rail the only barrier. Beck could blast me and do serious damage.

My heart pounded, and I threaded my arm through Tru's. Just in case. "I am listening."

Mica nodded. "Maelstrom has threatened to tear down my rocky coasts and dam Beck's estuaries if we don't hand you over. Instead, we propose an alliance. We will help protect you if you deliver true justice to Maelstrom when you ascend."

How did they know I'd be justice? Must be a god thing. I pursed my lips to hide a grin. *The enemy of my enemy is my ally.* "I appreciate your offer. Please elaborate on what your protection entails. Are you volunteering to travel with me and serve as guards?"

Beck glared. "I am no guardian!"

Mica elbowed him again. "Learn some tact, you drip." She rolled her eyes. "We'll follow discreetly."

Jasmine sniggered. "Seriously? You two stand out like bloodied corpses in a snow field."

Mica dipped her head to Jasmine. "We will don cloaks to disguise ourselves. We've done it before."

Allowing them into the palace would be foolish, but they could patrol outside, watching for Maelstrom or his priests. Provided they could keep up with our wagon for the two-hour journey.

Dariel spoke. "What are Maelstrom's weaknesses? How does he fight? What is his preferred weapon? When will he strike? Can he walk on land?"

Mica's eyebrows rose. "A simple cloak won't disguise him. His appearance is too odd. He draws attention wherever he goes; he thrives on it." She nudged Beck. "Tell them about his fighting style."

Beck's jaw clenched. "He favors a short sword, like yours." He gestured at Dariel's weapon. "Though he hasn't lifted a blade in eons. He's weakest at low tide and the new moons."

We were nine days from full moons. Low tide came twice a day. Unless we could lure him out of the ocean at a time of our choosing, that wouldn't help.

Jasmine lowered her arrow. "You only requested justice for Maelstrom. Does that imply you want Cali to turn a blind eye toward any injustices you've committed?"

Beck dropped his gaze to his bare feet. What were the odds he regretted a handful of transgressions?

Mica squeezed his hand and sighed. "We have both committed indiscretions in the heat of anger or jealousy. But we've been trying to make amends."

That sounded rehearsed. And vague. "How do you undo a murder and return a loved one to family when they're all long dead?" I glared at Beck. "How do you make amends for attacking me in the courtyard without provocation because you wanted something I possess?"

"Some things cannot be undone." Mica almost sounded repentant. "Beck and I have been working to bring fresh water back to The Wastes, creating places where people can flourish. Cragbarrow Oasis is now green all year and capable of sustaining a town. Xyla planted fish in the lake, providing a new source of protein for the inhabitants, and I've begun digging a trench that will convey water from the lake to my temple, where another village can thrive, provided they aren't afraid of the nagas. We also created an artesian well in Mooncliff. That settlement is growing."

Mica bowed her head to me. "Please. We need to redeem our past misdeeds. If you'll work with us to contain Maelstrom, we will continue helping the citizens of Kurik and Rigolan."

They were attempting to aid the populations of their kingdoms. They could be a positive example for the other deities. "Your desires are noble. I agree to your terms." I nodded at their enjoined hands. "And congratulations." Nice to know romance wasn't prohibited in the pantheon. "Will you follow us into High Point or meet us there?"

"Follow," Beck grumbled. The column of water whisked them to the far side of the river, where they stepped onto the bank near Charity. Cloaks and packs shot out and landed near them.

We hurried across the bridge. Mica walked behind the wagon, and I leaned against the hatch and chatted with her.

I'd be home in a few hours! I'd greet my family, find my counterpart, and ascend to goddess status before supper. Until then, I just had to avoid any more homicidal gods.

****

Tru gawked like a tourist and followed Newt down the river of people and carts cutting through the heart of the city. Through all their travels, Gray had never ventured into a place this big. The close-packed buildings, vendors hawking their wares, shoppers, horses, children…and the smell. *Gah!* The city had sewers, but trash and animal crap accumulated in ditches, corners, and alleys. The scooper crews should add more shifts.

A sparkle of light flashed, and Tru stared like a country hick. The palace bluestone walls and slate roof gleamed in the sun like jewels, pristine and elegant.

Cali had grown up in that magnificence, surrounded by servants and luxury. He couldn't even imagine how different her life had been from his.

A group of women gathered around a bubbling fountain. Of course, there'd be a magician in the capital city to provide running water and sewer management. Maybe even guide stones to light the roads at night.

Newt cut down a cleaner side street, and the sea of people parted to make way.

Tru didn't have to decide today. No one would force him before the emperor. Was it worth the risk of losing everything to fulfill a duty? Tru liked his life. But Jasmine's words haunted him. He could accomplish great things for commoners as a prince. But how much control would he have over his life? Would he be told when to eat, what to wear, where to be? It'd be a fine cage, but still a cage.

He couldn't return to the Evening Inn, either. It had been home for a time, but going back would be hollow. Could he stay with Cali? Be her high priest? She didn't need him. He'd get her to safety, then slink away.

Jasmine bumped his shoulder. "Have you decided?" Her eyes darted everywhere.

"Yes." A dirty child scampered into the street, and Tru hauled on the reins. The girl waved and disappeared down an alley. As a prince, would he have the power to save a person like that? Make the lives of commoners easier? "No."

"Hurry up. You're running out of time."

They rounded another corner. A massive stone wall encircled the palace, but the gates stood open, allowing a stream of carts and pedestrians into the courtyard. Most of them filed off to the left, probably to a service entrance. The soldiers went right, toward two large outbuildings.

"Time's up."

Tru scowled. "I haven't decided yet."

Newt led Tru to a central covered portico and dismounted. "I'll take care of the animals and stow the wagon. Grab your gear."

Tru hopped out and helped Charity unload their packs.

Jasmine strapped her sword to her back, tossed her quiver and her pack over her shoulder, and grabbed her bows.

"Newt, please take this food to the barracks kitchen." Cali set the crates near the edge. "Leave the rest here until I decide what to do with it." She slid out, pulled her hood up, and shouldered her bag. A beautiful smile blossomed on her face, and she turned to the massive double doors.

Beck and Mica walked through the gates and approached.

Dariel stepped toward them. "Walk the perimeter of the palace walls, keeping watch. If you spot Maelstrom, alert any guard."

Mica nodded, and the two headed back out.

Charity and Jasmine gathered beside Cali. She bounced on her toes. A breeze played at the edges of her hood and caught a few stray hairs. "I can't believe I'm here! We're going to pretend to be servants, so follow my lead."

Jasmine gestured for Tru. "You're requesting an audience with the emperor, yes?"

"No."

Cali's smile slid off. "Your kingdom needs you."

Like they hadn't been able to function all these years without him. "They don't even know I exist."

"Your parents have been grieving for a quarter century. They need to know you're alive."

"They've moved on with their lives."

Cali nodded at a second-floor balcony overlooking the courtyard. "Do you see that woman dressed in black?"

Tru squinted. A blonde woman in a fancy gown stood at the railing, gripping a pendant hanging around her neck, her head bent low. Every few moments, she lifted a handkerchief and dabbed at her eyes.

A squeezing ache spread through Tru's chest. "Who is she?"

"Queen Melissendra. Your mother."

She couldn't possibly still be mourning after all this time?

Cali clasped his wrist. "Your current life is a lie. You hate lies. Mend your mother's heart, do your duty, and seize your destiny, Tru. You have a family who love you, and they need to know you're alive."

"What's this about?" Dariel asked.

Tru turned. When had the enforcer snuck up on

them?

Cali dropped her hand.

Tru clenched his jaw. She was right. He'd been living a lie his entire life. A comfortable yet challenging one, but not his birthright. Maybe Sirini had dumped Cali in the bean field behind the stables so he'd find her *and* himself. Maybe this was his destiny.

Isn't that what he'd always wanted? A family? A place to belong? And it'd been handed to him in the most supernatural way imaginable. To turn his back on it now, without even meeting his mother, was unthinkable. But also permanent. He couldn't reveal himself, then slink off someplace else if he didn't like his new life. "I need an audience with the emperor."

"For what purpose?"

He bared his house mark to Dariel.

His eyes grew to soup-bowl size. "Ah. I'll set that up now. Shall we get this party inside and away from spying eyes?" He led them through the double doors, nodding at the two stationed guards.

Cali took Tru's hands. "We part ways here. I'll find you later."

What was he supposed to say now? *Please don't leave me to face this alone? Stay beside me, even though I'm still angry?* Except at some point that had melted away.

She stepped back, dropping his hands.

He nodded. "Later."

She turned to Jasmine. "Please go with Tru."

"I can't protect you if I'm not with you. Danger could lurk within these walls."

"I understand. But Tru needs a friend by his side while his world explodes, and I need to get out of sight.

When the audience is over, tell my father that I live, and ask him to meet me in Rosi's room. And to bring my mother."

Jasmine nodded. "I will do so."

Cali and Charity walked away, disappearing behind a massive staircase.

Tru scanned his surroundings. *Holy horse droppings, what an entryway!* A field of white marble flooring led to multiple hallways. An ancient wooden table squatted in the center of the foyer, topped with a spray of flowers in a silver urn the size of a wine vat. Dark-blue shiny fabric covered the walls. The stairs swept up to a balcony overlooking the grand space. A chandelier dripped with opulence and beeswax. Amber guide stones glowed overhead.

A blonde woman in a purple gown swished by.

"This way." Dariel took off down the left-hand hallway.

Jasmine fell into step beside Tru.

Dariel stopped outside a set of double doors guarded by two soldiers and opened a chest. "Place your weapons here. You'll get them back later."

Jasmine placed her bows in the trunk, followed by her quiver. She unbuckled her sheath and dumped her sword, the knife at her thigh, two boot knifes, a belt dagger, and a garotte she'd stuffed in a pocket.

Dariel pursed his lips. "Anything else?"

She scowled and drew two sharp pins from her hair knot. Multiple braids fell down her back to her waist. She tossed the pins into the chest. "That's it."

Tru added his weapons.

Dariel locked the chest. "Please wait here. I'll collect you when the emperor is ready."

"How long with that be?" Jasmine asked.

"Not sure. If you need something, tell one of the guards, and they'll call for a servant." Dariel entered the double doors and closed them behind him.

Nice. Abandoned in a strange place. At least it had a padded bench under a set of ridiculously tall windows. What was with these royals, wanting everything oversized? Tru was a big man, but even he couldn't jump high enough to brush the ceiling with his fingertips, and this was a damn hallway. Shoot, if he boosted Jasmine onto his shoulders, she'd be hard-pressed to touch the tiles. And were they really copper?

Tru sat on the bench and crossed his arms. *Goodbye old life.* It was fun while it lasted.

Chapter Twenty-Seven

I guided Charity to the servant's staircase, climbed to the second-floor family wing, and hurried to my bedchamber door but hesitated with my hand on the knob. Had they cleaned it out? Or had they left it as if I'd return? And did I want to know the answer? Maybe I should duck into Rosi's room.

No, I wanted to wash my face and change my clothes. My sisters would be thrilled to see me, but I didn't want to dirty their delicate garments when we embraced.

"What's wrong?" Charity whispered.

"Nothing." I entered.

The room hadn't changed. The boots I'd been wearing that fateful morning still lay on the floor next to the shoe rack. Someone had closed the wardrobe doors, straightened my vanity, and scoured the incense bowl of my shrine. The calming scents of lavender and sandalwood enveloped me. I was home again.

Charity dropped her bag and her jaw. "This room is bigger than my house!"

No time to reminisce. "We need servant clothing for you." I opened Grace's door. It was empty aside from the narrow bed and a dresser. She must have left when I died. My eyes watered, and I stepped back. "You can sleep in here if you'd like. My maid has left."

Charity smiled. "Can I be your new one? I can do

your hair and help with buttons and…what else does a maid do?"

"Don't worry about it. Let's clean up and find my sisters." I crossed to the basin and pitcher—which were empty. Of course. Why would fresh water be waiting for a dead woman? I picked up the container. "Stay here. I'll be right back."

"That's my job." She grabbed the vessel.

I hung on to it. "Do you know where to get water?"

She let go. "No."

"I'll be right back."

"I'm coming with you so I know where to go next time."

Ten minutes later, we'd washed and donned clean clothing. I opted for the blue dress I'd worn to my sacrifice and a cotton shirt, despite Charity begging me to wear one of the silk pieces in the wardrobe.

"I'm Calla, a serving girl. If I wear a fancy gown, everyone will know I didn't die." I laced up a tunic over the dress and stuffed my feet back in my hardy work boots. To complete the costume, I wrapped my apron over my hair and knotted it beneath my braid.

If anyone recognized me as Princess Cali, it would be a miracle.

Charity grabbed the linen scarf off my vanity and draped it over her head. "How's this?"

I laughed. "I guess it'll work."

"I'm ready. What's the plan?"

"First we greet my sisters and parents. Then a trip to the temple. I don't know what to do once I find my counterpart. Blast it! I should have asked Mica. Should we find her, instead?"

"I don't want to try locating her in the crowds."

"Good point. Once I know the process for my ascension, I'll find Prince Shaded. Maybe by dusk I'll be a goddess."

"I hope so." Charity bounced on her toes. "I can't wait to see your godly form! Will you have powers? Amazing strength? Wings? A glowing halo? Ooh, the ability to read our minds?" Her eyes widened. "That might not be fun, but you'll need some way to discern the truth."

"Maybe I'll be like Tru, able to smell lies. Let's go." I opened the door and scanned the hallway. All clear.

"Eyes lowered," Charity said. "We're servants now."

"Right." I hurried across the hall to Rosi's door and peeked inside.

She sat at her vanity, straightening a wire hair piece studded with sapphires and chatting with her maid, Dia. "If you can't work these in, maybe the pearls?"

I slowly closed the door. "Dia's in there. We should wait until she leaves."

Charity glanced around. "Out here? What if we're seen?"

Dia rushed out, racing past us without even looking at our faces.

Charity pushed me into Rosi's room and shut the door behind us.

"That was fast. Did you find the right—" Rosi turned. "Daffi, why are you dressed as a maid? That's not funny. We need to get ready…" Her gaze locked with mine, and all the color drained from her face. "Cali?" She pressed her fingers to her lips. "How can this be?" She rose and took two steps, hands extended. Her eyelids fluttered, her eyes rolled back, and her knees folded.

I rushed forward and caught her. Her weight pulled me to the floor. "Tru makes this look so easy, but she's heavy. A little help here?"

Charity and I lowered Rosi to the pink carpet and stuffed a pillow under her head. I tapped her hand. "Wake up."

Her eyelashes quivered, and she opened her eyes. "Am I dreaming?"

"No. I'm here."

"It's not possible. I don't believe it." She touched my cheek.

I smiled. "It's really me. I'm home."

Her gaze drifted across my face, and tears welled in her eyes. She cried out and wrapped her arms around my neck. Sobs wracked her body. "Where have you been?"

I hugged her tightly. "Running. Hiding."

Rosi thumped my back with her fist. "Why did you wait so long to let me know you survived?" She pulled back and clutched my shoulders. "You little wretch, Mother's been sick with grief, Father's been stomping around in a mood, and you waited seven days to show yourself?" She swatted me. "What is wrong with you?"

"I've had other issues—"

She laughed. "I'm so happy you're alive! Who else knows?"

I kissed her cheek. "You're the first, other than my new friends." I took her hands. "This is Charity. She's been my traveling companion and confidante, along with Priestess Jasmine and a stable hand named Tru. They've been protecting me and—"

"Why do you need protection?"

"That's a long story. Do you mind if I save it until everyone's here?"

"Who else is coming?"

I grinned. "I haven't sent out the invitations yet, but I'm hoping to only tell family members. Don't even tell Dia. Oh! Has Rhygan been found?"

Rosi bit her bottom lip. "No. There's been no word."

The door opened.

I let go of Rosi's hands, tucked my chin to my chest, and peered through the loose hair hanging beside my face.

Dia entered the room with three pairs of shoes. "I didn't know which—"

"Thanks. Those are great." Rosi climbed to her feet and took them. "Ask Daffi to come over right away, please. Without Valora. Then you're excused. I'll call you when I'm ready."

Dia frowned and backed out, closing the door.

Rosi clasped her hands. "We have to tell Mother immediately." She opened the door and yelled, "Dia, ask my mother to attend me, as well. Thank you."

I laughed. "Since when do you shout after servants?"

"Since my sister returned from the dead." She knelt on the floor and wrapped her arm around my shoulders. "I can't wait to hear your story."

Daffi entered, a long curl clutched in one hand. "What do you require? Valora hasn't finished—" Her gaze darted between Rosi and me. "—my ringlets." Her chin quivered.

Mother followed, the blue agate pendant engraved with my house mark glinting. "I'm running—" She pressed her hands to her mouth, and her green eyes teared up. "Cali? Is that you? How—" She spread her arms, beckoning me into them. "My baby."

I threw myself into her embrace. Her knees buckled, but I held her tight, and we cried together. Daffi and Rosi joined our group hug, and we all clung to each other and sobbed.

Goddess, I'd missed them so much.

"How is this possible?" Momma asked.

Daffi's voice trembled. "How did you survive?"

I squeezed her. "I'll tell you momentarily. Let me enjoy this."

Rosi patted Momma's shoulder. "Cry it all out. That helped me."

Daffi sniffed and withdrew, wiping away tears with her fingers. "Valora toiled so arduously on my eye cosmetics, and I've ruined them."

Rosi studied Daffi's face. "No, you're fine."

Momma cupped my cheek. "I still can't believe you're here. You're not a spirit?"

"I'm here."

She smiled around trembling lips. "Praise the goddess. You look healthy. How do you feel?"

"I'm great, now that I've seen you all."

"Where did you find a new maid?" Momma nodded at Charity.

"She's my friend from Borderline. I'll explain everything soon."

Daffi crossed to Rosi's wardrobe, passed out handkerchiefs, and sat on the bed. "Cali, where have you been? Is Maelstrom going to attack the palace to get you back?"

"He'd better not." I settled beside her.

Rosi and Momma climbed up with us and redistributed the pillows.

"Charity, please join us." I patted a free spot.

Her eyes widened. "I should step outside and guard the door."

I nodded. "If you want to. But you're welcome to stay."

Daffi cocked her head at Charity. "Why are you wearing a dresser scarf on your head?"

I laughed. "We're disguised as servants."

Mother clucked her tongue. "Cali, this is your home. Why would you worry about being seen by others?"

Charity headed for the door. "I'll be out there." She slipped out.

"It began when I dove into the ocean. It hit me like a punch to the throat, and I sucked in a mouthful of water. I was sure I'd drown."

****

Tru leaned against the window, his leg bouncing. *How much longer?*

The doors opened. "The emperor will see you now." Dariel swept his hand toward the room like he'd practiced it a million times. "Truthful and Priestess Jasmine of Borderline." His raised voice echoed.

Time for my life to crash and rebuild. He gained his feet and walked beside Jasmine through the doors, slowing his pace to take in the room. White marble floors and columns. Blue fabric walls and vivid tapestries. Guide stones hanging from the ceiling. Massive windows with sunshine reflecting off shiny surfaces. Enough space to hold horse races, cheering crowds, and beer vendors. And at the far end, a dais with two thrones and a bench, all built of highly polished black walnut, studded with gemstones, and padded with blue cushions.

Emperor Rhys stood before the larger throne. Tall, muscular, imposing…not a man to pick a fight with.

Although the laugh lines around his mouth and eyes spoke of a kinder side, and the gray streaks at his temples hinted more at wisdom than vanity.

The man had raised Cali. No reason to fear him. Tru bowed. "Thank you for seeing me, Your Imperial Majesty."

Jasmine curtsied, cocked her head, put one finger to her lips, and crept to a tapestry of children picking strawberries.

Emperor Rhys's gaze tracked her.

She grabbed one of her braids and pulled out a thin hairpin the length of her forearm.

Dariel scowled and started toward her.

She drew back the edge of the tapestry and jammed the hairpin through a small hole in the stone block.

Someone on the other side yelped and, with a whisper of fabric, ran away.

"He won't get far, Majesty." Dariel strode to the door and signaled for a guard.

"Thank you." The emperor grinned at Jasmine. "How did you know we had a spy?"

She crossed to Tru's side. "Sirini told me."

The emperor cocked one eyebrow. "Does she speak to you often?"

"Every day. She's quite friendly."

"I'm relieved to hear that. Is she the reason for your audience today?"

"No, we're here for Tru."

Dariel approached. "My men are on it." He stood guard between the dais and Jasmine, feet spread, hand on his knife hilt. He stared at her with narrowed eyes.

Emperor Rhys nodded. "What is on your mind, Truthful?"

The end of his freedom, but he couldn't say that. He wiped his sweaty hands on his thighs and cleared his throat. "I was told to present myself to you and show you my house mark." He loosened the laces on his tunic and pulled the edges back.

Emperor Rhys approached, his gaze locked on the tattoo.

Dariel tightened his grip on his weapon.

The emperor studied the tattoo, and a slow grin spread across his face. "Dariel, call three runners, please."

"But—"

"I'm in no danger. Go now."

Dariel bowed, turned on his heel, and hurried out a side door.

Emperor Rhys held out his hand to Tru.

Tru sucked in a quick breath. As a commoner, he'd be punished for attempting to touch the emperor. But since he initiated it, Tru repeated the gesture.

The emperor gripped Tru's wrist.

"I'm honored, Majesty. Thank you for this warm welcome."

"Where have you been all these years?"

Dariel returned with three boys.

The emperor addressed the first. "Fetch Queen Melissendra and the Princesses Finna and Farras. Tell them not to worry over their clothing. I need them immediately." He turned to the second boy. "Find Empress Bronwyn. Same message." He pointed at the third. "Find Ironweed. Skip the part about attire."

The three boys darted out the door.

Emperor Rhys turned back to Tru. "Sorry about the interruption."

"No apology is necessary, Majesty. I'm here to serve."

He smiled. "Your manners are impeccable. Who raised you?"

"My guardian called himself Gray. I don't know his real identity."

"Amazing." The emperor glanced at Jasmine. "Has Sirini told you anything about our young friend here?"

"Just to protect him with my life."

Tru's stomach tightened. "She did what?"

Jasmine slapped his shoulder and laughed. "The look on your face! Yes, Sirini commanded me to watch over both of you. When Xyla stabbed you, I seriously wondered if the goddess would zap me. Not a killing blow, just a warning." She rolled her eyes. "How was I supposed to know you'd tackle a goddess?"

"I can't wait to hear the details." Emperor Rhys turned to Tru. "You were attacked?"

"Several times."

The door opened, and a short, fat man entered. He shuffled forward, his tan robes swirling about his feet, and bowed. "Majesty."

"Ironweed, verify this house mark." Emperor Rhys pointed to Tru's chest.

Tru swallowed. If this man found the tattoo fake, what would happen? What was the punishment for impersonating a royal? Stocks? Imprisonment? A chill crept down Tru's spine. Death? What had he stepped into?

He should have fled Riverton when he had the chance.

Chapter Twenty-Eight

Ironweed squinted at Tru's chest. "Bend down a bit, if you please?"

Tru complied.

Ironweed placed his hand over the mark and closed his eyes. He cocked his head. He hummed deep in his throat.

What was he doing? Cali said the tattoo was etched with magic. Could Ironweed sense it somehow? Or worse, could he not find it at all? *Goddess, let this man verify it.*

Ironweed stepped away. "It is genuine."

Tru released his breath. One momentous challenge met. On to the next.

"Thank you," Emperor Rhys said. "Please remain, as you may be needed soon."

"I'm always at your service, Majesty." Ironweed retreated to the door.

A gorgeous older woman with auburn hair, brown eyes, and a copper gown swept into the room. "You called for me?"

Emperor Rhys opened his arms and kissed her cheeks. "Yes, my love. We're about to witness a miracle, and I thought you'd enjoy it." He turned to Tru. "This is Empress Bronwyn."

Tru bowed. "Pleased to meet you, Majesty."

"And your name?" she asked.

"I go by Tru, though I imagine that will change soon."

She shot a curious glance at her husband. "More details would be lovely."

Emperor Rhys patted her hand. "In a few moments. We await the arrival of three more...ah, here they are now."

The woman from the balcony entered, followed by two younger versions with matching blonde hair, green eyes, and cleft chins. They all wore black. The matron stroked an onyx medallion around her neck, engraved with a vertical line and a dot within two concentric circles.

His skin tingled. That was his house mark. She still grieved. Tru blinked and clenched his trembling hands. This was his mother and sisters. His family. Warmth spread through his body. He'd been waiting for this all his life, but now his tongue stuck to the roof of his mouth, and he couldn't come up with any words. *Greetings, Mother*, wouldn't suffice. Nor would *How are you,* or *Pleased to meet you*, or *Surprise!* A chuckle lodged in his throat, and he glanced at Jasmine.

She whispered, "You're good."

The blonde women curtsied to the emperor and empress.

"We are honored to serve you." The queen's voice was low pitched with a vibrant, almost liquid quality. Her gaze skimmed past Jasmine, slid to Tru, and locked on to him. Her face paled, and she clutched her medallion.

Emperor Rhys said, "Melissendra, you may wish to see this young man's—"

"House mark." She stepped toward Tru, and her

knees buckled.

He rushed forward and caught her. *Oh, sard!* Was he supposed to touch her? "I beg your pardon, Majesty."

She clung to him, fingers clenched in his stained shirt, her gaze darting from his eyes to his chin to his hair. Tears welled in her eyes. She cupped his cheek in one hand. "You look so much like your father. Can it be true?"

He pressed his lips. *Yes, I'm Tru.* But that wasn't her question. He bared his mark.

She traced it with the tip of her shaking finger. "My son. You've returned to me." Tears streamed down her face, and she smiled. "I've prayed for your return, and the goddess blessed me." She stretched on her toes, kissed his face, and wrapped her arms around his neck.

He held her, closed his eyes, and laid his cheek against her silky hair. She smelled like roses and cinnamon. He'd waited his entire life for his mother's hug, and it was worth every moment. A weight fell off his shoulders. He owed Cali and Jasmine a heartfelt *Thank you* for convincing him to present himself.

"Rhys, is that young man Prince Freidrick?" Bronwyn asked.

"Yes, my love."

"Why is he dressed as a commoner?"

Tru chuckled. Maybe the empress would find his tale amusing. He opened his eyes and caught her staring at him.

One of his sisters stepped toward him. "You're my brother?"

He smiled. "Yes."

Her eyes narrowed. She ripped her onyx necklace from her throat and threw it at his feet. "You should have stayed in your hovel!" She whirled and strode from the room.

His mother backed out of his embrace and caressed his cheeks with her fingertips. "That was your sister, Finna. I'm sure once the shock wears off, she'll apologize for her abysmal behavior. Farras, come greet your brother."

The other young woman approached, holding her skirts. She curtsied. "I am pleased to meet you, Freidrick."

"And I you."

Empress Bronwyn came forward, her slippers whispering against the marble flooring. "Melissendra, I'm so happy for you."

The two women embraced. They were friends? Tru glanced at Emperor Rhys. Were he and King Franklin close, as well? "What of my father? When will I meet him?"

Fresh tears welled in his mother's eyes, and Empress Bronwyn answered. "King Franklin passed away four days ago. His heart was weak, and the stress of the journey proved too great."

Tru's belly clenched, and he lowered his head. Sunlight pooled on his filthy boots, so out of place in this opulent venue of kings and emperors. He was late by four lousy days? Now he'd never get to hear his father's stories of his past. Never do father/son activities like hunting, fishing, or swordplay. Did his father even enjoy those things? An ache spread through Tru's chest, but his grief couldn't compare to his mother's. "I'm sorry for your loss. I wish I had arrived sooner to offer him comfort in his last hours."

She hugged him again. "I know he would have been

overjoyed to learn that you survived." She sniffed. "My son, I am elated to have you by my side, but you smell of horse. Perhaps we could retire to our suites and find you more suitable attire? Then you could tell us where you've been all these years and how you returned to us."

Tru grimaced. "I apologize. I've been traveling for the last quarter-moons, and there have been few opportunities to wash properly, Queen Melissendra."

Her eyebrows rose. "Come now. Call me Mother."

He nodded. "Thank you. Mother."

She glanced at Jasmine. "Is this your wife?"

Tru chuckled. "No, a friend. I'm not married."

Mother sighed. "That is probably for the best. All the young nobles are in residence to make alliances. Perhaps it's not too late to arrange a match for you."

He clenched his teeth. Not if he had anything to say about it. "There's no rush."

"Oh, but there is. You'll be crowned king tomorrow afternoon. You'll require a queen and heirs immediately."

Tru swallowed and choked on his spit. "But I just arrived."

She patted his arm. "I understand. But duty waits for no man. Come along. Farras, attend me, please."

Farras bobbed her head. "Yes, Mother."

Tru glanced at Jasmine. "Where are you off to next?"

"I need a word with the emperor, then I'll seek out our mutual friend."

Dariel stepped forward, hand on his sword hilt. "Do not presume, Priestess. No offense, but his safety is my sole concern."

Jasmine's eyes flared silver. A stiff breeze whipped

through the throne room and lifted her off the floor. Stray strands of dark hair fluttered around her face.

Oh, sard. Tru dropped to one knee and bowed, followed a moment later by the whisper of fabric as everyone else sank to the floor. He wouldn't want to be in Dariel's boots right now.

The goddess spoke through Jasmine with an eerie multitoned voice. "Emperor Rhys has no need to fear my servant, but I will permit you to remain, Enforcer Dariel, while she passes along her message. Do not stand in my servant's way again. She serves my will only."

Dariel swallowed hard and nodded. "Y-y-yes, Goddess."

Jasmine sank to the floor, and her eyes flicked back to the normal sky blue. She grinned. "That was exciting. She's never spoken through me before. Sorry if that frightened you, Dariel."

Color returned to his pale face, and he gained his feet. "No problem."

Tru helped his mother rise. "I believe it's time for us to leave."

She gripped his arm and led him to a side door, his sister behind them. "Has that happened before? How do you know that young woman?"

He'd love to stay and watch the emperor's reaction to the good news, but he needed this time to get to know his family and figure out how to escape being crowned king tomorrow.

****

"When we reached the highway, I knew I couldn't cross." Heat flushed my face, and I grinned. "Tru whisked me into his arms and dashed across."

Momma's jaw dropped. "Cali! Such improper

behavior."

"What was I supposed to do? Allow Tera to swallow me?"

The bedchamber door opened, and my father charged in, his eyes bulging like a madman's. He took in the room with one glance, and his gaze locked on me.

"Papa!" I flew to him.

He hoisted me up and squeezed. "I didn't know if I should believe her, but it's true. You're here." His shoulders twitched.

Jasmine came in behind my father and closed the door. I waved at her and rubbed my cheek against Papa's whiskers, soaking in his scent of applewood and sword oil. "I'm sorry I left you believing I was dead for seven whole days. I was afraid to return."

He cupped the back of my head with one huge hand and kissed my forehead. "I'm so happy you're here. Don't worry about it now." He twirled me around like he had when I was younger. "I'm never letting you go again."

I giggled. "You must, Papa, so I can finish my story."

He set me on my feet. "Did I miss much?"

"I'll start over."

Rosi groaned.

Papa glanced at the bed. "I'll pull over the sofa." He dragged it close.

"Mind if I stay?" Jasmine hauled over the padded vanity bench.

"You're always welcome." I smiled. "Ask Charity to come in. She was too embarrassed to remain, but with you in here, she'll be fine."

Jasmine fetched Charity, who settled on the floor

beside the bench. Momma sat with Papa on the sofa. Rosi, Daffi, and I climbed back onto the bed, smoothing our skirts and stuffing cushions behind our backs.

I started over on my tale. I left out the bits where I fell in love with Tru, held his hand, and kissed him, but it was impossible to hide the fact that we'd spent seven days together, some of it unchaperoned. Not that my reputation mattered since I wasn't going to marry. "Daffi and Momma came in, we all had a good cry, and now you're caught up."

Daffi's eyebrows scrunched. "You're going to be a goddess? How is that possible?"

Rosi beamed at Jasmine. "Will you teach me to be a guard when I pledge at the temple?"

Jasmine shrugged. "Sure. If you've got skills like Cali, you'll be a natural."

Papa leaned forward, and a sunbeam flashed off the golden torc around his throat. "Explain to me why you think you're in danger here."

"There are still deities out to kill me. Maelstrom, Sear, Sprout, Gale, Zelos, or Blanche could gain access to the palace." I found a tiny handprint on one of the lavender ruffles. "Rosi, who touched your dress?"

She brushed at the stain. "Dia's little brother came to visit. He had a sticky bun."

"Now you've got honey on the silk."

"Girls." Papa pulled us back on topic.

I scratched the gunk off the fabric. "Sorry. There's still danger, even now that I'm inside the palace. If the townspeople find out I survived, they'll think Maelstrom wasn't pleased with me and demand another. I don't want them clamoring for Rosi or Daffi."

Momma clenched her fists. "They aren't getting any

more of my daughters."

"That is illogical," Daffi said. "We will spread the theory that Maelstrom spared you. No more sacrifice is necessary."

"And when he attacks the palace to get to me, they'll know you lied." I squeezed her hand. "I know you want to believe I'm safe now, but I'm not. Plus, I still have to find Prince Shaded and ascend. If we don't locate each other before the crescent moons, we'll both perish."

Momma paled and leaned against Papa. "We'll just seal the gates. No one in or out until you've found that young man."

"We're already on lockdown, Eilee." Papa patted Momma's knee and looked to me. "Do you have a plan? Do you want our help?"

"I was thinking I could impersonate Rosi."

Daffi reared back. "Why not me?"

I rolled my eyes. "I can't pretend to be you. You're always saying stuff no one understands, like 'photosynthesis in the draven outlet proves the existence of a universal uvula.' The second I try to say something intelligent, everyone will know I'm a fraud."

Daffi laughed. "That made no sense! And do I really sound like that?"

"Yes." Rosi, Momma, and I responded.

"So if you're me, then I sit here in my room alone?" Rosi crawled off the bed and paced, shaking her skirts out.

"Yes. I'm sorry."

Charity raised her hand. "I'll stay with Rosi. I can guard the door and fetch anything she needs."

Rosi smiled. "That's a sweet offer."

It solved several problems. "And don't tell Dia."

"Why not?" Rosi asked.

"Servants talk. Even if she doesn't intend to gossip, all it takes is one slip, and suddenly the word is out, and we've got a mob in the portico again."

Papa nodded. "If it's only for a day or two, and Rosi agrees, it's a good plan. But I want Daffi and Jasmine with you, and I'll add another guard when you leave the palace."

I grinned. "I agree to your terms, Papa. Our first stop is the temple."

"Which means being outside in the sunshine," Charity added.

"I can fix that." Rosi grabbed her coin purse off the vanity, opened the door, and stuck her head out. "Dia— oh, there you are. Go buy two large parasols and matching gloves, please. You know which colors I like. Be quick!" She handed off the purse and closed the door. "Done. Parasols are all the rage in Olerio this year. And the Tulya party brought a different fashion trend that Charity and I can borrow." She patted Charity's shoulder. "Help me out of this gown. You and I have work to do."

Papa sprang from the sofa. "I'll leave this in your capable care, Rosi." He whisked me into his arms. "I'm overjoyed to see you again, Cali Cub. No unnecessary chances. Please." He kissed my cheek, set me on my feet, and left.

Rosi snapped her fingers at me. "Take off that ridiculous outfit and get into my dress. The next event begins in one hour. You need to hurry."

I untied my laces. "Do I have to wear that lavender thing? It's hideous."

"Cali!" Momma pulled the apron off my head. "It's

a fine gown for walking through the gardens, and it's already pressed."

Yet wrinkled from crawling around on the bed and sporting a honey handprint, but I didn't back-talk my mother. A walk in the gardens sounded divine after that last grueling week.

Chapter Twenty-Nine

"We're going to be late!" Daffi hurried down the stairs and shot out the front door.

Jasmine and I followed. A carriage awaited us, painted dark blue with brass accents. Two guards sat in the driver's seat, another hung off the back, and Dariel stood beside the open door. *Really, Papa? Four?*

Dariel bowed. "Ladies." He offered his hand.

Clobbering him with my new parasol wouldn't be ladylike. Rosi insisted the coral color contrasted nicely with lavender, but thank the goddess I didn't have to look at myself all day. Daffi's yellow gown didn't do any favors for her complexion, but it went with her sky-blue parasol. Dia should be ashamed of herself. With our island coloring, darker jewel colors served us better, despite Rosi's penchant for pastels.

Lucky Jasmine wore her gray priestess robe over leathers. Too bad I couldn't get away with that. The lace itched around the high neckline and wrists.

"Sirini's temple, please." I laid my gloved hand in Dariel's calloused one and climbed into the carriage. What a difference from the covered wagon. Padded blue velvet seats, windows with curtains, and brass hardware. I sat in one of the forward-facing benches, and Jasmine took the spot beside me.

Dariel entered, sat next to Daffi, and signaled the driver.

I pulled the curtain back and checked for sunbeams. Shade. Excellent. I shoved it aside and watched the activity in the surrounding streets.

A moment later, I spotted a familiar redhead. "Stop!" I opened the side door and hopped out while it was still rolling, Jasmine right behind me. "Mica!"

Several pedestrians offered shallow bows and scurried away.

The goddess turned and frowned at me. Then her gaze drifted to Jasmine, and recognition lit her face.

Lovely. Mica didn't recognize me in finery with my hair pinned up.

She spoke in a low voice. "Beck and I haven't seen Maelstrom, but a storm is brewing out at sea. It will hit landfall within two hours. Gale may arrive with it. I'd be happy to travel with you back to the palace."

I glanced at the sky. Dark clouds billowed in the south. "Jasmine?"

She rolled her eyes. "Don't worry, I can handle him."

Of course. But a squall and a battle would ruin the garden outing. "I think we'll be fine, Mica. I need to ask a personal question. Please don't be offended."

Her lips quirked up on one side. "Proceed."

"When you met your counterpart, how did you activate your spark? Is there a ritual? What's the procedure?"

She smiled, and her cheeks flushed. "When Beck and I spotted each other in the temple courtyard in Eldritch, we fell in love. I reached for him, he took my hand, and our sparks flared to fullness. As other deities despised each other on first sight, I'm assuming it was the touch, not the affection, that triggered the ascension."

"That's simple enough." I could come up with a way to touch Prince Shaded. "Thank you, Goddess."

She bowed. "Anything you need, Princess. Remember our agreement."

"I won't forget." I turned and plowed into Dariel's chest.

He caught my arm.

"Don't sneak up on me!" I tapped his hand. "Change of plans. We're heading to the gardens now."

He nodded. "And no more unplanned stops in the middle of a street."

"Agreed." I climbed into the carriage.

Daffi grinned. "Was that really the goddess of stone?"

"Yes. She's friendly. I like her."

Jasmine settled beside me, and the coach surged forward.

I stared out the window at my city. "Daffi, what's our goal? Are we to mingle? Act as tour guides? Remain aloof since we aren't husband fishing?"

Daffi giggled. "We're to be amiable—"

"You mean friendly."

"—and enjoy ourselves." She fluffed her skirt and picked off a chunk of lint. "And I chose the word I meant."

I grinned. "I love you."

"I know. Don't monopolize anyone's time. Compliment new fashions. Flirt with the men. And don't forget you're Rosi. If you introduce yourself as Cali, I will laugh instead of assist you."

Jasmine nudged me with her elbow. "I'll be behind you the entire time. If you slip, I'll incapacitate the witness and get you to safety."

Dariel scowled. "Please don't tell me you'll gut a royal on the off chance they discovers Cali's identity."

Jasmine glared at him. "Do you really believe I'd stab an innocent person?"

"No, but that word makes me pause."

Extra marks to Jasmine for not rolling her eyes. "I'll return Cali and the witness to the carriage where we'll have a chat on the ride back to the palace. Satisfied?"

He grunted.

"I won't slip." We were approaching the city center where a massive fountain sprayed water into the air, offering citizens a cool place to rest during the heat of the day. Us silly royals would skip that tantalizing respite to stroll through the hot walled gardens. Shade trees dotted the space, but most of the exotic flowers needed full sun. If we were lucky, breezes from the oncoming storm would whip through the garden walkways. Otherwise, we'd all be sweaty and tired long before the two hours slotted for the event slid by.

Maybe I'd find Shaded and ascend. "Was everyone required to attend this outing?"

Daffi frowned. "More like encouraged."

So he could be here this afternoon. I couldn't wait to meet the others. The Olerio family had visited often in my youth, but the others, especially Tulya and Rigolan, hadn't called on us in years. I remembered the Rigolan girls as standoffish, but maybe they'd been shy when they were children. When we were fourteen, Rosi and I had giggled over the adorable Kurik boys. They were bound to be drop-jaw gorgeous by now.

On that happy thought, the carriage stopped.

Dariel opened the door, stepped out, and scanned the surroundings. He offered his hand to Daffi, then me.

Jasmine hopped out.

The moment sunlight hit my face, my skin heated. I flicked the parasol open and settled it on my shoulder. *This may be a long afternoon.*

We'd parked near the gate to the walled gardens. Other young royals descended from carriages or horses and gathered in a loose circle. Daffi grinned like a child with a cookie and strode toward the group.

I followed, Dariel and Jasmine behind me.

A muscular blond man in olive silk and brown velvet dismounted a gray horse, gripping the reins and patting the animal's neck, his back to the crowd. A dark-haired woman with porcelain skin approached him, smiled, and said something I couldn't hear. He nodded, tied his mount to the hitching post, took her arm, and walked with her toward the group.

My breath hitched. It was Tru! Someone had trimmed his hair and dressed him in finery. His confident swagger was gone. He hooked one finger into the neckline and pulled his ruffled shirt away from his throat.

I sidled closer to them.

"I'm Princess Sorka from Kurik." The dark-haired woman gazed at Tru with her beguiling sapphire-blue eyes. Her crimson-and-black dress complemented her coloring. She'd paired it with a black hat and gloves. "I can't believe we haven't met yet."

My eyes narrowed. My oldest brother, Rhygan, had been courting her for the last several years, and she behaved like this in the presence of a new prince?

Tru cleared his throat. "I'm Tr—Prince Freidrick of Rigolan. I arrived this afternoon."

Her red-tinted lips formed a perfectly practiced O. "You're the foundling. Where have you been? Your skin is bronzed, and you're so…muscled." She ran her hand along his bicep and down to his wrists. "Oh no, your hands are calloused!"

All the better to slap you with, wench.

He gently pulled his hand from hers. "I've been working as a stable hand."

She batted her ridiculously dark lashes. "I wager you ride well." She wrinkled her nose. "How unfortunate for you to have been forced to live so below your station. I'm sure you're thrilled to be finished with it."

A fireball sizzled in my chest. *That little tramp!* How dare she suggest he give up the one thing that brought him joy?

Jasmine whispered in my ear. "What are you doing?"

"Plotting vengeance." I took another step in their direction.

Others of the group noticed Sorka and Tru, and the crowd shifted toward them like a school of fish.

A woman with mousy-brown hair reached his side first and offered her hand. "I'm Lynna of Olerio. Pleased to meet you." She wore a turquoise frock that clashed with her sage parasol.

"Charmed." He bowed and scanned the crowds, his brows furrowed. His gaze caught mine, and he froze.

Lynna threaded her arm through his, and the edge of her parasol grazed his cheek.

He leaned away from it.

"Shall we make our way to the gates?" she asked.

Queen Loraida of Olerio clapped her hands. "Attention. The chaperones have all arrived." She brushed a lock of auburn hair beneath the brim of her floppy hat and waved everyone closer. "Let us proceed into the gardens. Please do not stray from the graveled paths, do not pluck any of the blossoms no matter how well they'll match your gowns, and absolutely no liberties. Remember your stations." She picked up her skirts and swept toward the open gates.

Everyone followed, though several other women converged on Tru and Sorka, including a few of my sisters. Palama curtsied and offered her fingers to him.

Lynna clung to his arm like a leech, aborting his hesitant attempt to kiss Palama's hand.

"Let's go." Jasmine prodded me.

Tru caught my gaze again.

I trailed after Daffi. I was here to find Prince Shaded, not combust at all the female attention paid to Tru. I didn't own him, and he deserved to have an enjoyable afternoon with all the conniving princesses fawning over him like a frosted pastry.

Compared to all the other princes standing around, Tru was by far the most handsome. And the largest. His chest and shoulders dwarfed the others. And he needed a roomier pair of leggings. His thighs would burst the side seams if he squatted. Which he shouldn't do, as a prince, but who knew what he might do?

Daffi and I passed Queen Loraida, bobbing more than curtsying. She nodded back and gestured us through.

A line of chaperones stood inside the gates and filed off to follow couples into the gardens. Several were servants from Tulya, based on their darker skin tones, and wore bright, patterned scarves over their faces. Only their brown eyes showed above the colorful fabric. One of them moved to intercept Daffi and me, but Jasmine put out her hand. "We've got them."

The woman's gaze drifted from Jasmine to Dariel, both armed, and nodded.

"New fashion trend?" Daffi asked. "The facial scarf?"

I shrugged. "Could be."

We walked the gravel path around a bed of purple hyacinth and yellow daffodils planted in the shape of a massive daisy. Bees and butterflies liberally swarmed the blossoms.

Pensie and Prescia stopped. Were they waiting for Palama to catch up? The Olerio triplets hovered nearby.

I swallowed. Pensie used to tease me about being useless and not "needing" an education since I was going to die. Prescia had said cosmetics were wasted on me, as I didn't have to attract a spouse. But Palama had been the worst, excluding me from the "household management" courses given by our tutors because I'd never use the information. Maybe once I became the goddess of justice, they'd see some worth in me.

Daffi waved to them and moved on, pulling me along.

The scent of blooming flowers and saltwater rode a light breeze from the south, and the sun glinted off rocks, trellises, and polished torch-holders. I let go of the Batch Two bitterness and enjoyed myself. It was a gorgeous day. Holding Tru's arm and strolling by all the glorious displays would be magical. But I didn't have time to pry the gigglers off his arms. I needed to find Prince Shaded.

A swath of grass separated the daisy-shaped flower bed from the next exhibit, a marble statue of a long-dead empress. She lifted one hand into the air, as if to pluck an apple hanging in a nonexistent tree. The expression on her face suggested constipation. Sadly, birds found her outstretched arm a suitable perch, and their droppings robbed the sculpture of dignity. The gardeners should scrub her more often.

"Pardon," a familiar voice said behind me.

I turned to find Sorka and Lynna draped over Tru.

Daffi curtsied. "Greetings. I'm Princes Daffilee."

I bobbed. "Ca—Call me Rosi. Rosilee. That's my name." Heat flooded my face.

He smiled. "I'm Prince Freidrick. Pleased to meet you." He yanked on his hand, but Lynna wouldn't let loose.

"Beautiful day for a stroll." Daffi twirled her parasol on her shoulder, creating a slight breeze that lifted the stray hairs off my nape.

"Perhaps you ladies would care to join me?" Tru's gaze ran down my ruffled gown.

"In a half hour or so." Lynna glared at me. "I want to show him the weeping willow."

"Thank you for the offer, Prince Freidrick. We would love to." Daffi nudged my elbow.

"Yes. In a half hour." I gripped my parasol. Otherwise, I might punch Lynna.

Sorka plastered a fake smile on her face and waved at someone behind us. "Jayson!" She hurried toward my brother.

He greeted her and offered his arm. She latched on like a nursing kitten.

One floozy down, one to go.

"Come, Freidrick." Lynna pulled him down a side path. "The willow is this way." She "accidentally" stubbed her left toe against her right heel. She cried out and pitched forward, thrusting her bosom out.

Tru caught her around the waist before she hit the

gravel. "Princess, are you injured?"

She clung to his chest, her hands fisted in the silk and velvet fabrics. "You saved me."

Spots flared in my eyes. That was the oldest trick! And Tru fell for it? Smacking the path with her painted face would have served the plump tart. But no, he had to be a gentleman. And I couldn't resist poking fun at her. "Be more careful with your enormous feet, Lynna. It'd be a pity to tear your frock on this gravel."

Her eyes narrowed, and her lips pinched.

"Perhaps you should rest a moment before we continue." Tru led her to a bench, one arm hooked around her waist.

She smiled at him. "You're so sweet."

Goddess, save me from retching.

Two young men dressed in Kurik green approached. "Good afternoon, ladies. I'm Artur, and this is my brother, Edmun."

Daffi and I bobbed and grinned. My cheeks were beginning to cramp. These were the two boys we'd fawned over as girls. They'd grown into their bodies and held on to their pretty faces.

"Good afternoon. I'm Daffi, and this is my sister, Rosi. Are you enjoying the gardens?"

"They're well-maintained. Though they'd be more pleasurable in the right company." His gaze strayed down to Daffi's chest.

Oh, that was smooth. "I agree. Have you seen Prince Shaded? I was hoping he'd walk with me through the butterfly exhibit."

Artur's cheeks colored. "I haven't seen him today."

Another young man approached us, dressed in Tulya yellow with black accents, reminding me of a honeybee.

"Ladies, I'm Heath. Are these rogues bothering you?" He frowned at Jasmine and Dariel behind me. "How did you get saddled with commoners for chaperones?"

Heath didn't get a bob or a smile from me. "Priestess Jasmine is my dear friend. You would do well to mind your tongue, as she is armed."

He blinked at me twice, turned on his heel, and stomped away.

Daffi giggled. "Your words are sharp today. We're supposed to be polite."

I threaded my arm through hers and led her away from Artur and Edmun. "Oh, please. I offered him the same manners he showed us. And Edmun stared at his feet through the entire conversation. How should I react to that?"

She shrugged. "I don't know. Comment on the weather?"

"He'd do better to leave his brother's side and venture off on his own." *Maybe I can introduce Artur to Lynna.*

Daffi and I ventured deeper into the gardens, past flowering trees, babbling fountains, and topiaries shaped as ladybugs and caterpillars. Birds chirped. Bees buzzed. Flirting women giggled. A magic statue of a dancing girl twirled on a stone pillar. Young couples strolled the paths, sometimes stopping to view an exhibit. Princess Helene of Tulya and my brother Justyn lingered near a long, narrow trellis dripping with flowering vines. Their chaperone hovered discreetly a few steps away.

I passed into a curtain of green leaves and violet blooms. Three steps in, one of the vines curled around my neck. I clawed at it, gasping for breath.

More encircled my arms and hauled me off the ground. They were so tight I couldn't scream.

Chapter Thirty

Lynna chattered nonstop through the butterfly area, around the fountain, and into the bird sanctuary. *Good gods, can she be any more tedious?* Tru glanced up. Maybe one of the robins would let loose on her gown, and she'd run away.

Shouts and squeals came from up ahead. Was that Cali? He broke from Lynna's grasp. "Stay here."

"What?"

He ran toward the vine-covered arbor.

Daffi stood at the entrance, her fingers over her mouth, beside two other women with clenched hands. Daffi pointed inside. "Help her!"

He darted into the tunnel of greenery.

Cali hung suspended near the ceiling, jerking and twisting, encased in a mass of vines. Her face was blue, and she clawed at the creepers at her throat. Jasmine, Dariel, and a red-haired man slashed at leaves and trailers. For every branch they severed, another would entangle their blades.

Tru took three running steps, leapt, and hooked his arm around Cali's hips. His weight brought her down. She sucked in a deep breath. He shifted his grip, cradled her to his chest, and yanked hard to the left. The remaining vines encircling her body snapped.

"Get her out of here!" Jasmine sliced at a reaching creeper. "I'm behind you." She slashed again.

Cali gasped. "Thank you." She collapsed against his shoulder, breathing heavily.

Tru ran from the arbor and lowered her to the grass.

Daffi hurried over and shaded Cali's exposed face with a parasol. "How is she?"

His heart pounded. "I don't know. Ca—Rosi, can you hear me? Are you injured?"

She grabbed his hand and drew in deep breaths.

Jasmine took a protective stance, scanning the surroundings, sword ready. "How is she?"

Dariel and the other man took a spot near Cali's feet.

"She hasn't said." Tru yanked more vines from Cali's body and checked her throat. "She's not bleeding that I can see. She's breathing."

"What's going on?" Lynna pushed by Daffi to stare down at Cali. "What an undignified position, Princess Rosi. Already on your back for the new prince?"

Daffi shoved Lynna's shoulder. "Depart, shrew."

Lynna cried out, stumbled, and landed in the gravel on her ass.

The red-haired man gaped at Daffi. "That was rude, sis."

Cali giggled. "I'm fine. Just rattled. Is Sprout nearby?"

"I don't see him." Jasmine scoured the terrain. "But that was definitely him."

"We should get her back to the palace." Dariel gestured toward a group of onlookers. "Everyone please back away. Prince Justyn, are you available to help these people to safety?"

Justyn stared at Cali. "Are you expecting another plant attack?"

"Or a god." Cali sat up. "Thanks for the assist,

Justyn."

"You're welcome, Ca—sis." He winked.

Lynna held out her hands for assistance. The crowd backed away. Several women unsuccessfully hid grins behind their fingers.

Nice to know Tru wasn't the only one who had a problem with her.

Justyn hauled her up. He turned and addressed the people. "This area isn't safe. We all need to leave." He herded people out, Lynna attached to his arm like a leech. Unfortunately, most of them lingered, staring at Cali seated on the grass.

Tru helped her to her feet and brushed stray leaves and blossoms from her dress. "Are you sure you're all right?"

"Yes. Thank you. My vision was going dark when you ripped me down. You saved my life, T—Freidrick."

"You're welcome." He plucked a violet petal from her hair.

"Did I hurt your shoulder?" she asked.

"No, it's fine."

Daffi handed her parasol to Cali. "Take this. I'll find yours."

"Leave it." Dariel set his hand on Cali's arm and guided her toward the path.

"Incoming." Jasmine crouched, sword ready.

Tru turned.

A tall, thin man with pine-green hair stomped out of the trellis network and sneered. His tattered robe resembled a knot of autumn leaves sewn together. Vines and branches sprouted from his back and arms, writhing around him. "She's mine!"

Tru stood with Jasmine, blocking access to Cali.

"Jaz, do you have a spare weapon?"

She extracted a knife from her thigh holster and handed it to him. "I want that back."

"I'll do my best."

Sprout, the aptly named god of plants, roared and drew a blade.

The branches of a nearby weeping willow grabbed one of the straggling onlookers. She screamed and dropped in a dead faint. A blond man scooped her up and followed the fleeing crowd.

Justyn pushed Lynna and two others in the proper direction and turned back for his sisters. "Come on!"

Cali shoved Daffi toward him. "Run!"

"I'm not leaving you here." Daffi grasped Cali's hands.

"Go with her!" Jasmine yelled and charged Sprout.

Tru cut to the right and stepped too close to a holly bush. It poked him with its sharp leaves like hundreds of needle jabs, driving him into range of the creepers on Sprout's back. Tru slashed at them, severing two before a third wrapped around his wrist. He yanked back, snapping the vine.

Jasmine and Sprout circled each other, both searching for an opening.

Mica and Beck raced into the clearing and drew their weapons. "We'll deal with him. Gale's on his way." Mica darted between Jasmine and Sprout. "Get Justice to safety."

Sprout jabbed his blade into Mica's belly, and the steel shattered.

She grinned. "Marble wins." She attacked, and he backed away.

Beck snuck up from behind and seized Sprout's

throat. "Go! Now!" The creepers plunged into Beck's body.

Tru took off, Jasmine beside him.

Storm clouds rolled overhead, and fat raindrops pounded the ground. Within moments, it was a downpour. Tru squinted through the dark curtain and pushed on. They caught up to Dariel, Daffi, and Cali at the crap-covered statue.

A blast of wind grabbed Cali's blue parasol and flipped it inside out. She fought the gusts, folded it, and picked up her skirts with her free hand.

Tru wrapped his arm around her waist. "I've got you."

They raced by the daisy flowerbed, squinting against flying leaves and debris, and exited the garden.

In the parking zone, shrieking women dove into coaches. Footmen slammed doors, drivers flicked reins, and the area cleared. Several horses snorted and stomped at the hitching rail, abandoned by their riders. Those men must have found rides in the fleeing coaches.

Cali's carriage pulled up. A guard hopped off the back, opened the door, and offered his hand to Daffi. She grasped it and climbed inside. Cali held out her hand and lifted her skirt.

A gust of wind hit her and shoved her into Tru. She cried out.

"I've got you." He hoisted her into the vehicle.

Jasmine cursed. "We weren't fast enough." Water sluiced over her face and drenched her robes, but she raised her sword and stared into the darkness.

Tru slammed the door and spun, knife ready.

A massive man with flowing white hair and bulging muscles emerged from the mists, his leather clothing dry.

Gale, the god of storms. "Give me the spark, and everyone else lives."

"No." Jasmine charged him.

He lifted his palm, and a bolt of lightning hit her in the chest.

She collapsed in a sodden heap.

A chill swept through Tru's body. "No!" He ran at Gale, squinting against the howling winds and sleeting rain.

Gale held up his hand again.

Tru dropped to the ground, rolled on his shoulders, and gained his feet within striking distance of Gale.

He aimed for Tru's face.

Tru ducked and slashed at Gale's thigh. Blood spurted.

Dariel popped up at Gale's side and stabbed him in the shoulder.

He whirled and limped backward toward Cali's carriage, firing lightning bolts and gusts at Tru and Dariel.

Tru dodged, heart pounding, leaning into the wind, itching to sheath his knife in godly flesh. His belly wound, mostly healed, burned. Had it opened again?

A strike hit Dariel in the arm. He fell, grasping his bicep. A sharp gust caught him and shoved him across the parking area.

Gale stepped over Jasmine's body and neared the coach door.

It flew open, smacking him in the temple. He staggered back.

Cali leaned out and slapped him in the face with her parasol.

His nose snapped with a loud crunch. Blood gushed.

Great shot! Tru surged forward.

Cali flicked her parasol again, nailing Gale's throat.

He staggered back, gagging, clutching his neck.

Tru buried his knife in the god's kidney.

Gale blinked once, faded to mist, and floated away on the storm.

Tru sucked air and stared at Cali. "Well done."

"Jasmine!" Cali jumped out, ran to the priestess, and rolled her over.

She groaned and winced. "That hurt."

"You're alive." Cali hugged Jasmine. "Don't ever do that again! You scared me breathless. Let's get you home."

"I've got Dariel." Tru jogged to the enforcer and hoisted him up. "Can you walk?"

"Probably."

Tru helped Dariel into the carriage. "You're all set?"

Jasmine lay across the bench, her head and shoulders cushioned in Cali's lap. "Get in. There's room for you."

"I need to grab Lady. She's terrified." Tru tossed Jasmine's knife on the floor, shut the door, and stepped up to the driver's box. "Wait two minutes for me. I'm going to collect the rest of the horses, then I'll follow you back to the palace."

The driver nodded. "I understand."

"Don't lose me! I don't know the way."

The driver's jaw dropped. "Highness, I would never leave ya."

Tru grinned. "I appreciate it." He crossed to Lady and took a few moments to quiet her. Thankfully, the storm was abating. The wind had died, and the rain slowed to a drizzle. "You'll get a rub down and a treat in a bit."

She nuzzled his hair and snorted.

Tru gathered the reins of the three other horses, climbed into Lady's saddle, and fell in behind the coach. *What an outing*. If Cali hadn't been taught how to defend herself, or had been afraid to enter the fight, Gale might have won. Tru shivered. Cali would be dead instead of riding back to comfort and safety. Maybe it'd be best if she remained in the palace.

The return trip through empty rain-soaked streets went quickly. They passed through the palace gates, and the spooked horses nickered and tossed their heads at the scent of home.

The carriage stopped by the portico. Three guards rushed out to assist.

Tru rode Lady toward the stable.

"Highness." The driver hopped down. "I'll take them for ya. Get inside and warm up."

"I can do this. Lady needs a rub down."

The driver bowed. "I will see to it personally. Please, sir. Allow me ta carry out my duties. If the stable master finds ya brushing a horse, it's my hide he'll tan."

Tru'd been there before. He dismounted. "Very well." He pulled a coin from his pouch and handed it over. "Thank you."

The driver's eyes widened at the silver. "She'll receive the best care."

"And a treat?"

"An entire apple."

Tru slapped the man's shoulder. "I appreciate it."

Cali called his name, and he turned. She stood beneath the covered portico.

He crossed to her. "You shouldn't have waited for

me." He offered her his arm and escorted her through the double doors and into the crowd of waiting maids with drying cloths.

She squeezed his hand. "Thank you again."

He bowed. "It was my pleasure."

The maids descended on Cali, Daffi, and Jasmine. Within moments, they'd been whisked up the stairs.

"Highness." Another maid curtsied and handed him a drying rag. "Please come with me."

He scrubbed the cloth over his hair and followed. His mother would be so upset at his ruined outfit. The damn leggings had split in three places. And wasn't it bad for silk to get wet?

****

I followed Daffi as she headed for Rosi's bedchamber. Candles in mirrored sconces gave off a cheery glow and a bayberry scent. Jasmine walked beside me, her hand trailing along the polished stone wall. Her eyes were glassy. She veered hard to the right and slammed into Justyn's bedroom door. I grabbed her arm. "What's wrong?"

"A bit dizzy."

"Does your chest hurt?"

She massaged the spot where she'd been hit. "No."

"That's amazing. It knocked you out cold."

"Oh, I remember. My heart almost stopped." Jasmine rubbed her forehead. "I want a nap. Don't we have a meal in a few hours?"

"You're not attending. You're going to sleep until dawn. I can't believe you nearly died! Don't ever do that again." Tears welled in my eyes. "I'd miss you."

Charity and Dia stood outside Rosi's room.

Daffi pointed at Dia. "I need your assistance in my

room. Charity will remain with Rosi."

Dia cast a furtive glance at me and followed Daffi.

Charity trailed Jasmine and me into Rosi's room.

The moment the door closed, Jasmine collapsed to the rug and rolled to her back, arms spread. "I haven't ached like this since my training days."

Rosi and Charity descended on Jasmine and me, stripping off wet clothing.

"Find a sleeping gown for Jasmine." I ran a brush through my hair, catching missed pins in the tines. "She's not attending the meal."

"Yes, I am." She dug through her pack. "I'm your protector."

"I'll request Dariel."

"You'll get us both."

Rosi took the brush from me and attacked my hair. "Tell me about the event. Who did you speak to?"

Jasmine laughed. "The better question is, who did she offend?" She tugged on leather leggings.

Rosi gasped and slapped my shoulder. "Tell me you didn't!"

"Ow." I rubbed the sore spot. "Only people who deserved it. Lynna of Olerio. She was hanging off Tr—Freidrick like a harlot."

"And those boys." Jasmine pulled a cotton shirt from her pack and shook it. As if that would eliminate wrinkles.

"Artur, Edmun, and Heath." I glanced at Rosi in the mirror. "They deserved it, too. Artur stared at Daffi's chest, and Heath insulted Jasmine." My voice held steady, but my insides fluttered like a leaf in a windstorm. Gale had almost killed us! Would he enter the palace grounds once he recovered? And how had he found me amidst all those fancy frocks? Did I glow like a guide stone or something?

Charity opened the wardrobe. "Which one do you want for tonight?"

I swallowed. *Pull it together, Cali. The evening isn't over yet.* "My sapphire one." We'd all be expected to wear blue, but Rosi's only suitable dress contained too much lace. I'd replaced it with satin ribbon on my matching gown.

Rosi yanked too hard on the brush, and my head snapped back.

"Slow down, killer. My hair's not your enemy."

"The blue gown is in your room. I'll go get it. Charity, fix Her Highness's hair somehow."

Charity grinned and bobbed. "Yes, Princess."

An hour later, Daffi, Jasmine, and I descended the grand staircase for the evening meal.

With luck, I'd be seated beside Prince Shaded, touch his hand, and start my life as a goddess. Then Jasmine and Tru wouldn't be endangered anymore.

If Shaded doesn't show, I'll hunt him down.

Chapter Thirty-One

Bronwyn had outdone herself. One long table stretched down the center of the hall for the emperor and his wives, the visiting kings and queens, their younger progeny, and a few elevated guests. Dark-blue linens, fine white dishes, crystal goblets, and a vast centerpiece of fresh flowers and bayberry-scented candles offered an elegant and sophisticated dining experience.

Around the perimeter of the room were ten four-person tables with red tablecloths and napkins, white candles in glass votives, and pink rosebuds floating in bowls of tinted water.

All the dinner guests gathered near the walls, awaiting instructions. Most of the women wore their house colors: Acoris in sapphire, Kurik in malachite green, Rigolan in onyx, Tulya in citrine, and Olerio in turquoise. Three of my sisters opted to break up the monotony and showed up in cream.

The men chose the safe choice of black, although Tru wore brown.

My heart fluttered. How could a man be that handsome?

The young woman next to me whispered to her neighbor. "I hear Prince Shalek isn't feeling well. He's in his room suffering."

Poor man. Hopefully, Shaded wasn't sick.

Bronwyn raised her hand and smiled. "Welcome,

everyone. Tonight's event will be special. I'd like all the ladies to sit two per table."

Prime, nineteen females could not fill twenty seats. Same with the men.

She must have noticed because she zeroed in on Jasmine. "Priestess, please join Rosilee to fill the last space."

Jasmine's eyes widened, and she opened her mouth.

I nudged her. "She'd be honored, Your Excellency."

Bronwyn scanned the other guests and settled on my cousin, the younger son of the Pearl Islands governor. The kid was only sixteen. "Lord Geary, please fill in the remaining seat."

He paled. "Yes, Excellency." He glanced at his older brother, Valen, but received a glare.

I waved my fingers at Geary. He hurried to my side. I leaned toward him and whispered, "You'll be fine. Just eat, nod, and smile."

He swallowed. "Sure."

Bronwyn continued. "The men will find empty seats, and the soup will be served. Use the allotted time to visit. When the maids clear the place settings, all you handsome men will rise and shift to another seat. A third and fourth moves will occur before the main course and the dessert, ensuring you dine with half the eligible women." Her gaze drifted across Jasmine. "It will be enjoyable."

Sounded like a lot of work to me, but I didn't have to move.

Bronwyn splayed her hands. "Please, ladies, find your places. Sit beside someone you don't know well." She shook her fingers at Pensie and Prescia. "No sisters seated together."

That put an Acoris woman at every table but two.

With the rustle of skirts and the swish of ruffles, we all chose our seats. Daffi and Helene sat at the table to my right. To my left, Jerys had to endure Lynna for the entire meal.

Jasmine joined me. "I feel like a fool," she whispered. "I can't eat and protect you at the same time. And do I have to speak?"

"I'll carry the conversation. And Dariel's behind me. He'll keep watch."

Bronwyn called out, "Gentlemen, please select your first dining guests."

Geary plunked himself into the chair beside me. He hooked a finger into his collar and scratched his neck, then ran his hand through his dark-brown hair.

I smoothed his ruffled hair. "Calm yourself. It'll be fine."

Artur took the other chair. "Evening, Princess." He ignored Jasmine and Geary.

The soup course had better fly.

Servants filed through the room, placing steaming bowls before diners.

The savory scents of butternut squash, sage, cinnamon, and nutmeg perfumed the air. Toasted squares of seasoned bread and sprigs of parsley dotted my orange starter course. I picked up my soup spoon.

Jasmine and Geary watched me, then selected the proper utensil from the place setting.

They were so out of their element. I couldn't resist. "First, dip into the center and skim the surface to the far side." I demonstrated.

Geary blushed.

Jasmine kicked me under the table. "I know how to

eat."

I grinned.

Silverware clanked against dishes amidst the low murmur of voices, interrupted occasionally by giggles or squeals of joy. Some of these women were laying it on too thick. Lynna's eyelashes would fall off if she continued batting them like that.

Rindi sat by Tru. A lump formed in my throat. She'd be the perfect match for him, politically. I couldn't hate her, but marriage should be for love, not peace agreements.

"Rosi, what are your future plans?" Artur plunged his spoon into his soup and scooped like he was digging a hole.

Why can't it be Tru at my table? "As the n—seventh daughter of the emperor, I've been promised to the Temple of Sirini, where I'll serve as a guard. Would you like to see my boot knife? I sharpened it this afternoon."

Jasmine nudged me with her foot again.

Artur choked and wiped his mouth. "No. Thank you. You're not to marry?"

"Not in this lifetime."

"Lucky," Geary muttered into his bowl.

"What are your plans?"

He shrugged. "I'm a cousin, so I'll be expected to wed and produce heirs. But I won't ever reach the throne."

Artur was from Kurik. Who had that throne? I'd paid attention during that class. "Simon is the heir of Kurik, yes?"

Artur shoveled more butternut squash. "Yes. His twin, Sidel, is second in line. I'm third. I was hoping to make a match with your sister Jerys or perhaps one of the

Tulya cousins."

I scanned the room. "I'm not familiar with them. Are they here now?"

He pointed—*pointed!*—across the room at two dark-haired women in yellow. "That's Hilma and Hildi. They have no shot at the throne, so they'd be approved by my father."

"How lovely for them." I finished my soup and signaled for a servant.

Jasmine and Geary picked up their dirty bowls and handed them to the girl, who blushed and scurried off.

I leaned toward Geary. "You're supposed to let her take them."

Artur sneered. "Uncouth commoners."

Geary glared. "I'm a minor noble."

Jasmine fingered her knife hilt. "And I'm armed."

Bronwyn stood. "Gentlemen, please rise and move to another table. Take your napkin."

Thank the goddess. I patted Geary's hand. "Sit with Daffi."

Chaos ensued. Some men went left and others right, but after several well-timed instructions from Bronwyn, they all found seats.

A dark-haired man with sapphire-blue eyes bowed before taking the seat by me. A blond gentleman with olive-green eyes and a cleft chin took the other chair.

All the spit in my mouth dried up. He looked so much like Tru; they must be related. This was one of the Rigolan triplets! "Good evening, gentlemen. I'm Rosilee. This is my friend, Priestess Jasmine."

The blue-eyed crown prince smiled at me. "Simon of Kurik." He bobbed his head at Jasmine. "Thank you for filling in. I hope you're not too uncomfortable."

"I'm fine. Thank you for noticing my personhood."

Simon laughed. "You were stuck with Artur?"

She grinned.

The blond man nodded at me. "I'm Shanen of Rigolan. Call me Shane. I met you two days ago on the hayride, but I don't blame you for not remembering me."

My smile faltered. If he wanted to continue a conversation he'd begun with Rosi, I'd be hard-pressed to succeed. And he was the wrong triplet. "I apologize."

"No problem." He spread his napkin in his lap. "I'm used to being confused with my brothers. Sometimes we play pranks and pretend to be each other. Have you ever done that?"

I choked back a chuckle. "Occasionally."

Servants brought out appetizers: crab-and-mozzarella-stuffed mushrooms, savory lamb and blue cheese bruschetta, lemony tapenade and roasted asparagus tips with crusty bread rounds, and salty-sweet prosciutto-wrapped figs. My mouth watered, and I picked up the appropriate fork.

Jasmine studied hers, selected the correct one, and stared at her plate.

"Try the mushrooms. You'll like crab."

"I will?" She speared one and sniffed it.

Shane smiled. "You don't have to eat it if you don't want to."

"I'm not one to waste food." She ate everything on her plate, though I noticed she swallowed her asparagus whole with a swig of wine.

Simon led a lively discussion of the trade dispute between Kurik and the Jewel Islands. Shane agreed that the latter were robbing Kurik with the unfair tariffs and proposed new terms, if the leaders of both nations would simply listen to his ideas.

He made sense, but no one wanted my opinion. "What of the rumors of a civil war? I hear troops are amassing on the border."

Shane wiped his mouth with the back of his hand. "I haven't heard anything."

Bronwyn rose. "Entrée shift. Don't forget your napkins."

Simon stood and bowed. "Ladies, thank you for a lovely appetizer course."

Shane grabbed his napkin—so he knew it existed— darted to an empty spot by Helene, and kissed her fingers.

The scuff of shoes on marble and the susurrus of silks and velvets lasted a few moments until all the men found a new place.

One of Shanen's brothers sat beside me, and Tru took the other spot. "Ladies." He nodded at Jasmine and gave me a smile.

I offered him my hand, and he kissed my fingers.

Lynna glared at me.

I winked at her and turned my attention back to Tru. "Thank you for joining us."

"My pleasure."

The other suitor bowed. "Good evening. I'm Shaded, but everyone calls me Shade."

My counterpart. *Finally!* My stomach churned, but I smiled and held out my hand.

Shade stretched his hand across the table to Tru. "Cousin. Nice to meet you."

Tru rose from his chair slightly to complete the gesture. "Thanks. I appreciate that."

"I'm Rosi." I waggled my fingers at Shade again.

He took my hand, planted a sloppy, moist kiss on it, and released.

Absolutely nothing happened.

He gulped his wine and grinned at Jasmine. "A priestess! Never dined with one before."

"What a treat for you," Jasmine answered.

I stared at my hand. Why did nothing happen? Had I done something wrong? Did it take more than a touch? *Oh no*. Did I have to fall in love with this man for the spark to ignite? But that made no sense. Maelstrom and Tera hated each other, yet they'd both ascended.

I met Tru's gaze.

He shook his head slightly.

Shade wasn't Shade. He'd lied about his name. That sneaky fart. He was either Shalek or Shanen. I scoured the room for the man who'd introduced himself as Shane over appetizers. I hadn't touched him because he wasn't the correct triplet. But what if he was? What if both were playing games and giving out wrong names?

Shane was seated with Rhyada and Hildi. The moment this meal ended, I'd rush over and take his hand.

A servant brought our entrées: salmon filets with capers and lemon, baby pea pods and carrots in butter, and rice with fresh herbs and mushrooms.

Counterfeit Shade mixed it all together on his plate and shoved a forkful to his lips. "I heard you two had a nasty encounter in the garden today. What happened?"

I lowered my gaze. This course would last an eternity.

"A simple misunderstanding. Nothing major." Tru forked a bite of fish. "But the squall ruined her gown and my silk shirt. My mother was indignant."

Fake Shade laughed, displaying a mouthful of half-chewed food. "I bet she was! Auntie Mel takes fashion seriously."

I choked on my rice. He referred to the queen as Auntie Mel? Probably not to her face. "Shady—er, Shade, do you live in the castle with the royal family?"

"Sure. We've got part of the south wing. My brothers and my mother." He stirred his meal vigorously and accidentally whacked a passing servant with his elbow.

His mother had neglected to teach him dining manners. "And your father?"

He shrugged. "He died a month before we were born. He'd just turned twenty, and wham, dead. Can you believe that?"

Tru and I glanced at each other, and a flash of hurt crossed his features. I laid my hand over Tru's and squeezed his fingers. He'd recently lost his birth father, too—the older brother of Shade's father, who was the youngest of identical triplets. He either hadn't known to seek out his counterpart, or he'd failed in the attempt.

"I'm sorry for your loss."

"It's all right. I never knew him." Shade scraped the edge of his utensil against his plate and collected the puddle of butter.

My appetite vanished. "Freidrick, you'll be crowned tomorrow. Are you excited?"

"More like terrified." Tru picked at the remnants of his salmon.

Shade laughed. "Don't blame you. Shanen was to get the throne if Finna would've married him. But now you're here, and that's blown. She's livid."

I frowned. "Isn't Finna your first cousin? Why would they marry?"

"To keep the torc in the family." Shade drained his wineglass and signaled for another. "In Rigolan, women don't have inheritance rights. Finna wants to rule, but she's gotta marry Shanen to get it. If she marries one of these other fops"—he gestured to the room of suitors—"the rule goes to his family. Twisted setup if you ask me."

Indeed. And poor Finna.

Bronwyn rose. "Dessert course. Change seats."

"Ladies, it was a pleasure dining with you." Tru kissed my hand, then Jasmine's. He nodded to Fake Shade. "Cousin."

Shade stood, dumping his napkin on the floor. "That was fun." He dashed off to sit with Rindi.

Tri grimaced. "His manners need work." He squeezed my hand. "I'll see you later?"

A swarm of dragonflies took flight in my stomach. He wanted to spend time with me? Why? He'd be expected to marry one of my sisters. Or Sorka. Or maybe Helene. Meeting me later might jeopardize his chances of making a good match. "Are you sure?"

He leaned down to whisper in my ear. "The rose garden, after the meal."

The scents of sandalwood and horse made the dragonflies flap harder. A romantic setting for a secret rendezvous. "I'd love to."

Chapter Thirty-Two

Tru touched my wrist with his fingertips, smiled, and drifted over to Palama's table.

Jasmine leaned toward me and lowered her voice. "What are you doing? Stop flirting with him."

"Sorry." She was right. I needed to concentrate on finding my counterpart. Then stop the civil war. I scanned the room for Shanen. He was two tables over with Finna—or was it Farras?—and Prescia. The moment the dessert course finished, I'd dash over and grab his hand like a brazen trollop.

I sighed. Within the hour, I'd be a goddess. At that point, it'd be totally inappropriate to take a stroll through the rose garden with Tru.

One of the Olerio triplets slid into the empty chair beside me. "I'm Lev." He'd slicked his bright-red hair back into a tail, and his brown eyes glimmered. "Nice to see you again, lambkin."

We'd met many times before, but as he wore the same face as his brothers, supplying his name was courteous. He was also most likely to marry my sister Pensie, so he'd be an enjoyable companion. No pretense of flirting expected. "I'm Rosi."

Jasmine rolled her eyes. "You can ignore me."

Moments later, my cousin Valen sank into Tru's vacated chair. "Evening, ladies." His green eyes and sun-kissed brown hair matched mine, though his curls wrapped around his ears. His island skin was darker than mine, and his seafoam shirt showcased his glorious coloring.

I smiled. "Greetings, cousin. Aren't you supposed to be flirting with the eligible women tonight? Why sit with me?"

"Because if I hear one more irritating giggle, I'll lash out and say something inappropriate." He signaled for a glass of wine. "I know you won't titter or flirt with me, so you're a safe dessert companion."

Lev laughed. "Then I'll take her attention. Thank you, Valen."

"You're welcome."

A servant presented plates of almond cake with glazed violets and honey.

Jasmine picked up the last fork, frowned, and flicked the petals. "Can I eat this?"

"If you want to. Or leave it on the plate." The scents of almonds and honey swirled around the table. "Lev, how goes the courting ritual? Has Pensie agreed to marriage?"

"Actually, I found Prescia more compatible. Pensie fell for Lane." He leaned closer and lowered his voice. "Don't tell anyone, but Palama and Lucas despise each other. It might not work out for the six of us to stay together."

"Oh, that's a shame." A servant filled my teacup. A floral scent wafted from the dark liquid, and I sipped. It had the perfect tartness to cut the sweetness of the cake. "Has Lucas been looking elsewhere?"

"I think he and Hilma may make an alliance."

I scoured my memory for the genealogies. Hilma of Tulya was nowhere near her throne. Maybe a second cousin? She'd make a wonderful match for Olerio's crown prince. I nodded. "Well done. And what of Palama?"

"I hear she's set her eyes on Rigolan's new prince."

My fork clattered against the plate. She'd be suitable for him, politically, but not as strategic as Rindi or Rhyada.

Yet my throat tightened, and I blinked. What a fool, hanging on to him as if we had any chance. Meeting him in the rose garden was imprudent and selfish. Rigolan needed a southern queen to maintain the peace and keep the north from seceding. I risked not only the safety of the realm but my sisters' happiness by mucking about where I didn't belong.

Whoever he married should have his heart. I'd skip the meeting tonight.

Jasmine's foot nudged mine, and I looked up. She smiled at me.

I tucked my chin to my chest and blinked furiously. The last thing I needed was Valen and Lev to fuss over me. Which they would if they saw tears.

"Speaking of Freidrick, I hear he's being crowned tomorrow." Valen slurped his tea and winced. "My apologies. That was rude."

"Forgiven." I reached for mine. Maybe it'd open my throat.

"You going to finish your cake, Rosi?" Valen asked.

"No."

"May I?"

I passed him my plate.

He grinned. "Thanks, cousin."

"You two know each other well?" Lev asked.

Valen had a mouthful of cake, so I responded. "We

grew up together. His father and my mother are siblings, and I spent time on the islands as a child. Valen's like a brother to me."

Lev nodded. "That's great. My cousin, Lynna, is a pain. I avoid her as much as possible."

Couldn't blame him. "Who's she hoping to match with?"

"She's aiming for Freidrick, but she'll be lucky to come away with Heath or Edmun. Or maybe Geary."

I laughed. "You're kidding! Geary's at least six years her junior."

"I know, but the way she's driving away all the others, she'll be stuck with the leftovers. It'll serve her right, though I feel sorry for the boy."

Valen wiped his hands on his napkin and laced his fingers over his stomach. "Geary would be fortunate to get a woman like Lynna, but most likely he'll take a local bride. As will I."

"Didn't I see you earlier with Hildi?" My eyes were about to cross from trying to keep everyone straight.

"Yes, but she's set her eyes on Sidel."

"He's the younger Kurik heir?"

Valen scrunched one side of his mouth. "Yes. The one with the—according to every woman in the palace—gorgeous blue eyes."

I laughed. "I know who he is. And his eyes *are* amazing. Like sapphires in candlelight." Paired with his pale skin, black hair, and lean muscular build, the entire man was breathtaking.

"Could we not talk about him? Or matchmaking? I wanted to enjoy the dessert course." Valen finished his tea and leaned back. "I'm more interested in hearing about the scuffle in the gardens today. I missed it, but

I've heard rumors that you were at the heart. What happened?"

If I told him, he'd spread the tale. I shrugged and relied on Tru's story. "It was a misunderstanding. Then the squall hit, and everyone ran for cover. I got drenched."

"What kind of misunderstanding? I heard there were swords involved. Did you challenge someone to a duel?"

Lev perked up. "What? I didn't hear about any of this. Please tell us."

I stared at Jasmine. How was I to get out of this?

Bronwyn rose.

Bless you, Prime!

She clapped. "That concludes our event. Thank you for participating. I hope you enjoyed this whimsical exercise." She brought her hands together beneath her chin. "For those who wish to continue socializing, the parlor has been readied with games, seating areas, and a tea service. Our next scheduled event is tomorrow at midday when Prince Freidrick will be crowned." She sought the room for him and flashed him a smile. "Following the ceremony, we will enjoy snacks. The afternoon will be free for resting or shopping, followed by an evening meal here. Thank you."

A few of the guests applauded or offered thanks in subdued voices. Moments later, people rose from their seats with a rustle of fabrics.

I picked up my skirts and headed directly for Shanen, Jasmine on my heels. I had to dart around several people and furniture, but I made it to his side and grabbed his hand.

Nothing happened.

Damnation! Wrong triplet. I whirled to search the

room for the other one.

"Did you need something?" Shanen set his hand on my elbow.

He probably thought the hand grab was the instigation of something more intimate. I didn't care. "I'm trying to find your brother. I thought you were him."

He grinned. "Believe me, you'd prefer my company to his. He's an absolute boor."

"I know. I ate part of a meal with him." I stretched up on my toes to scan the crowd, but with all the people milling, it was impossible to find Fake Shade. Though odds were the triplet who remained in his bedchamber was the one I needed. I grabbed Shanen's hand again. "Your third brother isn't here, but I'm anxious to meet him."

Shanen's eyes narrowed, and his grin widened. "Is that how it is?"

"He's the only man at the event I haven't been introduced to, and I want to remedy that. Do you think he'd be willing to join me tonight?"

Shanen stroked his thumb across my skin. "I'll run up to our rooms and ask. If he's amenable, he'll arrive in the rose garden in one hour. If not, I'll be there to pass along his regrets."

"Thank you." I withdrew my hand and curtsied. "Good evening."

Jasmine guided me through the crowd and out the side doors into the service corridor. "If I may, you've agreed to meet with two separate men in the rose garden tonight. Should I anticipate a knife fight?"

I led her to the back stairwell. "No." I'd run from Tru if I spotted him. Unless I found Shaded first. Then I could tell Tru we were finished. A deep ache spread through my chest. I didn't want to give him up. But I had to.

We arrived at Rosi's door to find Dia leaning against the wall.

I smiled. "You may assist Daffi tonight."

She curtsied. "Yes, Princess Calilee." She turned away.

Oh no! I grabbed her shoulder. "I'm Rosi."

She ducked her head. "Please, Highness, I've been in Princess Rosilee's service for six years. I know the difference between the two of you."

This could be a disaster. "Come with me." I opened the door to Rosi's room and stepped inside, Jasmine and Dia behind me.

Rosi's eyes widened, and she covered her face with her hands.

Brilliant disguise, sister. "Dia knows."

Rosi sighed at her maid. "I'm sorry. It's supposed to be a secret."

Dia bobbed. "I understand, Highness. I would never betray your confidence."

"Thank you." I crossed to the vanity. If I were to ascend tonight, I couldn't do it in this gown. "Please help me. I want my mulberry frock, black boots, and black shawl. And let's do something different with my hair. Loose, maybe?" I began pulling pins and decor from my curls.

This was it. I'd finally ascend. Would it hurt, changing to an immortal? I'd love a pair of wings, though maybe that was asking too much. It would attract attention.

Tru would love them.

I gripped the vanity stool. Would my feelings for him change, as well? What if I felt nothing for him as a goddess? What if my personality altered, and I turned into an aloof, uncaring being who only dispensed justice? Sweet Sirini, would I be as hated as the other gods?

Within twenty minutes, Jasmine and I headed to the ground floor. My stomach had soured, and I pressed my hand against my belly. I had to break out of this foul mood.

Bronwyn's rose garden spread out behind the southern wing of the palace. Detouring through the parlor would be quicker, but diners were socializing there. Instead, I led Jasmine through the breakfast room and out onto a paved terrace lined with miniature maple trees and boxwood hedges. A breeze whispered through the branches and left goose bumps on my arms. Guide stones delineated the path.

I took a right and passed through a wide trellis packed with grapes. We emerged into another torch-lit area that featured a four-tiered fountain and stone benches. One young couple occupied a bench, holding hands, their chaperone neatly hidden in the shadows. Was that Justyn and Finna? Or maybe Farras?

I hurried by. "Pardon us."

I pushed between two rose topiaries into Bronwyn's garden. She tended the plants herself, though gardeners cared for everything else, including the lawn surrounding the beds and the kidney-shaped goldfish pond at the center. Moonlight flashed on water and the wrought iron foot bridge that arched over it.

Every raised bed showcased a different species of rose and a life-sized statue of a previous empress. Low-lying geranium, pansies, and salvia complemented each arrangement. Bluestone pavers wove between them to wrought-iron benches, birdbaths, and a beehive. The path terminated at the entrance of a small labyrinth of silver ornamental grasses that featured a gazebo in the middle, illuminated faintly by amber guide stones.

It was a great place for covert meetings between lovers. Or counterparts.

"Do you see anyone?" I whispered.

"Not in this light," Jasmine answered. "Why are you whispering?"

"I don't know."

The murmur of fabric against plant-life made me whirl.

Prince Shaded of Rigolan approached, a smug grin on his handsome face.

Finally! Time to become a goddess.

Chapter Thirty-Three

Arguing with his mother or the valet did no good.
Tru donned the heavy maroon "brocade"—whatever that
was—jacket over his cotton shirt and suede leggings.
The seamstress had altered several of his father's
garments to fit better, but not the jacket. Tru held out his
arms, and the shoulder seams threatened to strangle him.
If he wasn't careful, he'd have more split stitching for
his mother to fuss over.

The valet brushed a pair of black shoes to a gleam
and handed them to Tru.

He laced them up and waved off a cloak. "It's a
warm evening, and I won't be long."

"Do you need a chaperone?" Mother hovered in the
common area, watching him through the open doorway.

Finna laughed and sprawled in an oversized chair,
hooking one leg over the arm. "How is he to take liberties
if you send along a watcher? Really, Mother, think this
through. Freidy needs quality time alone with his
inamorata."

Her tongue had grown sharper in the few scant hours
they'd spent together, but how could he blame her? He'd
stolen the throne from her by just showing up. Tru stood,
adjusted his collar, and headed toward them. "Rosi has a
chaperone, so I won't need one. And this isn't a lover's
meeting. We're friends. She's to become a priestess." He
swatted Finna's slippered foot, knocking her leg off the

chair. "And please don't call me Freidy, or I'll call you Finnie in front of Justyn."

She glared.

"Mother, the parlor will be crowded." He tugged at the jacket sleeves, but they'd never fully cover his wrists. "Is there another route to the rose garden?"

She circled him, her fingers trailing along the tight seams. "Go through the breakfast room to the terrace and turn right. Follow the path until you reach the gardens. Maybe you'd better take this off and wear the cloak. The threads are already pulling." She didn't wait for his approval but yanked it down his arms.

"Thank you, Mother." He took the dark green cloak from the valet and fastened it with a malachite and silver pin. "I'll be back soon."

"Don't leave her too early, brother," Finna said. "Make sure she's satisfied."

"At least I have someone to meet up with tonight, sister."

Finna sputtered.

Tru smiled. "I'll see you in the morning, Mother." He kissed her cheek and left.

Her instructions were perfect, and a few minutes later, he entered the rose garden. A familiar raised voice drew him to the far side, where he found Cali, Jasmine, and one of his cousins.

"You've lied to me twice!" Cali planted her fists on her hips. "Do you find this amusing? Because I do not."

His cousin's eyes widened. "I assure you, Princess, I'm Prince Shaded."

The dandelion stench smacked Tru in the face, and he sneezed.

Cali pointed at him. "See? Confirmation you speak

falsely."

The man stared at Tru. "How does he prove anything?"

"Because Sirini gave him a gift. He smells lies."

Tru winced. He didn't want his cousins knowing that. Yet.

Her eyes narrowed. "Deceive me one more time, and I'll tell Queen Melissendra that you call her Auntie Mel. Now where is Prince Shaded?"

The man gazed at his boots. "You're correct. I'm Shale. My brother didn't want to come, so he asked me to take his place."

"Why doesn't he want to meet me?" Cali asked.

Shale shrugged. "I don't know. He told me to find out if you kiss well."

Tru's fists clenched. *That slime!*

Cali slapped Shale's face. "How dare you!"

Exactly.

Shale cradled his reddened cheek. "What was I supposed to think? You grabbed Shane's hand shamelessly, and you asked to meet Shade in this romantic spot…" He glanced at Tru. "Why is he here? Are you into threesomes?"

Cali surged forward and growled.

Growled! Tru grinned. This was more entertaining than sparring with Finna.

Jasmine hauled Cali back. "He's not worth it."

Cali's narrowed eyes glittered in the torch light. "Tell Prince Shade that I have important information, life-or-death stakes, both his and mine. I'm not interested in a kiss. I simply want to pass along the message. Are you capable of delivering that, or should I march up to your suite and ask the guards to break down the door?"

Shale swallowed. "I can deliver it."

"Excellent. I will remain here for one hour tonight, or he can find me tomorrow."

Shale bowed and backed away. "Good evening." The moment he disappeared into shadows, his footfalls pounded fast and heavy on the paving stones.

"You'd better run, you slug." She grunted, then turned to Tru. "I pity you being related to him. His eating habits are even more atrocious than his social manners."

Tru took her hands in his. "I'm sorry you haven't located your counterpart. If he hasn't found you by the coronation tomorrow, I'll call for him and hold him until you arrive."

"Call all three of them. Otherwise, they'll send another substitute. They act like children, impersonating each other." She shivered and released his hands to pull her shawl tighter.

"Would you like my cloak?" He unfastened the pin.

"No, I'll be fine. I need to stay in case Shaded shows up. I won't impose upon you."

An hour? He'd remain all night. "I'll keep you company. Shall we walk?"

She smiled and took his offered arm.

Jasmine blended into the shadows. "I'll be nearby."

They walked between the raised beds and caught up on their day—the first time in a quarter-moons they'd been apart. Cali laughed at his barbed taunts to his sister and cooed over his hatred of the new, stupid clothing.

He sighed. "My mother refuses to allow me leather leggings. Suede is the closest, though she prefers cotton or linen. I swear, I'm going to rip that flimsy fabric and ruin all my father's garments."

"You should hire a team of seamstresses to make

you new things."

"It's in process, but it takes time."

She giggled. "I'm sorry you're having a hard time adjusting."

"No, you're not! You just laughed."

"Because it's funny." She steered him toward the fishpond and out to the center of the footbridge. Moonlight glinted off the water. Tiny splashes hinted at fish, frogs, or bugs. A faint breeze rustled the lily pads and cattails.

"What a beautiful place." He caught her gaze. "To share with a beautiful woman."

She leaned back against the railing. "Tru, this is wrong. We shouldn't be here."

He placed his hands on either side of her hips and pressed his lips to her forehead. "I know. But why waste the moonlight?"

Her fingers splayed across his chest, and the heat of her skin sent a shiver down his spine.

She sighed. "We won't fall out of love if we continue in this manner. And I thought you were angry at me."

"It's not possible to stop loving you." He nuzzled her hair, caught in her honeysuckle perfume. "I was angry, but I couldn't hang on to it. I ache to hold you, Cali. It's driving me insane, watching you with other men."

Her arms encircled his waist. "It's worse for me, seeing you with all those women, because I know you'll marry one of them. We need to quit our feelings for each other. Your wife deserves your heart. She won't be willing to share it with me. Especially if she's one of my sisters."

"I'm not marrying one of your sisters, Cali." He couldn't resist. He cupped her face and pressed his lips against hers.

Her soft curves melted into him. Heat flared at her touch. Then her tongue met his, and fire exploded in his core. He wrapped his arms around her as cicadas buzzed, frogs croaked, and the pond burbled.

He kissed her jaw, her ear, her neck. "I'll find a way to be with you, Cali. No one will keep us apart." He kissed her cheek and tasted salt. He pulled away. Moonlight reflected on the moisture. "Oh, beloved. I didn't mean to make you cry." He brushed her tears away. "What's wrong?"

She rested her forehead against his chest. "There is no way for us, Tru. It's foolish to hang on to that dream." She stepped back. "This is unfair to both of us. Please, go. I'll wait here for Shade and fulfill my destiny. You go inside and forget me."

He grasped her hands. "I can't forget you."

"You must." She turned and ran toward the gazebo, stomping through the grasses instead of following the labyrinthine path.

Jasmine glared at Tru and followed Cali into the structure.

He swallowed around the lump in his throat. Everything was ruined. Life would be miserable without her. He had to find a solution because he simply couldn't let her go. His heart would burst.

Nor could he leave the area while she lingered. He found a bench in the shadows of an ornamental tree with a view of the gazebo. If Shaded showed up, Tru would watch Cali become a goddess.

An hour later, she and Jasmine left.

Fine. Once he was king, Tru would make sure she and his cousin met.

****

The following morning, Tru endured Finna's verbal barbs over the meal. Couldn't she see how it hurt their mother? But no, Finna had no compassion for anyone. At least Farras tried to be friendly and helpful.

There'd been no sign of his cousins.

The team of tailors finished his new suit an hour before the ceremony began. Tru accepted the valet's help, because without the assistance, he'd be late.

Thankfully, the burgundy silk shirt didn't strangle him. Instead, it had a V-neck to showcase his house mark and leave his throat bare for the royal torc.

Sweat pooled in his armpits. Why did he have to be king? He'd rather hand it to Finna and hang out in the stables. Or serve as Cali's head priest wherever she chose to live. Which would probably be High Point, unless Sirini demanded elsewhere. Regardless, he'd follow her.

But not with a damned torc around his neck.

He strapped his father's bejeweled sword to his belt and slid his knife into a sheath on the other hip. The blades were purely ceremonial.

He brushed his hands down the well-fitting gray suede leggings. *What a heel.* Cali had twenty-two days to find her counterpart or die, and he was anxious about his crowning? He was better than that. He picked up Cali's bone button, caressed it, and slipped it into his pocket.

"Are you ready, dear?" Mother stood in the doorway of his bedchamber. She'd retired her mourning frock to don a silver gown with black lace and onyx jewelry.

"Almost." He pinned an onyx medallion to his gray

vest and presented himself. "Does this meet with your approval?"

She smiled, and her eyes turned glassy. "You look like your father on his coronation day. He wore gray and burgundy, as well." She opened her arms.

He embraced her. "Thank you, Mother."

"For what?" She pulled away and cupped his face in her hands.

"For welcoming me so warmly."

"I love you, Freidrick. Sirini blessed me by returning you to me after I lost Franklin. I will do anything to keep you happy."

Some things she could not do, and he wouldn't ask. He offered his arm. "Shall we?" His sisters, also dressed in silver and black, fell in behind him and his mother.

The main hallway was crowded with other guests heading for the ceremony. Those around him smiled and congratulated him as they made their way down the grand staircase and into the throne room.

Emperor Rhys wore a sapphire silk shirt, gray brushed suede leggings, and black boots. Empress Bronwyn sat beside him in a blue gown with gray ruffles. Duchess Dorana and Duchess Eilee perched on the bench in sapphire and white.

Stanchions with velvet ropes created an aisle up the center leading to the dais. Tru escorted his family to the front. He nodded to the emperor's children and caught Cali's gaze.

Her cheeks flushed, and she dropped her gaze.

He slid his hand into his pocket and caressed the bone button. He'd find a way.

Beck and Mica glided down the aisle, dressed in silks. She smiled. "It's a fine day for a coronation."

The crowd gaped, eyes wide.

Tru bowed. "You honor me."

Beck scanned the full front rows. "Mind if we stand?"

Justyn and Jayson rose and bowed. "Please, take these seats as our most honored guests." Cali's brothers moved to the side wall.

Beck and Mica took the emptied spaces between Jerys and Prescia. Both women blushed and stared at their fingers.

Mica patted Jerys's hand. "We don't bite."

Tru stifled a smile with clenched lips. Maybe having deities present wasn't a common event. Cali changed everyone's world.

Emperor Rhys approached the edge of the dais. "Welcome, honored guests." His voice carried through the room, but his gaze lingered on Beck and Mica before shifting. "Crown Prince Freidrick Cromwell Rigolan. Come forth."

The entire room silenced like an empty tomb.

That was his full name? *How pretentious.* Tru kissed his mother's cheek and turned to Emperor Rhys. "Your Excellency." He stepped forward and dropped to one knee, palms sweating and heart pounding.

"Rise."

Tru stood and squared his shoulders. The Rigolan torc lay on a black satin pillow on a pedestal, and he cringed. He wasn't ready for this burden. He had no clue how to rule a kingdom.

The emperor launched into his speech, explaining the form of government, the allegiance of the kings to the emperor, and on and on.

Tru held his rigid stance. His gaze wandered to the

empress and the other wives. All three offered faint smiles and held adoration for the emperor in their eyes. They loved him, even though the first two were political matches.

Some arranged marriages produced loving relationships. His mother and father were further proof. But others… If Finna married Shanen, they'd be at each other's throats. What was wrong with these people? Forcing their offspring to marry for strategy, peace, or stability. They were excellent goals, but at what cost? Weren't there other ways to prevent war or cement treaties?

Emperor Rhys picked up the Rigolan torc, stepped off the dais, and stopped before Tru. They were the same height, eye to eye. "Do you solemnly swear to uphold all the laws of the realm, to perform your duties to the best of your ability, to protect the welfare of your people, and to bring honor to the sacred responsibilities of your station?"

Tru nodded. "I do swear."

Emperor Rhys held up the torc for the crowd. Sunlight flashed against the gold-and-bronze choker covered in intricate scrollwork. He gripped the two ends and stretched the opening, his powerful arms bulging from the strain. Large onyx stones set in the knobby buffers winked. He wrestled the torc around Tru's neck and released it. It sprang back to its original shape. Emperor Rhys positioned the buffers to rest on Tru's collarbone above his house mark. "Congratulations."

The weight of the bauble bore down on Tru like an iron yoke. "Thank you."

Rhys bellowed at the crowd. "King Freidrick Rigolan!"

"King Freidrick!" they called back, followed by cheers. Some tossed streamers of ribbon into the air. Others flung flower petals.

Finna threw a copper coin at him. It bounced off his chest and rolled away.

He ignored her and stood before the crowds like an exhibit they'd paid to view, his hands clenched behind his back. Thank the goddess it was over. Now for the reception, which hopefully served ale. And a lamb chop. His stomach growled.

Emperor Rhys crossed to Mother and bowed, kissed her fingers, and offered congratulations. She blushed and giggled like a woman half her age.

Tru smiled. She deserved some happiness.

Farras approached. It was still odd, seeing his own green eyes staring up at him from someone else's face. But he wouldn't trade his family for the world now that he'd found them.

She curtsied. "Brother, they await you to lead the way. Shall we?"

He offered his arm. "Thank you. I haven't yet learned all the protocols. Where is the reception?"

"The Blue Room, through there." She motioned with her chin to a side door.

He turned to the front row. "Water and Stone, would you care to join us?"

Beck and Mica nodded. She took his arm, and he walked her to Tru's side.

"I can't believe you came," he whispered as he headed for the door.

"We were invited," Beck growled.

Mica patted his arm. "Seemed rude to turn down the offer."

Cali must have done that. Or maybe Jasmine, placing extra guards around Cali? He escorted Farras through the doorway, and the crowd fell in behind them.

The gathering did not serve ale, lamb chops, or anything more substantive than tiny appetizers that often slipped through his fingers before he could get them into his mouth. He was laughed at a few times, but he didn't care.

Beck and Mica walked one loop through the room, then took up positions near the doors. Their gazes never left Cali. Someone was bound to notice. Maybe Jasmine should warn them they were conspicuous.

The moment he set his plate down, Lynna and Palama latched on to his arms. His mother expected him to mingle with everyone, including the other kings and queens, but hauling the two princesses around grew old. He found a sofa to seat three and dropped into it. Visitors could come to him.

His mother rescued him. "Freidrick, please attend me."

Palama and Lynna began to rise from the sofa.

Mother raised her eyebrows. "I do not require your attendance, ladies."

Lynna clenched her teeth but bobbed her head. "Certainly."

Palama picked up her skirts and hurried away.

Tru offered his arm to his mother and whispered, "Thank you!"

She patted his hand. "My pleasure. I'd like to introduce you to King Shalamon of Kurik and his queens."

Tru sighed. The afternoon would take forever.

Chapter Thirty-Four

Prince Shaded did not attend the morning meal in the breakfast room. Or the coronation. Jasmine and I wove through the crowds exiting the throne room, then milled through the Blue Room for hours. We found Shale, again masquerading as Shade, but the open-mouthed laugh full of food gave him away. Later, I spotted one of them ducking out onto the patio, but by the time I got there, he'd disappeared.

I clenched my teeth and stomped back to the Blue Room, Jasmine at my side. "When I find that ill-mannered slug, he'll wish he'd crawled to me in the rose garden with a peace offering and a contrite heart."

"What sort of peace offering?" She snagged a cheese-stuffed mushroom off the buffet table and popped it into her mouth.

"I don't know. Flowers. Sweets. His brothers in restraints."

A servant with a tray of wineglasses walked by, and I helped myself. I gulped it down and set it back on the tray.

Jasmine grinned. "Maybe you'd better take Tru up on his offer. And if he can't get the three men in the same room at the same time, your father certainly can."

"Now there's a thought." I curtsied to the Tulya queen who caught my gaze and hurried across the room toward Daffi.

She and Jerys huddled in a corner behind a potted plant in a couple of padded chairs they'd dragged over. They both wore sapphire gowns and comfortable slippers. Jerys had piled her auburn curls atop her head while Daffi had braided her hair and coiled it at the back of her neck. They slumped as if they'd just run footraces in the back greens.

Jerys would become suspicious if I asked her to leave, so I'd have to be careful what I said. I perched on the arm of Daffi's chair. "No sign of Shade anywhere."

She patted my hand. "I'm sorry. Everyone I've interviewed says they've only seen two of them at one time. I gathered the trio have never appeared together at any event in the past eight days." She frowned. "Although they must have arrived together. Maybe I can locate the driver or the footman of their carriage."

"Don't bother. I've come up with a different plan."

Jerys smiled, leapt from her chair, and hugged me. "You're not Rosi!" she whispered in my ear. "Why didn't you tell me you'd survived?"

I patted her back. "I'm trying not to endanger Rosi and Daffi. Keep it to yourself, please. I couldn't bear to lose either of them to an angry mob."

"Who else knows?" Jerys pulled away but kept her arm around my shoulders.

"Papa, my mother, Rosi, Daffi, and Justyn. I assume Papa informed Bronwyn and Dorana, also, but I'm not sure."

"Tell me what's going on and who you're searching for." She glanced at Jasmine. "And who your shadow is."

I told Jerys everything except my romantic feelings for Tru.

She scanned the room. "I can't believe you traveled

with the lost prince. Is he a good man?"

"The best. Kind, compassionate, humble, and selfless."

She whipped around to stare at me, and her lips slid into a grin. "Someone's taken a fancy to an eligible young king."

My shoulders tensed. "He's not for me. Please drop it."

She nodded and squeezed my shoulder. "I'm sorry. I didn't mean to upset you. So how can I help? I'm sure the three of us can corner one man without asking Papa."

Daffi laughed. "I suggest we march up to his suite and bang on the door. If he didn't attend the coronation, surely he's still in his room."

A chill shot down my spine. "What if he left the palace days ago and no one's seen him because he isn't here?" I had twenty-one more days to find him, or we both died. If he ran off, how would I track him? If he departed the same day he arrived, he had a twelve-day head start. But where would he have gone?

"Why would he leave?" Jasmine asked.

"I don't know." I smoothed my hands down my skirt. "Maybe he left with a lover. Have any of the event women disappeared? Or were we expecting someone who never arrived?"

"Everyone who should be present is here. Except Rhygan." Jerys returned to her chair.

What if Shaded was behind Rhygan's disappearance? This entire time, I'd been thinking of Shaded as a good man, a worthy counterpart. But what if he was like Maelstrom, power-hungry? The world would be better off without another god like that.

Maybe I shouldn't find him. Maybe that's why

cornering him had been so hard—Sirini was keeping us apart. If we didn't ascend, he'd die, and everyone would be spared from him.

No. I couldn't think like that. Sirini hadn't protected anyone from Maelstrom, so why would she interfere with Shaded? My mind was going places it shouldn't.

Jerys continued. "I don't think your missing man could have left the palace without someone noticing. Remember no one could leave without an armed escort due to Rhygan's disappearance. So Shaded had to sneak by guards to get out."

Jasmine rolled her eyes. "Or dress as a servant and leave with an empty delivery wagon. Merchants pass through the gates all day."

I shook my head. "The guards know all our delivery drivers. If they spotted someone they didn't personally know, they'd investigate." Although, if he were truly motivated, maybe he'd found a way? I grunted. "This isn't helpful. I must believe he's here, or I'm in trouble."

Daffi rose. "Let's visit his suite. If he's not there, his servants will know if he has disappeared."

The four of us made it halfway across the room before Tru stepped into our path, his gaze locked on mine.

He bowed. "Ladies. Are you enjoying the reception?"

Daffi curtsied. "It's been lovely, thank you, but we must withdraw to rest before the evening meal. Congratulations on your ascension."

"Thank you. I look forward to seeing you all later tonight." He kissed her hand, and she brushed by him. He repeated the gesture with Jerys's fingers, and she followed Daffi. He reached for my hand.

My heart would shatter if he kissed me. I grabbed my skirts and curtsied. "Until tonight." I hurried after my sisters. Behind me, Jasmine muttered something to him, but I couldn't catch the words. I was too busy blinking.

She fell into place beside me. Tru appeared at my other side.

I stared up at him. "What are you doing?"

"Aiding you in your quest for my elusive cousin. He'd better have a great excuse for missing my coronation."

I stopped. "You can't leave. This is your reception."

"It's almost over. The food's been put away, and servants are hovering to clean up the mess." He nodded toward the patio. "The moment your father stepped outside with the Olerio and Kurik kings, the crowds thinned. My mother already left. I'm sure it's fine."

Lynna slithered over, her skirts hiked high enough to show off her pink ruffled stockings. "My lord, are you leaving already?"

He hooked my arm in his. "Yes. I have something I must attend to. Hopefully, I'll see you at tonight's meal."

She glared at me but curtsied. "I look forward to it."

Tru hauled me out of the room at a hurried pace, trailing Daffi and Jerys.

I grinned. "You've mastered the verbal etiquette."

"She won't leave me alone. If you'd agree to marry me, she'd have to move on."

I gasped and stopped mid-step, my heart thumping hard enough to drown out Jasmine's snicker. "What did you say?"

He pulled me aside, out of the path of Helen and Simon. Or maybe it was Sidel. I couldn't tell the difference. Did Tru just propose to me in the middle of a hallway?

His eyes burned with intensity. "I've been strongly encouraged by my mother to wed one of the emperor's daughters. They didn't say which one." He dipped to one knee and took my hand. "Will you marry me?"

My jaw dropped, and I staggered backward. Jasmine caught me. My breath lodged in my throat. My vision went spotty. In a moment, I'd faint and escape this delicious horror. "Get up."

His eyebrows rose. "What's your answer?"

"Get up!" I took a step back and scanned the hallway. If anyone saw him like that, I'd be locked in my room until he was safely married to Rindi or Rhyada. I was too low in the lineup. Damn, because of the spark, I wasn't even *in* the lineup. He couldn't marry me if his life depended on it. Which it did.

He was still on his knee, brows furrowed.

I grabbed his hands and hauled him to his feet. Or at least I tried. He didn't budge. I released him, hiked up my skirts, and ran. My satin slippers had no traction on the polished marble floor, and I skidded into a bench. Limping, I continued down the hall, tears welling in my eyes, my shin throbbing.

How could he! Wasn't it enough he stole my heart, kissed me senseless, then broke me? No, he had to stab me in the back with that dangerous, ridiculous, incredibly sweet proposal that he didn't have permission to offer.

I clamped my hand over my mouth and clambered up the stairs. If his enemies found out what he'd just done—and he had some now that he was a king—we'd both be in danger. They might not try to kill me to harm him, but they'd sure make my life miserable.

At the second-floor landing, I turned right.

Jasmine caught my arm. "They went up one more flight." She pointed after my sisters, climbing the treads at a ladylike pace.

I nodded and hurried after them, sniffing and blinking. I didn't even have a handkerchief. Or a pocket to hold one. This dress was useless.

Jasmine handed me a scrap of cotton cloth.

"Thank you." I patted my face and tucked the wet rag into my bodice.

At the third-floor landing, Daffi and Jerys went left and headed down a hallway of guest suites. I followed, my heart threatening to climb up my throat. *How could he!*

Daffi stopped before the correct door. Her gaze swept my damp face, and she hugged me. "What's wrong? Why are you weeping?"

Fresh tears welled, but I blinked. "I'm fine. Just a bit of a shock. Let's finish this." As a goddess, I'd be out of Tru's reach forever. My chest tightened, but I squared my shoulders. *Shaded, you sneaky fungus, prepare to face my wrath.*

Jerys knocked on the door.

A male servant answered. "Yes, Highness?"

Jerys smiled. "We're searching for Prince Shaded. Is he by chance in residence?"

"No, Princess. I am here alone."

"Have you seen the prince recently? We're worried about his health."

The servant frowned. "His Highness is not sick."

I pushed by Daffi to peek over the servant's shoulder. "Have you seen all three of the Rigolan triplets together in the past few days?"

"I brought them breakfast this morning." He gestured behind him to a table near the window. "They ate before heading out for the day's festivities."

Oh, thank the goddess. At least I wouldn't have to chase him around the Five Realms. "Thank you, sir. May I leave a message for Prince Shaded with you?"

He nodded. "I would be honored to pass it along."

"Princess Rosilee requests the honor of dining with him tonight at the banquet."

"It will be delivered."

I sighed and turned toward the stairs. One hurdle tripped over, one larger one to go.

****

Tru considered chasing Cali, but to what end? And why had she reacted so strangely to his proposal? She was supposed to squeal, say yes, and offer him a delectable kiss. Instead, he received…what was that? Was she angry?

He entered his family suite and unbuttoned his vest. If the day grew any warmer, he'd be tempted to strip down to his underclothes. Then again, that would upset his mother.

She'd changed into a gray cotton frock and sat reading at the dining table in the corner of the common area.

"Good afternoon." He kissed her cheek. "Did you enjoy the events?"

"I'll admit, they tired me." She pushed the book away. "Sit. We have much to discuss."

He obeyed, slinging his vest over the chair back. "Regarding?"

She poured him a cup of tea.

The lemony scent reminded him of Cali, and his

chest ached.

His mother set the teacup near his hand. "You're the king now, so these decisions are no longer mine. It is time you learn your duties." She nodded at the tome. "This is Rigolan's financial ledger. Can you, by chance, read and do sums?"

He sipped the tea. Tart and sweet. "Yes, my guardian taught me reading, writing, history, and arithmetic."

"Excellent." She tapped the first column. "These are expenditures. The next is income. The final is a running balance of our coffers."

He scanned the lines. "We aren't bringing in as much as we spend."

"You're quick."

"Who manages our finances?"

"We've an advisor, but your father frequently checked the work. Since he passed, I've been doing it." She sighed. "I can't tell you how grateful I am that you can take on that duty. It is so stressful."

He squeezed her hand. "I'm happy to relieve you of this burden. Is our financial advisor here?"

"Yes, as are three others."

"I'd like to meet them."

She twisted her teacup on the saucer. "Shall I have them sent for now?"

"Yes, as well as Finna and Farras."

She rang a bell.

He scanned the ledger page, then flipped back several.

A young woman in servant's attire approached and bobbed. "Yes, Majesty?"

Mother gave the instructions, and the servant headed

for the door.

He spotted something odd. "One moment."

The servant turned back. "Yes, Your Grace?"

"Also fetch the man who runs the emperor's stables, please."

She hurried away.

"Why would you need to see him?" Mother asked.

"I have a question." Tru studied the ledger.

Mother called for a full teapot and more cups. Finna and Farras arrived and scurried into their bedchamber.

Someone knocked, and Tru rose.

Mother grabbed his hand. "Darling, you are not a servant. You should not answer doors."

"Who else is here to do it? You sent the maid away."

She shrugged. "They will wait until she returns."

Ridiculous. He opened the door.

A tall, thin man in a silk red robe bowed. "Sire. I am Nickel, your financial advisor. I'm honored to make your acquaintance."

An ironic name. Had he taken it for his position, or had his mother saddled him with it? "Pleased to meet you. I'm Freidrick."

"King Freidrick," Mother corrected from beside him. "Son, do not omit your title to anyone who isn't family or a close friend." She glared at Nickel. "Come in. Tea?"

Nickel bowed. "I would not impose upon you, Majesty."

Tru beckoned the man in and closed the door. "I have questions regarding our finances. Are you available for a few hours?"

"I am always at your service."

Tru sat and waved for the man to take a chair.

"Darling, remind me later to teach you protocol with servants and advisors."

"Yes, Mother."

Nickel pressed his lips flat.

Tru poured another cup and slid it to Nickel. "We're waiting on others."

Finna flounced from her room in a crimson gown. "You bellowed for me, Highness?"

"No, I asked politely. Please join us." I waved at an empty spot.

She paled. "Why?"

"Because I need advisors I can trust."

She chuckled. "You trust me?"

"That remains to be seen. Have you been training to rule?"

"Since I was four."

"Then you have experience I lack. Would you care for tea?" He picked up the pot and poured the last of it into a tiny cup with pink flowers.

"Darling, honestly, you must not serve others!" Mother took it from me. "You are the king. Act according to your station."

"I apologize, Mother."

Her eyes bulged a bit. "And stop agreeing with me on everything. You're allowed to argue sometimes. Your sister certainly does." She speared Finna with a sharp look. "Sit, child, and quit gaping like a landed fish."

Finna plunked herself into a chair and stared at Tru. He slid the teacup toward her.

Farras entered and curtsied. "You wished to see me, Sire?"

"Please join us. I've added you and Finna to my cadre of advisors."

Farras grinned like she'd been offered cake and slipped into the seat beside him. "I've never been an advisor. What makes you believe I know how?"

"I merely want your input on certain matters."

"What topics, may I ask?" Nickel sat stiffly.

This will be so enjoyable. Tru crossed his arms. "First, the funds you've extorted."

Chapter Thirty-Five

Nickel sputtered. "I beg your pardon?"

Someone knocked.

Mother glared at Nickel. "Answer that. Don't try to run."

He hurried across the room and opened the door.

A man in stained leathers bowed, his hands folded at his waist. "I was told ya needed me, Sire? I work in da stables."

"Please come in." Tru picked up the ledger and met the man in the middle of the room.

Nickel remained by the open door, fidgeting with his collar.

Three more men appeared at the door and bowed. "Majesty?"

Mother nodded. "Please come in. Freidrick, these are your advisors."

They'd be excellent witnesses. "Nice to meet you." Tru stuck out his hand.

The three glanced at the queen.

Mother rolled her eyes. "Darling, you don't shake hands with servants."

He'd never get used to that. "Pardon me. Have a seat, gentlemen."

They crossed to the table but lined up by the window.

Tru would learn their names eventually. He nodded

at the stable hand. "Thank you for coming."

He bowed and cast nervous glances at the others. "How may I help ya, Sire?"

"How many horses are in the barns now?"

He stared at his boots. "Ah, fifty-six, I believe, Sire."

Truth, though Tru didn't expect this man to lie. "How many are there normally?"

"Thirty or so. It fluctuates depending on the season and visitors."

"How much do you spend, per month, on hay? I'm looking for an estimate."

The man spit out a number that matched what Tru normally spent at the Evening Inn.

"Thank you." Tru dug a silver from his pouch. "Sorry to disturb your work."

He put his hands up. "Sire, ya need not tip me. I'm happy ta serve."

"And I may call on you again. You have the thanks of Rigolan." Tru placed the coin in the man's hand and returned to the table. "Nickel, show the man out, then report back to me."

"Darling, what was that about?" Mother asked.

"I'm unraveling a mystery."

Finna grinned. "Darling, do you think you've discovered a revelation regarding hay?"

"Yes. And I love how that nickname sounds rolling off your lips. You may call me darling from now on." He winked at her. "I insist."

She scowled.

The three advisors pursed their lips.

Nickel sat. Sweat beaded on his forehead.

Tru spun the ledger toward him. "Look at the

amounts paid for hay. Either you are an absolute fool and have been swindled by the world's most expensive dealer, or you're triple-charging and pocketing the extra. Care to explain?"

Nickel stared at the book. "Really, Sire, there is nothing wrong with these figures. Rigolan feeds more horses than Acoris."

The dandelion stench left Tru's eyes watering. "I ran a stable for the last six years. I know the costs involved."

Mother turned to Finna. "How many horses do we own?"

"Fifteen."

She addressed the advisors. "Does that sound correct to you?"

All three nodded.

Nickel opened his mouth, closed it, then opened again.

Tru put up his hand. "Sirini gave me an incredible gift. I can smell lies."

"What?" Mother's eyes widened.

The three advisors exchanged glances.

Finna laughed. "Oh, please. You expect us to believe that?"

Tru leaned back in his chair, crossed his arms, and smiled. "Say something that I can't know the answer to, and I'll tell you if you lied."

Nickel dabbed his forehead with his handkerchief.

Finna grinned. "I'll play. I was born in Quickswallow."

The disgusting combination of dandelion and sour milk wafted off her lips. "Lie."

"Lucky guess. I'm in love with Jayson."

"Untrue."

Her nostrils flared. "I saw you kiss Princess Rosi in the gardens last night."

Oh, sard! Had she… He sneezed at the dandelion stench. *Thank the goddess.* "Another lie. That was low, even for you."

Farras joined. "My favorite color is pink."

Tru glanced at her pink frock and grinned. "True. But anyone would know that."

Finna tried again. "I'm in love with Justyn."

"True. And congratulations. I hope you'll make a match soon."

Mother's hands flew to her chest. "That has *not* been approved, young lady. Please tell me you haven't accepted a proposal."

Finna's chin quivered, but she squared her shoulders. "I would never do anything so foolish, Mother."

Nickel pushed the ledger away. "Sire, I may have been swindled by thieves who overcharged for the hay."

The stench of the lie lodged in the back of Tru's throat. "That is false. Your next statement will not be, or I will call for enforcers. Captain Dariel is a friend of mine. I'm sure he can get the truth from you."

Nickel's shoulders slumped, and he dabbed his face with his handkerchief again. "Sire, I can explain. I—"

"I don't want an excuse. Answer my question. Did you embezzle funds?"

His chin hit his chest. "Yes."

"The food expenses also look high. Shall I call the Acoris chef to enlighten us on the cost of meat, or will you admit that your sticky fingers have been dipping into more than one account?"

Nickel scrunched his eyes shut. "Yes. I've been

embezzling from multiple places."

That was easy enough. "Thank you for your candor. You will repay everything you stole, plus twelve percent interest, before the summer solstice."

Nickel froze. "You're not going to have me imprisoned?"

"How would you pay back what you owe if you're locked up?"

His jaw dropped, and he slurped his tea. It had to be cold by now. "Thank you, Sire. You are generous."

"You're also fired." Tru pointed to one of the advisors. "Would you send for an enforcer, please? This man needs to pack his bags and return to Rigolan."

Mother glared at Nickel. "You stole from us after all we've done for you? My son has been exceptionally lenient. If you run before you've paid your debt, there is no place in this world you can hide from *my* wrath."

Nickel bowed his head. "You are gracious, my queen. I will not flee."

The enforcers took a few minutes to escort the thief back to his room, which gave Mother time to collect a fresh pot of tea from a servant and refill cups. Finna asked the girl to fetch cakes, as well. Tru convinced the advisors to find seats at the table, and he learned their names. They all settled and munched on sweets.

Tru addressed the advisor with streaks of gray in his beard. "Do we have a copy of Rigolan's laws here?"

"Yes, Sire."

"Excellent." *Now to make a difference for my new home country.* "I need to know about the secession concerns, the trade disputes, and how to add new laws to our canon, and I don't have a lot of time. I'm meeting with Emperor Rhys in two hours."

****

Prince Shaded skipped the evening meal. I should show up at his bedchamber door late that night. I almost had Daffi convinced, but Jasmine intervened.

"Ask Tru to call for his cousins. That'll solve the issue." She sat on the floor of Rosi's bedroom, mending a tear in her robe. "If it doesn't, your father can summon them. They won't dare refuse that."

"But it means waiting until tomorrow." I paced, kicking my skirt with each step. "Do you think Shade is avoiding me on purpose?"

"Why would he?" Rosi grabbed my arm and steered me toward the vanity bench. "Sit down. You'll wear a track in my carpet." She began unbuttoning my gown.

"Maybe he's figured out his spark, and he doesn't want to ascend yet." I attacked my hair with a brush. "Or maybe he thinks I'm a lunatic."

"I think he's being elusive because he shares his brothers' wicked humor." Daffi dug through Rosi's wardrobe and tossed a clean sleeping gown at me. "You'll find him. Don't fret."

"How can I help it? I'm down to twenty-one days. To come so far yet miss him while he's residing in the same building with me?" I stood and stripped. "It's almost comical."

Charity gathered the dress and hung it up.

Daffi pulled the sleeping gown over my head and guided my wrist toward the sleeve hole.

I swatted her away. "I'm not an infant."

"You're acting like one."

I stuck my tongue out at her and climbed into the garment. Of course, she was right. I had no reason to panic. I'd find the rotten bug wart tomorrow, even if I had to call upon the throne of the Five Realms. "I'm sorry. I'm about to crawl out of my skin."

"It doesn't help that Tru skipped the evening meal." Jasmine used her teeth to cut her thread. "You haven't worked out your difficulties with him yet, so it's also eating you."

My entire body tensed. "I don't want to talk about that."

Charity perked up. "What happened?"

"Nothing." I crawled under the bed covers.

Jasmine rolled her eyes. "Tru proposed to her in a hallway."

"What?" Rosi, Daffi, and Charity said it at once and converged on me.

"Tell us everything!" Charity demanded.

Heat flooded my face. "It was stupid. I don't think he even meant it. He dropped to one knee in a public space where *anyone* could have seen him. It was one of the stupidest things he's ever done."

Charity sighed. "I've been wanting him to do that to me for years." Tears welled in her eyes, and she blinked. "He's way out of my reach now, but why didn't you say yes?"

I hauled the sheet up to my chin and ran my fingers over the decorative stitches set in the hem. I'd added them years ago, since Rosi hated sewing. "Because he must marry someone worthy of the station. I'm a ninth daughter. Ninth! He could settle for a third, but his rank deserves better." My eyes burned. *Not now!* Crying didn't accomplish anything. I needed my sarding counterpart so I could get on with life.

Rosi sighed. "You rely too much on the protocols. Where have they gotten you? Sacrificed to a god. You should have said yes."

"He didn't have permission to ask! How humiliating would it be if I accepted, then he was forced to withdraw it because my father or his mother said no?" I rolled to bury my face in the pillow. "I want to sleep now."

After a bunch of shuffling, Charity, Jasmine, and Daffi left.

Rosi climbed into the bed and slung her arm over me. "I'm sorry you had to endure that. I envy you, though. You've fallen in love and had your first kiss. I've met all the young men here, and none of them seem interested in me. I'm destined for life in the temple with no hope of falling in love or marrying."

A knot formed in my chest. "You're lucky. You'll escape the heartache I'm enduring."

"Perhaps. Or maybe you'll get a happy ending." She rolled over. "Sleep on it. You'll feel better tomorrow."

Only if the morning brought an ascension to godhood, and I could run away from Tru.

The morning of my eighth torturous day of searching for an elusive counterpart, Daffi, Jasmine, and I arrived early in the breakfast room and nibbled food for two hours, waiting for the Rigolan triplets. They never showed. Neither did Tru. I was going to have to knock on his door and ask him for a favor.

Could I? Look into his olive-green eyes and not touch him? Would I tear up like a love-starved damsel pining for her lover, or could I maintain my composure?

Getting Papa's help would be easier. Those idiot triplets couldn't turn down a request from the emperor. My shoulders relaxed. That would work.

"Have you finished your mask yet?" Daffi sipped the last of her tea.

"What mask?" I chased a bit of cold sausage around my plate. Papa hadn't come to breakfast, either. Where was he?

"For the masquerade ball tonight." Daffi smiled and waved at one of the Tulya women who entered the room.

If she'd been five minutes later, she'd have missed the food. Servants were already gathering dishes.

"I didn't know there was a ball." I rose and waited for Jasmine.

She shoved the last bite of toast in her mouth and joined me, still chewing.

"I'm not in a hurry. Finish your meal."

She swallowed. "I'm good. Where are we going now?"

"To find mask-making supplies," Daffi said.

"To find my father." I located the steward. My father was unavailable for audience, even with his daughters, until late afternoon. I couldn't work up the courage to knock on Tru's door, nor could I convince Jasmine to go in my stead. So the three of us invaded the sewing room.

Daffi dug through a décor basket and found two peacock feathers. "What about these?"

Good grief, sister, really? "They'd stick off the sides of my face like massive ears."

"No. They're gorgeous. I'll add them to my mask. They match my teal dress."

I sifted through a bowl of sequins. No one said the mask had to be fancy. A simple strip with eye holes would work. I set the bowl back in the cubby and crossed to the fabric bolts. "I'll wear my pine-green gown." Who was I kidding? I didn't want to go to the dumb ball. I didn't want to dance with strange men, and if Tru asked me…I couldn't do it. "Maybe I'll let Rosi attend, instead."

"What if Shaded shows up?" Jasmine rummaged through a basket of buttons and came up with a pale wood chip that resembled one of Sirini's tokens.

I sighed. "What if he doesn't? It's his pattern of late."

Jasmine found another button and passed the pair to me. "These belong on your mask."

I flipped them over, and a chill shot down my body. They were prayer tokens. And both said "Justice." Two buttonholes were drilled below the word. "How did these end up in here?"

"I don't know. Maybe it's a sign that you'll ascend tonight while wearing those." She crossed to the bolts and hauled out a remnant of dark-green silk. "Does this match?"

My heart rate picked up. This was seriously spooky. "Perfectly. But that doesn't make sense. I hired a seamstress in town to make that dress. We shouldn't have matching scraps here."

Daffi smiled. "Then it's a double sign from Sirini. Let's add a spray of feathers around the tokens." She flicked through the basket for two burgundy ones. She draped them over the pine fabric and laid the coins over the shafts.

The combination was stunning.

I sighed. "You win. Let's create my mask and spend the day resting. If I don't find Shaded tonight, tomorrow morning I'll bolster my courage and ask for Tru's help. Or Papa's." I glanced at Jasmine. "Or maybe I need Sirini for this one."

Jasmine squeezed my hand. "Let's tackle this day first."

Right. Because what could go wrong at a masquerade ball?

Chapter Thirty-Six

I studied my reflection. *Absolutely ridiculous.* I'd
sewn the buttons near my temples with feathers
sprouting off and ended up with the bushy ears I'd teased
Daffi about. My mask turned out gorgeous, but it didn't
conceal my identity. The moment I walked in with Daffi,
everyone would recognize us as the emperor's youngest
daughters. Whose stupid idea was it to don a mask when
it did nothing to conceal identities? The concept of
"masquerade" was to hide, not mildly decorate.

Jasmine entered Rosi's bedchamber in her normal
gray robe, probably with leather leggings and boots
beneath. Maybe I should have dressed as a priestess.
Now that would be a fun disguise.

The shutters bashed against the window frame. Was
a storm brewing? I glanced out. Dark clouds moved in
from the south. I shuddered. Was that Gale?

Charity smiled at me. "You look beautiful!"

I locked the shutters. He couldn't get into the palace.
Could he? "I look absurd. No one will be fooled by this
mask."

Rosi flicked my skirts to straighten the ruffles. "The
idea of the mask isn't to fool people. It's to offer an air
of mystery."

"There's no mystery at all." I crossed to stand beside
Daffi in her teal dress with peacock feathers sprouting
off her face like seriously overgrown eyebrows. "Do

you, for even one instant, believe that she and I are Lynna or the Tulya girls? If nothing else, our coloring gives away our identities." Lynna was short and round, the Tulya twins had darker skin, and the other bachelorettes had auburn, blonde, or black hair. There was zero chance of being mistaken for any of them. "This event is a farce."

"It'll be fun." Daffi brushed a feather away from her eye. "We get to dance with handsome men."

"Are you kidding? Most of them have paired off and will accompany their preferred partner the whole evening."

"Except Freidrick," Daffi said. "He'll dance with you."

I clenched my teeth. "Maybe I don't want to."

"Suit yourself. I will if he asks. Same with all the others. Even Geary."

That poor boy. "You think he'll be there?"

"Why not? His brother and parents will be." She pulled a hand fan from a pocket and flicked it open. It was a lighter shade of teal from her dress, and she'd attached more peacock feathers to it. She held it before her face so only her eyes showed. "Is this mysterious?" She waggled her eyebrows, and the feathers on her mask fluttered.

I laughed. "Oh yes. That's lovely. Please do that all night."

She batted her eyelashes at me. "Only for you, dear sister, to release you from this foul mood. Enjoy yourself."

The only way that would happen is if I found Shaded and touched him. Then my heart would stop pounding, my fingers might stop quaking, and my breath could even out. Maybe. Once I became a goddess, should I continue dancing? Or should I leave before anyone realized two new deities were in their midst? And what of Tru? I should find him and say goodbye, even though it'd gut me. Oh goddess, what was I supposed to do?

Jasmine opened the door. "Let's get this started. The sooner you find Shaded and touch him, the sooner you can take your mask off."

"Good point." I hoisted my skirts and headed for the ground floor, Daffi at my side.

Father and Bronwyn, also masked, greeted guests at the ballroom door. They hugged Daffi and me and propelled us in.

We entered and froze. Musicians tuned their instruments in the far corner. Massive candelabras and guide stones gave off romantic lighting and soothing scents. Swaths of blue fabric hung from the ceiling, studded with sparkly silver and gold sequins that twinkled in the candlelight. Long tables piled with candles and flowers also held bowls of fruit juices and wines, glassware, and finger snacks. Padded benches lined the walls for exhausted dancers to rest. Masked chaperones stood between the seats, and servants with face scarves hurried about.

The room had never looked so gorgeous.

Several masked males chatted in the center of the room. Daffi and I arrived exactly on time yet still managed to be the first women in attendance.

Fine by me. I swept toward the group and searched for blond heads. The sooner I found Shaded, the better.

Instead, I found my brothers Jayson and Justyn, my cousins Valen and Geary, and the Olerio triplets. I curtsied to them, Daffi in perfect unison beside me, and pasted a fake smile on my cheeks. "Good evening, gentlemen."

"Ladies," they said with a bow.

Jayson held out his hand to me. "Rosi, may I speak with you a moment?"

"Certainly." I took his hand, and he led me away from the crowd.

He hugged me and whispered in my ear. "Cali, Justyn told me you'd survived! Why didn't you tell me?"

Some tension melted from my shoulders, and I explained in hushed tones, keeping watch on the doors.

He nodded. "That makes sense. Anything I can do to help you?"

"I need to find Prince Shaded. If you spot him tonight, haul him to my side."

Jayson grinned. "With pleasure." He froze and stared across the room.

Finna and Farras swept in, wearing varying shades of pink. Rose petals and sequins covered their masks, and their blonde hair hung in loose curls over their shoulders.

I squeezed Jayson's hand. "Which do you favor?"

"Farras. Her sister's tongue is too sharp. Excuse me." He strode toward the pair and welcomed them with a kiss to each of their hands. He lingered over the second woman. Finna's mask had a few red rose petals whereas Farras's were pure pink. Nice of them to alter their costume slightly so we could tell them apart. *Insert sarcastic eye roll.* As if children with matching faces hadn't been playing similar stupid tricks for eons.

Tru and his mother came in behind the sisters, and my breath lodged in my throat. He wore a berry-colored shirt, more purple than red, with charcoal suede leggings and black boots. His mask was a simple strip of gray suede with eye holes. No adornments. His gold and onyx torc reflected candlelight and reminded everyone of his status. He was the prize tonight.

He caught my gaze and smiled.

More people filed into the room, including Lynna and Sorka, who hurried to Tru's side. He still held my gaze. They chattered and finally drew his attention to themselves. Simpering puff pastries. He could do better. He excused himself from them and strode toward me.

I swallowed, shoving my heart back down into my chest.

Jasmine put her hand on my shoulder. "Easy."

"Good evening, Rosi." He bowed and kissed my fingers.

I curtsied. "Highness."

"You look lovely."

"As do you."

He laughed and leaned closer. "I found my worthless cousins and demanded all three show themselves at tonight's event or risk my wrath."

My heart puddled. "That was sweet. Thank you."

"I'd be honored to escort you to the doors and await their arrival."

"I appreciate the offer, but Rindi just entered. You should greet her." I totally lied. I had no idea if it was Rindi or Rhyada, but it had to be one of them.

"If that is your wish." He backed away, then turned to my sister.

She smiled. It was Rhyada. Rindi had a slight chip in her front tooth, courtesy of one of Rhygan's pranks.

Palama pinched me above the elbow. "You can't marry him," she whispered in my ear, "so leave him for those of us who have a shot!" She plastered on a smile and swooped in on him.

I rubbed my sore arm. "I hope she ends up with Shalek."

"Come." Jasmine guided me toward the doorway. "I'll wait with you."

I hurried but was stopped several times by young men welcoming me. I let them kiss my fingers and bow but kept part of my attention on the newcomers.

Tru appeared by my side and spoke with a low voice. "Here they come."

My heart pounded like a kick drum, and I stretched up on my toes. The dark Tulya women entered, then three blond men. They bowed to Tru.

"Reporting as requested, Sire," the first man said with a bit more spit than necessary. They all wore matching black clothing with copper accents and silk masks.

I grabbed his hand. Nothing happened.

He grinned and leaned in as if to kiss me.

I took a step back. "Mind your manners, Shalek."

He pursed his lips. "I know the game. You want Shade." Someone behind me caught his eye. He muttered, "Excuse me," and walked away.

The second man offered his hand. "Princess. I'm Shane." He kissed my fingers.

Nothing happened.

I smiled. "Enjoy your evening."

Prince Shaded drew near, and the dragonflies in my stomach took flight. This was it! My life would change forever. I'd be immortal. As would he. My hands trembled, and I held out my fingers.

He didn't take them. Instead, he shoved his behind

his back. "Princess. I'm ill and should not be here tonight." He glared at Tru. "It would be wise if you didn't touch me."

Liar. He wasn't sick, unless he was referring to his twisted sense of humor. I'd come too far to waste this moment, and I didn't want to die. I reached for him—and froze.

Did I really want this? As a goddess, I'd never perish, but I'd watch all my loved ones grow old and pass away. Papa and Momma. My siblings. Cousins. Nieces and nephews. Friends. My heart clenched. Tru. A wave of dizziness hit, and I stumbled.

Tru caught me. "Ca—Rosi? What's wrong?"

I clung to him.

And what if Shaded didn't want to be a god? I couldn't make the choice for him. If he preferred mortality, if I didn't ascend…I'd have twenty more days with my family, to be something more than a single stocking, to make a difference in the lives of the people around me.

It wasn't fair! I'd wanted to have an impact before I died. Help the helpless, defend the weak, punish the abusers. I hadn't found Flick yet. He'd been crippled for fourteen years, and in all that time, I'd been unable to find him and mend the horrendous wrong done to him. Twenty days wasn't enough.

But if I truly desired justice, then I had to let Shaded decide for himself. Maybe he'd prefer to die. How could I take that choice from him? "May I have a private word with you?"

He frowned. "Why?"

"It's a matter of grave importance. Please."

He sighed. "Fine."

I led him to a quiet alcove with padded furniture and a tall potted tree. Shaded took a chair. Tru and I perched on a bench. Jasmine shielded us further with her body.

I folded my hands in my lap. *Sirini, guide my words. Please.* "Sirini gave an extra blessing to us. A spark of divinity." I explained how it worked. How we had twenty-eight days to find each other. How the other gods discovered they could steal our sparks to increase their own strength.

His eyebrows furrowed. "I wondered why I couldn't go outside without the elements attacking me. I couldn't go near candle flames, either, or a water pump. I've been hiding for a week."

I nodded. "Zelos, Gale, and Sear want your spark. I was attacked by Beck, Xyla, Zephyra, Sprout, Tera, and Gale."

His jaw muscles jerked. "What are we supposed to do?"

"To ascend, we touch each other. If we never do, we will both die. It happened to your father; he never found his counterpart, and his heart failed."

Shade's face paled, and he sat forward, his elbows resting on his knees. "This spark means we become…gods?"

"Extreme injury can kill us, but otherwise, we'll live forever. Mica told me of her experiences. Joy and purpose, sorrow and loneliness, unending repetition but also incredible opportunities. Yet for all the darkness, it is a blessing."

Shade scrubbed his hand over his face. "I lost my father before I even met him. That wound has never healed, and I'll endure it again when my mother and brothers pass?"

I winced. "It will hurt. But we could also do great good."

"Sure. Watch my family and friends die. Try to help other people, only to see them make the same mistakes over and over."

I reared back. That was a tad cynical. "There would also be good. People would rely on us as they do Zelos and Beck."

Shade's eyebrows furrowed, shifting his mask on his face. He ripped it off and balled it in his hands. "Like I need more duties. People don't worship gods for the fun of it. I'd have to earn it. Although offerings sound like a perk."

He was worried about responsibilities? "If we don't touch, we both die in twenty days. Is that what you want?"

Tru threaded his fingers through mine.

Shade rubbed his chin. "I don't want to be the cause of your death, but I'm not sure I'm ready for this. May I have some time to talk to my brothers and mother?"

I nodded. "Will you decide soon? I don't wish to put it off until the last moment."

"Tomorrow night?"

Tension leaked from my stiff shoulders. "Fine. We can enjoy the ball as humans."

He grinned. "You'll forgive me if I don't ask you to dance." He glanced at our laced fingers in my lap.

I smiled. "Have a pleasant evening, Prince Shaded."

Jasmine shifted, allowing him to leave the alcove.

Tru squeezed my hand. "I'm sorry you didn't ascend tonight. Hopefully, he'll come to you tomorrow for the touch."

But what if he didn't? What if he wanted to die,

instead? I swallowed. "Let's enjoy this evening, please. Will you dance with me?"

"Every one of them, Your Highness."

So sweet. My insides melted into a gooey puddle. "I doubt you'll be allowed to monopolize one woman's time. You have suitors."

Tru helped me rise. "They can wait."

Bronwyn signaled for the tuning musicians to quiet, and everyone turned toward her.

Lynna and Palama, on opposites sides of the ballroom, picked up their skirts and scurried across the hardwood floor, their gazes glued to Tru.

It was too good to last. "Your admirers missed you." I released his hand, curtsied, and retreated to let the more suitable matches have the first dance. *If I can only release my feelings for him and heal my battered heart.*

Chapter Thirty-Seven

Tru offered his arms to Lynna and Palama. Or maybe she was Pensie. He couldn't tell. Did it matter? "Good evening, ladies." They turned to face Empress Bronwyn.

She welcomed everyone and pointed out the refreshments. "My only instruction tonight is to not dance with the same partner for two songs in a row." She smiled. "Mingle. Have fun." She waved to the musicians. "Let the dancing begin!"

Four stringed instruments and a tuned drum broke into a lively song.

Palama—or Pensie—squeezed his arm. "May I have this first one?" She wore a purple gown with tiny white pearls. More of them swirled across her purple mask in a wave pattern.

Men and women began an intricate set of weaving steps with bobs and swishes. Tru cringed. "I'd be delighted, Princess, but I confess I may embarrass you." Where was Cali?

She glided into the dance on the arm of Simon. Or maybe it was Sidel. Tru couldn't tell the twins apart, especially from this distance. Not that it mattered. Oddly, Jasmine remained at the edge of the room, gaze locked on Cali.

The blonde princess at his side laughed. "They're simple. I'm sure you'll catch on quickly. Follow my lead." She tugged him toward the center.

"I get the next one," Lynna stated, then latched on to Lev. Or Lane. Or Lucas. The number of twins and triplets in the room was ridiculous.

Tru picked up the steps within moments without treading on anyone's feet or skirts. His guardian had taught him some of these combinations. Maybe all the dances utilized similar footwork and he wouldn't embarrass himself, after all. He smiled when the music ended and kissed her fingers. "Thank you, Princess."

"Call me Palama." She batted her eyelashes. "May I have another dance later?"

"Of course. Although I assumed men were to do the asking."

She grinned. "This lady doesn't take chances." She curtsied and turned to accept another man's arm.

Lynna slipped her hand into his. "My turn."

He moved her hand to his forearm and led her into the next round with more difficult steps. He caught on, though, and made it through. He spotted Cali with one of her brothers, laughing and gliding with liquid grace.

The song ended, and Tru bowed to Lynna. "Thank you, milady."

"Another? Please?"

Gods above. He'd never get rid of her, would he? "Sadly, the empress stated no two in a row. We cannot disobey."

Lynna scowled and stomped toward a refreshment table.

Tru danced with Rindi and Helene before finally catching Cali without a partner. He offered his hand. "Shall we?"

The musicians began a slower number. He copied

the other men, drawing Cali close, one arm around her waist, the other holding her hand. Warmth spread through his body at her touch. *May this song never end—*

The clash of steel against steel echoed through the room. A woman screamed.

Tru whirled.

An instant later, Jasmine appeared beside them, her sword drawn.

"What's happening?" he asked.

"Maelstrom." She backed toward a side door, pulling Cali with her, and handed Tru a weapon. "Get her out. I'll take care of the flatfish."

The stench of brine wafted through the room. Armed priests in blue-green robes swarmed around the dancers, herding them to the center of the room. Two of them cut off Tru's escape route.

Jasmine attacked one, thrusting her sword at his belly. "Get her to safety!"

The priest parried the thrust with an ear-shattering clash.

Tru grabbed Cali's wrist and ran for the door.

Two more priests stepped into their path and pointed to the middle of the room. "That way. No one leaves."

Tru cut to the right, but they were surrounded. "Hide among the other women."

She yanked her hand from his. "I won't endanger them to save myself."

One of the priests stabbed at her, and she backed away.

Women screamed. Men shouted. Metal clanged.

Tru blocked Cali with his body, taking small steps backward, gaze locked on the armed priests glaring at her.

Jasmine killed her opponent and engaged another.

A priest snuck up behind Cali and grabbed her shoulder. Tru darted forward and turned aside the thrust aimed at her back.

She grasped the priest's wrist and twisted his hand until his arm pivoted at an unnatural angle. She ducked beneath his reach, whirled, and threw a palm strike at his nose. The cartilage cracked and gushed blood. He cupped his face. She hauled her knee up, striking his chin. He fell back, stunned. She picked up his sword and buried it in his belly.

Gods above, what an amazing woman! Tru parried an incoming thrust and delivered an upper cut with his left fist. The priest staggered back and knocked Geary over.

Cali ran for her cousin. "Stop! I'm the one you came for. Let the others go."

"I'm the one you want!" Shade stood several steps away from Cali, shielding Jerys. He waved his hands above his head. "I'm the spark. Leave her alone."

His cousin's quality character finally emerged, thank the goddess. Tru guided Cali closer to Shaded, keeping the blade between her and the priests.

The emperor's soldiers rushed into the room and spread out. Where had they been, and how had armed priests accessed the palace?

The space rang with the clash of weapons, grunts of pain, and plenty of female shrieking, but the blue-green robes outnumbered the guards three to one.

A nearby priest parried a blow from Dariel and backed into Jerys. She grabbed a handful of his hair, hooked her leg around his ankle, and threw him on the ground. Dariel skewered the priest through the heart.

Shade scooped up the dead man's sword and engaged another priest.

Dariel forced his way to Cali.

Tru stabbed at the sea of blue-green robes, but they were succeeding. The dancers were shoved into a tighter group.

Justyn and Jayson attacked a priest with only their bare hands, fists flying, feet kicking. Palama darted behind her brothers and kicked their opponent in the nethers. His face turned purple, and he sagged forward, clutching his jewels. Justyn grabbed the priest's sword and stabbed him.

"Stop, or she dies!"

Fighting continued around them, but Tru turned toward the voice. Where had Jasmine gone? He found the speaker and froze. One of the priests held Daffi to his chest with a knife to her throat.

"Dreaf!" Cali ran toward them. "Let her go!"

Tru caught her around the waist.

Daffi's eyes narrowed. She thrust her elbow back into Dreaf's sternum, flicked her fan, and stabbed him in the thigh with the blade protruding from the back edge. Where had she found a weaponized accessory?

Dreaf let out a whoosh of air and buckled, crushing her in his arms. She dropped the fan and clawed at his hand. His knife slipped, and a bead of blood welled on her skin. She froze.

Cali screamed and pulled at Tru's hand around her waist. "Let me help her."

He tightened his grip. "No. He'll kill her."

Tears filled her eyes, her gaze locked on Daffi only a handful of steps away.

Dreaf straightened and pressed the knife deeper. A

thin stream of blood trickled down Daffi's neck. She sobbed and stared at Cali.

Emperor Rhys bellowed, "Hold!"

His soldiers immediately took two steps back from their opponents, swords raised.

Rhys stomped toward Daffi and Dreaf, a simple chipped sword in one hand, probably liberated from one of the priests. He tore off his mask and tossed the weapon at Daffi's feet. "We yield. Release my daughter."

"Tell your guards to disarm."

"You heard him!" Rhys yelled.

The clatter of steel landing on the hardwood floors echoed painfully.

Dreaf smirked. "Now behold your master."

Maelstrom strode into the room with a gust of salty wind, the gill slits at his neck flaring. He wore grass sandals, kelp green leggings, and a sky-blue shirt. A turquoise cape billowed around him, held in place by a purple-and-white seashell.

Tru was no expert, but after spending a few days with his sisters, he knew Maelstrom's color choices clashed with his seafoam green skin.

The god of the sea locked his gaze on Emperor Rhys. "Give me what's mine, and maybe I'll spare the rest."

Rhys took two steps closer to Daffi. "Release my daughter. Then I'll discuss terms."

"You are in no position to bargain!" Maelstrom flicked his fingers, and two priests thrust their swords at Rhys's throat. "I will have my sacrifice. Appease me, or I'll drink from all of you."

Shaded eased toward Cali and held his hand out. "The others have a better shot of surviving if we do this now," he whispered.

Tru's heart pounded. Maybe two gods could take out one, even with all the armed priests standing around. "Take him down, Justice."

Cali grinned and took Shade's hand.

****

Our hands met. A tingly warmth spread through my fingers, shot up my arms, and bloomed in my chest. The dragonflies in my belly exploded. The small hairs on the back of my neck rose. My scalp prickled.

My eyesight wobbled for a moment, then sharpened. Every sweaty pore on Shade's face came into focus. Several paces to my right, the pulse at Papa's throat quickened. His gaze met mine, the laugh lines around his eyes etched with worry. The coarse threads in my mask irritated the skin above my eyebrows.

And the smells! Sweet Goddess, how would I learn to live with this? Multiple perfumes, sweat, and the overpowering salt.

Ladies whimpered. Fabric rustled. Shaded breathed heavily. Maelstrom's gill slits swished like crepe paper against rough stone.

Power surged in my veins—but how could I access it? What were my new abilities? How could I eliminate this threat?

I glanced at Shade. He was staring at his hands. Did he have extra strength? Speed? An ability to draw weapons from thin air? Flight? Invisibility? Impervious skin?

Tru leaned toward me. "Did it work?"

I ripped my mask off. "Yes."

"Silence!" Maelstrom sneered at me. "You. Come forward and kneel before me."

I took a step toward him, my heart pounding. *Sirini, I need some guidance here! Please?*

Jasmine joined me, her hands free of weapons, and matched my pace. Where was her sword? Her knife? Was she going to take him out with her fists?

Maelstrom smiled at her. "I did not ask for you, but I accept your life as a sacrifice. Kneel, and I will deal you a swift death."

She squared her shoulders. "I offer you a chance to save your worthless hide, worm. Call off your priests and leave, or you'll lose everything."

One side of his mouth quirked up. "Your insolence has cost another life." He looked around and pointed at Sorka. "I want that tall, lithe morsel." His hand shifted. "And that one."

Priests wove through the dancers, seized Sorka and Jerys, and dragged them, thrashing and screaming, to Maelstrom. The priests pushed both women to their knees.

Sorka cried, staring at his sandaled feet. "Please don't kill me."

Jerys scowled. Probably planning her attack strategy.

My entire body trembled. He'd kill us all. "Leave them alone. I'm here."

Maelstrom grabbed Sorka's throat with one hand and Jerys's with another. "I want what's mine." His fingers tightened around their necks, and blood seeped. They gasped, clawing at him.

"No!" I surged forward and shoved him.

He fell back and cracked his head against the hardwood floor. "You disrespectful wench!" He drew his belt knife and came at me.

Jasmine threw herself between us.

He bellowed and jammed the blade into her chest, sinking it to the hilt.

She dropped like a stone.

My breath stopped.

Jasmine lay unmoving at my feet, eyes dull, blood soaking into her gray robe.

I staggered back. A moan slid out of my lips, and I clamped my hand over my mouth. She was dead? My friend, my protector, was gone just like that? As a goddess, I might have survived that blow. Why had she taken it for me? My vision blurred, and I blinked. This couldn't be. "Sirini!" The cry left my throat raw, but I tried again. "Save your servant!"

"That old bat is sleeping." Maelstrom pulled the knife from Jasmine's body and advanced on me. "Now. Kneel."

I took another step back, and my foot slipped on Sorka's gown. She and Jerys lay on the floor, staring sightlessly at the ceiling, deep bruises and lacerations on their throats. My chest tightened, and I moaned. He'd killed my sister and the future empress. He'd probably slaughter everyone in this room because I'd fought him in the water. Was that only nine days ago?

Maelstrom took two more steps toward me.

I took two back. My heart pounded in my head, drowning out the whimpers and tears.

Behind Maelstrom, two servants in face scarves crept up to Jasmine, grabbed her hands, and pulled her away. One met my gaze. Eyes that matched mine stared back at me. Rosi? What was she doing here? She should be safely hidden in her bedchamber with—Charity, the other woman rescuing Jasmine.

Charity laid her fingers at Jasmine's throat, looked at me with tear-filled eyes, and shook her head. Jasmine was truly gone.

This had to end. If I gave him my life, maybe he'd spare the rest. "I yield." I picked up my skirt and stepped toward him. "Take me. Let the others go."

"Don't." Shade grabbed my elbow and stopped me from kneeling. "Maelstrom, I freely offer my spark if you'll let everyone else go free."

Maelstrom grinned, then laughed. "You think I'd be satisfied with only one when I could have two? What kind of fool are you?" He closed the distance and lashed out with his knife.

Shade sucked in his gut and skipped back, but the weapon sliced through silk and skin easily. He folded his hands over his bleeding belly and staggered. His face paled and flickered as if a veil of water separated me from him.

No! Not him, too. Tears welled in my eyes.

His gaze caught mine, and he…rippled. Changed. One moment he was a man; the next he was a horse. A beautiful, powerful, blond stallion.

I clutched my hands to my chest. What kind of god was he that he could shift forms?

He opened his horse lips. "I'll find help!" With a clatter of hooves against hardwood, he dodged Maelstrom and ran out the doors.

"Get him!" Maelstrom pointed after Shade.

Four priests raced out the doors, chasing the stallion.

A chuckle bubbled up from my throat. I'd have never guessed that in a million years. A talking horse. Could I do something like that? What would I want to be? Something strong that could withstand a blow from that sharp blade. A great horned dromodon! I pictured one and willed my body to change.

Nothing happened.

Maelstrom snickered. "Now you're mine." His eyes narrowed, and he charged me, his knife aimed at my belly.

My thoughts slowed. Several women screamed. My brothers and father bellowed. A priest near me cheered. As the blade came at me, I couldn't run, couldn't move. Couldn't breathe. I'd spent how many days fleeing, escaped countless attacks, and struggled every day to stay alive, and it all ended here? Light glinted off the steel, and I watched it plunge toward my now immortal body. One blow wouldn't kill me—he'd take his time. But to save my sister, I'd endure it. I'd welcome every strike if it meant keeping her alive.

Tru darted between Maelstrom and me, knocking me back. The blade plunged into his side below his ribs. He gasped and buckled.

I clamped my fingers over my lips. *Oh, goddess, no…*

Tru's shoulders bunched, and he punched Maelstrom in the nose.

The cartilage snapped, his head flew back, and blood gushed. He swayed and fell on his ass, clutching his face.

"No!" I wrapped my arm around Tru's waist.

He took two steps back, and his knees gave out. I slowed his fall, but he hit the floor and cried out.

"I've got you." Tears obscured my vision. I pulled his shirt free of his belt and fumbled with the buttons. How bad was the wound? *Please don't let it be fatal…* Dark blood soaked into the cloth and dripped onto the floor. The coppery stench lodged in the back of my throat. I tore the silk away from the blade.

It'd sunk in all the way to the hilt.

Chapter Thirty-Eight

An icy pit blossomed in my guts. Tru wouldn't survive. Not even a team of surgeons could repair that damage. My Tru would perish. He'd given his life to protect mine, and I'd still have to die to save Daffi.

I glanced back at Maelstrom. He was on his hands and knees, trying to staunch the blood with the blue-green robe of one of his priests.

He'd be busy for a few moments. I turned back to Tru.

His mother, Queen Melissendra, cradled his head in her lap. Tears streamed down her face. "Stay with us, darling." She stroked his hair.

He winced. "I'm trying."

His sisters crept closer. Finna ripped a row of ruffles off her dress, packed it around the wound, and pressed down.

Tru cried out. Sweat coated his pale face, and his breathing grew shallow.

My poor Tru. I couldn't do anything for him. "Please don't die. I don't want to live without you." I wiped tears from my cheeks and clasped his hand. "Why did you do this?"

He swallowed. "You can't fail, Cali. Fight him, or everyone will suffer."

"But Daffi—"

"You Acoris women have the heart of true

warriors." His hand slid from mine. "The realm needs justice."

"Tru?"

"Fight."

Maelstrom howled and surged off the floor. "You'll pay for that!"

Heat flared in my chest. *How dare he!* Who gave him the right to invade my home, endanger and kill my sisters and my friend, and stab my Tru? That idiot would regret his mistakes. I launched myself at him. "You slug!" I feigned a punch to the ribs. He deflected the blow with his forearms, and I slapped his ruined nose.

He shrieked and reared back, holding his face.

"Slime!" I punched him in the throat.

He lurched away, gagging.

"Fungus!" I stomped toward him and shot my knee at his privates.

He twisted his hips and blocked with his thigh. His hands clamped around my neck. "I've had enough of you!"

Sharpened fingernails pricked my skin. But I wouldn't be a repeat of Sorka and Jerys. I thrust my face down to my thighs, breaking his hold, and kicked him in the knee.

It hyperextended. He bellowed and punched me in the temple.

Pain flared through my head, and my vision darkened at the edges. I wobbled back a few steps. Blinked. Lost my balance and fell. My hip slammed into the hardwood floor with another eruption of searing agony.

The clop of hooves on marble announced the arrival of Shade and the summoned help. Waves of citizens flowed into the ballroom, armed with kitchen utensils or farming tools, led by Mica and Beck seated on stallion Shade. Mica jumped off and ran toward me.

Two priests intercepted her and broke their swords on her marble skin.

She grinned. "Funny, that happened to the previous four priests, as well." She tore into them with her bare hands, and others swarmed around her. Beck and the others joined in, but they were still overmatched.

I crawled toward Tru.

Maelstrom landed on me.

I collapsed to my stomach. My chin bashed against the floor, shooting pain through my skull. My breath whooshed out between my lips, and my ribs burned.

He wrapped his arm around my neck and hauled my head back to lie smashed against his chest, my spine bent painfully in the wrong direction. His finger trailed down my cheek, and he sniffed my hair. "Finally." He tightened his grip on my neck.

I gasped and clawed at his flesh. My throat caught on fire. My brain throbbed to the beat of my pounding heart. Stabbing pains shot down to my hips. It couldn't end like this! I bucked. I threw my elbow back. I tried to roll to my side, but I wasn't strong enough to unseat him.

No! He couldn't win. I glanced at Daffi to my left. Tears streamed, and blood dripped down her skin. I couldn't save her. I was too weak. Pathetic. Useless.

The throbbing in my head increased. I opened my mouth and sucked in air, but Maelstrom's grip was too tight. I couldn't breathe.

I caught Papa's tear-filled gaze. His jaws clenched against the sword points resting at his neck. I'd lose him, too. Momma stood behind him, eyes red, shoulders slumped, surrounded by Batch Two.

Beck hit the floor by my shoulder. He growled, rolled to his knees, and pounced at someone else.

Beck and Mica were mighty, but they couldn't take on all these priests and Maelstrom. We'd all die. He'd steal their sparks, along with mine and Shade's.

I'd failed them all. I was utterly useless. Unnecessary. A failure. I would die. As would Papa, still gazing at me. He loved me. As did Daffi, Rosi, and the rest of my siblings. Even Bronwyn, in her way, cared for me.

Maybe I wasn't totally useless. The token I'd drawn that morning outside the throne room read "service." I'd thought Sirini meant I should dive into my sacrifice willingly. And I'd plucked "home" several times, as well. Maybe Sirini wanted me to serve my family. There was no higher purpose, no greater destiny.

But I'd also drawn "retribution." Maelstrom could not win, even if he managed to kill me, because Sirini would guarantee that moldering beast got what he deserved. It might not be today, but why shouldn't it?

I locked gazes with Tru. Sweat dripped into his pinched brows, yet his beautiful olive-green eyes didn't waver. I couldn't speak, couldn't tell him how much I loved him. Maybe we'd be together in the afterlife.

Beck stumbled over Finna, blood streaming down his transparent skin in multiple places, and lay still on the floor. She ripped another ruffle off her dress and turned to him.

Darkness clouded my peripheral vision, but I kept my gaze on my beloved Tru.

"Cali." He stretched his hand toward me. "We've been wronged. We need Justice!"

Fire exploded in my core. It doused the pain and flooded me with strength. My throat opened. I inhaled deeply. This was more like it. Silvery-blue light blossomed in my chest like a heat halo from an inferno, traveled down my arms, and flew from my fingertips.

Maelstrom catapulted off me and landed in a heap.

I rolled to my feet and shot up, hovering above the dance floor like a floating lantern, my loose hair swaying in invisible air currents. Silvery-blue light flickered around my body like lightning. I scanned the room. Maelstrom's priests ringed it. A dozen dead ones and twice that many slain citizens lay scattered on the floor.

People stared at me, wide-eyed and silent.

Justyn and Jayson smiled and fell to one knee. "Kneel before the goddess," they commanded.

Some complied. Others just gawked.

Mica, covered in blood, cradled Beck's head in her lap. Despite his wounds, which were rapidly closing, he winked at me.

She clapped. "Well done! Smoke him, Justice."

Maelstrom's eyes grew wide, and he scrambled back on hands and heels.

"Hold!" My voice echoed through the chamber as if spoken by thousands.

Maelstrom froze like a marble statue, unable to slink away. So did his priests.

Power coursed through my veins giddily. "Mica, free my sister and father from those blades, if you please?"

"Gladly." The goddess crossed to Daffi, grabbed the blade with her impervious hand, and yanked Dreaf's arm away from Daffi's neck.

She squirmed out of his grasp and hurried to our

mother.

Mica disarmed the two priests holding Papa captive and tossed the weapons aside. Their eyes tracked her movements, and sweat dripped down their faces, but they couldn't break free.

Papa wrapped his arms around Momma and Daffi, though his gaze never left me.

Bronwyn, tears streaming down her face, ran to Jerys and cradled her body.

I turned my attention to the cowering Maelstrom. "Your victims have cried out for justice. Prepare to be judged." A pale-blue beam of light shot from my forehead to his.

His eyes bulged, and he whined like a kicked puppy.

"Her eyes are glowing!" a woman shouted.

Several people gasped.

I glared at Maelstrom. The bully became the victim, but I had no pity. Now he'd meet true justice, wielded by Sirini's servant, and receive what he deserved. The light crept across my vision, obscuring everything around me until only a field of blue remained.

I invaded his memories.

He swam from his underwater temple, shooting through the blue-green sea. Something broke the surface above and sank. He stroked toward it. He caught the squalling infant and choked the child. The baby turned blue, and a multicolored, sparkling orb rose from the boy's chest. Maelstrom grabbed it, absorbed the spark, and released the corpse. The lifeless body drifted to the ocean floor and settled on a bed of coral.

Another memory. A young girl entered the water kicking and flailing. Maelstrom snatched her, killed her, and stole her divinity. Again. And again. Every crime against innocents reenacted like a grisly theatrical production. Every spark he'd stolen, every ship he'd sunk, every life he'd ended for his own gain or pleasure. I relived them all from his viewpoint.

Impartial, I was not. Anger seethed in my chest like a swarm of bees. The field of blue retreated.

Maelstrom managed to turn his hands palm up. "Have mercy, Princess."

"I am Calilee, the goddess of justice." My polyvocal tone reverberated off the walls. "You deserve only judgment."

He swallowed.

"All life is sacred and should be protected. The laws of this land shield the innocent and vulnerable, and the harsh punishments levied against abusers reflect that. You have failed in your duties as a servant of Sirini and protector of your people. You are guilty of nine hundred twenty-two acts of murder, seven hundred ninety-six assaults, sixty-eight kidnappings, forty-eight rapes, two hundred eighteen incidents of property destruction, and thousands of thefts. I sentence you to death."

His eyes bulged. "What?"

A comforting mass settled between my shoulder blades in the same place Jasmine wore her blade. *Nice!* My godhood came with a weapon. I grasped the hilt of my new sword and held it aloft. It flickered with blue light, as if constructed of liquid fire. Excellent balance. No discernable weight. Minimal heat. The perfect length for my petite size.

I flicked my wrist, and the blade separated Maelstrom's head from his body. The heat seared the flesh, and not a drop of his blood hit Bronwyn's polished hardwood. His head struck the dance floor with a muffled *whump*, and the corpse crumpled.

Several women screamed.

I'd warned them the execution was coming. What did they think would happen?

A blazing ball of sparkling light, larger than the wagon I'd lived in for a week, drifted up from Maelstrom. All the sparks he'd stolen from others. His power.

Not anymore. I ran my hand through it and absorbed the entire thing. Heat flared from me like ripples in a disturbed puddle, and a tingle surged across my skin.

Everyone who still stood dropped to one knee and bowed their heads. Murmurs rose from their ranks, muted and hurried.

Justyn chuckled. "That's my sister!"

Nervous giggles and shushes followed.

"Cali?"

I turned. Jasmine looked up at me.

"How is this possible?" I floated down and threw my arms around her. "I'm so glad you're alive."

She returned the hug. "I am, too. I was floating, looking for a blade to sheath in that worm, when Sirini said, 'Not now, child,' and shoved me back into my body. Now help Tru. He's fading fast."

How could I have forgotten? Charity and Rosi moved aside, and I knelt beside my beloved. Blood soaked his clothing, the floor, Finna's hands, and the ruins of her ruffles she'd packed against the wound. His skin held a blue tint, and his eyelids dropped over waxy eyes.

"Tru?" I picked up his limp hand.

He grinned. "That was awesome, Cali."

Tears welled in my eyes, and I blinked. Jasmine had

told me to help him, which meant I could. But justice didn't come with a gift of healing. Though I did possess a massive dose of divinity. If I could take sparks, then I could sarding well give them, too. "I can heal you, but I won't act against your will." I ran my fingers down his cheek. "I will transform you into a god if you approve. You'd be immortal, though. You'd have to relinquish your throne."

He licked his lips. "No more wool or twill clothing that itches? No more long meetings with sneaky advisors? No more barbs from Finna?"

She swatted his shoulder. "No, you'll always have those."

I chewed my lower lip. Humor wouldn't make this an easier decision. I had to paint the entire picture. "You'll watch your mother and sisters grow old and die. You'll outlive your friends. You'll serve Sirini with your powers instead of living out your dreams."

His grip tightened on my hand. "I don't want a life without you. If I agree, will you be with me for eternity?"

Tears dripped down my cheeks. "Absolutely."

"Then I accept your terms, my love."

"Thank you." I splayed my fingers across his chest, reached inside for the sparkly mass, and willed part of it into Tru.

Silvery-blue light spilled down my arms and into him.

He gasped, and his back arched, lifting him up except where his heels met the floor and his skull rested on Melissendra's lap.

His spilled blood flowed back into the wound. From Finna's hands, the ruffles, the shirt, even the puddle on the hardwood, it all seeped back into him. The knife hilt vibrated. The blade worked its way out of his flesh and clattered to the floor. His broken skin knitted together, flared pink, then faded to his normal coloring.

He settled back and groaned. "That sarding hurt."

Melissendra gasped. "Darling! Language."

"Sorry, Mother."

I smoothed his hair back. It'd turned from sandy blond to stark white, but it suited him. His eyes were clear and bright, his skin a healthy tan. "How do you feel?"

"Amazing." He lifted his hands and stared at them. "Strong. Powerful."

His sisters backed away from him.

His mother rained kisses down on his face. "My son!"

Tru sat up and stroked her shoulders. "It's fine, Mother. I'm whole again."

"And a god!" She chuckled through her tears and cupped his face. "I'll never lose you."

"Does he need a counterpart?" Rosi asked.

Jasmine cocked her head, and her eyes blazed silver. "No. Cali gave him part of her spark, so they're sharing the power and the counterpart."

Sounded fine by me. I rose. "I still have work to do. Rise so I can finish with these despicable priests."

Tru gained his feet and helped his mother up. "I have one thing to do before you continue." He scanned the room. "Emperor Rhys? Prince Justyn? Would you please join us?"

My father and brother wove through the crowd and bowed to Tru.

"No need for that." He grabbed his torc in both hands and effortlessly pried it off his neck. He handed it to Papa. "I'm no longer eligible to rule Rigolan, but this afternoon I signed several new laws into effect. Women now have inheritance rights." He held out his hand to Finna. "Sister, I name you my heir."

Her chin trembled, and she clutched her hands to her chest. "What?"

"You will be queen as soon as the emperor can schedule the ceremony. It is yours by rights. Will you have it?"

She nodded. "Yes. Thank you, darling."

He laughed. "You're welcome. Also, you have our blessing to marry Prince Justyn. I cleared it with Emperor Rhys and Mother already. The alliance will stop the civil war before the first battle begins."

"But—how—you didn't know you would step down this evening. Why did you meet with them about me?"

"I wanted you to be happy."

Finna squeaked and covered her mouth with her fingers. "Why, brother? After the way I've treated you? You could name anyone else your heir."

"You've been training for it your entire life. And you're my sister. I love you."

"What about me?" Shanen pushed through the silent crowd. "I've been in training, *and* I was planning to marry her. You're ready to ruin all my blessings, too?"

"I'm sure Finna will find a use for you, cousin." Tru winked at her.

She hurried to Justyn's side. "We can marry!"

He kissed her, right there in front of everyone.

Queen Melissendra wrinkled her nose at Justyn.

Our audience cheered. Hands patted Justyn and Finna's shoulders, and Farras beamed at Jayson. Maybe she'd have her happily-ever-after, also.

That reminded me I still needed mine! I grabbed Tru's hand.

He caressed my cheek. "Thank you, Cali."

I sank to one knee.

The crowd gasped.

Daffi laughed. "Cali, really?"

Absolutely! "Truthful ex-King Freidrick of Rigolan, will you marry me?"

He blessed me with the most gorgeous smile. "Yes, I will." He hoisted me to my feet, wrapped his arms around me, and kissed me until my toes curled.

The crowd clapped and made a great deal of noise.

Father raised his hands. The people hushed. "If you wish to return to your suites now, please do so. The goddess needs to finish doling out justice."

No one moved. Prince Xavier, the bold Tulyan prince, cleared his throat. "If you don't mind, Your Excellency, we'd like to bear witness."

The Olerio triplets agreed.

Father nodded. "Very well. Justice, I believe the priests await your judgment."

"In a moment. I want to know Tru's domain." I scanned the space and found Jasmine behind me. As usual. "Can you find a bowl of tokens, please?"

"Certainly." She waved to a trio of priestesses huddled in the corner. The same three who'd offered me blessings the day I was sacrificed to Maelstrom.

They came forward and blessed me, fingers touching foreheads, lips, and chests.

"How may we be of service?" the gray-haired woman asked.

"May I have the honor of the tokens?" Jasmine held out her hands.

The small blonde priestess set the bowl in Jasmine's care.

She turned and presented it to Tru. "You know what to do."

Chapter Thirty-Nine

Rosi joined me, and Daffi pushed through the crowd to our side.

I raised my eyebrows.

Daffi shrugged. "I couldn't see from back there."

Tru nodded at us and dipped into the bowl. He withdrew a metal chip and placed it in Rosi's hand. He set a bone disc in Daffi's. The last, a wooden coin, he laid in mine. "Ladies, please read them for me."

Rosi held hers up. "Wisdom."

"Wisdom!" Daffi bounced on her toes.

What mine said was no mystery. I tossed it back in the container and curtsied to Tru. "You're the god of wisdom. You and I will serve Sirini together in harmony."

Jasmine held out the bowl to Shaded. "Care to know your domain?"

"Sure." He flickered back to man form, still wearing his finery. He picked three tokens from the bowl, read them, and tossed them back in.

She frowned. "Well?"

"I'll make an announcement later. Right now, Justice has work to do."

I was dying to know his domain, but if he wanted to keep it a secret, fine. I took Tru's hand. "Come help me with these priests." I crossed to the empty floor space where I'd judged Maelstrom. "Captain Dariel?"

389

He stepped forward, his sword in hand, and bowed. "Yes, Highn—Goddess?"

"May I have your assistance, please?"

"It would be my honor."

"I don't wish to float around the room like a stray leaf. Have your men gather the priests and line them up. You might send someone for a wheelbarrow, too." I scowled at Dreaf. "There may be many corpses tonight."

A tiny flicker of fear cut through the defiance in Dreaf's eyes.

Excellent. He needed to sweat over his crimes. I pointed at him. "Put him first."

Dariel bowed again. "It will be done." He barked a few orders, and everyone in the room shifted. Guards picked up immobile priests and set them in rows. Palace staff brought in six wheelbarrows. Maelstrom's corpse was tossed into one with a dull thunk.

Sirini's priestesses gathered around Sorka and Jerys and began the death chant. As they laid hands on the bodies, Sorka gasped and sat up.

The crowd cheered.

Jerys moaned and rolled to her knees. "This is most undignified. Mother?"

Bronwyn helped Jerys rise and kissed her temple. "The goddess gave you back to us. We will sacrifice accordingly."

Sorka scrambled to her feet, tears welling in her eyes, and grasped her mother's hand. "What's going on? Why was I lying on the floor?"

The queen hugged Sorka. "I'll tell you later. Come." They moved toward the group and were absorbed by loving hugs and whispers of encouragement.

Someone cried out. "They're all rising!"

Around the ballroom, the slain guards, citizens, and palace employees who'd rushed to our aid took ragged breaths and sat up. The priests stayed dead, as they should.

"Praise be to Sirini!" Jasmine shouted.

The entire room echoed the call. The Tulya twins helped a butler to his feet, which spurred other royals to offer hands of assistance.

Having multiple witnesses, both royal and commoners, from all over the realms suited my purposes. If tales of this event spread, citizens might trust me when I showed up in their villages or cities. I'd have to travel, since most people couldn't afford a trip to the capital. I waved everyone forward. "Find a good vantage to witness this occasion and ensure word circulates of what happens this day in your home kingdoms."

Justyn and Jayson hauled benches over for the foreign queens and Papa's wives. The townspeople filled in the space behind the royals.

Mica and Beck approached. He'd healed from his wounds and wore a satisfied smile.

Mica reached for my hands. "Welcome to the pantheon, Justice. Tomorrow, if you're free, we can meet, and I'll teach you what I know." She bowed to Tru. "I include you as well, Wisdom."

I curtsied. "We'd be honored. Shall I have a guest suite prepared for you?"

"That is most generous."

Bronwyn signaled for a servant.

Dariel bowed to me. "Goddess, all is ready for you."

"Thank you."

Tru whispered in my ear. "What kind of help will I give you?"

His breath tickled and sent a delicious shiver to my core. "Stand behind me, hands on my shoulders, and demand justice for the victims. If you're touching me when my powers activate, it might trigger yours, too. I'm dying to know what you do!"

"Me, too."

I counted sixty-two priests and sighed. This would take time, but worse, I'd have to witness their wicked acts.

Tru's hands settled on my shoulders and gave a light squeeze. Sweet man. And I got to spend eternity with him! Despite the gravity of the chore ahead, I grinned.

He bellowed, "Goddess Calilee, the victims of these men beg for justice!"

The silvery-blue glow blazed around me. Tru's hands flared with sparkling white light. It worked! I rose into the air with him behind me, white-and-blue lightning crackling around us. A beam shot from my forehead to Dreaf's, and a second one connected me to Tru's. I was sucked into Dreaf's memories, and Tru's warm presence enfolded me.

I am here with you, he said in my mind.

Thank you. That was an interesting new skill. We'd have to explore that further. Did we need to be linked to speak that way? We'd find out later—we had eternity.

We relived every horrible act Dreaf had committed in his life, and my stomach churned. Babies tossed into the sea. Screaming children thrown off the Ridge. Multiple murders. Assaults. Rapes. Thefts. Bribery. Extortion. And most recently—I gasped. A kidnapping, and it wasn't too late to save the victim! The visions ended. "Murder, rape, assault, and kidnapping all justify a death sentence." With a flick of my wrist, his despicable life was over. "Captain Dariel, send soldiers to the catacombs beneath the ruined temple. Prince Rhygan is locked in a dank cell."

Empress Bronwyn cried out.

"He lives." I smiled at her. "He's spitting mad, but he's healthy."

She blinked and nodded.

I half expected her to go with the guards, but she remained on the bench with Dorana and my mother.

"Why did they take him?" Bronwyn asked.

"Someone in Tulya hired the priests to kidnap Rhygan, intending to use him as leverage to broker a match between him and Helene. But the messenger they sent couldn't make it past the gate guards on his first several tries, nor could he pass the note off to a soldier without being captured, so they gave up." Idiots. They couldn't free him, since he knew who'd taken him, and they'd planned to kill him soon.

I turned to the next priest.

That was horrible, Tru mind-spoke. *Did you go through that with Maelstrom?*

I swallowed. *Yes, only much worse. He'd had thousands of years to commit his crimes. Let's finish this quickly.*

What can I do to help? he asked.

I'm not sure. Have you discovered your power?

Not yet. I'll experiment.

We dove into the next priest's memories, and within moments, he was sentenced. In a half hour, I executed thirty priests. Each body was loaded into a wheelbarrow and hauled away before another was brought up. Sickening. Yet the crowd stayed as witnesses.

Four soldiers escorted Rhygan into the ballroom.

Bronwyn cried out and rushed to hug her oldest son. Papa was two steps behind her.

Rhygan wore wrinkled homespun, and his long auburn hair was pulled back in a simple tail. The priests had treated him well—I'd witnessed it through memories—other than keeping him against his will.

And I floated above him like a lantern on a pole. I wanted to embrace him, too, but I'd have to fight through everyone else. Not only our brothers and sisters, but Princess Sorka and Prince Simon both ventured into the hug-fest.

Rhygan kissed Sorka, earning ooh's and hoots and laughter. He smiled. Then his gaze tracked up to me and Tru, and his jaw dropped. "Cali?"

I waved. "I'll hug you when I'm finished here. Do you wish to clean up?"

He grinned. "I'd rather watch whatever you're doing." He scanned the room, one arm hooked around Sorka's waist. "And hear what I've missed."

Bronwyn hauled him to the bench and placed him in her spot. She circled behind and stood, beaming, with her hands on his shoulders. Papa joined her. Sorka knelt on the floor beside Rhygan and leaned against his knees. He took her hand. So sweet. Now that Finna was marrying Justyn, Rhygan was free to marry for love.

As fun as the romance and homecoming was, I should finish my grim task. I called for the next priest. Two soldiers picked up a terrified man and settled him before me.

Sixty-one executions later, my stomach roiled like the sea in a windstorm. Being Justice was gruesome work. But finally, the last remaining priest stood before me. He'd been frozen in a cowering position, his hood covering his head, his hands folded and hidden in his sleeves—he hadn't been holding a sword like his brethren. I sighed. He'd be a slimy rat like the rest of them, but it wouldn't be justice to execute him simply because he was one of Maelstrom's priests.

The beam connected the last man to Tru and me. His comforting presence enveloped me, and I dove into the memories.

In the dark of night, the priest lifted a sleeping infant from a cradle and snuck out of the nursery. With the babe snuggled to his chest, he crept through a maze of darkened corridors, slipped out a narrow door, and disappeared into the shadows.

And it ended. That's the only crime this man had ever committed in his life? Granted, kidnapping a child was heinous, but it was tame compared to what the others had done. And it'd happened years ago.

Still, the punishment was death. I raised my sword.

Wait. Tru stirred behind me. *He seems familiar. I want to see his face.*

We floated to the floor.

Tru approached the priest. "Allow him to move, please, Cali."

"You are freed."

The priest's shoulders hunched farther, and he took a step back. "Please don't kill me. I had good reason for what I did."

Tru flicked the man's hood back.

His bald head gleamed in the candlelight. He had blond facial hair on his upper lip and chin but kept the rest clean-shaven. His cheeks were rough and ruddy, and wrinkles lined his squinting eyes.

"Look at me," Tru commanded.

The priest sighed, squared his shoulders, and raised his head. He wore Tru's face. Same olive-green eyes, cheekbones, even the cleft in his chin.

Was this man Tru's kinsman?

****

"Gray!" Tru's guardian had aged and shaved his head, but it was him. After all these years! A weight lifted from Tru's shoulders. He laughed and embraced the priest. "It's good to see you again. Where have you been? Why are you serving Maelstrom? You hate him."

Gray relaxed and wrapped his arms around Tru. "You grew into a fine young man. I'm sorry to see the torc found your throat, though. I'm glad you shed it so quickly."

Mother appeared at Tru's side and gasped. "Fenton!" She grabbed Tru's arm and yanked. "Unhand that cur! How do you know him?"

Tru clapped Gray's shoulder and stepped away. "He's my guardian, Mother. He's the man who raised me."

"The man who kidnapped you." Cali threaded her fingers through Tru's.

Mother glared at Gray. "You stole my son. How could you?"

Finna and Farras approached. "He looks like Father." Farras cocked her head. "You're our uncle?"

He nodded. "I am."

When Tru was growing up, Gray had been patient and kind, always offering encouragement and affection, always acting as a father despite never allowing Tru to use that term. Now it made sense. His guardian was his uncle, not a stranger who found a lost child in the forests.

Mother poked Gray in the chest. "You treasonous

wart! You will die for what you did." She waved at Cali. "Cut him down."

Tru pulled his mother away. "Don't be so hasty. I want to know why he took me."

"It doesn't matter. It gutted me, and I want him punished." She wrapped her arms around Tru's waist and squeezed.

Emperor Rhys approached. "Would you like to retire to a private place for this discussion?"

Cali smiled. "That would be lovely, Father." She placed her sword on her back—it just hung there without a scabbard like it was part of her body—and gestured toward a side door. "Follow me, please."

Bronwyn stood, one arm around Jerys. "While they take care of that last business, we shall clean up this mess." She glanced around the space and pressed her hand to her temple. "Oh, my. Guests, you are excused. Guards, please help the servants putting the room to rights and wipe up the blood." She blew a loose chunk of hair from her eyes and hurried to direct the staff.

Cali led the group into a smaller room decorated in blue and white that featured several intimate seating arrangements.

Tru's mother trembled. He patted her wrist. "It will be fine." He steered her to a padded sofa across from Gray. His sisters sat on either side of her and held her hands. He joined Cali on a bench, Emperor Rhys took the chair by Gray, and—Tru grinned—Jasmine squatted on the floor to Cali's right.

Gray stripped off the blue-green robe and dumped it on the floor. He clasped his shaking hands in his lap and stared at them.

Emperor Rhys nodded at Tru.

He laced his fingers through Cali's. "Gray—"

"Fenton," his mother corrected.

"Fine. Uncle Fenton. Please tell us why you took me."

He took a deep breath. "I grew up the crown prince. My earliest memories were instruction on how to behave. What subjects to study. What to eat. What to wear. I had no freedom, only duty. I wanted to play music, but instead my time was packed with history, math, and law. I wanted to learn how to hunt with a bow. Instead, I was taught swordplay and horseback riding. I wanted to travel. Instead, I was held inside and guarded like a delicate work of art."

Mother rolled her eyes. "The same as every other royal child. Quit whining."

Fenton's jaw clenched. "I was a slave to the throne. A puppet. Not allowed my own thoughts or interests, only what would benefit my kingdom. But it was my duty, and I submitted. Until I was told to marry a princess from Olerio. She was beautiful, of course, but shy, young, and…giggly."

"I'd been taught how to be a proper queen!" Mother glared. "I was not giggly."

Whoa! Tru hadn't expected that. He leaned forward. "What happened?"

Fenton shrugged. "I was in love with someone else."

Mother blew air out her lips. "A merchant's daughter. Low-born and unworthy."

"Thrift was wonderful!" Fenton's eyebrows furrowed. "Sweet, compassionate, funny…she made me happy. She lived outside the gilded palace and knew what life could be. And I wanted it. Her." He looked at Tru. "I abdicated my position, married Thrift, and left.

Melissendra wed my younger brother, and I was free to do what I wanted for the first time in my life."

Mother picked at her fingernail. "Traitor."

Fenton continued. "We settled outside of Quickswallow and farmed."

"Lived in poverty," Mother muttered.

"Please let him speak." Tru sighed. "Were you happy, Uncle?"

"Immensely. Until I learned that Melissendra gave birth to a male child. I realized you'd be subjected to the same torture I'd endured. My heart ached for you. Thrift was due to deliver soon, but all my thoughts were on rescuing you."

"You mean stealing him!"

"Mother, stop. Please."

Fenton grimaced. "She's right. I stole you, believing I'd saved you from the torment and misery I'd gone through. I told Thrift I'd found you in the wilderness, abandoned. She welcomed you as her own. A week later, she gave birth to our son, but he didn't survive."

Cali gasped. "That poor dear."

Tru rubbed his thumb against her hand.

Fenton nodded. "If not for Tru, Thrift may have died from grief."

"*I* almost died from grief!" Mother surged from the scttee.

Finna and Farras pulled her back.

"You have no idea what you did to me!" Tears welled in Mother's eyes.

"Oh, I know what you went through. Thrift suffered greatly. But you had two daughters to console yourself. She only had her adopted son. To take him from her would have killed her." Fenton brushed at a stain on his leather leggings. "We told our neighbors Truthful was ours. When soldiers came looking for the missing heir, we rubbed coal dust in his hair and disguised his house mark." He glanced up at Mother. "I felt guilty for taking him. It ate me. But I couldn't take him from Thrift, and I couldn't bear to think of him imprisoned in the palace."

Tru frowned. "Why don't I remember Thrift?"

Fenton's eyes misted. "She passed away during your second year. I couldn't remain on the farm with the bittersweet memories, so I sold everything. You and I hit the road and traveled the realms."

"Until Borderline."

Fenton nodded. "I wanted to settle down again. The life I'd given you was adventurous and educational, but it wasn't what you needed. You'd been asking about family, wanting to know if I'd ever marry and hold a real job. If we'd ever live in a house. When I met Hawk and Eve, I realized you'd be happy there. I worked and started saving to buy a plot of land."

Pain jolted through Tru's chest. "Yet you abandoned me."

"I had to. Rigolan soldiers showed up. They would have recognized me." Fenton scrubbed his hands over his face. "I thought I'd leave for a few days, wait for them to pass on, then return. But they spotted me and gave chase. I ran to High Point, blended into the city, and found refuge at Maelstrom's temple. I only intended to stay for a day or two. I didn't realize it was a lifetime commitment. They wouldn't allow me to leave."

"Until today. Why didn't you try to send word to me? Or tell me who I was?"

Fenton's brow furrowed. "I left you a box with a note explaining everything and some mementos from your cradle. Did you not find it?"

Of all the sarding... "It was *your* box. I didn't want to be disrespectful by opening it."

He sighed. "Do you still have it?"

"Yes."

"Open it. Later."

"I will." Now that he had the truth, what would Cali do with Fenton? The penalty for kidnapping was death, but Tru couldn't bear that. It would be like losing his father all over again. No, worse. Tru had never met his birth father, but he'd spent fourteen years with Fenton.

Tru had to somehow spare his uncle's life.

Chapter Forty

Would thought-speak work outside of Cali's judgment sessions? Only one way to find out. *Cali, can you hear me?*

Yes! She blessed Tru with a radiant smile. *This is an amazing gift.*

I don't want you to execute Fenton.

She squeezed his hand. *I don't blame you. But he should be punished. What do you suggest?*

Tru turned to his mother. "As Fenton's victim, you have the right to demand justice and his execution, but may I suggest a different outcome?"

"No." She looked down her nose at Fenton. "He deserves it."

"Yes, he does. But it would break my heart to lose him again, and I've thought of a way he could atone for his crime."

Mother's jaw clenched. "He could never atone. He must die."

Fenton winced.

Tru continued. "What if he returns to Oakencrest to serve as a life-long advisor to Finna? He was raised to rule, and his knowledge base has swelled from all his years living on his own. He can sympathize with both royals and commoners, giving him a unique perspective. He would be an invaluable asset to the throne."

Mother stared at Fenton, her chin twitching.

Finna's lips pressed into a thin line. "I don't need his advice."

"She needs advisors she can trust," Tru said. "He would not betray her."

Mother bit her lower lip. "He betrayed me! I see no evidence he's changed."

Tru, justice demands his execution. I can't let him escape his fate after the way I cleansed the ballroom today. No one would trust me again. There must be restitution.

Anything to spare his life.

Cali rose and drew her sword. "I can guarantee his loyalty." Her power surged, and the lightning enveloped her rising body. Her blade flickered and danced with flames of blue fire. Her glorious brown hair floating on the currents, she pointed the weapon at Fenton, and she spoke with that chilling polyvocal tone. "Rise."

He swallowed, stood, and bowed. "I am at your service, Justice."

Cali's eyes swirled with silvery-blue light. "Fenton of Rigolan, you are offered a chance at redemption. Speak now and swear upon this Sword of Retribution that you will honor your word and serve Rigolan's throne with integrity and devotion for the remainder of your days or until released from service by the rightful ruler."

Fenton's spine stiffened. "I do so swear, Justice. I humbly thank you for this opportunity. I will not disappoint you or the throne of Rigolan."

Cali plunged her weapon into his chest.

Fenton gasped.

Sard, no! Tru jumped up. "Cali, what are you doing?"

Fenton stared at the sword impaled through his

heart. "You didn't accept my oath?"

Cali hauled the blade out.

Fenton fingered the spot. No injury, no blood, not even a hole in his shirt. "I yet live?"

"Your oath is sealed. Should you break your word, that wound will become reality, and your heart will stop. Finna, do you accept my judgment? Will you collect retribution from him in the form of service to the realm?"

Her eyes narrowed, but she nodded. "As long as he's punished if he fails."

The lightning faded, and Cali settled to the floor. Her eyes lost the silvery glow. "Sorry about that, Fenton. I didn't know that last part would happen." She held out her hands to him, and he took them. "I am pleased you survived."

He smiled. "As am I." He crossed to Mother and sank to his knees before her. "I cannot undo the wrong I have committed against you, but I will turn all my efforts to aiding Finna. If you desire, I will strive to never be in your presence."

Mother's chin quivered. "That's not necessary." She rose. "Come, daughters." They left the room in a swirl of lace, tattered ruffles, and dangling threads.

Tru embraced Fenton. "I'm so happy to have you back in my life again."

"Will you be in residence at the palace?"

Tru looked to Cali. He'd be wherever she was.

She shook her head.

"I'm afraid not." Tru smiled. "But I'll come visit as often as possible."

Cali winked and turned to Jasmine. "I took a wagon-sized amount of spark from Maelstrom tonight. Do you suppose Sirini would allow me to give it away?"

Jasmine's eyes swirled silver. "For now, guard it. I will distribute it when you find people worthy to bear it. I chose you for your heart and trust you to serve my will."

Cali hugged Jasmine. "Thank you." She hopped from her seat and grabbed her father's hands. "Papa, you and I have things to discuss. Will you be available tomorrow morning?"

He smiled. "I will always have time for you, Cali Cub."

"As will I." Tru winked. "I will take every opportunity to worship you, my love."

She wrapped her arms around his neck and kissed him. "I love the way you adore me."

Sirini, thank you for sending Cali to the bean field.

****

Five days later, I dug out my travel coat and gave Charity the black pearls and silver beads. "Take Jasmine with you. She'll get a better price."

Charity nodded. "You won't leave without us, will you?"

"Certainly not. You've got several hours." I turned back to my wardrobe, shoved Tru's things to the side, and pulled out the raspberry frock. Leathers were great for the road, but I'd need gowns for calling on royals. And why hadn't Tru packed all his new shirts? I'd find room for the purple one—I loved the way it fit him through the chest.

I laid the dress in the long knapsack. The matching slippers went into a smaller pack, along with shirts, stockings, underclothing, grooming kit, and Tru's forgotten items. The bag was full to bursting. No matter what Tru asked, I'd never get all my things into two bags.

Rosi entered wearing leather leggings, a white

cotton shirt, and a yellow brocade tunic. "When are you meeting Mica and Beck?"

"They're traveling with us for the first few days." I held up my sapphire and aqua dresses. "I only have room for one more. Which do you like?"

She studied them. "Both. I'm sure we can stuff them in." She picked up the aqua one and laid it atop the raspberry frock. After a bit of squishing, she tucked in both dresses, closed the flaps, rolled it into a hay-bale shaped bundle, and tied the knots.

Daffi stuck her face in. "Servants are gathering our packs. Place yours in the queue."

I grabbed the bags and dumped them in the hallway beside Tru's small rucksack—no wonder he'd left things behind.

Two footmen and a maid gathered packs and hauled them down to the awaiting carriages.

Rosi bounced on her toes. "I'm so excited! I've never been on a journey like this. When are we leaving?"

"When Charity and Jasmine return." I scoured my bedchamber for anything I might have forgotten, but I'd lived for six days with the bare necessities. Forgetting something wouldn't be a hardship. Papa had given me a bulging pouch full of coins, so we could always shop later.

Jasmine assumed it would take us two years to complete one full circuit of the Five Realms. By the time we returned to High Point, the construction of our temple should be completed. I loved the irony—Maelstrom's tithing gift to me would finance the project. Building it atop his crumbling one and using the catacombs beneath was frosting on the cookie.

Tru had plans for a library at the site. One of his new

powers was a head full of knowledge, and he couldn't wait to begin writing it down. He'd arranged for one of our wagons to be stocked with blank books, ink, and quills. Some would be gifts to the priestesses to copy their Writs of Sirini for distribution to all the temples, but Tru was certain he could fill entire tomes.

Daffi hopped onto the bed. "We're ready. Everything is packed, and the maids and drivers are standing by. All we need is passengers."

Charity entered, breathing heavily, hand to her chest. "Sorry. Ran up the stairs. We're back."

"That was quick." I grabbed my coat.

"Jasmine asked another temple guard to take care of it. We're dying to get on the road again!" She brushed her hand down her leathers. "Visiting the palace has been my dream since I was a child, so I can't believe I'm anxious to leave."

I led the procession to the grand entry. "Where's Tru?"

"Waiting for us." Rosi's boot scuffed against the marble floor.

We entered the throne room. Papa and Tru stood on the dais, chatting. Bronwyn sat in her chair, eavesdropping. Dorana and Momma perched on their bench with red-rimmed eyes.

It was roughest on Momma. The other wives would hold on to their children for a few more weeks before the wedding ceremonies and the mass exodus. By summer solstice, only Rhygan would remain.

Three priestesses came through the side door, bearing a bowl of tokens. "Are you ready for your blessings?" the oldest asked.

"Yes." I reached for the bowl, Rosi and Daffi on

either side of me.

Sparks shot from my fingertips and zapped my sisters.

Rosi gasped and clasped her hands to her chest. "What did you do?"

A chill skittered across my skin. "I didn't do it." I turned to Jasmine.

She grinned. "Sirini gave them sparks! They'll become demigods, as well."

Daffi stared at her flared fingers. "I feel different. More…robust."

Rosi's eyebrows furrowed. "You said 'become.' We're not goddesses yet?"

"You'll need to find your counterparts." Jasmine cocked her head to the side. "Actually, they don't exist yet. Cali will need to get close enough to a worthy person for sparks to jump into them."

Cold swept through my body. "And if we don't find those people within twenty-eight days?"

Jasmine's lips pursed. "Rosi and Daffi will die."

Tears welled in my eyes. *This again?* When I went through it, I'd known who I was searching for—a triplet my age. But this was different. Were we looking for two specific people, or would any two "worthy" people suffice? "Please tell me Sirini gave you more guidance than that."

"Sorry." She held out the bowl of tokens. "Want to find out your domains?"

Rosi's face paled. "I guess so." She pulled three tokens and held them in her clenched fist. Daffi did the same. They spoke together. "One, two three."

Rosi sighed. "I'll be the goddess of mercy."

Daffi read hers, and tears welled in her eyes.

"Order." She smiled. "Our strengths lie together, at least." She tossed her tokens back in the bowl and wrapped her arms around us.

The blonde priestess shook the bowl, rattling the tokens. "Draw your blessings."

Rosi's eyebrows scrunched, but she plucked a metal chunk off the top. "Service."

Daffi drew a wooden one. "Service."

I didn't roll my eyes. "What are the odds?" I fished out a bone token. "Service."

Jasmine clapped her hands. "That's lovely, people, you know what to do. Now if I may, we've got work to do. Counterparts to find. People to serve. Destinies to fulfill. Evil people to afflict with goodness. Say your goodbyes, and we'll be on our way."

Papa hugged the three of us. "Find those counterparts quickly, daughters. I can't bear to lose any of you."

"We'll do our best." Rosi hugged Prime and Dorana. Daffi and I followed her.

How could this get worse? Twenty-eight days!

Jasmine opened the throne-room doors.

People lined both sides of the hallway all the way to the grand foyer.

Ah, road stinks. They'd make me cry again.

Rhygan opened his arms. "I'll miss you while you're gone. Please write."

"I will." I squeezed him and stepped forward.

Rindi embraced me. "I'll beat you to Tulya, and by then I'll be a bride."

"Congratulations. We'll celebrate when we get there." If Rosi and Daffi survived. It'd take more than a month to reach Tulya.

Rhyada was next. "You'll have to stay extra time in Rigolan, for Frei—Tru's sake."

"I'm sure we will." With Rosi and Daffi as goddesses.

Palama, Pensie, and Prescia smiled. "Clean up the realm, Sister." They kissed my cheeks, and I moved on.

Justyn picked me up and swung me around. I squealed. "You've always been the strongest of us all," he whispered. "Can't wait to see you again and hear of all the chaos you've left in your wake."

Should I tell him about Rosi and Daffi? But why worry him unnecessarily? We'd find the counterparts, and we'd see our brothers again someday. I wiped my eyes. "Thank you."

Jayson and Jerys clasped me between them. "Sirini bless you."

Queen Melissendra and Fenton stood together. He bowed over my hand. Melissendra hugged me. "Take care of my son and plan an extended stay when you reach Oakencrest."

"Your will be done, Majesty."

I said goodbye to Finna and Farras, Shanen and Shalek—or was it Shalek and Shaded? Thankfully, sparks didn't fly into them. Although having them for my sisters' counterparts would have relieved the stress. What were the opposites for mercy and order? Selfishness and mess? This could be disastrous.

We bid farewell to the Tulya men, the Olerios, and the Kurik offspring. They'd all be in-laws soon. The remainder were noble parents of the event crowd, dignitaries, advisors, and guests, followed by palace personnel and guards.

Dariel bowed to me. "If you find villages in need of

enforcers, send word, and I'll assign someone."

"Thank you." If my tears would stop, I might be able to see all these people I'd known my entire life. Would sparks fly into any of them? No. Of course not. Finding two worthy people for my sisters' counterparts couldn't be that easy. Finally, I made it to the front doors and stepped onto the portico.

A magnificent blond horse waited.

I laughed. "I wondered if you'd show up to say farewell."

He flicked back to a man, dressed in pale leathers. "Actually, I'm hoping you'll take me with you. I have a lot to learn about my new state of being."

"We'd love to have your company. How long do you need to prepare?"

He winked. "I already tossed my bags in."

"You may wish to stay in man form. Otherwise, Tru might hitch you to a wagon."

"I would not!" Tru kissed my cheek. "I'm glad you're coming, Shade. We should know each other better."

Jasmine mounted the driver's seat on the lead wagon. "Shade! You're with me."

He climbed up.

Beck perched atop a large white stallion beside the next carriage.

Mica hung out the window, chatting with him. She waved at Rosi, Daffi, and Charity. "Join me!"

Tru boosted me into the driver's seat of their coach. "Want to learn how to drive?"

"Absolutely." With me at the front of the procession, I might see more people and home in on those counterparts quicker than if I were inside a carriage.

I might have been a useless princess, but I'd be Sirini's servant for the rest of eternity.

Epilogue

We'd barely made it through the palace gates when I spotted a beggar, his crippled hand outstretched. My heart raced. *Finally!* I patted Tru's forearm. "Stop the wagon."

"Already?"

I hopped down before it'd stopped completely. "Flick?"

He turned his grubby face up to me and gasped. "Lady?" He trundled to his feet and bowed. "My apologies. I'll go somewhere else."

"I want to speak with you."

He stopped, but his gaze hovered on his filthy, encrusted bare feet. His clothing hung from his thin frame in tatters.

Heat streamed through my core. This poor young man needed more than justice, but my gift didn't come with healing. But I could right the wrongs. My power flared, and I rose into the air, blue lights glistening around me.

Flick gasped and struggled to his knees. "Goddess."

People descended from the carts, wagons, and horses and gathered.

"What are you doing now, Cali?" Rosi asked.

"Dispensing justice." A shimmery thread shot from my forehead to Flick's, and I relived our first meeting— from my childhood viewpoint.

Ahead, a scrawny street child hovered near a meat pie vendor's cart, eyeing the crispy treats and licking his lips. Why didn't Papa send some of our food down here? The boy's bones stuck out beneath his skin. I had enough coins in my pouch now to buy him a few.

A taller street boy ran toward us, his bare feet slapping on the wooden boardwalk. As he passed the vendor, he nabbed one of the pies, shoved the entire thing in his mouth, and darted down the alley.

The vendor turned, leaning hard on his cane, and stared at the hole in his wares. "Thief!" He grabbed the scrawny boy's arm. "Ya'd steal from me, ya ungrateful wretch?"

"He didn't do it." I released Grace's hand and ran toward them. "The tall one did."

The vendor scowled at me. "Ain't no tall one." He shook the skinny boy. "This one did it. Naughty Flick!" He raised his cane above his head.

Flick ducked and lifted his arm, shielding his head. I screamed. The merchant's cane descended, and Flick's hand bones snapped. He wailed and curled around his mangled fingers, his other arm still caught in the vendor's grip.

"He didn't do it!" I lifted my skirts and kicked the mean man in the shin. "You scoundrel, how could you hurt him? That was unfair."

He pushed me away and brought up the cane for another blow.

My guard grabbed the stick and wrenched it away from the vendor. "That's enough. The crime for theft is stocks, not a beating. Or broken bones." He knelt beside the boy. "Let me see."

He sobbed and held out his swollen hand. It was

already turning purple.

The guard scowled. "You'll need a surgeon. Come with me."

"I want my ma!" He turned and ran.

The vendor glared. "You just let him get away? I demand justice!"

"Then you'd be beaten for hitting an innocent." I stomped toward him, but Grace grabbed my shoulder.

My guard handed the vendor a copper. "This should cover the pie. No more hitting people. If you need assistance, call for an enforcer."

The vendor rolled his eyes. "As if there's ever one around when you need one."

The vision shifted to a shack near the abattoir.

"Mama!" Flick raced inside. His hand felt like it was on fire. He showed it to her.

She tsked. "This needs a surgeon, Flick, but it'd cost more than we ken afford. Lemme bind it for ya." She wrapped his hand in strips from a stained cleaning rag.

She did her best, but the hand never worked right after that. He learned to eat with his other, but a one-handed boy couldn't get hired on to do odd jobs. He mostly begged in the streets as he grew up, trying to help his mother keep food on the table, but there was never enough.

Then she grew sick and died. He was evicted from their shack and slept on the streets, eating scraps from garbage heaps, finding used clothing in rag bins, and relying on the goodness of strangers—and there were too few of those.

Tears streamed down my face. Flick had grown up sickly, bone-thin, and incapable of providing for himself. Now, at the age of nineteen, his body was failing him.

He'd die within the year if no one intervened.

I couldn't undo the years behind him, but I could make things right. I drew my sword.

His eyes widened, glowing oddly blue in the light of my blade.

"Justice rights the wrongs done to you." I went with my intuition and touched his shoulder with the glowing tip.

He screamed and jerked away, cradling his hand to his chest. The bones twisted and writhed into the proper places.

I hadn't expected that!

His legs lengthened. His chest filled out. His shoulders and arms grew. He was still too thin, but he was healthy now. His scream cut off, and he stared at his newly healed limb. It was slimmer than the other, but it worked. "Praise be." He glanced at me, then fell to his knees and pressed his forehead to the cobbles. "Thank you, Goddess. How shall I serve you in return?"

I floated down to the cobbles, and my glow faded. "Do good to others when you can." I dug five gold pieces from the hem of my coat and handed them to him.

His eyes widened. "I can't take this much. I am unworthy—"

"Nonsense. You're a citizen of the Five Realms, and you deserve better than what you've endured. Buy yourself new clothing, find a bathhouse, and make yourself presentable. Then report to the palace gate and tell them Cali sent you. They'll find you a job and give you a place to live."

He bowed. "Your generosity is only surpassed by your beauty. Thank you, Goddess."

I smiled. "You're welcome." I threaded my fingers